Anonymous

Statutes of the Province of Quebec, Passed in the Thirty-Ninth Year of the Reign of Her Majesty Queen Victoria

Anonymous

Statutes of the Province of Quebec, Passed in the Thirty-Ninth Year of the Reign of Her Majesty Queen Victoria

Reprint of the original, first published in 1875.

1st Edition 2024 | ISBN: 978-3-38525-185-4

Verlag (Publisher): Outlook Verlag GmbH, Zeilweg 44, 60439 Frankfurt, Deutschland
Vertretungsberechtigt (Authorized to represent): E. Roepke, Zeilweg 44, 60439 Frankfurt, Deutschland
Druck (Print): Books on Demand GmbH, In de Tarpen 42, 22848 Norderstedt, Deutschland

STATUTES

OF THE

PROVINCE OF QUEBEC,

PASSED IN THE

THIRTY-NINTH YEAR OF THE REIGN OF HER MAJESTY

QUEEN VICTORIA;

And in the First Session of the Third Parliament,

BEGUN AND HOLDEN AT QUEBEC ON THE 4th DAY OF NOVEMBER, AND CLOSED BY PROROGATION
ON THE 24th DAY OF DECEMBER, ONE THOUSAND EIGHT HUNDRED AND SEVENTY-FIVE.

THE HONORABLE RENÉ-ÉDOUARD CARON,
LIEUTENANT-GOVERNOR.

QUEBEC:
PRINTED BY CHARLES-FRANÇOIS LANGLOIS,
PRINTER TO THE QUEEN'S MOST EXCELLENT MAJESTY.

ANNO DOMINI, 1875.

VICTORIÆ REGINÆ.

CAP. I.

An Act for granting to Her Majesty certain sums of money required for defraying certain expenses of the civil government for the fiscal years ending on the thirtieth day of June, one thousand eight hundred and seventy-six, and on the thirtieth day of June, one thousand eight hundred and seventy-seven, and for other purposes connected with the public service.

[Assented to 24th December, 1875.]

Most Gracious Sovereign,

WHEREAS it appears by messages from the Honorable Préamble. Réné Edouard Caron, lieutenant-governor of the province of Quebec, and the estimates accompanying the same, that the sums hereinafter mentioned are or may be required to defray certain expenses of the government of this province, not otherwise provided for, for the fiscal years ending on the thirtieth day of June, one thousand eight hundred and seventy-six, and on the thirtieth day of June, one thousand eight hundred and seventy-seven, and for other purposes connected with the public service ; may it therefore please Your Majesty, that it may be enacted, and be it enacted by the Queen's Most Excellent Majesty, by and with the advice and consent of the Legislature of Quebec, that :

1. From and out of the consolidated revenue fund of the province of Quebec there shall and may be applied a sum not exceeding, in the whole, eighty three thousand two hundred and eighty eight dollars, for defraying the several charges and expenses of the civil government and $83,288.00 for the year ending the 30th June, 1876.

public service of this province, or which, in the interest of the public service, may require to be so paid and applied, whether for account of this province or otherwise, for the current financial year ending on the thirtieth day of June, one thousand eight hundred and seventy-six, which are set forth in the schedule A, annexed to this act, and for the other purposes therein mentioned.

$1,792,096 00 for the year 1876-1877.

2. From and out of the consolidated revenue fund of this province, there shall be, and may be applied, a sum not exceeding, in the whole, one million seven hundred and ninety-two thousand and ninety-six dollars, for defraying the several charges and expenses of the civil government and public service of this province, or which, in the interest of the public service, may require to be so paid and applied, whether for account of this province or otherwise, for the current financial year ending on the thirtieth day of June, one thousand eight hundred and seventy-seven, which are set forth in the schedule B, annexed to this act, and for the other purposes therein mentioned.

Proviso :

3. Nothing herein or in the schedules hereunto annexed, nor yet any payment or application whatever of moneys hereby appropriated, or of any part thereof, shall be held to import that such moneys are so paid or applied for charges or expenses of this province properly so called, or are not otherwise provided for, or are to be finally carried to account of the said consolidated revenue fund; but on the contrary, every such payment and application shall be held only to be made provisionally from such fund, and subject to all rightful adjustment in account hereafter, in respect of the Dominion and of the province of Ontario, and of all special funds which the same may at all affect, and otherwise.

Accounts to be rendered to the legislature.

4. Accounts in detail of all moneys expended under the authority of this act, shall be laid before both houses of the legislature of this province, at the then next session thereof.

Moneys expended accounted for to Her Majesty.

5. The due application of all moneys expended under the authority of this act, shall be accounted for to Her Majesty, her heirs and successors, through the lords commissioners of Her Majesty's treasury, in such manner and form as Her Majesty, her heirs and successors, shall be pleased to direct.

Act into force.

6. This act shall come into force on the day of the sanction thereof.

SCHEDULE.

SCHEDULE A.

Sums granted to Her Majesty, by this act, for the fiscal year ending on the 30th June, 1876, with indication of the purposes for which they are granted.

SERVICE.	—	—
I. LEGISLATION.	$ cts.	$ cts.
Expenses of Elections.........	....	13,000 00
III. ADMINISTRATION OF JUSTICE.		
Prison Inspection	....	400 00
IV. EDUCATION.		
Salaries of School Inspectors...............	....	1,000 00
V. COLONIZATION.		
Colonization Roads, 1st class...............	....	11,000 00
VI. PUBLIC WORKS AND BUILDINGS.		
Rents, Insurances, Repairs, &c., of Public Buildings, generally...	12,268 00	
Repairs of Court Houses and Gaols...............	2,900 00	
Gaspé Court House and Gaol, to complete fence for prisoners' yard.	720 00	
Gaol for Females, Montreal...............	36,000 00	
		51,888 00
	....	6,000 00
Tanneries Land Suit...............		83,288 00

SCHEDULE B.

Sums granted to Her Majesty, by this act, for the fiscal year ending on the 30th June, 1877, with indication of the purposes for which they are granted.

SERVICE.	—	—	—
	$ cts.	$ cts.	$ cts.
I. LEGISLATION.			
Legislative Council :			
Salaries and contingent expenses, including printing, binding, &c..................	....	26,443 00	
Legislative Assembly :			
Salaries and contingent expenses, including printing, binding, &c..................	....	61,300 00	
Expenses of Elections.....................	....	5,000 00	
Parliamentary Library.....................	....	3,000 00	
Clerk of the Crown in Chancery :			
Salary, covering ordinary contingencies......	....	800 00	
Printing, binding and distributing the Laws......	....	5,500 00	
Law Clerk :			
Salaries of office	3,400 00		
Contingencies, comprising extra clerk........	600 00	4,000 00	$106,043 00
II. CIVIL GOVERNMENT.			
Public Departments :			
Salaries and contingencies.................	....	....	147,900 00
III. ADMINISTRATION OF JUSTICE, &C.			
Administration of Justice.................	....	350,754 00	
Police..................................	....	21,400 00	
Prison Inspectories.....................	....	45,000 00	
....	....	4,100 00	
Carried forward			421,254 00
	....	....	$675,197 00

SCHEDULE B.—*Continued.*

SERVICE.	—	—	—
	$ cts.	$ cts.	$ cts.
Brought forward............	....	....	675,197 00
IV. EDUCATION, &c.			
Superior Education :			
Superior Education, proper $71,000 00			
High Schools, Quebec and Montreal 2,470 00			
Compensation to Roman Catholic Institutions for grant to High Schools 4,940 00	78,410 00		
Common Schools.......................	155,000 00		
Schools in poor Municipalities.................	8,000 00		
Normal Schools...........................	46,000 00		
Salaries of School Inspectors..................	25,500 00		
Books for Prizes............................	3,500 00		
Journals of Education............	2,400 00		
Superannuated Teachers.....................	6,600 00		
Schools for the Deaf and Dumb	12,000 00		
		337,410 00	
Literary and Scientific Institutions :			
Medical Faculty, McGill College, Montreal......	750 00		
School of Medicine, do	750 00		
Natural History Society, do	750 00		
Montreal Historical Society, do	400 00		
Numismatic and Antiquarian Society,do	100 00		
School of Medicine Bishop's College, Lennoxville.	750 00		
Literary and Historical Society, Quebec.....	750 00		
Institut Canadien, do	500 00		
Académie de Musique, do	100 00		
Aid towards publication of "Le Naturaliste Canadien."	400 00		
Towards providing aid to secure publication of reports of decisions of Law Courts, at Montreal.	1,000 00		
		6,250 00	
Arts and Manufactures :			
Board of Arts and Manufactures................	....	10,000 00	
			353,660 00
Carried over	....	....	1,028,857 00

SCHEDULE B.—*Continued.*

SERVICE.	—	—	—
	$ cts.	$ cts.	$ cts.
Brought over...............	....	....	1,028,857 00
V. AGRICULTURE, IMMIGRATION AND COLONIZATION.			
Agriculture :			
Board of Agriculture.......	4,000 00		
Agricultural Schools...........................	2,400 00		
		6,400 00	
Immigration :			
Immigration and repatriation...................	....	45,000 00	
Colonization :			
Colonization Roads, 1st class...................	40,000 00		
do 2nd and 3rd class.......	8,000 00		
		48,000 00	
Aid towards the establishment of Beet-root Sugar manufactories.....	....	5,000 00	
			$104,409 00
VI. PUBLIC WORKS AND BUILDINGS.			
Rents, Insurances, Repairs, &c., of Public Buildings generally....	44,076 00		
Inspections and Surveys.......................	4,000 00		
Public Departments, to build...................	100,000 00		
Bridge across the Ottawa River to Calumet Island, provided the township in which such bridge is situated furnishes an amount sufficient to complete it..........................	1,000 00		
Workman's property, Gabriel Street, Montreal, to purchase.............................	16,000 00		
Towards making the Railway bridge over the St. Maurice suitable for vehicles, or if not found desirable, towards reconstructing the bridge over the St. Maurice near Three Rivers, provided the City of Three Rivers and the other adjoining municipalities furnish funds sufficient to complete said bridges..............	15,000 00		
		180,076 00	
Chargeable to Building and Jury Fund :			
Rents of Court Houses and Gaols.	527 00		
Insurances of do	3,600 00		
Repairs of do	18,500 00		
Bonaventure Court House and Gaol, to heighten wall and to build house for Keeper..........	2,500 00		
Court Houses and Gaols, new Districts, to construct fireproof safes..........................	6,000 00		
Quebec Gaol, for heating apparatus.............	8,000 00		
		39,127 00	
			219,203 00
Carried forward.............	....	....	1,352,460 00

SCHEDULE B.—*Continued.*

SERVICE.	—	—	—
	$ cts.	$ cts.	$ cts.
Brought forward...............	....	....	1,352,460 00
VII. CHARITIES.			
Lunatic Asylums.............................	192,506 00		
Belmont Retreat Inebriate Asylum, Quebec......	700 00		
Marine and Emigrant Hospital, do	2,666 67		
Lying-in Hospital, care of the Ladies of the Good Shepherd, Quebec........................	1,333 33	197,206 00	
Miscellaneous.			
Corporation of the General Hospital, Montreal..	4,000 00		
Indigent Sick, do ..	3,200 00		
St. Patrick's Hospital, do ...	1,600 00		
Sœurs de la Providence, do ..	1,120 00		
St. Vincent de Paul Asylum, do ..	600 00		
Protestant House of Industry and Refuge, do ..	800 00		
St. Patrick's Orphan Asylum, do ..	640 00		
University Lying-in Hospital, do ..	480 00		
Magdalen Asylum, (Bon Pasteur,) . do ..	720 00		
Roman Catholic Orphan Asylum, do ..	320 00		
Sœurs de la Charité do ..	800 00		
Do. do. for their foundling hospital (so long as there is none in Quebec,) do ..	400 00		
Protestant Orphan Asylum, do ..	640 00		
Lying-in Hospital, care Sœurs de la Miséricorde,do..	480 00		
Bonaventure Street Asylum, do ..	430 00		
Nazareth Asylum for the Blind and for destitute children, do ..	1,230 00		
Dispensary, do ..	320 00		
Ladies' Benevolent Society for Widows and Orphans (including late House of Refuge,) do ..	850 00		
Home and School of Industry, do ..	320 00		
Carried over...................	18,720 00	197,436 00	1,352,460 00

SCHEDULE B.—*Continued.*

SERVICE.	—	—	—
	$ cts.	$ cts.	$ cts.
Brought over..............	18,720 00	197,436 00	1,352,460 00
St. Bridget Asylum, Montreal..	800 00		
Frères de la Charité de St. Vincent de Paul, do ..	500 00		
Hospice de Béthléem, do ..	500 00		
Hospice de St. Joseph du Bon Pasteur, do ..	200 00		
Protestant Infants' Home, do ..	400 00		
Women's Hospital, do ..	500 00		
Eye and Ear Institution, do ..	250 00		
Charitable Ladies' Association of the Roman Catholic Orphan Asylum, and Nazareth Asylum, Quebec..	1,140 00		
Indigent Sick, do ..	3,200 00		
Asylum of the Good Shepherd, do ..	800 00		
Hospice de la Maternité, do ..	340 00		
Ladies' Protestant Home, do ..	750 00		
Male Orphan Asylum, do ..	420 00		
Finlay Asylum, do ..	420 00		
Protestant Female Orphan Asylum, do ..	420 00		
St. Bridget's Asylum, do ..	750 00		
Dispensary, do ..	200 00		
Sisters of Charity, for old and infirm persons, do ..	200 00		
Hôpital du Sacré Cœur de Jésus, do ..	1,000 00		
do Dispensary do ..	200 00		
Indigent Sick, Three Rivers.	2,500 00		
Sœurs de la Charité, for foundling hospital, do	400 00		
General Hospital, Sorel	500 00		
St. Hyacinthe Hospital, St. Hyacinthe.......	500 00		
Ouvroir de St. Hyacinthe, St. Hyacinthe.......	200 00		
Hospice Youville, St. Benoit	200 00		
Carried forward	36,010 00	197,436 00	1,352,460 00

SCHEDULE B.— *Continued.*

SERVICE	$ cts.	$ cts.	$ cts.
Brought forward..........	36,010 00	197,436 00	1,352,460 00
Asile de la Providence, Côteau du Lac......	200 00		
Hospice St. Joseph, Beauharnois........	200 00		
Hospice Ste. Marie, Ste. Marie de Monnoir	200 00		
Asile de la Providence, Mascouche..........	200 00		
Hôpital St. Jean, St. Jean............	200 00		
Sisters of Charity, do	200 00		
Hospice La Jemmerais, Varennes...........	200 00		
Hospice Sœurs de la Provdce, St. Vincent de Paul....	200 00		
Hôpital de la Providence, Joliette............	200 00		
Hospice de Laprairie, Laprairie..........	200 00		
Hôpital St. Joseph, Chambly..........	200 00		
Asile de la Providence, Ste. Elizabeth......	200 00		
Sœurs de la Providence de N.-D. de l'Assomption..	200 00		
Asile de la Providence, Ste. Ursule.........	200 00		
Hôpital Ste. Anne Lapocatière	200 00		
Sœurs de la Charité, Rimouski..........	200 00		
Hôpital St. Ferdinand d'Halifax	200 00		
Hospice Yamachiche	200 00		
Sherbrooke Hospital and Orphan Asylum	500 00		
Sœurs de la Charité, Lanoraie	200 00		
Hôpital St. Paulin	200 00	40,740 00	
Reformatory Schools	8,140 00		
Industrial Schools	7,000 00	15,140 00	
			253,086 00
Carried over............			1,605,546 00

SCHEDULE B.—*Continued.*

SERVICE	—	—	—
	$ cts.	$ cts.	$ cts.
Brought over..........	....	....	1,605,546 00
VIII. Miscellaneous Services.			
Miscellaneous generally............................	....	20,000 00	
For expenses connected with the Philadelphia Exhibition............................		5,000 00	
To provide pure vaccine lymph for public distribution............................		200 00	
To pay for copying Registers of St. Gervais, County of Bellechasse.		600 00	25,800 00
IX. Collection, Management and other Charges on Revenue.			
Municipalities Fund, C. S. L. C. cap 110, sec. 7....		5,000 00	
Registration Service through Crown Lands Department............................	.50,000 00		
Surveys do do	24,000 00		
General Expenditure by Crown Lands Department, including Jesuits' Estates, Clergy Lands, Crown Domain, Seigniory of Lauzon, Woods and Forests, &c	63,550 00	137,550 00	
Quebec Official Gazette.................		14,200 00	
Stamps, Licenses, &c.................		4,000 00	160,750 00
			1,792,096 00
To cover special warrants for expenditure already made belonging to the fiscal year ended 30th June, 1875, see Public accounts 1875, page 47.	40,404 49		

CAP. II.

An Act respecting the construction of " the Quebec, Montreal, Ottawa and Occidental Railway."

[Assented to 24th December, 1875.]

WHEREAS the " North Shore Railway Company " Preamble. and the " Montreal, Ottawa and Western Railway Company," heretofore known as the " Montreal Northern Colonization Railway Company," have severally signified to the lieutenant-governor their inability to carry out the construction of the said lines of road, and whereas they have severally expressed their readiness to surrender to the government of the province of Quebec the property and rights of the said corporations, if the government would undertake to construct the said lines of railroad, with the branches thereof, to the Grand Piles and St. Jerome ; and whereas it is in the public interest that the said roads should be constructed, and therefrom prolonged as hereinafter set forth ; Therefore, Her Majesty, by and with the advice and consent of the Legislature of Quebec, enacts as follows :

1. There shall be a railway constructed, commencing at Railway to be the port of Quebec, and extending from deep water in the constructed, said port, *via* Montreal, to such point in the county of Pontiac as may be most suitable for connecting hereafter the said railway with the subsidized portion of the Extent. Canada Central railway, and with any other railway as the lieutenant-governor in council may hereafter decide, including therein a branch line from the city of Three Branches. Rivers to the Grand Piles, and another from St. Therese to St. Jerome ; and such railway shall be styled and known as " The Quebec, Montreal, Ottawa and Occidental Name. Railway."

2. The said railway shall be a public work belonging Shall be public property. to the province of Quebec, held to and for the public uses of the said province, and shall be made with a guage of four feet eight and one half inches, and on such grades, in such places, in such manner, with Mode of construction, localization, &c. such materials, and on such specifications, as the lieutenant-governor in council shall determine and appoint, as best adapted to the general interests of the province, the whole subject to any existing contracts which the legislature of the province of Quebec may hereinafter or hereby ratify and confirm.

3. The construction of the said railway and its management shall be under the control of three commissioners, Commissioners. to be appointed by the lieutenant-governor in council, who shall hold office during pleasure.

Their designation

Irresponsibility.

They shall be known by and under the name of " the commissioners of the Quebec, Montreal, Ottawa and Occidental Railway," and when acting as such, within the powers conferred by this act, they shall incur no personal liability.

Engineers.

4. The lieutenant-governor in council shall and may appoint a chief engineer, and engineers, over the whole or over any section or part of the said road, who shall hold office during pleasure, and to whom the said commissioners shall intrust the general superintendence, under their instructions from time to time, of the works to be constructed or completed under the present act.

Secretary and other officers.

5. The commissioners shall and may, subject to the approval of the lieutenant-governor in council, appoint and employ a secretary, such engineers, surveyors and other officers, and also such agents, servants and workmen, as in their discretion they may deem necessary and proper for the execution of the powers and duties vested in and imposed on the said commissioners in virtue of the present act.

Power of the commissioners.

6. The commissioners shall have full power and authority, by themselves, their engineers, agents, workmen, servants and contractors, and the servants and workmen of such contractors,

To explore;

1. To examine, explore and survey the present projected line of railway from Quebec westward, and the country adjacent thereto ;

To enter on lands.

2. And for that purpose to enter into and upon any public land, or the land of any corporation or person whatsoever ;

To make surveys.

3. To make surveys, examinations or other arrangements on such lands necessary for confirming, altering, establishing or locating the site of the railway, and to set out and ascertain such parts of the lands as shall be necessary and proper for the railway ;

To fell or remove trees.

4. And further to fell or remove any trees standing in any woods, lands or forests where the railway shall pass, to the distance of four rods from either side thereof.

Resolutions of the N. S. R. C , confirmed.

7. The resolution passed on the eleventh day of August last by the directors of the North Shore Railway company, and subsequently to wit, on the 22nd day of November, 1875, as ratified and confirmed by a resolution of the shareholders of the company, purporting to vest and convey all the property of the said railway company in and to the said province of Quebec, shall, at all times and places, be held to be full, final, complete, and effectual to all intents and purposes whatsoever; and all the property and rights of action of the said Effects. corporation and all the franchises and privileges thereof shall be, and the same are hereby, vested in Her Majesty, to and for the public uses of this province; and the enregistration of a copy of the said resolutions, in any registry office in any registration division of this province, in which any Enregistralands are situated, which have at any time heretofore been tion and its conveyed or bonded to the said company, shall have the effect. same force and effect, as if such lands had been specially mentioned in the said resolutions, and separately, and specially and expressly therein described, any provision of any law or act to the contrary notwithstanding.

8. The transfer and assignment passed on the second Assignment day of November, one thousand eight hundred and seven- of the Montty-five, before Mtre. Dumouchel, notary public, by and and Western between the Montreal, Ottawa and Western Railway com- R. C. conpany, and the province of Quebec, purporting to vest and firmed. convey all the property of the said railway company in and to the said province of Quebec, shall be held to be full, final, complete and effectual to all intents and purposes whatsoever; and all the property of the said corporation, and all the rights and privileges thereof, thereby Effects. conveyed or intended so to be, shall be, and the same are hereby, vested in Her Majesty, to and for the public uses of this province; and the registration of a copy of the said transfer and assignment, in any registry office in any re- Enregistragistration division of this province, in which any lands tion and its are situated, which have at any time heretofore been con- effect. veyed or bonded to the said company, shall have the same force and effect as if such lands had been specially mentioned in the said contract or agreement, and separately, specially, and expressly therein described, any provision of any law or act to the contrary notwithstanding.

9. The contract passed at the city of Quebec, on the Contract with twenty-fourth day of September, last past, before Mtre. Hon. Mr. Mc- Ph. Huot and colleagues, notaries, between the Honorable firmed. Charles B. deBoucherville, representing the province of Quebec, and the Honorable Thomas McGreevy, for the construction and completion of that portion of the said railway between deep water in the port of the city of Quebec, and the city of Montreal, and the branch thereof to Grand Piles, is hereby ratified and confirmed.

10. The contract passed before Mtre. Dumouchel, no- Contract with tary public, at the city of Quebec, on the sixteenth day of Donald, con- November. in the year of Our Lord one thousand eight firmed. hundred and seventy five, between the Honorable Charles B. deBoucherville, representing the province of Quebec, and Duncan MacDonald, for the construction and com-

pletion of that portion of the said railway between the
city of Montreal and the village of Aylmer, in the county
of Ottawa, with the branch to St. Jérôme, is hereby ratified
and confirmed.

The Quebec railway act shall apply.

11. The provisions of *The Quebec Railway Act* 1869,
so far as they are applicable to the undertaking hereby
authorized, and in so far as they are not varied by or
inconsistent with, the provisions of this act, shall apply to
the said Railway to the extent to which they are applicable thereto, and be construed to form part of the present
act.

The deposit of plans, heretofore made may be of use.

The said commissioners in locating the railway hereby
authorized to be constructed, at any place or point where
the same is not already located, shall be entitled to avail
themselves of the deposit heretofore made by the Montreal,
Ottawa and Western Railway company, or by the Montreal
Northern Colonization Railway company, in the office of
the Clerks of the Peace for the districts or counties
through which the said railway was intended to pass,
and shall forthwith cause a complete copy of such plans
and books of reference to be deposited in the office of the

Copies shall be deposited in the Public Works department.

department of public works, and such deposit shall be
held to be a compliance with the provisions of *The Quebec
Railway Act* 1869, in respect of plans and surveys, and
shall be held to be a sufficient basis for any proceedings
to be taken under the said railway act, to the same
extent and in the same manner as if the said commissioners had made and corrected maps or plans and books
of reference, and had deposited them and copies of them,
in conformity with the first and second sub-sections
of the eighth section of the said *Quebec Railway Act,*
1869. And the copies now deposited in the said office of
the said clerks of the peace, and the copy to be deposited
in the department of public works in conformity hereto,
shall be treated, received, dealt with and accepted in
every respect as if the same had been made and deposited
by the commissioners under the provisions of the said
eighth section.

The line, heretofore adopted, is the true line, but may be changed.

The line heretofore adopted by the Montreal, Ottawa
and Western Railway, unless the same be changed by the
said Commissioners, is hereby declared to be in future;
the line of the Quebec, Montreal, Ottawa and Occidental
railway between Montreal and Aylmer, and of the
branch to Saint Jerome, but such location shall be subject to all such alterations as shall be made therein, in
conformity to the said eighth section of the said railway
act ; which alteration shall be made in the manner prescribed in the said section.

Proceedings respecting expropriation or acquisition

In cases where proceedings have been commenced by
the said Montreal, Ottawa and Western Railway, or by
the Montreal Northern Colonization Railway, for the

·expropriation or acquisition of lands for the purposes of commenced the said railway, and have not been completed, the com- may be conti-missioners shall have the right to continue such proceed- nued ings under the provisions of the said *Quebec Railway Act,* 1869, provided the proprietors, or persons interested in such lands, shall file with the commissioners a written Consent re-consent thereto ; but the said commissioners may discon- quired. tinue all anterior proceedings, on the part of the said company, and may commence such proceedings *de novo* May be com-under the said *Quebec Railway Act ;* and in the valuation menced, *de* of such properties allowance may be made to such pro- *novo.* prietors, or parties interested, for any actual and material damage which has been caused to them by the discon-tinuance of such previous proceedings. But no construc- Damages to tive or general damages shall be awarded in relation be paid. thereto.

The deposit of maps, plans and books of reference, Deposit of wherever made by or on behalf of the said North Shore plans made Railway company, and all valuations, tenders, deposits R. C. of use. of money, and all other steps and proceedings taken by or on behalf of the said company, towards the acquisition or expropriation of any land or property required for the purposes of the said railway, shall enure to the benefit of the said province, and the said commissioners shall have the power to take up such proceedings at whatever stage Proceedings they may have arrived, and to continue and complete the of acquisition same in the same manner as might have been done by the and expro-said company ; and they may discontinue such proceedings priation. and begin others, according as they may deem advisable.

12. The said commissioners may enter into contracts Contracts and stipulations with all persons, corporations, guardians, with capable tutors, curators and trustees whatsoever, not only for those repre-themselves, their heirs, assigns and legal representatives, senting the but also for and in the name of those whom they re- incapable. present, whether minors, absentees, lunatics, married women, or persons otherwise incapable of contracting, in relation to the purchase of any land or other pro-perty necessary for the construction, maintenance and use of the railroad, upon such prices as may be agreed be-tween them ; and they may also enter into contracts and stipulations with such persons and corporations, in res-pect of the amount of compensation to be paid for all damages sustained by them, by reason of anything done in virtue and under the authority of the present act.

13. As to that portion of the said railway between Ayl- Construction mer aforesaid and the point in the county of Pontiac of the por-tion between which shall be determined upon, as most suitable for Aylmer and crossing the Ottawa river to connect such portion of the Pontiac. said railway, with the subsidized portion of the Canada Central Railway, the said commissioners shall build the Tenders.

same by tender and contract, after the plans and specifications therefor shall have been duly advertised; and they shall accept the tenders of such contractors as shall appear to them tó be possessed of sufficient skill, experience and resources, to carry out the work or such portions thereof as they may contract for; provided always, that the said commissioners shall not be bound to accept the lowest, or any tender, if they should deem it for the public interest not to do so, and provided also that no contract under this section shall be concluded by the commissioners, until first duly sanctioned by the lieutenant-governor in council.

Assent of the lieut.-gov.

Stipulations in the contract. **14.** The contract, to be so entered into shall be guarded by such securities, and contain such provisions for retaining a proportion of the contract moneys, to be held as a reserve fund, for such period of time and on such conditions, as may appear to be necessary for the protection of the public, and for securing the due performance of the contract.

Certificate required before payment. **15.** No moneys shall be paid to any contractor until the chief engineer shall have certified that the work, for or on account of which, the same shall be claimed, has been duly executed, nor until such certificate shall have been approved of by the commissioners.

Members of the Legislature. **16.** No member of the legislature shall be a commissioner, under this act, or shall hold, or be appointed to any office of emolument under the commissioners, or be a contractor, or party to any contract with the commissioners, for the construction of the railway or any part thereof.

Inspection of the commissioners' proceedings. **17.** The lieutenant governor, in council, or any person or persons appointed by him, shall have power to inspect all contracts, and proceedings of the commissioners and to examine their accounts at all times.

Salary of the commissioners and employees. **18.** The lieutenant-governor in council shall fix the rate of salary or compensation for the commissioners and the chief engineer, and shall approve of all other salaries to be awarded by the commissioners, subject in all cases to the revision and confirmation of the legislature.

Suspension of works. **19.** The lieutenant-governor in council shall have the power, at any time, to suspend the progress of the work until the then next session of the legislature.

Payments made to the commissioners. **20.** The treasurer of the province, shall from time to time pay to the commissioners, on their demand, all moneys required under this act, for the purposes thereof, in such manner, at such times, and in such sums, as may, from time to time, be ordered by the lieutenant-governor in council.

21. The commissioners shall furnish quarterly accounts, (or oftener if required by the lieutenant-governor in council), to the treasurer of the province, of all expenditure and liabilities made and incurred under this act. *Accounts to be furnished.*

22. The commissioners may make such arrangements with the Canada Centra railway company, as shall be approved by the lieutenant-governor in council, for the extension of the said Canada Central railway, from the eastern terminus of the subsidized portion thereof, or from such other point of junction with the said subsidized portion thereof, as may be selected, to the Ottawa river, opposite the western terminus of the railway hereby authorized to be constructed, or for the construction of a bridge over the said river at the said last mentioned terminus ; and also, to make such arrangements for the transit of rolling stock, goods, freight and passengers over the said subsidized portion of the said Canada Central railway, and over the Canada Pacific railway, or any branch thereof, as shall be approved by the lieutenant-governor in council, but such arrangements shall only be binding and conclusive, after having been approved by the legislature of the province of Quebec. *Arrangements with the Canada Central.*

23. For the construction of that portion of the said railway lying between the said point fixed or to be fixed in the county of Pontiac, and the eastern terminus of the said subsidized portion of the Canada Central railway in the province of Ontario, or such point thereon as may be selected as a point of junction, the said commissioners shall also have full power and authority, in their quality of such commissioners, to apply to the parliament of the Dominion of Canada, for authority to construct such portion of the said railway, subject to such regulations as the lieutenant-governor in council may prescribe, and on such terms and conditions, and with such powers, franchises and limitations, as the said parliament of the Dominion of Canada may think proper to grant and confer. *Commissioners may apply to the federal parliament respecting the portion from Aylmer to Pontiac.*

24. All that portion of sections two and five of the act of this province, 34 Vict., chap. 21, of section three of the act of this province, 36 Vict., chap. 42, and any other provision of law, whereby a grant of lands has been given or reserved to the North Shore Railway Company or Grand Piles branch thereof, or to the Montreal, Ottawa, and Western Railway Company, are hereby repealed ; and the said lands are hereby re-united to the public lands of the province of Quebec, as fully and completely, as if the said sections or provisions had never been passed *Grant of lands to the two Cos. repealed.*

Loan of
$3,000 C00 by
the commis-
sioners.

25. The said commissioners are authorized to raise by way of loan, a sum not exceeding three millions of dollars, for the construction of the said road and its branches, and for such purpose to issue bonds or debentures, and they may, by the lieutenant-governor in council, be authorized

Guarantee.

to guarantee in the name of the province, that the said railroad shall be completed and put in operation.

Debentures.

26. Such bonds or debentures shall be signed by one of the commissioners and countersigned and registered in a special book by the secretary of the said commissioners, and they shall be certified, as having issued under this act, by the treasurer of the province.

Interest.

They shall be made payable in thirty years, and shall bear interest at a rate not exceeding six per cent per annum, payable semi-annually, on presentation of the interest coupons thereunto annexed.

Coupons.

The interest coupons annexed to the debentures shall be signed by the secretary of the said commissioners.

When and
where pay-
able.

27. The bonds or debentures issued by the said commissioners may be made payable in Canada or elsewhere, and in currency or sterling, as they shall deem most expedient to facilitate the negotiation thereof.

Disposal of
the bonds.

28. The said commissioners may sell the bonds or debentures issued in virtue of the present act and dispose of the same at such prices as they may agree upon, and the lieutenant-governor in council shall approve or direct ;

Interest gua-
ranteed.

and they may guarantee the due payment of the principal and interest of the said debentures by first mortgage or hypothec on the said line of railway, and the lands,

Mortgage.

buildings, rolling stock, plant, and upon all other property, and revenue, and the commissioners shall be bound, from time to time, to execute any deed or other instrument which the lieutenant governor in council may ap-

Mode of gua-
rantee.

prove, which may be requisite to perfect the charge intended to be created by such mortgage or hypothec, and to perfect the securities thereby intended to be given, and to enable such charge to be made completely effectual by registration thereof, in accordance with the laws of this province.

Mortgage to
whom made.

29. Every such mortgage or hypothec may be from time to time made to any corporation, or to any person or persons in the United Kingdom, or in the Dominion of Canada or elsewhere, as trustees for the holders of the said debentures ; which debentures shall refer to such mortgage or hypothec, and shall be countersigned by the

Trustees.

trustees, or one of them, or by some person in their name duly authorized by them in that behalf, for the purpose of identifying such debentures as those which are to be secured by such mortgage or hypothec ; but any bank, or company lawfully incorporated for financial purposes, may be also appointed trustees, and they are hereby authorized to accept such appointment and perform the duties connected therewith, as described in such mortgage or hypothec.

30. Every such mortgage or hypothec may contain an authority to the trustees to take possession of, to work and sell the railway, lands and other property therein comprised, upon default by the commissioners to pay the interest of the debentures to be secured thereby, or any part thereof, within such delays respectively, and upon such terms and conditions, as the said commissioners shall agree on, and the lieutenant governor in council approve or direct, as set forth in such mortgage and hypothec. *Trustees may take possession in case of non-payment.*

31. Every such mortgage or hypothec, upon being duly registered in accordance with the laws of this province, by the registration thereof or of an authentic notarial copy thereof, in the registry offices for all the registration divisions in which shall be situate any part of the railway, lands or other property intended to be affected thereby, and without the registration of any of the debentures issued shall, for the purposes of this act, and of the loan to be made in virtue thereof, take effect in priority from the date of its registration, without reference to the date or dates at which the debentures to be secured thereby shall be issued, and at whatever subsequent date or dates they shall be issued ; and except when otherwise provided in the mortgage or hypothec, all the debentures to be issued, upon the security thereof, shall be secured thereby *pari passu*, and without any preference of one over the other, in consequence of the respective dates of issue thereof, or for any other reason. *Effect of the enregistration. Priority.*

32. The trustees may, at all times, in their own names, and without the concurrence or co-operation of any of the debenture-holders, enforce all the rights which such mortgage or hypothec shall purport to confer upon them, and all contracts into which, for the purposes of benefiting or protecting the debenture-holders, they may enter with the said commissioners respecting the construction of the railway, or with any other persons, in precisely the same way as if such contracts, and such mortgage or hypothec had been made to them for their own benefit, and that they were the holders of all the debentures issued thereunder and intended to be secured thereby ; and for such purpose they may, if necessary, bring or defend in their own names, any actions or suits in any court in the province of Quebec. *Power of the trustees.*

Accounts to be rendered by the trustees. **33.** It may be a condition of such mortgage or hypothec that upon the said trustees assuming to take possession of and work the said railway, they, the said trustees, shall be bound and obliged to render periodical accounts to the commissioners, of the earnings and receipts of the said road, and to pay over to the said commissioners any surplus of revenue over and above what is required for the payment of the claims of the said debenture-holders, and over and **Surplus of revenue.** above the expense of working and maintaining the said road, the whole subject to such penalty, as in and by the said mortgage may be stipulated for and provided.

Sinking fund. **34.** A sinking fund is hereby established, to which the said commissioners shall pay an annual sum of one per cent, on the amount of the bonds or debentures issued in virtue of this act, and such sum shall be by them paid over to the provincial treasurer, in equal semi-annual payments, and shall be invested by and permitted to accumulate under, the management of the said treasurer.

Redemption of debentures. **35.** Such sinking fund may be employed in the redemption of the debentures so issued, in accordance with the instructions of the provincial treasurer, as approved by the lieutenant-governor in council.

Orders of claims. **36.** From and out of the revenue of the said road, after payment of the current expenses for the maintenance and working thereof, the first claims to be paid shall be the interest on the bonds and debentures issued by the said commissioners under the present act, and the sums to be devoted to the sinking fund established under section 34 ; the interest payable to the municipal corporations as hereinbefore stated shall be the second claim ; and the **Balance.** balance shall be the property of the crown and shall form part of the consolidated revenue fund of the province.

Municipal grants invested in the road. **37.** The municipal grants or subscriptions for stock mentioned in schedule A hereunto annexed, made under the several by-laws authorizing the same in favor of the said North Shore Railway company, and of the said Montreal, Ottawa and Western Railway company, hitherto known as the Montreal Northern Colonization Railway company, shall be and are vested in the Quebec, Montreal, Ottawa and Occidental Railway, and shall be paid to the treasurer of the province.

Municipal grants and by-laws obligatory. **38.** The corporations which have made such grants or subscribed for the said stock shall not be admitted to plead by way of exception, or for the purpose of modifying their engagements, the lapse of time, or negligence on the part of the companies, or either of them, in fulfilling the conditions or any of the conditions, under which the said grants or subscriptions for stock were made ; and the said several by-laws are hereby declared to be obligatory, legal and effectual for all purposes whatsoever ; and the said corporations shall be respectively bound and obliged to execute, issue and deliver to the provincial treasurer, the total amount of their said respective bonds or debentures, the issue whereof is authorized by such by-laws, and the treasurer may when necessary, and as the case may require, negotiate such bonds or debentures. Delivery and negotiation of municipal debentures.

39. The several amounts of the subscriptions of the municipal corporations, to the capital stock, of the "North Shore Railway Company," or of the "Montreal Northern Colonization Railway Company," and of the bonuses granted to such companies, including the sums already paid, shall be deemed to be invested in the said road, and shall bear interest, to be paid by the said commissioners to the said corporations, at such rate, not exceeding five per centum per annum on their respective amounts, as the annual revenue of the said road will admit of, after payment of the cost of maintenance and running expenses, of the interest on bonds or debentures issued under section 25, and of the sinking fund established under section 34,—such interest not to begin to run, until after the whole of the said road shall have been completed and put in operation. Interest to be paid on such grants

40. The balance of the various subsidies or grants accorded by the acts of this province now in force, to "The North Shore Railway company," and to "The Montreal Northern Colonization Railway company," and the sums subscribed by the cities of Quebec, Montreal and Three Rivers, and the several other corporations and municipalities shall be paid by the treasurer of the province to the said commissioners for the purposes of this act, and shall be expended on the parts of the road, in respect of which such subsidies, grants and subscriptions were given ; and the said payments shall be made subject to the terms of the proviso, relating to the road from the city of Three Rivers to the Grand Piles, and to the establishment of steam navigation on the St. Maurice, contained in sub-section 1 of section 16 of the act of this province, 37 Vict., cap. 2, and also subject to the proviso contained in section 21 of the said act. Balance of subsidies and municipal grant, to be paid to the commissioners.
How spent.

41. The lieutenant-governor in council may grant to the said commissioners for the construction of the railway to be built in virtue of the present act, another additional subsidy of two millions three hundred and twenty-seven thousand dollars, as representing the value of the grant in land accorded to the North Shore and Montreal Northern Colonization railways. Additional subsidy of $2,327,000.

Lease of the road.   **42.** The lieutenant-governor in council may, so soon as the said road or any section thereof shall have been completed, lease the said road or section thereof to any person or persons, or to any corporation, subject to the approval of the legislature.

General investment in the road.   **43.** And to avoid all doubts it is hereby enacted that " the Quebec, Montreal, Ottawa and Occidental railway " is hereby vested with all the rights, powers, immunities, franchises, privileges and assets, heretofore by any act granted unto either the North Shore Railway company, or the Montreal Northern Colonization Railway company, subject nevertheless to any alterations, limitations or restrictions herein contained, and so far as this legislature may or can do, with all the rights, powers, immunities, franchises, privileges and assets granted by the parliament of the Dominion of Canada to the Montreal, Ottawa and Western Railway company.

Directors abolished.   **44.** Notwithstanding anything to the contrary in any of the hereinbefore recited acts, or in any of the by-laws hereinbefore alluded to, the said several corporations shall not be entitled to appoint or to be represented by any directors in the management of the affairs of the company ; and the directorate contemplated and provided for by the provisions of the said acts is hereby abolished.

Rights of individual shareholders vested in the commissioners.   **45.** The contracts or agreements hereinbefore alluded to for the transfer of the rights and assets of the North Shore Railway company and of the Montreal, Ottawa and Western Railway company, to the province of Quebec being ratified, the rights of the individual shareholders, in the said companies, shall be transferred to and vested in the said commissioners in their quality, to and for the uses of this province.

Stock refunded.   The stock of individual shareholders in the said companies, or so much thereof as shall have been paid up, shall be refunded to them.

Federal legislation may be asked for,   **46.** And it is further enacted that the said commissioners, in their said quality by and with the consent of the lieutenant-governor in council, may be and they are hereby authorized to apply to the parliament of Canada, for any legislation which may be deemed necessary for the purposes of this act.

Act into force.   **47.** The present act shall come into force on the day of the sanction thereof.

SCHEDULE A.

Municipal subscriptions and grants to the Montrea
Northern Colonization Railway.

The city of Montreal ....$1,000,000 in stock.
The county of Ottawa..................... 200,000 "
The parish of St. André.................. 25,000 "
The village of Ste. Thérèse de Blain-
    ville............ .... 12,000 "
The village of Ste Thérèse .... 12,000 "
The village of St. Jérôme .... 15,000 "
The parish of St. Jérôme................. 10,000 "
The village of Ste. Scholastique........ 10,000 "
The village of St. Jérusalem d'Argen-
    teuil (Lachute)............................ 25,000 Bonus.
The village of la Côte St. Louis........... 25,000 in stock.

II. Municipal subscriptions to the North Shore Railway.

The city of Quebec........................$1,000,000 in stock.
The city of Three Rivers................. 100,000 "
The parish of St. Sauveur de Quebec. 25,000 "

CAP. III.

An Act to amend the law respecting subsidies in money
made to certain railways.

[Assented to 24th December, 1875.]

HER MAJESTY, by and with the advice and consent of the Legislature of Quebec, enacts as follows:

1. The lieutenant-governor in council may, upon resolution of the directors of any company entitled to a subsidy in money, convert such subsidy into a guarantee, and payment by this province, in favor of the holders of bonds or debentures of such company, of interest at the rate of five per centum per annum, on a capital which at such rate produces a sum in interest, equal to the subsidy granted for each mile of road, together with interest thereon, until the whole subsidy be paid. *Conversion authorized in payment of the interest.*

2. Any payment on a subsidy already made by this province, may be returned to the provincial treasurer, and thereafter converted into a like guarantee, for such part or portion of the subsidy returned. *Subsidies already paid returned.*

3. The payment of the interest shall be made semi-annually, for every ten miles or more of road completed, continuous and uninterrupted. *Payment.*

Subsidy of the Montreal, Chambly and Sorel comp'y changed as regards a certain part of the road. '

4. The subsidy of one thousand dollars per mile granted to the Montreal, Chambly and Sorel railway company, (now amalgamated with and known as the Montreal, Portland and Boston railway company), for that part of the said road from Sorel to Chambly, and from Chambly to St. Jean, shall be withdrawn, and used, applied and paid on the line of the said Montreal, Portland and Boston railway *via* Chambly, West Farnham and Frelighsburg,

Proviso.

to the frontier of this province ; provided that between this day and the first day of August next, the directors of the said Montreal, Portland and Boston railway company, pass a resolution to such end, and that such resolution be approved by a majority of the votes of the shareholders thereof, and by the lieutenant governor in council, and

Proviso.

provided that the directors of such company have given satisfactory evidence to the lieutenant-governor in council that the company has paid to the proprietors the cost of the right of way, and the damage to their properties.

Subsidy to the company of the South-Eastern railway change for a certain portion.

5. The subsidy of two thousand five hundred dollars per mile granted to the South-Eastern railway company, for that part of the said road heretofore known as the Richelieu, Drummond, and Arthabaska counties railway, for a length of fifty-five miles, from Drummondville to the Arthabaska branch (Grand Trunk,) and all that portion of the said road to the east of Drummondville, shall be withdrawn, and used, applied and paid on the line of the said South-Eastern railway, from Sorel

Proviso.

to Sutton Junction *via* Acton and Waterloo ; provided that between this day and the first day of August next, the directors of the said company pass a resolution to that end, and that such resolution be approved by the majority of the votes of the shareholders thereof, and by the lieutenant-governor in coun-

Proviso.

cil ; provided also, that the said company return to the municipality of the townships of Wendover and Simpson, the bonds or debentures subscribed by such municipality to the said road, or the amount thereof, save and except the interest already paid thereon ; and provided that in any case, the apportionment of the said subsidy added to the present subsidy, does not exceed the total amount of $4000 for each mile of road.

Proviso.

Nothing hereinabove contained shall affect the road to L'avenir.

Certain delay extended.

6. The delay accorded by section 2 of the act of this province 38 Vict., ch. 3, is extended until the first day of the month of October next.

Interpretation.

7. Nothing in this act contained shall be construed as extending the period for the accomplishment of the conditions which such companies are bound to fulfil to be entitled to a subsidy in money, save in so far as is prescribed in the section preceding.

8. This act shall come into force on the day of the sanction thereof. [right margin: Act into force]

CAP. IV.

An Act authorizing the issue of Provincial Debentures, for the payment of the subsidies granted to railway companies.

[Assented to 24th December, 1875.]

HER MAJESTY, by and with the advice and consent of the Legislature of Quebec, enacts as follows :

1. The lieutenant-governor in council may authorize the provincial treasurer, to contract a loan and to that end to issue, sell and negotiate bonds or debentures in the name of the province, to an amount not exceeding eight hundred and sixty thousand pounds sterling [right margin: Loan of £860,000. sterl.]

2. Such bonds or debentures shall be issued in the form, and according to the mode and conditions which the lieutenant-governor in council shall deem expedient to prescribe, in the interests of the province. [right margin: Debentures, their form,&c.]

Such bonds shall be payable in thirty years, in currency or sterling, and shall bear interest not exceeding five per centum per annum. A sinking fund of one per centum per annum shall be established for their redemption. [right margin: Sinking fund.]

8. The amount raised by such loan and issue of debentures, shall be employed in the payment of the subsidies granted by the various acts of this legislature. [right margin: Employment.]

4. This act shall come into force on the day of the sanction thereof. [right margin: Act into force]

CAP. V.

An Act to amend the Act 38 Vict., chap 4, respecting the manufacture of sugar from beet-root.

[Assented to 24th December, 1875.]

HER MAJESTY, by and with the advice and consent of the Legislature of Quebec, enacts as follows:

1. Section 1 of the act of this province, 38 Vict., chap. 4, is replaced by the following : [right margin: 38 V., c. 4, s. 1 replaced.]

" 1. With the object of securing to the province the benefit of European capital and experience, the lieutenant-governor in council may grant an annual subsidy of seven thousand dollars, during ten years, for the establishment of the manufacture of sugar from beet-root in the province." [right margin: Annual subsidy of $7,000 during 10 years.]

CAP. VI.

An Act to further amend " the Quebec License Act,"
(34 Vict, ch. 2), and the several Acts amending
the same, and to extend the application thereof.

[*Assented to 24th December, 1875.*]

HER MAJESTY, by and with the advice and consent
of the Legislature of Quebec, enacts as follows :

34 V , c. 2, s.
43, § 4 amend-
ed anew.

1. Paragraph 4 of section 43 of the " Quebec License
Act " as amended by the act of this province, 37 Vict., ch.
3, s. 9, is amended anew by adding at the end thereof, the
following words : " each time these sales are not made by
a licensed auctioneer," and by adding in the french version the word " non" at the beginning of the third line
of the said paragraph.

Idem, § 5
amended.

Penalty for
refusal to pay
duties on sale
by auction.

2. Paragraph 5 of section 43 of " the Quebec License
Act " is amended by adding thereto the words following :
" And any person, not being a licensed auctioneer,
who refuses or neglects, within thirty days after any such
sale, to pay to the revenue officer of the district, within
the limits of which such sale has taken place, or to any
other person by him to that end authorized, all moneys
which he owes by reason of such sale, shall incur a penalty of twenty dollars for each day during which he shall
so refuse or neglect to pay ; and the moneys due by reason
of such duties may be recovered with costs by the said
revenue officer, at the same time and in the same suit, as
the amount of the penalties; and in default of payment
of the amount of judgment, including the penalty, costs
and duties, if they have been claimed, the offender may be
condemned to imprisonment for any time not less than
one month, nor exceeding three months."

Rights on im-
movables sold
by auction.

Exception.

3. All immovables sold by public auction or outcry in
this province and adjudged to the highest bidder, shall be
subject to a duty of one dollar for each hundred dollars
of the price at which they are sold, and at and after the
same rate for every greater or less sum, save and except
the part of the price of shares belonging to minors, when
sold by licitation under authority of law.

Sections 39, 40, 40a (37 Vict., ch. 3, s. 8,) 41, 42, 44, 45,
46, and paragraphs 1, 2, 3 and 5 of section 43 of " the Quebec License Act," as also the preceding section, shall
apply to immovables, in the same manner as to merchan-
dise or effects, and shall be interpreted as if the words
" or immovables," were inserted after the word " effects,"
wherever the latter word occurs in such sections and
paragraphs.

4. No person, unless he has obtained a license for such License re-purpose, under the authority of this act, shall open or ex-quired to ex-hibit, in this province, any circus or equestrian exhibition, caravans,&c. or any menagerie, caravan or show of wild animals, under a penalty of two hundred dollars for each representation or exhibition, recoverable in the manner specified in section 6 of this act, and in default of payment, and of property and effects to be taken in execution and sold to the amount required, to imprisonment for any term not less Penalty. than one month nor exceeding four months, on sentence of a judge of the superior court, district magistrate, or a justice of the peace, upon summary petition.

5. Any person opening or exhibiting a circus or eques- License to be trian exhibition, or a menagerie or show of wild animals, shown. shall be bound to show the license required for such purpose, to the revenue officer, or to any one of his deputies, or to any other person thereunto authorized by the revenue officer, on mere written or verbal application on their part, and in default of his so doing, such person shall be deemed not to possess such license, and shall be punished in consequence.

6. The revenue officer, or one of his deputies, or any Recovery of other person thereunto authorized by the revenue officer, fines. may, by a warrant of distress, signed by a judge of the superior court, a district magistrate or any justice of the peace, seize the goods and chattels, even such as are in ordinary cases exempt from seizure, to whomsoever they may belong, which form part of any circus or equestrian exhibition, or of any menagerie or show of wild animals, for the opening or exhibition of which, no license has been taken out, or in respect of which there has been any refusal to show the license required, and he may without any other preliminary formality, sell and adjudge by public auction, the goods and chattels so seized, up to the amount of the penalty incurred and the costs of sale, and this without any judgment being required.

7. The revenue officer of the district, on receipt of the Grant of the duties and fees exigible, shall deliver to any person ap- license. plying therefor, the license required under section 4 of this act.

8. There shall be paid to the revenue officer by every Duties on person who takes out a license to open or hold a circus or licenses. equestrian exhibition, a menagerie or caravan or show of wild animals,

1. In each of the cities of Quebec and Montreal, and within a radius of three miles of each of such cities, $100, for each day of representation or exhibition ;

2. In every other part of the province, $50 for each such day.

Term of the license.

9. Every license granted under the two preceding sections shall state the number of days for which the duties have been paid, and shall become inoperative at the close of the last of such days.

One license only is required, in certain cases.

10. One license only shall be required for the opening or holding at the same place and on the same days, of a circus or equestrian exhibition and of a menagerie or show of wild animals, if they form part of the same troop or company.

Interpretation, &c.

11. The provisions of the second part of " the Quebec License Act," and the amendments thereto, and more particularly those respecting the granting, the form and the cancelling of licenses, the fee to be paid, the reduction of the duties exigible and the application of those collected, shall apply to licenses required by section 4 of this act, and to cases of infraction in relation thereto, in the same manner as if they were here anew enacted; save in so far as would be inconsistent with this act.

34 V., c. 2, s. 125, repealed.

12. Section 125 of " the Quebec License Act, " as amended by the acts of this province, 37 Vict., ch. 3, and 38 Vict., ch. 5, is repealed and the following substituted therefor :

Duties payable.

" 125. There shall be paid to the revenue officer by every person who takes out any of the following licenses, the following duties respectively, that is to say :

Inns; and sale of spirituous liquors.

1. For every license to keep an inn, hotel, tavern or other house or place of public entertainment, and for retailing brandy, rum, whiskey or any spirituous liquors, wine, ale, beer, porter, cider, or other vinous or fermented liquors,
    a. In the city of Montreal, $200, if the annual rent of the place for which such license is demanded, is less than $400,—$300, if such rent is $400, or upwards ;
    b. In the city of Quebec, $125, if such rent is less than $400,—$175, if such rent is $400 or upwards ;
    c. In any other city in the province, $80 ;
    d. In any incorporated town, $70 ;
    e. In any incorporated village, under the operation of the municipal code, $60 ;
    f. In any organized section of the province, not within any such city, town or village, $50 ;
    g. In any unorganized territory, not within the limits of any municipality, $35 ;

Inns; and sale of wine & beer.

2. For every license to keep an inn, tavern, or other house or place of public entertainment, and for retailing wine, ale, beer, porter, cider, or other vinous or fermented liquors, but not brandy, rum, whiskey, or other spirituous liquors,
    a. In each of the cities of Quebec and Montreal $75 ;
    b. In any other city of the province, $50

c. In any other organized section of the province, $40 ;
d. In any unorganized section of the province, $30 ;

3. For every license for retailing brandy, rum, whiskey or other spirituous liquors, wine, ale, beer, porter, cider, or other vinous or fermented liquors, in any restaurant, saloon or refreshment room, *Saloons ; and sale of spirituous liquors.*
    a. In the city of Montreal, $200 ;
    b. In the city of Quebec, $100 ;
    c. In any other city, $80 ;
    d. And in any other incorporated town, $60 ;

4. For every license to keep a " temperance hotel, " for the reception of travellers and others, but not for retailing brandy, rum, whiskey, or other spirituous liquors, nor wine, ale, beer, porter, cider or other vinous or fermented liquors, $9 ; *Temperance hotels.*

5. For every license to vend or retail, in any store or shop, brandy, rum, whiskey, or other spirituous liquors, and wine, ale, beer, porter, cider, or other vinous or fermented liquors, in a quantity not less than three half-pints at any one time, *Retailing spirituous liquors in a shop or store.*
    a. In each of the cities of Quebec and Montreal, $60, if the annual rent of the store or shop, for which the license is demanded, does not exceed $100,—$80, if such rent exceeds $100, but does not exceed $200,—$100, if such rent exceeds $200, but does not exceed $400,—and $125, if such rent exceeds $400 ;
    b. In any other organized section of the province, $50 ;
    c. In any territory unorganized, beyond the limits of a municipality, $20 ;

6. For every license to retail on board any steamboat or other vessel, brandy, rum, whiskey, or other spirituous liquors, wine, ale, beer, porter, cider, or other vinous or fermented liquors, the sum of $150 ; *Retailing spirituous liquors on any steamboat.*

7. For every license to retail on board any steamboat, or other vessel, wine, ale, beer, porter, cider, or other vinous or fermented liquors, but not brandy, rum, whiskey, or other spirituous liquors, the sum of $100 ; *Retailing wine and beer on any steamboats.*

8. For every auctioneer's license, *Auctioneers.*
    a. In each of the cities of Quebec and Montreal, $60, together with an additional sum of $25, for every assistant, agent, servant or partner named therein ;
    b. In every other part of the province, $40, together with an additional sum of $15, for every assistant, agent, servant or partner named therein ;

9. For every separate license taken out by an auctioneer, for one or more assistants, agents, servants or partners, employed as criers ; *Assistants, &c., of auctioneers.*

a. In each of the cities of Quebec and Montreal, $25, for each such assistant, agent, servant or partner, who is therein named ;

b. In any other part of the province, $20, for each such assistant, agent, servant or partner, who is therein named ;

Pedlers.

10. For every hawker's or pedler's license, for one judicial district only, the sum of $20, and for every additional district, the sum of $10 ;

Billiard-tables, &c,

11. For every billiard-table subject to be licensed under this act, when not more than two are kept by the same person, and in the same building, $75 each, and when more than two are kept, for a third and a fourth table $60 each, for a fifth and a sixth, $50 each, and for every table beyond six, $30 each ;

Mississippi-tables, &c.

12. For every bagatelle-board, pigeon-hole board, or Mississippi-table, $25 ;

Pawnbrokers.

13. For every pawnbroker's license, $100 ;

Ferry.

14. For every ferry license such sum as may be fixed by the lieutenant-governor in council, under the provisions of section sixty-five of this act ;

Powder.

15. For every license to keep or use a powder-magazine, $50 ; and for every license to sell or to keep for sale gunpowder,

a. In the cities of Quebec and Montreal, wholesale and retail..$20 00

Retail only.. 8 00

b. In any city of the province, other than those of Quebec and Montreal, wholesale and retail..... 10 00

Retail only.. 5 00

c. In any incorporated town, wholesale and retail. 5 00

Retail only.. 2 50

d. In country parts, wholesale and retail............ 2 50

Retail only.. 1 00

Interpretation.

A quantity of more than twenty-five pounds, or a dozen canisters of one pound each, sold at any one time, shall be deemed to be sold wholesale, and any less quantity than that hereinabove mentioned shall be deemed sold by retail."

37 V., c. 3, s. 17, amended.

13. Section 16 of the act of this province, 36 Vict., ch. 3, as replaced by the act 37 Vict., ch. 3, s. 17, is amended by substituting the following for the first paragraph thereof :

Dues for wholesale spirituous liquors.

" There shall be paid to the revenue officer, by every person who takes out any such license, under this act, $100, if the annual rent of the place for which the license is asked does not exceed $200,—$125, if such rent exceeds $200, but does not exceed $400,—and $150, if such rent exceeds $400.

Case of license deter-

14. In the case of paragraphs 1 and 5 of section 125 of " the Quebec License Act," as amended by this act, respecting the cities of Quebec and Montreal, and in the _{mined by the annual value.} case of section 13 of this act, if the annual rent cannot be established by the valuation roll, or if the place for which the license is demanded, is the property of the person asking for such license, or is occupied by him otherwise than as tenant, the amount to be paid on the license shall be determined by the annual value of such place.

15. The inn, hotel, or tavern, house or place of public What com-entertainment, shop or store, for which a license is de-prises the inn. manded comprises all the apartments and stories of the same building communicating with each óther, as also yards, coach-houses, stables and other dependencies, forming part of the establishment for which the license is demanded, any lease or agreement to the contrary notwithstanding.

16. The annual rent or the annual value in accordance Mode of establishing with which the price of licenses is in certain cases deter-the rent or mined, shall be the same as those established in the annual value. valuation roll in force in the city or municipality for the purposes of municipal taxation.

17. Any person applying for a license, the price where-Certificate, of is determined by the amount of the annual rent or of duced. the annual value, as the case may be, shall be bound to produce, together with his application, a certificate from the clerk or secretary of the city or municipality, establishing the amount of such rent or annual value, as set forth in the valuation roll.

18. Each such clerk or secretary shall ·be bound to Duty of the municipal furnish the certificate specified in the preceding section, clerk, or sec.- on demand made to him therefor, under a penalty of fifty treas dollars for each contravention, o., in default of payment, Penalty. of imprisonment for three months.

19. Paragraph 5 of section 2 of the act of this province, _{38 V. c. 5, s. 2, ¶ 5 repealed.} 38 Vict., chap. 5, is repealed.

20. Section 2 of·" the Quebec License Act," as amended 34 V. c. 2, s. 2 further by the act 37 Vict., chap. 3, s. 1, is further amended by amended. substituting the words " seventy-five dollars," for the words " fifty dollars," and the words " thirty-five d•llars" Penalty. for the words " twenty-five dollars."

The provision added by the act 38 Vict., chap. 5, to sec-38 V., c. 5, s. 2 amended. tion 2, of " the Quebec License Act," is amended so as to read as follows :

" But if such contravention takes place in the city of Penalty in Montreal. Montreal, the person committing the same shall incur a penalty of ninety-five dollars, whereof fifteen, on recovery, shall belong to the informer, fifteen to the revenue officer.

3

and the balance to the province. If the whole penalty and costs are not fully recovered, the amount collected shall be first employed in payment of costs, and the balance shall be distributed in the proportion of the sums aforesaid.

34 v., c. 2, s. 6, amended
Penalty.

21. Section 6 of "the Quebec License Act," is amended by substituting the words "seventy-five dollars" for the words "fifty dollars."

s. 31 amended.
Penalty.

22. Section 31 of the same act is further amended by substituting the words "seventy-five dollars" for the words "fifty dollars."

36 v., c. 3, s. 13, amended.
Penalty.

23. Section 13 of the act of this province, 36 Vict., chap. 3, is further amended by substituting the words "seventy-five dollars," for the words "fifty dollars."

34 v., c. 2, s. 130 and 131 repealed.

24. Sections 130 and 131 of "the Quebec License Act" are repealed.

s. 184 replaced.

25. Section 184 of the same act, as amended by the act of this province, 36 Vict., chap. 3, s. 7, is replaced by the following :

Use of penalties if the whole is paid

"184. The penalties recovered under this act shall be disposed of in the following manner, that is to say:

1. If the whole of the penalty and the amount of the costs have been recovered, forty dollars of the penalty shall belong to the revenue officer, subject to the obligation of paying one half of such sum to the informer, if there be an informer, and the balance shall be paid over to the treasurer, to form part of the consolidated revenue fund;

If only one part is paid.

2. If the whole amount of the penalty and costs has not been recovered, the amount recovered shall be applied, first to the payment of the costs, and the balance shall be divided between the revenue officer, the informer, if any, and the treasurer of the province, in the proportion mentioned in the preceding sub-section;

Case of conviction on view.

3. In the case of convictions on view, the penalty, or as much thereof as shall be recovered, over and above costs, shall be paid, one-third to the corporation of the municipality within the limits of which the offence has been committed, one-third to the revenue officer, and the other third to the treasurer, to form part of the consolidated revenue fund;

Suits by the revenue officer.

Sub-sections one and two of this section, shall apply only to suits instituted by and in the name of the revenue officer.

Exception for Montreal.

This section, nevertheless, is subject to the application of the provision added to section 2 of "the Quebec License Act," by the act of this province, 38 Vict., chap. 5, s. 1, as amended by this act

Who recovers the penalties and costs and

In all cases, the penalty and the costs, or the amount recovered, shall be payable into the hands of the magistrate sitting in such causes, or if such magistrate is a district magistrate, or police magistrate, into the hands of apportions his clerk ; and such magistrate or clerk shall thereupon, them. without delay apply, divide and apportion the amount recovered, in the manner prescribed by this section."

26. No place in which spirituous, vinous or fermented Conditions liquors are sold or retailed, or in which there are one or required for more billiard tables, shall be deemed not to fall within clubs. the application of " the Quebec License Act, " as regards the sale of liquors, or the keeping of billiard tables, on the pretext that such place is for the use of a club or other association of the kind, unless the profits made in such place belong to the shareholders of, or subscribers to, such club or association, and that the latter are legally constituted by act of incorporation, and unless they are *bonâ fide* proprietors of all the furniture of the establishment and owners or lessees of the building.

27. The foregoing provisions shall form part of " the InterpretaQuebec License Act ; " may be cited under the numbers tion. assigned them by this act ; shall apply to the same references as the provisions for which they are substituted or which they amend, and shall have in general the same force or application as the said license act.

28. This act shall come into force on the day of the Act into force. sanction thereof.

CAP. VII.

An Act to compel assurers to take out a License.

[*Assented to 24th December*, 1875.]

HER MAJESTY, by and with the advice and consent of the Legislature of Quebec, enacts as follows :

1. Every assurer, carrying on in this province, any Assurers business of assurance, other than that of marine assurance bound to take exclusively, shall be bound to take out a license, before a license. the first day of May, in each year, from the revenue officer of the district wherein is situate his principal place of business or head agency, and to remain continually under license.

2. The price of such license shall consist in the pay- Price of such ment to the crown for the use of this province, at the liense. time of the issue or delivery of any policy of assurance, except of marine assurance. and at the time of the making or delivery of each premium receipt or renewal, respecting any policy issued before or after the coming into force of this act, of a sum computed at the rate of three per cent as to assurances against fire, or of one per cent as to other assurances, for each hundred dollars or fraction of one hundred dollars of the amount received as premium or renewal of assurance, by the assurer, his agent or employee.

Mode of payment.

And such payment shall be made by means of one or more adhesive stamps equivalent in value to the amount required, to be affixed by the assurer, his agents, officers, or employees, on the policy of assurance, receipt or renewal, as the case may be, at the time of the drawing up, issue or delivery thereof.

Fraction reckoned as a cent.

3. When the amount to be paid, in virtue of the preceding section shall include a fraction of a cent, such fraction shall be reckoned as one cent.

Penalty on default of payment, against the agent or his employee.

4. Any person, who for or on behalf of an assurer bound to take out a license under the present act, or in the name of such assurer, shall deliver any policy of assurance, receipt for premium, or renewal, without such policy, receipt or renewal being stamped to the amount required, shall be liable, for each contravention, to a penalty of fifty dollars, or in default of payment, to imprisonment for any term not exceeding three months.

Penalty against the assurer.

5. Every assurer, bound to take out a license under the present act, for whom or in whose name, any policy of assurance, or any premium receipt or renewal, shall have been delivered, without the same having been stamped to the amount required, shall be liable, in each case, to a penalty not exceeding fifty dollars, or in default of payment, unless such assurer be a corporation, to imprisonment not exceeding three months.

Obligation of cancelling stamps.

6. Any person who affixes stamps under this act, shall be bound to cancel the same, at the time of so affixing the same, by writing, stamping or printing with ink, on each of the stamps affixed, the date of the affixing thereof, in such manner as to obliterate and cancel each such

Penalty.

stamp so completely, that it cannot be again used, under a penalty of fifty dollars, for each contravention, or in default of payment, of imprisonment for any term not exceeding three months.

Effect of the issue without stamps.

7. Policies of assurance, premium receipts or renewals, not stamped as required by this act, shall not be invoked, and shall have no effect in law or in equity, before the courts of this province.

Definition of the word " assurer."

8. The word " assurer" used in this act, means and includes all persons, firms, corporations, and all companies, societies or associations, whether incorporated or unincorporated, carrying on the business of assurance on life, or against fire or accidents, or the business of guaranteeing public functionaries or other employees, or any other assurance business whatsoever.

9. The provisions of the second part of "the Quebec License Act" and the amendments thereto, and specially the provisions and amendments respecting the granting, form and cancelling of licenses, the fee to be paid, the recovery and application of penalties, and the application of the duties levied, shall apply to the licenses required by this act, and to cases of contravention in respect thereof, in the same manner as if they were herein anew enacted, save in so far as they are inconsistent with this act. *The Quebec License Act shall apply.*

10. This act shall not affect any policy, premium receipt or renewal, in relation to assurances, wherein the interests assured are beyond the limits of this province. *Assurances not affected.*

11. Section 13 of the act of this province, 31 Vict., chap. 2, shall apply to this act. *31 v. c. 2, sec. 13, shall apply.*

12. The stamps required as the cost of the license in virtue of this act, shall only be so required from and after the first day of the month of May next. *Act into force as to law stamps.*

CAP. VIII.

An Act to aid the grant for the purposes of the Administration of Justice.

[Assented to 24th December, 1875.]

HER MAJESTY, by and with the advice and consent. of the Legislature of Quebec, enacts as follows :

1. A duty of ten cents payable to the crown, for the uses of this province, shall be levied on each receipt, bill of particulars, and exhibit whatsoever, produced before the superior court, the circuit court or the magistrate's court. *Duty on exhibits, &c.*

2. The duty mentioned in the preceding section shall form part of the consolidated revenue fund of the province, and shall be levied in the same manner as other duties on law proceedings, now payable to the crown; and all the provisions of law applicable to such latter duties, shall apply with the same effect, to the duty imposed by this act. *Use of the duty: its collection.*

3. The corporation of any city, town, village or municipality, within the limits of which any person shall have been sentenced to imprisonment in the common gaol of *Municipal corporations bound to pay* for certain prisoners. the district, in virtue of the act respecting vagrants (Canada 32-33 Vict., chap. 28,) or for contravention of the by-laws of such city, town, village or municipality council, shall be bound to pay to the sheriff of such district, a sum of twenty-five cents for each day, during which such person shall be detained in the gaol.

Duty of the sheriff. **4.** It shall be the duty of the sheriff of every district to demand, at the end of each month, the sums due during such month by corporations, under the preceding section, and on refusal of payment, the sheriff may in his own name, sue for the recovery thereof, by action of debt, before any competent court.

Act into force. **5.** This act shall come into force on the first day of February, eighteen hundred and seventy-six.

CAP. IX.

An Act to amend the act of the late province of Canada, 27-28 Vict., chap. 5, respecting the affixing of Stamps on law proceedings.

[Assented to 24th December, 1875.]

HER MAJESTY, by and with the advice and consent of the Legislature of Quebec, enacts as follows:

27-28 v., c. 5, s. 18, amended. **1.** Section 18 of the act of the late province of Canada, 27-28 Vict., chap. 5, is amended by adding thereto after the words "in the case" the words following: "or to the prothonotary or clerk of such court."

Interpretation. **2.** This act shall form part of the act amended by the preceding section, and shall apply to the same references as such act.

CAP. X.

An Act to amend the act of this province, 32 Vict., chap. 11, respecting the sale and administration of Crown Lands.

[Assented to 24th December, 1875.]

HER MAJESTY, by and with the advice and consent of the Legislature of Quebec, enacts as follows:

Effect recognized to certain documents signed by an agent. **1.** All licenses of occupation, certificates of sales or receipts for moneys paid on the sale of public lands, and all location tickets issued and signed by any crown land agent, in favor of any person who has purchased public

lands, shall have the same effect in respect of such person
and his assigns, and shall confer upon them the same rights,
powers and privileges, in relation to the lands for which
they have been issued, and shall subject them to the same
conditions, as if such person had obtained from the commissioner of crown lands an instrument in the form of a license of occupation in conformity with section 16 of the
act 32 Vict., chap. 11.

2. All licenses of occupation, certificates of sales, or
receipts for moneys paid on the sale of public lands, and
all location tickets granted or drawn up before the passing
of this act, by the commissioner of crown lands or any of
his agents, so long as the sale or concession to which they
relate, is in force and has not been rescinded, shall have the
same force and effect and shall equally profit the person
in whose favor the same have been granted, or his heirs,
and his legal representatives in virtue of an instrument
registered in conformity with the provisions of the act
hereinbefore cited, in the same manner and to the same
degree, as the instrument in the form of license of occupation specified in section 16 of the said act.

*Effect recog-
nized to cer-
tain docu-
ments al-
ready made.*

3. This act shall not affect pending cases.

*Pending
cases.*

4. This act shall come into force on the day of the
sanction thereof.

*Act into
force.*

CAP. XI.

An Act to amend chapter 23 of the Consolidated
Statutes for Lower Canada, respecting the sale and
management of Timber on public lands.

[*Assented to 24th December*, 1875.]

WHEREAS it is not always desirable to have annual
sales of timber limits, and whereas it is necessary
to make more ample provision for the preservation and
re-growth of timber on crown lands in this province ; Her
Majesty, by and with the advice and consent of the
Legislature of Quebec, enacts as follows :

Preamble.

1. Nothing contained in section 2 of the act of this
province 36 Vict., chap. 9, shall be construed in such
manner as to render it obligatory to have an annual sale
of timber limits.

*36 v. c. 9, s.
2, amended
and inter-
preted.*

2. It shall be lawful for the lieutenant-governor in
council, upon the recommendation of the commissioner
of crown lands, to set aside certain portions of the forest

*Reserve of
forests.*

lands of the crown vacant at the time, to remain forest.

Management of those reserves. **3.** The territories so set apart shall be reserved for the production and culture of timber, and shall be worked and managed, and the timber thereon be cut, as shall be ordered from time to time, by regulations made by the lieutenant-governor in council.

Cut on such reserves. **4.** The timber cut from and upon such reserves shall be sold at public auction.

CAP. XII.

An Act respecting the internal economy of the Legislative Assembly, and for other purposes.

[Assented to 24th December, 1875.]

HER Majesty, by and with the advice and consent of the Legislature of Quebec, enacts as follows :

Commissioners named for the execution of this act. **1.** The speaker of the legislative assembly, for the time being, and three members of the executive council of this province, for the time being,—who may be appointed by the lieutenant-governor in council as commissioners under this act, they and each of them being also members of the legislative assembly, and the names and offices of whom and their appointment as commissioners being communicated to the legislative assembly, by message from the lieutenant-governor in the first week of each session of the legislature,—shall be, and they are hereby nominated, constituted and appointed commissioners for the purposes of this act ; and any three of **Quorum.** such commissioners, whereof the speaker of the legislative assembly for the time being shall be one, shall be, and they are hereby authorized to carry this act into execution.

Estimate prepared by the clerk of the Legislative Assembly. **2.** An estimate shall annually be prepared by the clerk of the legislative assembly of the sums which will probably be required to be provided by the legislature for the payment of the indemnity and mileage of members, and of salaries, allowances and contingent expenses of the house, and of the several officers and employees thereof under his direction, and of the stationery of the house during the year commencing on the first day of July of each year.

Estimate by the sergeant-at-arms. An estimate shall also be annually prepared by the sergeant-at-arms of the legislative assembly, of the sums which will probably be required to be provided by the legislative assembly, for the payment of salaries or allowances of the messengers, door-keepers and servants of the house under his direction, and of the contingent expenses under his direction during the year as above mentioned.

Such estimates shall be submitted to the speaker for his approval, and shall be subject to such approval and such alterations as the speaker shall consider proper; and the speaker shall thereupon prepare an estimate of the sums requisite for the several purposes aforesaid, and shall sign the same. Estimate by the speaker.

Such several estimates of the clerk, sergeant-at-arms and speaker, shall be transmitted by the speaker, to the treasurer for his approval, and shall be laid severally before the legislative assembly with the other estimates for the year. Approval of such estimates.

3. An estimate shall also be annually prepared by an officer acting for that purpose, under the sanction of the legislative council and the legislative assembly, of the sum which will probably be required to be provided by the legislature for the printing services during the year commencing on the first July in each year, which shall be transmitted to the treasurer of the province for his approval, and shall be laid before the legislature, with the other estimates for the year. Estimate for printing services. Approval.

4. All sums of money voted by the legislature upon such estimates, or payable to the members and to the speaker of the legislative assembly, under the act of this province 33 Vict., chap. 4, shall be paid over to, and held by the treasurer of the province, subject to the order of the said commissioners or any three of them, of whom the speaker shall be one, and shall be paid or transferred to them or their order, at any time, and in such sums as they may deem requisite. Disposal of the sums.

5. All the sums specified in the preceding section shall be paid according to the orders of the commissioners, from time to time issued, and the speaker shall to that end appoint an officer, who shall be styled the accountant to the legislative assembly, and shall require from such latter person, in order to guarantee the faithful accomplishment of his duties, security to an amount which the commissioners shall deem advisable. How pa Accountant: security to be given by him.

An account shall be opened in one of the banks of Canada, in the name of the accountant, and the commissioners hereinabove mentioned shall pay or transfer, from time to time, such sums as they shall deem requisite, to the credit of the accountant, by means of an order signed by the speaker and two others of the commissioners. Bank account.

Case of death or removal of the accountant.

In the case of the death or removal from office of such accountant, the monies standing to his credit in the account aforesaid, shall be forthwith paid by the bank to the commissioners.

Disposal of the sums voted for printing.

6. The sums voted by the legislature for parliamentary printing shall be paid over to the treasurer and employed by him to the paying of printing services.

Bank account.

For these services an account shall be opened in one of the banks of Canada, in such name as the legislative council and the legislative assembly may direct, and such sums as shall be deemed necessary shall be paid or transferred to the name of the person so selected, as the work progresses, to be accounted for in the printing account annual balance sheet.

Case of a surplus.

7. In case the sums voted by the legislature shall in any year be more than sufficient to pay and discharge all charges thereon, the commissioners shall within six weeks after the end of the session, after retaining in their hands a sum sufficient to answer all demands in respect of the same, which may be likely to arise before the beginning of the next session, pay the surplus to the treasurer of the province to form part of the consolidated revenue fund of the province.

Speaker continued as commissioner after the dissolution.

8. For the purposes of this act, the person who shall fill the office of speaker at the time of any dissolution of the legislature, shall be deemed to be speaker until a speaker shall be chosen by the new legislature.

Vacancy in that charge.

In the event of the death or disability or absence from the province of the speaker, during any dissolution or prorogation of the legislature, the three remaining commissioners may execute any of the purposes of this act.

Enquiry into misconduct of an employee.

9. If any complaint or representation shall be made to the speaker for the time being, of the misconduct or unfitness of any officer, employee, messenger or other person attendant on the legislative assembly, now or hereafter to be appointed, it shall be lawful for the speaker to cause an enquiry to be made into the conduct or fitness of such person.

Suspension or removal of the same.

If thereupon the speaker is convinced that such person has been guilty of misconduct, or is unfit to hold his situation, he may, if such officer, employee, messenger or other person has been appointed by the crown, suspend him and report such suspension to the lieutenant-governor ; and if he has not been appointed by the crown, then the speaker may suspend or remove such person as the case may be, and such person shall be accordingly so suspended or removed as the case may be.

10. Immediately after the passing of this act, the Oath of clerk of the legislative assembly shall take and subscribe allegiance. the oath of allegiance before the speaker, and all the other officers, employees and messengers of the legislative assembly shall take and subscribe the oath of allegiance before the clerk of the legislative assembly.

Any officer, employee or messenger who shall be in future appointed, shall before his entry into office, take and subscribe the same oath.

The clerk of the legislative assembly shall preserve a register of all such oaths.

11. For the purposes of this act, all sums payable to This act shall members of the legislative assembly, under the act of this apply to sums province 33 Vict., chap. 4, and all sums voted and already voted. appropriated for the payment of salaries, allowances, contingent expenses and stationery of the legislative assembly, for the fiscal year expiring on the thirtieth day of June, one thousand eight hundred and seventy-six, and for the fiscal year expiring the thirtieth day of June, one thousand eight hundred and seventy-seven, shall be deemed and taken as having been based upon the estimates mentioned in the second section of this act, and shall be subject to the several provisions of this act, in respect to the mode of payment thereof respectively, and of the disposal of any surplus thereof.

12. All sums of money which, under the eighth sec- 33 v., c. 4, tion of the act of this province 33 Vict., chap. 4, might amended. heretofore have been advanced to the clerk of the legislative assembly, shall after the passing of this act be paid over to the treasurer for the purposes and under the authority of this act.

So much of the fourth, seventh and of the ninth sections of the said act, as respects the clerk of the legislative assembly, shall be repealed after the passing of this act, and the accountant shall thereafter perform the duties assigned to the clerk.

13. This act shall come into force on the first day of Act into force. January, 18¯^

CAP. XIII.

An Act to amend " the Quebec Election Act, " (38 Vict., chap. 7.)

[Assented to 24th December, 1875.]

HER MAJESTY, by and with the advice and consent of the Legislature of Quebec, enacts as follows :

38 v., c. 7, s. 2, sub-sec. 4 amended.   **1.** Sub-section 4 of section 2 of " The Quebec Election act" is amended by adding at the end thereof the words, " and who derives the revenue therefrom."

S. 14 amended   **2.** Section 14 of the same act is amended by substituting the number " 11" for the number " 12."

S. 26 replaced   **3.** Section 26 of the same act is replaced by the following :

List by clerk, *ad hoc*.   " 26. The mayor and the officers of the council, in so far as the same is incumbent upon them, shall be bound to deliver to the clerk *ad hoc* on his demand, the valuation roll, which is to avail, as the basis of the list of electors, under a penalty not exceeding two hundred dollars, or in default of payment, of imprisonment not to exceed six months."

S. 27 replaced.   **4.** Section 27 of the same act is replaced by the following :

Examination of the list on complaint.   " 27. The list of electors may be examined and corrected by the council of the municipality, in the thirty days next after the publication of the notice, given in virtue of section 21, upon complaint in writing to such effect, under either of the two sections following, and not otherwise."

S. 29 replaced   **5.** Section 29 of the same act is replaced by the following :

Person complaining.   " 29. Any person believing that the name of any person entered on the list, should not have been so entered, owing to his not possessing the qualifications required for an elector, or believing that the name of any other person, not entered thereon, should be so entered, owing to his possessing the qualifications required, may file a complaint in writing to such effect within the same delay of fifteen days."

S. 41 replaced   **6.** Section 41 of the same act is replaced by the following :

Appeal.   " 41. Any person may appeal from any decision of the council correcting or amending the list, to the judge of the superior court for the district, within the fifteen days following such decision, by petition in which shall be briefly set forth his grounds of appeal."

7. Section 42 of the same act is replaced by the follow- S. 42, replacing :   ed.

"42. If the council has neglected or refused to take into Appeal.
consideration, within the time prescribed, a complaint
duly filed, any person may appeal to such judge therefrom,
in the manner and within the delay prescribed in the preceding section."

8. Sections 59, 60, 89 and 91 of the same act are amend- Ss. 59, 60, 89
ed, by substituting for the words "three hundred," and 91
wherever they occur in such sections, the words "two amended.
hundred."

9. Section 89 of the same act is further amended by S. 89 amend-
striking out the words : "upon receipt of the writ of elec- ed.
tion."

10. Section 96 of the same act is amended by striking S. 96 amend-
out the third sub-section thereof.   ed.

11. Section 99 of the same act is amended by adding Sec. 99
thereto the words following : "and sections 128a, 128b, amended.
128c, and 128d, of 'the Quebec controverted elections
act, 1875.'"

12. Section 101 of the same act is amended by substi- S. 101, french
tuting for the last word of such section, in the french version,
version, the word "Saguenay."   amended.

13. Section 109 of the same act is amended by insert- S. 109 amending therein, after the words "one-half," the words follow- ed.
ing : "the number."

14. Section 137 of the same act is amended by adding S. 137 and
thereto the words following : "as also of the different orm K
polls established by him, together with the territorial amended.
limits of each of such polls."

Form K of the same act shall be amended and applied
in conformity with the preceding provision.

15. Section 135 of the same act is amended by adding S. 135 amend-
thereto the following provision :   ed.

"Nevertheless, if he has been elected, he may dispose Eligibility.
of the property specified in his declaration, provided that
at all times during his term of membership, he is the
owner of lands or tenements within the province, of the
value of two thousand dollars, over and above all rents,
hypothecs, incumbrances and hypothecary claims."

16. Section 149 of the same act is amended by insert- S. 149 and
ing therein, after the words "form O," the words follow- form O
ing : "without a line on the right of the names."   amended.

Form O shall be changed in consequence.

S. 170 amended.

17. Section 170 of the same act is amended by striking out the words following : " or other mark on the right hand side," and by inserting therein, in the place of such words so struck out, the following words : " with a pencil."

S. 229 amended.

18. Section 229 of the same act is amended by adding thereto, after the number " 226," the number following : " 227."

Canvassing.

19. The payment of money or other valuable consideration, made to any person, to engage him to work, or for having worked, as a canvasser, shall be corrupt practice, within the meaning of the provisions of " The Quebec Election act."

Interpretation.

20. The preceding provisions shall form part of " the Quebec Election act," shall apply to the same references as the provisions for which they are substituted or which they amend, may be cited in the same manner as such provisions, and shall in general, have the same force or application as " the Quebec Election act."

Act into force.

21. This act shall come into force on the day of the sanction thereof.

APPENDIX.

Form O, of " the Quebec Election Act " as amended by 39
Vict., chap. 18, s. 16.

Ballot Paper.

18	**1**	**DUREAU.** [Jean Dureau, town of Sorel, county of Richelieu, merchant.]	
Election for the Electoral District of	**2**	**MEUNIER.** [Joseph Meunier, city of Montreal, 10, Fontaine street, Montreal.]	
	3	**RICHARD.** [Antoine Richard, of the parish of St. Henri, county of Lévis, farmer.] .	×
	4	**RICHARD.** [Joseph Richard, of the town and county of Lévis, advocate.]	

CAP. XIV.

An Act to amend " The Quebec Controverted Elections Act, 1875," (38 Vict., chap. 8.)

(Assented to 23rd November, 1875.)

HER MAJESTY, by and with the advice and consent of the Legislature of Quebec, enacts as follows :

1. " The Quebec Controverted Elections Act 1875," is amended by inserting at the end of the first paragraph of section 56, the following words : " and article 275 of the code of civil procedure shall apply." 38 v., c. 8, s. 56 amended.

2. The same act is amended by inserting therein, after section 56, the section following : Sect. 56a inserted.
" 56a. All proceedings respecting the trial of an election petition shall be suspended, during the sessions of the Legislature of this province, and during the eight days which precede and the three days which follow such sessions, on the mere application of the sitting member." Suspension of the proceedings.

3. The same act is amended by inserting therein, after section 128, the following sections : Sections 128a, b, c, d, inserted.
" 128a. If the election is set aside on account of any corrupt practice on the part of one or more agents, without the knowledge and consent of the candidate, such agents may be condemned jointly and severally with the respondent, to pay, in whole or in part, the costs awarded to the petitioner." Corruption by agents.
" 128b. The judge or court shall order that such agents be summoned to appear to be heard, within a fixed delay. Summons of agents.
If they do not appear, they shall, on the proof already taken, be condemned to pay the costs, in whole or in part, as shall be deemed just. Judgment.
If they appear, the judge or court, after having heard the parties and the proof adduced, shall render such judgment as law and justice require."
" 128c. The petitioner may execute the judgment for the costs against any agents so condemned, in the same manner as against the respondent." Execution against agents.
" 128d. The agent so condemned may be imprisoned for any term not exceeding two months, in default of payment of the amount of the judgment.". Imprisonment.

4. The foregoing provisions shall form part of " The Quebec Controverted Elections Act, 1875," shall take their place in the body of such act in the places indicated by this act, may be cited under the numbers assigned them, Interpretation.

4

and shall in general have the same force or application as
" The Quebec Controverted Elections Act, 1875."

Pending
cases.

5. Sections 128*a*, 118*b* and 128*c*, added by section 3 of
this act shall not apply to pending contestations.

Act in force.

6. This act shall come into force on the day of the
sanction thereof.

CAP. XV.

An Act to further amend the law respecting Public
Instruction.

[Assented to 24th December, 1875.]

HER MAJESTY, by and with the advice and consent
of the Legislature of Quebec, enacts as follows :

I. OF THE SUPERINTENDENT OF PUBLIC INSTRUCTION.

31 v., c. 10 re-
pealed.
Superinten-
dent.

1. The act of this province 31 Vict., chap. 10, is repealed ;
and the department of public instruction is restored to
the charge of a superintendent.

Appointment.
Salary.

Security.

2. The superintendent of public instruction shall be
appointed by the lieutenant-governor in council, shall
hold his office during pleasure, shall have an annual
salary of four thousand dollars, and shall give security, in
conformity with the act of this province, 32 Vict., chap. 9.

Powers.

3. The superintendent of public instruction shall
possess all the powers, functions, rights and obligations
conferred or imposed by law, on the superintendent of
education, at the time of the coming into force of this act.

Powers.

4. He shall further discharge all the duties which the
lieutenant-governor in council may see fit to assign to
him, respecting :
1. The establishment or encouragement of art, literary
or scientific societies ;
2. The establishment of libraries, museums or picture
galleries, by such societies, by the government, or by
institutions receiving government aid ;
3. The support of competitions and examinations, and
the distribution of diplomas, medals or other marks of
distinction, for artistic, literary or scientific labors ;
4. The establishment of schools for adults, and the
instruction of laborers and artisans ;
5. All which in general relates to the support and
encouragement of arts, letters and science ;

6. And the distribution of the funds placed at his disposal by the legislature, for each of such objects.

5. The superintendent of public instruction shall Publication compile and publish statistics and information, respecting of statistics and informaeducational institutions, public libraries, and art, literary tion. and scientific societies, and in general respecting all subjects connected with literary and intellectual progress.

6. The superintendent shall annually draw up, in Budget of the accordance with the directions of the council of public public in- instruction, or of the committees thereof, as the case may struction. be, a detailed statement of the sums required for public instruction, and shall submit the same to the government.

7. The superintendent of public instruction, in the Superinten- exercise of all his functions, is bound to comply with the dent acts ac- directions of the council of public instruction, or with cording the those of the roman catholic committee or protestant of the coun- committee, as the case may be, in conformity with sec- cil and com- tion 16 of this act.

8. Two secretaries of the department of public Secretaries instruction may be appointed, as may also all other and officers. officers required for the due administration of the laws respecting public instruction.

9. All documents, whether originals or copies, signed Authenticity by a secretary or assistant secretary of the department of documents of public instruction, shall be authentic, and make proof signed. of their own contents without it being necessary to prove the signature.

10. The department of public instruction shall form Department part of the civil service of the province; and the lieute- forms part of nant-governor in council shall designate the functionaries vice. of such department who shall be members of the board of examiners for the civil service.
Section 4 of the act of this province 31 Vict., chap. 8, is 31 v., c. 8, s. repealed. 4, repealed.

II. OF THE COUNCIL OF PUBLIC INSTRUCTION.

11. After the coming into force of this act, the roman Catholic part catholic portion of the council of public instruction, of the coun- shall be composed of the bishops (ordinaries) or adminis- cil. trators of each of the roman catholic dioceses comprised in the province, either in whole or in part, who shall ex officio form part thereof, and of an equal number of other roman catholics to be appointed by the lieutenant- governor in council.

Delegate.

Each such bishop or administrator, if he is unable through illness or absence from the province, to be present at the meetings of the council, or at those of the committee of which he forms part, may appoint a delegate to represent him, and such delegate shall have all the rights of the person appointing him.

Protestant part.

12. The protestant portion of the council of public instruction shall be composed as provided for by section 1, of chapter 16 of 32 Victoria.

Idem.

13. Whenever the number of roman catholic members, nominated by the lieutenant-governor in council, shall be augmented by more than seven, the number of the protestant members of that council shall be augmented, in the same proportion and in the same manner.

Super. is memb. of the council and committees.

14. The superintendent shall be *ex-officio* president of the council of public instruction.

He shall be also *ex-officio* a member of each of the committees thereof, but he shall only be entitled to vote in the committee, of the religion to which he belongs.

Persons added to the protestant committee.

15. The members of the protestant committee may add to their number five persons, to assist in the labors of their committee.

Such persons shall not form part of the council of public instruction, but shall have, in the protestant committee, all the powers of the members of such protestant committee.

Exclusive jurisdiction of the committees.

16. Everything which, within the scope of the functions of the council of public instruction, respects specially the schools, and public instruction generally, of roman catholics, shall be within the exclusive jurisdiction of the roman catholic committee of such council.

In the same manner, everything which within the scope of such functions respects specially the schools and public instruction generally of protestants, shall be within the exclusive jurisdiction of the protestant committee.

Donations, legacies, etc., to the committees.

17. Each of such committees may receive by donation, legacy, or otherwise *à titre gratuit*, money, or other property, and may dispose of the same in its discretion, for the purposes of instruction.

Each such committee shall possess, in respect of property so acquired, all the powers of a body politic and corporate.

Idem.

18. In the event of any person making a legacy to the council of public instruction, without stating the committee for which he designed the same, the legacy shall belong to the committee of the religion, to which the testator belonged, at the time of his death.

If the testator belonged neither to the roman catholic religion, nor to the protestant religion, the legacy shall be divided between the two committees, in the proportion of the roman catholic and protestant populations of this province.

19. The sums of money which shall have been granted to roman catholics or protestants, for the purposes of public instruction, or any part thereof which shall have not been expended, shall remain at the credit and disposal of the committee which had the control thereof. Surplus of the sums voted.

20. Each such committee shall have the sittings or meetings thereof separate, and it may fix their period and number, establish its quorum, settle the mode of procedure at its meetings, appoint a chairman and secretary, and revoke such appointments at pleasure. Meetings of the committees.

21. The chairman of each committee shall have, on all questions, in which the votes are equal, a second or casting vote. President thereof.

22. Special meetings of each of such committees may be convened by the chairman, or by the superintendent of public instruction, by notice given at least eight days in advance. Special meetings.

If two or more members of either committee require in writing the superintendent or chairman of their respective committee, to convene a special meeting of such committee, it shall be the duty of the superintendent or of the chairman to convene it, in the manner prescribed by the provision preceding.

23. School inspectors, professors, directors and principals of normal schools, the secretaries, and the members of board of examiners, shall be appointed or removed by the lieutenant-governor in council, on the recommendation of the roman catholic or protestant committee of the council of public instruction, according as such appointments or removals respect roman catholic schools or protestant schools. Appointment of the inspectors, principals, professors and secretaries.

24 An appeal may be had to the committee of the council of public instruction, which it concerns, from any decision or action of the superintendent of public instruction, or of any person discharging his duties by delegation or otherwise. Appeal from the decisions of the superintendent to the committees.

25. All provisions in any act or law, inconsistent with this act, are repealed. Repeal.

Act in force{ **26**. This act shall come into force on the first day of February next.

CAP. XVI.

An Act to amend the Laws respecting Education in this Province, in so far as regards schools, in the city of Montreal.

[*Assented to 24th December*, 1875.]

HER MAJESTY, by and with the advice and consent of the Legislature of Quebec, enacts as follows :

$25,000 yearly, for school houses· **1**. The roman catholic school commissioners and the protestant school commissioners of the city of Montreal, notwithstanding any provision to the contrary contained in the thirty-fifth section of the act thirty-two Victoria, chapter sixteen, including therein the amounts which they are authorized to lay aside by the third section of the act thirty-fourth Victoria, chapter twelve, and of the second section of the act thirty-sixth Victoria, chapter thirty-three, may respectively lay aside a portion of these revenues not exceeding the sum of twenty-five thousand dollars per annum, to acquire real estate and to construct school houses in the said city.

Debentures. And all the debentures which the said commissioners may hereafter issue, for the purpose of borrowing any sum of money for the purchase of land and the construction of school houses, in the said city, may be made redeemable within a period not to exceed thirty years next after the date of their issue and not afterward, and the said thirty-fifth section of the said chapter sixteen, of the act thirty-second Victoria, and the third section of the act thirty-four Victoria, chapter twelve, and the second section of the act thirty-sixth Victoria, chapter thirty-three, are in consequence hereby amended.

32 v., c. 16, s. 35, 34 v., c. 12 s. 3, and 36 v., c. 33, s. 2, amended.

Secretary and Treasurer : salaries. **2**. The said roman catholic school commissioners and the said protestant school commissioners of the city of Montreal, may hereafter fix and determine the salary of their secretary-treasurer, notwithstanding any provision to the contrary ; and they may also appoint a secretary and a treasurer separately and fix and determine their salary.

CAP. XVII.

An Act to authorize the catholic school commissioners
of the school municipality of St. Henri, county of
Hochelaga, to raise a certain sum, and purchase real
property and erect buildings thereon, for school
purposes.

[*Assented to 24th December, 1875.*]

WHEREAS, the catholic school commissioners for the Preamble.
school municipality of St. Henri, county of Hochelaga, have by their petition prayed to be allowed to acquire
real property, and erect buildings for educational purposes and establish within the limits of the said school
municipality all such schools as the said commissioners
may deem necessary, and for this purpose to raise a sum
not exceeding $50,000, and whereas, it is expedient to
grant their prayer: Her Majesty, by and with the advice
and consent of the Legislature of Quebec, enacts as
follows:

1. Notwithstanding any provision of the law on educa- Acquisition
tion now in force in this province to the contrary, it of properties
shall be lawful for the catholic school commissioners of and loan of
$50,000.
the school municipality of St. Henri, county of Hochelaga,
to acquire within the limits of their municipality,
immoveable property, to·build one or more school houses
thereon, and to establish therein all such schools as the
said commissioners shall deem advisable, and for these
purposes to raise a sum not exceeding fifty thousand
dollars.

2. It shall be lawful for the said commissioners to Bonds.
borrow money, to·issue debentures or bonds to the
amount of the said sum of fifty thousand dollars, or else
to impose a special tax to raise the said sum, the said tax Tax.
to be spread over as many years as the said commissioners shall deem advisable, provided that the annual Proviso:
tax does not exceed ten thousand dollars.

3. The said special tax shall be raised and collected in Collection of
the same manner as the annual taxes, the said commis- the tax.
sioners having for the raising and collection of such
special tax, the same rights granted by law for the levying and collection of the annual taxes; and such tax
shall not be levied, nor such bonds or debentures shall
be issued, nor such loan contracted, except after the Formalities
observance of the following formalities, that is to say: required.

4. The said commissioners, after passing a resolution Resolution.
to levy the said tax, issue the said bonds or debentures,

Notice.

or effect the said loan, shall cause their secretary-treasurer to give notice of the place and hour in which the said resolution shall be submitted for the approval of the ratepayers qualified to vote at the election of school commissioners.

Publication.

5. The said notice shall on two consecutive sundays, be read at the church door of the roman catholic church of the village of St. Henri, and a copy thereof shall be posted up on the first Sunday, upon the door of the said church.

Meetings.

6 The meeting shall be held in the place indicated in the said notice, within the limits of the said municipality; it shall commence at the hour of ten in the morning, and shall be presided over by the chairman of the commissioners, or by another rate-payer appointed by them.

Approval of the rate-payers.

7. At the place, and on the day and hour indicated, the said chairman shall open the meeting by explaining the purpose thereof, and shall demand of the rate-payers then present if they approve of the said resolution. If no one objects thereto during the space of one hour, the said chairman shall declare the said resolution approved; but if ten rate-payers qualified to vote as aforesaid at the election of commissioners, shall within the said hour oppose the said resolution, the chairman shall immediately open a poll to record the votes of the rate-payers. The

Poll.

said poll shall remain open until four of the clock in the afternoon, and on the following day from ten in the forenoon until four in the afternoon.

Votes.

8. The votes of electors in favor of the resolution shall be recorded under the word "yea," and the votes of those against it, under the word "nay."

Consequence of the vote.

9. If at the close of the poll, the "yeas" are in a majority, the said resolution shall be held to have been approved, and the tax may be levied and collected, or the said loan may be effected, or bonds issued; if the "nays" are in a majority the said resolution shall remain without effect.

If, however, the "nays" are in a majority, the commissioners may, at the end of a year, again submit the said or any other resolution to the approval of the rate-payers, in the manner above prescribed.

Tax required.

10. No issue of bonds or debentures shall take place, and no loan be effected, until there shall, by the resolution authorizing the same, be imposed upon the taxable property of the catholics only, liable for the payment of such loan or bonds, an annual tax sufficient to pay the

yearly interest, and at least two per cent in addition to Sinking fund
the interest, to form a sinking fund, until the said debt
is extinguished.

11. The rate-payers, proprietors of such real estate, Voters.
shall alone have the right to vote upon the approval or
disapproval of such resolution.

. **12.** The delay to contest the proceedings had under Delay to con-
such resolution, shall be thirty days and no longer. test.

CAP. XVIII.

An Act to amend chapter 21 of the Consolidated Statutes for Lower Canada, respecting Interments and
Disinterments.

[*Assented to 24th December, 1875.*]

HER MAJESTY, by and with the advice and consent
of the Legislature of Quebec, enacts as follows :

1. Sub-section one of section two and section eight of C. S. L. C., c.
chapter twenty-one of the consolidated statutes for 21, ss. 2, 8,
Lower Canada, intituled : " An Act respecting Inter- amended.
ments and Disinterments," are amended to read as follows :
   " 2. On a petition being presented to any judge of the Order for
superior court, either in term or in vacation, by any per- leave to dis-
son praying for leave to disinter a body or bodies buried inter given by
in any church, chapel or burial-ground, with a view to sup. court.
erection, repair or alienation of a church, chapel or burial-
ground, or with a view to re-interment of the said body
or bodies, in another part of the same church, chapel or
burial-ground, or in another church, chapel or burial-
ground, or with a view to the reconstruction or repair
of the tomb or coffin in which a body has already been
buried, and indicating, in the case of a proposed removal '
of any body or bodies, the part of the same church,
chapel or burial-ground, or the church, chapel or burial-
ground, to which it is proposed to effect the removal, and
on proof being made on oath to his satisfaction of the
truth of the allegations contained in such petition, such
judge may ordain that the body or bodies shall be disin-
terred as prayed for."
   " 8. Before proceeding to any disinterment in any Permission of
roman catholic church, chapel or burial-ground, under the Ec. autho-
this act, permission to that effect shall be obtained from rity, required.
the superior ecclesiastical authority of the roman catho-
lic diocese, in which the same is situate."

CAP. XIX.

An Act respecting the interment in roman catholic cemeteries.

[Assented to 24th December, 1875.]

Preamble.

WHEREAS it is expedient to prevent all conflict between the ecclesiastical and civil authority, respecting roman catholic cemeteries in this province ; Her Majesty, by and with the advice and consent of the Legislature of Quebec, enacts as follows :

Interment of rom. cath. regulated by relig. authority.

1. It belongs solely to the roman catholic ecclesiastical authority to designate the place in the cemetery, in which each individual of such faith shall be buried after death ; and if the deceased, according to the canon rules and laws, in the judgment of the ordinary, cannot be interred in ground consecrated by the liturgical prayers of such religion, he shall receive civil burial, in ground reserved for that purpose and adjacent to the cemetery.

Act in force.

2. This act shall come into force on the day of the sanction thereof.

CAP. XX.

An act respecting the compilation of statistics of births, marriages and causes of death in the Province.

[Assented to 24th December, 1875.]

HER MAJESTY, by and with the advice and consent of the Legislature of Quebec, enacts as follows :

Compilation by the Dept. of Ag. and P. W.

1. The department of agriculture and public works, shall make and publish annually, a compilation of births, marriages and deaths, and also of the various diseases and causes of death in this province, by means of such information as it shall obtain under the following sections.

Blanks sent to prothonotaries.

2. The commissioner of agriculture and public works, shall, from time to time, transmit to all the prothonotaries of the superior court in this province, blanks or forms of information to be filled in and completed with the number of births, marriages and deaths and with that of the diseases and causes of death.

Distribution by them.

3. On receipt of such blanks or forms, each prothonotary shall be bound to transmit a sufficient number of copies thereof to all persons who, in the district, are authorized by law to keep registers of the acts of civil status, and to all owners or administrators of cemeteries in such district.

4. Every person authorized to keep a register of the acts of the civil status and every owner or administrator of a cemetery, shall fill up and complete the blanks or forms of information which shall have been transmitted to them, and return them during the first six weeks of every year to the prothonotary of the district, who shall be bound to forward them without delay to the commissioner of agriculture and public works. *Blanks fulfilled, where and when forwarded.*

5. In case of an epidemic, should the lieutenant-governor so order by a proclamation to that effect, such blank forms shall be transmitted direct to the department of agriculture and public works, by those who shall have filled them up, and thus within the time specified in the proclamation. *Case of an epidemic.*

6. In localities where a cemetery is common to several parishes, the forms shall not be filled up, in so far as the deaths, diseases and causes of deaths are concerned, except by the owners or administrators of such cemetery. *If a cemetery is common to several parishes.*

7. The father, or in case of his death or absence, the mother of every child born, who shall not have caused such child to have been baptized or who, as in the case of persons of a creed other than the roman catholic one, shall not have caused the birth of such child to be registered by those persons authorized to keep a register of the acts of civil status, shall be bound to have the birth of such child registered within four months from the date of its birth, at the office of the secretary-treasurer or of the clerk of the municipality or city wherein is situate his domicile, or else with the nearest justice of the peace. *If the children are not baptized.*

Such justice of the peace shall, during the two first weeks of the month of January in each year, make to the secretary-treasurer or to the clerk of the municipality or city, his annual report of the births by him registered under the preceding section.

8. Every secretary-treasurer or clerk of a municipality or city, in whose office such births or reports of birth shall have registered shall each year, in the month of January, transmit a statement of such births to the department of agriculture and public works. *Duty of the clerk or sec.-treasurer.*

9. Any contravention to any one of the provisions of the two foregoing sections shall be punishable by a fine not exceeding fifty dollars. *Penalty.*

10. This act shall come into force the day of the sanction thereof. *Act in force.*

CAP. XXI.

An Act to amend the Act of the heretofore Province of Canada, 24 Vict., chap. 24, respecting the practice of vaccination.

[Assented to 24th December, 1875.]

HER MAJESTY, by and with the advice and consent of the Legislature of Quebec, enacts as follows :

24 v., c. 24, s. 1, amended. **1.** Section 1 of the act of the late province of Canada, 24 Vict., chap. 24, is amended by adding thereto the words following : " if the authorities of such hospital have been required so to do, by the lieutenant-governor in council.

CAP. XXII.

An Act to amend the game laws in this Province.

[Assented to 24th December, 1875.]

HER MAJESTY, by and with the advice and consent of the Legislature of Quebec, enacts as follows :

31 v., c. 26, s. 7, amended. **1.** Section 7 of the act of this province, 31 Vict., chap. 26, is amended, by substituting for the word " fourteen " the word " five."

id. s. 10, replaced. **2.** Section 10 of the same act, as amended by the act of this province, 32 Vict., chap. 38, s. 5, is replaced by the following :

Otter, beaver, musk-rat. " 10. No otter shall be hunted, trapped or killed between the first day of May and the first day of October, in any year, no beaver between the thirtieth of April and the first of September, no musk-rat between the first of June in any year and the first of April following, for the districts of Quebec, Saguenay, Chicoutimi, Montmagny, Kamouraska, Rimouski and Gaspé, and between the first of May in each year, and the first of April following, for the remainder of the province."

Property of effects confiscated. **3.** All beasts or birds, or any part thereof, confiscated under section 6 of the said act 31 Vict., chap. 26, shall belong to the person who shall have seized the same.

Game-keepers and agents of fisheries, justices of the peace for certain acts. **4.** Every game-keeper appointed by the commissioner of crown lands and all agents of fisheries, shall, so long as their functions continue, be *ex-officio* justices of the peace, for everything in relation to the due execution of this act, and of all other acts respecting game in this province, and they may exercise all the powers thereof, without possessing the qualification required by law.

5. This act, as also the act of this province 32 Vict., chap. Interpreta-38, shall form part of the act 31 Vict , chap. 26, and shall be tion. read and interpreted as forming one and the same act therewith.

CAP. XXIII.

An Act to amend the Law respecting the rights and liabilities of Innkeepers.

[*Assented to* 24*th December,* 1875.]

HER MAJESTY, by and with the advice and consent of the Legislature of Quebec, enacts as follows :

1. Every innkeeper, boarding-house-keeper and lodg- Lien. ing-house-keeper shall have a lien on the baggage and property of his guest, boarder, or lodger, for the value or price of any food or accommodation furnished to such guest, boarder, or lodger, and in addition to all other re-medies provided by law, shall have the right in case the Right to sell. same shall remain unpaid, for three months, to sell by public auction the baggage and property of such guest, boarder or lodger, on giving one week's notice by adver- Notice re-tisement in a newspaper published in the municipality in quired. which such inn, boarding-house, or lodging-house, is situate, or in case there shall be no newspaper published in such municipality, in a newspaper published nearest to such inn, boarding-house, or lodging-house, of such in-tended sale, stating the name of the guest, boarder or lodger, the amount of his indebtedness, a description of the baggage or other property to be sold, the time and place of sale, and the name of the auctioneer ; and after such sale such innkeeper, boarding-house-keeper, or lodging-house-keeper may apply the proceeds of such sale in pay Proceeds of ment of the amount due to him, and the costs of such ad- the sale vertising and sale, and shall pay over the surplus (if any) to the person entitled thereto on application being made by him therefor.

2. No innkeeper shall, after the passing of this act, be Responsibili-liable to make good to any guest of such innkeeper, any ty of the inn-loss of, or injury to goods or property brought to his inn, ed in certain nor being a horse or other live animal, or any gear apper- cases. taining thereto, or any carriage, to a greater amount than the sum of $200.00 dollars, except in the following cases (that is to say) :

1. Where such goods or property shall have been stolen, lost, or injured through the wilful act, default, or neglect of such innkeeper, or any servant in his employ ; '

2. Where such goods or property shall have been deposited expressly for safe custody with such innkeeper ;

Provided alway, that, in case of such deposit, it shall be lawful for such innkeeper if he think fit, to require as a condition of his liability, that such goods or property shall be deposited in a box or other receptacle fastened and sealed by the person depositing the same.

Exception.

3. If any innkeeper shall refuse to receive for safe custody, as before mentioned, any goods or property of his guest, or if any such guest shall, through any default of innkeeper, be unable to deposit such goods or property, as aforesaid, said innkeeper shall not be entitled to the benefit of this act, in respect of such goods or property.

Innkeepers bound to keep posted up.

4. Every innkeeper shall cause to be kept conspicuously posted in the office, and public rooms, and in every bed-room in his inn, a copy of the second section of this act, printed in plain type ; and he shall be entitled to the benefit of the said section in respect of such goods or property only as shall be brought to his inn while such copy shall be so posted.

Interpretation.

5. In the construction of this act the word "inn" includes an hotel, inn, tavern, public house, or other place of refreshment, the keeper of which is now by law, responsible for the goods and property of his guests, and the word "innkeeper" means the keeper of any such place.

Art. 1816 c. c. amended.

6. Article 1816 of the civil code is hereby amended in the particulars above mentioned,

CAP. XXIV.

An Act to amend article 210 of the civil code.

[Assented to 24th December, 1875.]

HER MAJESTY, by and with the advice and consent of the Legislature of Quebec, enacts as follows :

Art. 210 of c. c. amended.

1. Article 210 of the civil code is amended, so as to read as follows :

Separation from bed or board.

"210. The separation renders the wife capable of suing and being sued, and of contracting a n, for a that relates to the administration of her property ; but for all acts and suits tending to alienate her immoveable property, she requires the authorization of her husband, or upon his refusal the authorization of a judge.

CAP. XXV.

An Act to amend article 2179 of the civil code.

[*Assented to* 24*th December*, 1875.]

HER MAJESTY, by and with the advice and consent of the Legislature of Quebec, enacts as follows :

I. Article 2179 of the civil code is amended by adding thereto the paragraph following : Art. 2179 c, c. amended.

"He is also bound, upon payment of the fee lawfully exigible, to communicate the index to immovables to all persons who desire to examine the same without ~~renewal.~~"

CAP. XXVI.

An Act to declare from what day the delay for the renewal of the registration of hypothecs, after the *cadastrage*, shall begin to run.

[*Assented to* 24*th December*, 1875.]

WHEREAS article 2172 of the civil code provided that the registration of all hypothecs should be renewed within eighteen months after the proclamation bringing the provisions of article 2168 into force, which said proclamation is required by articles 2169 and 2176 to fix the day on which such provisions shall so come into force ; and whereas by section four of the act of this province, 35 Vict., chap. 16, the said delay of eighteen months is extended to a period of two years; and whereas the English version states the said period to be from the *date* of the proclamation, and the French version states it to be from the *day* of the proclamation ; Preamble.

And whereas doubts have arisen as to the time from which the said period of two years should run ; and whereas the intent of the said fourth section of the above mentioned act is that the said period should run from the day on which the provisions of article 2168 are put in force, and it is expedient to remove the doubts which have arisen ; Therefore, Her Majesty, by and with the advice and consent of the Legislature of Quebec, enacts as follows :

When the de-   **1.** The delay of two years granted by article 2172 of
lay begins to the civil code, as amended by the Act 35 Vict., chap. 16,
run.   for the renewal of the registration of hypothecs required
              by such article 2172, is declared to run, and shall in
              future begin to run, from the day fixed for the coming
              into force of the provisions of article 2168 of the civil
              code, in the proclamation to that end issued.

Pending   **2.** This act shall not affect pending causes.
causes.

CAP. XXVII.

An Act to supply the loss of certain Registers of Acts
of Civil Status, of the Parish of *Ste. Marie de
Monnoir*, in the County of Rouville.

[*Assented to* 24*th December*, 1875.]

Preamble.   WHEREAS on or about the sixth of November, 1875,
             the duplicates containing the original registers of
the baptisms, marriages and burials of the parish of *Ste.
Marie de Monnoir*, in the county of Rouville, for the
current year (1875), whereof one contained the acts of
baptisms, marriages and burials of such parish, for the
months of November and December, 1874, have been
secretly removed from the *sacristie* of such parish, and
whereas there is reason to believe that they have been
burned, which may be the occasion of serious injury to
divers families and individuals ; and whereas it is expedient to remedy the disappearance of such registers ; Therefore, Her Majesty, by and with the advice
and consent of the Legislature of Quebec, enacts as
follows :

Duty of the   **1.** It shall be the duty of the prothonotary of the
prothonotary superior court, at St. Hyacinthe, to cause a faithful tran-
script to be made in a book authenticated, in accordance
with article 1236 of the code of civil procedure, of all
entries of baptisms, marriages and burials, for the
months of November and December, 1874, contained in
the duplicate registers of civil status of the parish of *Ste.
Marie de Monnoir*, for the year 1874, now deposited in the
archives of his office.

His certi-   **2.** Such officer shall, under his own hand, certify each
ficates.   of such entries, as being a true and faithful copy of the
corresponding entry of the duplicate in his possession, and
afterwards shall forward such book to the *curé* of the
parish of *Ste. Marie de Monnoir*, to form part of the archives of such parish.

3. Such book shall be marked by the prothonotary as Designation of the book. follows : " New duplicate of the registers of baptisms, marriages and burials, &c., (*as the case may be*), of the parish of *Ste. Marie de Monnoir,* for November and December, 1874, made in conformity with the act 39 Vict., chap. 27."

4. The *Curé* now in office of the parish of *Ste. Marie de* The *curé* and vicars are commissioners. *Monnoir,* and his vicars, as shall all such persons as may replace them in the office of *curé* or vicar, shall during the whole period for the execution of the provisions following, be commissioners entrusted with the task of ascertaining all the baptisms, marriages and burials which have taken place in such parish from the first day of January, 1875, to the day of the disappearance of the registers, and of making entries in the new authenticated duplicates, in conformity with article 1286 of the code of civil procedure.

And each of such persons may act alone for the purposes of this act.

5. One of such commissioners, in a public written Notice required. notice, shall cause the object of this act to be known, and shall invite all persons interested, or 'who may be in a position to supply the loss of the original registers, to appear at the time and place specified in such notice, and to bring with them and produce any extract or certificate of baptisms, marriages or burials, made during the period mentioned in section four, and all family records or memoranda which they may possess of such baptisms, marriages or burials, or to give testimony under oath, in respect of all information which they themselves possess, or which may be obtained from them.

Each commissioner is authorized to administer the oath Oath. required, to all persons who may be so interrogated.

6. On proof made under oath by one or more witnesses, Entry of acts established. or on any other evidence, establishing that a baptism, marriage or burial has taken place in such parish, during the period hereinabove mentioned, the commissioner shall make an entry thereof in two registers, and each dupli- Signature. cate inscription shall be signed by the commissioner and by the witnesses interrogated under the oath. If the latter cannot sign, mention thereof shall be made.

Mention shall also be made of any extract or other proof Mentions required. in writing produced by the witnesses.

7. The commissioners, after having completed their Designation of the book. registers, shall mark each of them, as follows : " New duplicate of the registers of baptisms, marriages and burials of the parish of *Ste. Marie de Monnoir,* for 1875, made in conformity with the act 39 Vict., chap. 27."

Deposit of duplicates.   **8.** One of such duplicates shall be lodged in the office of the prothonotary of the district, and the other shall remain among the archives of the parish of *Ste. Marie de Monnoir.*

Authenticity of registers.   **9.** Each of the duplicates or registers specified in sections 3 and 7 of this act, shall be authentic, and shall have for all purposes whatsoever, the same force and effect, as if it had been made at the time, and in the form required by law.

Other proof allowed.   **10.** Nothing in this act contained shall prevent the proof, in any manner permitted by law, of any baptism, marriage or burial, which occurred during the period hereinabove mentioned, and which could not be proved and entered under the authority of this act.

Act in force.   **11.** This act shall come into force on the day of the sanction thereof.

CAP. XXVIII.

An Act to remove doubts respecting the authenticity of certain registers of acts of civil status, in the county of Rimouski.

[*Assented to 24th December,* 1875.]

Preamble.   WHEREAS, in authenticating certain registers destined for acts of civil status, in the office of the circuit court sitting at Matane, in the county of Rimouski, the seal of such court was not affixed thereto, and whereas doubts have arisen in respect thereof, and it is expedient to remove such doubts ; Her Majesty, by and with the advice and consent of the Legislature of Quebec, enacts as follows :

Prothonotary bound to affix the seal.   **1.** The prothonotary of the superior court, in and for the district of Rimouski, upon presentation of any register of civil status, which appears to have been authenticated in the office of the clerk of the circuit court sitting at Matane, by the clerk or deputy clerk, without however having been sealed with the seal of the court, shall be bound to affix the seal of the superior court on each such register, in the manner prescribed by the article 1236 of the code of civil procedure.

Duty of the custodians of the registers   **2.** Every custodian of any register in the condition specified in the preceding section, shall be bound to present such register to the prothonotary, and to require the affixing of the seal thereon, in the manner hereinabove set forth, within six months after the coming into force of this act.

3. The prothonotary shall annex to each register upon which he shall have so affixed the seal of the superior court, a certificate setting forth that in affixing the seal thereon, he has acted in conformity with this act. Special certificate.

4. Each such register so sealed with the seal of the superior court, shall be in all respects as authentic as if the seal had been affixed thereto at the time required by law. Authenticity of the registers.

CAP. XXIX.

An Act further to amend the Municipal Code.

[*Assented to 24th December*, 1875.]

HER MAJESTY, by and with the advice and consent of the Legislature of Quebec, enacts as follows :

1. Article 52 of the municipal code of the province of Quebec, is amended by substituting in the second line, the word " proprietors," for the word " electors." Art. 52, amended.

2. The following article shall be inserted after article 350 : Art 350a added.
" 350a. The delay to take proceedings in the manner specified in articles 350, 708, 925, 926, 927, 1064 and 1067 shall be thirty days, in lieu of the various delays accorded by the said articles, which are to such extent repealed. The delay to return the writ of appeal, in the terms of article 1070, shall be forty days."

3. Article 365 is amended by striking out in the second line thereof the words " of each year," and substituting therefor the words, "every second year." Art. 365, amended.

4. Article 366 of the said code is repealed, and the following substituted therefor : Art. 366, amended.
"366. The valuators shall enter upon their duties, so soon as they have made oath well and faithfully to discharge all the duties of their office. Road inspectors, rural inspectors and pound-keepers shall enter upon the discharge of their duties immediately after service of the notice of their appointment.'

5. The following article is inserted after article 380 of the municipal code of the province of Quebec : Art. 380a, added.
" 380a. Whenever a road inspector is personally interested in any work or other matter within his jurisdiction,

and neglects or refuses to execute or supply that which he is bound to execute or supply, as interested in such work or matter, the secretary-treasurer of the local municipality wherein such inspector has jurisdiction, possesses in relation to such inspector the same rights, powers and obligations as the inspector himself, in relation to all persons interested in the same work or matter.

In respect of works to be performed in common, the inspector so interested is always *in mora*, to fulfil the obligations attaching to such works."

Art. 407, amended.

6. Article 407 of the same code is amended by adding to the first paragraph thereof, the number "380*a*," after the number 380.

Art. 484*a*, added.

7. After article 484 the following article is inserted:

"484*a*. To establish and manage alms-houses or other establishments of refuge for the support of the necessitous; and to aid charitable institutions established in the municipality."

Art. 495, amended.

8. Article 495 of the said code is amended, by adding thereto the following words: "the apportionment of the moneys to be levied for the payment of the interest and the sinking fund annually shall be based on the roll in force at the time of such apportionment, without prejudice to the rights of debenture holders. "

Art. 635. amended.

9. Article 635 of the same code is amended by adding after the words "brought into," the words "or produced in."

Art. 789, amended.

10. Article 789 of the same code is amended, by inserting after the words "any special," in the first paragraph thereof, the words "or public."

Art. 810, amended.

11. Article 810 of the same code is amended by striking out the following words, at the end of the said article:

"Nevertheless any *procès-verbal* homologated by a board of delegates, can only be amended or repealed on petition by the majority of the rate-payers interested, who are mentioned in the *procès-verbal.*"

Art. 836, amended.

12. Article 836 of the said code is amended by striking out the word "must," and by inserting after the words "front road," the following: "and all the persons interested in by-roads must," and by adding at the end of the said article the following words:

"Nevertheless the owners or occupants of land, who maintain the fences along any front road, not being that on which they are obliged to work, shall pay to the per-

son bound to maintain such road, the excess of work
occasioned by the fact that as such fences cannot be taken
down, the person liable for the work on such road has
additional labor."

13. Article 840 is amended, by adding at the end of the
first paragraph " with the consent of the proprietors, "
and by striking out the second paragraph. Art. 840, amended.

14. Article 873 of such code is amended, by adding
to the second paragraph, the words following : " If such
special officer is selected from among the persons
interested in the work to be performed on such water-
course, he shall not be entitled to any fee for his services
or loss of time, from the parties interested, but he may be
paid by the council who appointed him. " Art. 873, amended.

15. Article 884 is amended, by adding thereto, the
following words : " or within the delays fixed by the
council." Art. 884, amended.

16. The following article is added, after article 1001 of
the same code : Art 1001a, added.
" 1001a. The secretary-treasurer shall be entitled to
ten cents for each hundred words or figures, for all
notices, lists and other documents in relation to the sale of
lands indebted for taxes, and further to the repayment of
any sum advanced by him to defray the cost of publication, in the *Quebec Official Gazette*, and in other journals,
and to one dollar and fifty cents for each certificate of
adjudication, or for every deed of sale, and moreover the
costs of the registration thereof, until such time as such
fees are otherwise established by a resolution of the
county council. "

17. Article 1004 of the said code is amended, by adding
at the end of the second paragraph, the words following :
" and to constituted ground rents." Art. 1004, amended.

18. Article 1009 is amended, by substituting for the
words " by the warden and by the secretary-treasurer, "
the words " by the secretary-treasurer." Art. 1009, amended.

19. Article 1013 of the said code is amended, by adding
in the sixth line after the words " except claims, " the
following : " to constituted ground rents." Art. 1013, amended.

20. The following article shall be inserted after article
1030 of the same code : Art 1030a, added.
" 1030a. If the judgment has been rendered on debentures or coupons issued in virtue of a by-law made by a
county council, in conformity with article 974 of this code,

or of any special act to the same effect as such article, the apportionment to be made by the sheriff shall be in accordance with the terms of such by-law, and in the same proportion as the apportionment made by the county council under article 974; and in such case mention shall be made both in the judgment and the writ of execution that the county corporation has been condemned in virtue of such by-law."

Art. 1049, amended.   **21.** Article 1049 is amended by adding in the third line after the words " of the judgment," the words following : " the property of the person so condemned, shall be seized and sold, up to the amount of the penalty and costs, and in default of property sufficient ;" and by substituting the word " shall," for the word "may."

Art. 1050, amended.   **22.** Article 1050 of the said code is amended by adding in the third line, after the words " under penalty," the following : " of seizure or."

Art. 1061, amended.   **23.** Article 1061 of the same code is amended by adding thereto the following paragraph :
" 3. From every decision given by any municipal council, under articles 734, 738 and 746a, in relation to any valuation roll."

Art. 1064, amended.   **24.** Article 1064 of the same code is amended by inserting in paragraph 1, after the words " or to their clerk." the words following : " or at the office of the municipal council, if any municipal council is in question."

36 V., c. 21, s. 29, repealed.   **25.** Section 29 of chapter 21 of 36 Victoria is hereby repealed.

Act in force.   **26.** This act shall come into force on the day of the sanction thereof.

C A P .   X X X .

An Act to amend "the Quebec Police Act," (33 Vict., chap. 24.)

[*Assented to 24th December*, 1875.]

HER MAJESTY, by and with the advice and consent of the Legislature of Quebec, enacts as follows :

33 V., c. 24. s. 32, amended.   **1.** Section 32 of the act of this province, 33 Vict., chap. 24, is amended by substituting the following for the first sentence thereof :

" Each city, town or municipality, in which any detachment of the police force shall be stationed, shall pay annually to the treasurer of the province, for each police officer or man so stationed therein, the sum which shall be agreed upon between the lieutenant-governor in council, and the council of such city, town or municipality."

2. Notwithstanding anything to the contrary contained in " The Quebec Police Act, " it shall at all times be lawful for the lieutenant-governor in council to withdraw from any city, town or municipality, any police force stationed therein, if he deem the same advisable ; and as soon as such withdrawal shall have been decided on any act or part of an act authorizing or requiring such city, town or municipality to maintain therein a police force at its own expense, or in any manner having respect to such police force, shall come again into force, as if " the Quebec Police Act" had never been passed, and this even in the case of such act or part of an act having been repealed. *The lieut.-gov. may withdraw any police force.* *Effect.*

3. It is further enacted that the lieutenant-governor in council may increase the amount to be charged to the city of Quebec, for the support of the provincial police, and the said city shall be bound and obliged to pay such increase, any provision to the contrary notwithstanding. *Sum to be paid by Quebec.*

4. This act shall come into force on the day of the sanction thereof. *Act in force.*

CAP. XXXI.

An Act to define the jurisdiction of the magistrate's court and that of district magistrates, in civil matters.

[*Assented to* 24*th December*, 1875.]

WHEREAS certain doubts have arisen as to the extent and jurisdiction in civil matters of magistrate's courts and of the district magistrates holding the same, in this province; Therefore, to remove the said doubts, Her Majesty, by and with the advice and consent of the Legislature of Quebec, declares and enacts as follows : *Preamble.*

1. The jurisdiction of the magistrate's court and of the district magistrates holding the same is declared not to have been extended or in any manner altered or affected by the 7th section of the act of this province, 37 Vict., cap. 8 ; and notwithstanding anything in the said act *Jurisdiction defined.*

contained, the jurisdiction of the said courts and of the said magistrates was and is regulated by the act of this province 35 Vict., cap. 9, and the acts antecedent thereto.

Pending cases. **2.** This act shall not in any manner affect pending suits or judgments heretofore rendered.

Act in force. **3.** This act shall come into force on the day of its sanction.

CAP. XXXII.

An Act to extend the jurisdiction of the fire commissioner for the city of Quebec.

[*Assented to 24th December*, 1875.]

HER MAJESTY, by and with the advice and consent of the Legislature of Quebec, enacts as follows:

Jurisdiction extended to the *banlieue* and Levis. **1.** The jurisdiction of the fire commissioner for the city of Quebec, as defined by the acts of this province, 31 Vict., chap. 82, and 32 Vict., chap 29, is extended to the *banlieue* of the city of Quebec and to the town of Levis, wherein such commissioner may exercise his powers, in the same manner and to the same effect as in the city of Quebec.

Salary. **2.** The annual salary of such commissioner is raised to the sum of fourteen hundred dollars, payable in the same manner and by the same parties as the salary received by him before the passing of this act.

Act in force. **3.** This act shall come into force on the day of the sanction thereof.

CAP. XXXIII.

An Act to amend and consolidate the various acts respecting the notarial profession, in this province.

TABLE OF CONTENTS OF THE ACT.

TITLE FIRST.

TITLE SECOND.

ORGANIZATION OF THE NOTARIAL PROFESSION.

[*Assented to 24th December*, 1875.]

Preamble.   WHEREAS there are a great many laws and statutes relating to the notarial profession, and much inconvenience results from such multiplicity of enactments of different sources; and whereas, for these reasons, it is advisable to amend and consolidate the laws respecting such profession ; Therefore, Her Majesty, by and with the advice and consent of the Legislature of Quebec, enacts as follows :

TITLE FIRST.

APPLICATION OF THE ACT,—INTERPRETATIVE AND DECLARATORY PROVISIONS.

Application
of the act.   **1.** This act applies to the province of Quebec.

Interpretation of the texts.   **2.** When there is any difference between the French and English texts of this act, the French text shall prevail.

Former admissions confirmed.   **3.** All admissions to the study or practice of the notarial profession, heretofore made by the various boards of notaries, or by the provincial board of notaries in this province, if they have not been cancelled, are confirmed, notwithstanding any irregularities which may have occurred in the proceedings of the said boards. All certificates of admission or of admissibility granted by any of the said boards, and all commissions granted by the governors, lieutenant-governors, or administrators of this province, under the seal thereof, appointing a candidate a notary public, and permitting him to practise as such, in the said province, unless the same have been cancelled, are likewise confirmed; subject however to all sentences of suspension, disability or interdiction.

Old certificates and commissions confirmed.

Proviso.

TITLE SECOND.

ORGANIZATION OF THE NOTARIAL PROFESSION.

CHAPTER FIRST.

OF NOTARIES, THEIR FUNCTIONS, RIGHTS, PRIVILEGES AND DUTIES.—
TABLE OF PRACTISING NOTARIES.

Object of the notarial profession.   **4.** Notaries are public officers, appointed to execute deeds and contracts, to which the parties are bound, or desire to give the character of authenticity attached to acts entered into under public authority; to assure the date thereof, to have and preserve the same in safe keeping, and to deliver copies, or authentic extracts therefrom.

5. Notaries are appointed for life, with jurisdiction throughout the province of Quebec, in every part of which they have the exclusive and concurrent privilege and right of practising; they may abandon the practice of their profession, and resume the same whenever they so please. Time and place of practice of notaries.

6. They are bound to give their services on immediate payment of their fees and disbursements, except upon grounds which justify their refusal. Bound to act.

7. They are under the protection of the law, and are protected in the execution of their professional duties; any person assaulting a notary, in the execution of his duty, or opposing him therein, is guilty of a misdemeanor, and may, on conviction be condemned to the same punishment, as if he had been convicted of an assault on a peace or revenue officer, in the execution of his duty. Protection.

8. Notaries are not bound to accept any municipal office under a municipal council, nor any office relating to a municipal or school corporation. Exemption

9. The profession of a notary is inconsistent with that of a surveyor, physician or advocate; and the exercise of the functions of a notary is inconsistent with the simultaneous exercise of those of a prothonotary, or deputy prothonotary in Her Majesty's superior courts of this province, of a sheriff, or deputy sheriff, or of a registrar, or deputy registrar, saving the reservation hereinafter made. Incompatibility with certain professions and duties.

10. Every notary, appointed prothonotary deputy prothonotary, sheriff, deputy sheriff, registrar or deputy registrar of any county or registration division, since the first day of January eighteen hundred and seventy four, has been bound to select between such occupation, and the practice of his profession of notary, and to transmit his declaration to that effect to the board of notaries, and to the office of the superior court for the district where he last practised as such notary. Selection to make. Declaration required.

But whenever he shall have elected to continue in the discharge of such office of prothonotary, deputy prothonotary, sheriff, deputy sheriff, registrar, or deputy registrar, he may retain his minutes, repertory and index in his possession, and deliver copies or authentic extracts from deeds passed before him, and up to such time deposited in his minutes. Privileges retained.

Re-entering into practice. **11.** He may also re-enter upon the practice of his profession as a notary, so soon as he shall have ceased to fill the office of prothonotary, deputy prothonotary, sheriff, deputy sheriff, registrar, or deputy registrar, upon transmitting a counter declaration to that effect.

Idem. **12.** The same rule applies whenever any notary has abandoned the practice of his profession, to follow any other employment, hereinabove declared inconsistent with the exercise of the profession of a notary.

Penalty for plurality of offices. **13.** Any notary, who continues to practice as a notary, or has any share or pecuniary interest whatever in the practice of another notary, and at the same time holds any of the offices specified in sections 9 and 10 of this act, is liable to a penalty not exceeding two hundred dollars, recoverable in the manner provided by section 181 of the present act; and the deeds or contracts, which he shall Deeds of notaries not practising. have so passed as notary, as also those passed before any notary considered as not practising within the meaning of this act, do not possess any authentic character.

Removal from office. **14.** It is lawful for the authority to that end constituted by this act, to remove from his office any notary lawfully convicted, under such authority :

1. Of having illegally joined with the exercise of his profession, that of those public offices, the simultaneous exercise of which is herein declared inconsistent therewith ;

2. Or of having joined with his profession, any of the professions declared inconsistent with that of a notary.

Keeping office in certain places not allowed. **15.** No notary can habitually practise his profession, that is to say, keep his office, in the offices of prothonotaries, sheriffs, or registrars, under the penalties and consequences mentioned in the two preceding sections.

Firm of notaries; their signature. **16.** Two or more notaries practising their profession together, cannot sign deeds or contracts passed before them, in the name of their firm. They may, however, use the signature of their firm in advertisements, notices, petitions and other documents not being notarial deeds.

Practice on Sundays, &c. **17.** Notaries may lawfully, if they so wish, draw deeds, make and date acts of voluntary jurisdiction on Sundays, *fêtes d'obligation* and legal holidays; they may not do so in acts of contentious jurisdiction.

If parties are unknown. **18.** The names, calling, residence and identity of the parties, if none of them are known to the notaries, must be certified to by a witness known to them and possessing the qualities required in an attesting witness to any instrument.

19. A notary cannot execute a deed or contract to which he is a contracting party. Notary is not a party to his deed.

20. Every notary is bound to keep exposed in his office, a roll in which shall be entered the names, additions and places of residence, of all persons, who, within the limits of the district in which he resides, are either interdicted or merely assisted by a judicial adviser, and also the names of curators or judicial advisers given to such persons, together with mention and date of the judgments relating thereto; and this, immediately upon the notification which the clerk or prothonotary of the district, in which the notary keeps his office, is obliged to give him without delay, and gratuitously. Roll of incapable persons, exposed in the office.

21. Notaries are entitled to emoluments or fees for the deeds which they execute, and the professional services they render, over and above their costs and expenses; these fees are regulated by the tariffs made by the board of notaries, or, in default of such tariffs, by a valuation before the court, by one or more members of the profession. Fees and expenses for services.

The tariffs of the several boards of notaries heretofore established according to law, remain in force till the board of notaries has otherwise determined, by the substitution of other tariffs. Old tariffs.

And in the class of professional services susceptible of emoluments or fees, are included, amongst others, travelling expenses, vacations, written or verbal consultations, and examination of deeds and papers. Other fees included.

The oath of the notary is admitted as to the nature and duration of the services rendered. Oath.

22. Parties to acts executed before a notary are jointly and severally liable for his disbursements and fees. Liability of parties to fees.

23. The furnishing of copies, extracts, title-deeds or deeds of any nature whatsoever, is not to be considered a presumption of payment of the costs and fees of a notary. And no notary is bound to furnish copies or extracts of any deed, to third parties, or even to the parties themselves, if he is not paid the original cost of the minute, if at the time prescription has not been acquired. Previous payment required.

24. Notaries may prepare the non-contentious proceedings specified in the third part of the code of civil procedure, and submit the same to the judge or to the Proceedings which notaries may prepare.

prothonotary : and may especially sign, in the name of the applicants, without any special power, requests or petitions for the summoning of a family council, in relation to tutorships, curatorships, sale or alienation of the property of minors or interdicted persons, partition or licitation, homologation *en justice*, the affixing and the removal of seals, as also all other petitions, or proceedings in which the action of the judicial authority, or of any other public authority whatever, is to be asked for.

Code of pro-
cedure.

25. All communications, copies, or extracts of any deed or document, forming part of the *greffe* of a notary, and every deposit of certified copies of *adirés* or lost deeds, are regulated by the code of civil procedure respecting compulsories.

Disposal of
deeds.

26. Notaries shall not allow any minutes, or papers annexed thereto, to go out of their possession, except in the cases provided for by law.

Notary not
obliged to
guarantee.

27. A notary, who passes a deed, is not obliged to inform the contracting parties of any fact within his knowledge, although such fact may be prejudicial to one of the parties. With the exception of his own acts, he is not the warrantor of anything recited in the deed passed before him : he is not even bound to declare the debts, the titles of which were previously passed before him.

Idem.

28. The omission by the acting notary to declare the hypothecs and charges in his own favor, on the immovable property alienated or hypothecated, is not detrimental to him, unless in the deed, the owner declares such immovable free and unencumbered.

Custody ; care
and alteration
of deeds.

29. Notaries must in no case, suppress, destroy or alter any minute when once signed by them, nor deliver it to the parties or to any of them, under penalty of deprivation of office, in addition to the other penalties provided by law. If it be useful or necessary to make changes, the parties can do so by another deed, and not otherwise.

Who may be
notaries.

30. The following persons and no others may be admitted as notaries public, in this province ; all British subjects either by birth, or effect of law, resident in the province, being of good conduct and morals, lay persons, males, of full age, and ascertained to be of sufficient intelligence, the whole upon examination and certificates as hereinafter provided.

A candidate
minor.

31. Upon his term of clerkship being completed, a candidate, of minor age, for the practice of the notarial profession, may present himself to undergo his examination ; but his certificate of admission is not given to him, nor can he practise, until he attains his majority.

32. On admission to the profession, a notary before practising, must take, before one of the judges of the superior court, the oaths of office and allegiance. The taking of such oaths must be preceded by the production of the certificate of admission, registered in the office of the provincial registrar. He must cause the whole to be enregistered with the board of notaries, together with a deposit of his official signature, which he cannot change, without the authority of the board of notaries. Oaths of office and allegiance.

Enregistration.

33. Every notary who practises as such before he has fulfilled such provisions, is liable for each offence, to the penalty hereinafter prescribed. Penalty.

34. Moreover, before having the right of acting and practising as a notary, he is obliged to enregister, in the board of notaries, a declaration as to the locality where he intends to practise. Such declaration must contain his surname, christian names, and that of the parish or township, county and district, where he intends to reside. In default of so doing, he is liable to the same penalty. Declaration required.

Penalty.

TABLE OF PRACTISING NOTARIES.

35. Any notary, who, at the time of the passing of this act, has not transmitted to one of the secretaries of the provincial board of notaries, a declaration signed by himself, containing his surname, christian names, residence and the date of his admission to the practice of the notarial profession, and the different localities (by parish, township, county and district), where he has practised since such admission (mentioning the time during which he has practised in each locality), must transmit the same to the board of notaries, within three months next after the passing of this act, if he has not done so, under the act of 1870, concerning the profession of notary. Declaration.

36. Any notary, who, having transmitted such declaration, has, since such transmission, and at the time of the passing of this act, changed his domicile, and removed to another township or parish, must, within the three months next after the passing of this act, transmit to one of the secretaries of the board of notaries, another declaration mentioning such change, and also the county and district, in the same manner as the declaration required by the preceding section. Change of domicile.

Declaration.

37. Any notary who changes the domicile mentioned, in his last declaration, for another, in another parish or New declaration.

township, is bound to transmit to one of the said secretaries, within fifteen days from such change, a new declaration containing, in addition to the foregoing, the name of the parish, township, county and district, where he intends to reside and practise.

Penalty.   **38.** Refusal or neglect in transmitting the declarations above mentioned, renders the notary in default amenable to disciplinary penalties.

Delivery of lists by the secretaries.   **39.** The secretaries, on or before the first of March in each year, are bound to transmit to the treasurer a list, certified by them, of all declarations received by them during the year.

Contents of the first list.   **40.** The first list, thus transmitted to the treasurer, must contain concisely the surnames, christian names and domiciles of the notaries, which the said secretaries find mentioned in the declarations received by them up to the date of such transmission to the secretaries, together with the declarations of election of domicile, made by recently admitted notaries, immediately upon their admission by the board of notaries.

General roll of notaries practising and not practising.   **41.** The two secretaries shall jointly prepare for the first of May, in each year, a general table of notaries practising in the province of Quebec, in alphabetical order, by districts and by names, mentioning the date of the commission, the parish or township, county and district where the notaries are practising at the time of the publication of such table. This table must also contain in a special category, and with the same details of residence, the surnames and christian names of non-practising notaries.

Payment required.   **42.** The table specifies merely the names *of such notaries as are not indebted in any arrears of contribution to the said board.

Statement and Treasurer's list.   **43.** On the first of April of each year, the treasurer of the board transmits to the two secretaries a statement of the receipts and expenditure of the board, and a list certified by him, of the notaries who have paid, at that time, the arrears then due of their contribution up till the last day of the month of February preceding. The table is drawn up according to such list.

Date and distribution of the roll.   **44.** The table must be prepared and printed by the end of April of each year, and transmitted by the secretaries, post-paid, to each of the notaries entered therein, as also to prothonotaries, clerks and registrars, who are **Exposition.** bound to expose it in a conspicuous place in their office, to be consulted when required, under pain of disciplinary penalties against notaries, and of a penalty not exceeding twenty-five dollars against prothonotaries, clerks and registrars. Penalty.

45. The first table shall be prepared and printed by the end of April, eighteen hundred and seventy-six. First table.

46. Any practising notary, whose name is not inscribed on the above mentioned table, through non-transmission of his declaration of election or change of domicile, or through non-payment of his arrears of contribution to the common fund of the board of notaries, is liable to disciplinary penalties and fines. Penalty for practicing without being inscribed.

47. Any notary, whose name, through his own neglect, is not inscribed on the general table of notaries, must, to have it so inscribed, transmit to the treasurer of the board, in addition to the arrears of contribution by him due to the fund of the board, a sum of eight dollars to cover the expenses necessary to forward to notaries, prothonotaries, clerks and registrars, a certificate to avail in lieu of inscription on the table. Inscription of notaries in arrears.

48. So soon as the notary newly admitted to the practice of the notarial profession has enregistered his declaration of election of professional domicile, prescribed by the thirty fourth section of this act, the secretary who has received such declaration, must transmit to notaries, prothonotaries, clerks and registrars, the surname, christian name, and elected domicile of the recently admitted notary. On reception of such notice, the notaries, prothonotaries, clerks and registrars, enter the name of the new notary upon the table exhibited in their office. Inscription of the new notaries.

49. The board is authorized to draw up rules, from time to time, in relation to the preparation, publication, distribution and modification of the general table of notaries, and even to alter the periods of its annual preparation and publication. Rules relating to table of notaries.

CHAPTER SECOND.

OF NOTARIAL DEEDS, OF THEIR FORMS OR FORMALITIES, AND THEIR EFFECT—OF MINUTES, BREVETS, COPIES AND EXTRACTS—OF REPERTORIES AND INDICES—OF THE PRESERVATION, DEPOSIT OR TRANSFER THEREOF.

SECTION FIRST.

Of deeds en minutes.

50. Notarial deeds are such as are executed before one or more notaries public; they are considered authentic, Notarial deeds.

and of themselves make proof of their contents in law.
They are drawn up *en minutes*. or *en brevets*. A deed *en minute* is that which a notary executes and retains in his office,
to deliver copies or extracts thereof, and thus differs from
a deed *en brevet*, of which he delivers the original to the
parties, whether in single, duplicate or multiple. The
formalities required · in notarial deeds are prescribed
in the civil code and in the code of civil procedure.

Who writes
them.

51. Notaries are not bound to write themselves the
deeds which they receive; they may employ another person, or use printed or written blanks.

Minutes
made separ-
ately.

52. Notaries must receive and inscribe the minutes of
their deeds separately in such manner as to facilitate their
production when legally required.

Specifications
required.

53. Every notarial deed must specify the name, official
quality and place of residence, and contain the signature
of the notary who executes it, the names, qualities and
domiciles of the parties, with a description of the procurations, or powers and authorizations produced, the
number of the minute, the place where the deed is passed,
the fact of the reading of the deed, the signature of the parties, or their declaration that they do not know how or are
unable to sign, and the cause, after being asked to sign ;
the presence, the name, official quality, residence and
signature of the assistant notary, or the presence, the
names, quality and residences, of the requisite witnesses,
and the date of the deed. It must mention the number, and

Marginal
notes, &c.

approval of the marginal notes and foot-notes, the
acknowledged number and nullity of words erased or
struck out, the number and approval of lengthened
lines. The deed is concluded by the signatures of the parties, of the assistant notary or the witnesses, and by

Closing of the
deed.

that of the acting notary. Whenever a deed to which
several persons are parties, has been signed or executed
by each of them on different days and at different places,
it shall be lawful for the notary to specify such plurality
of dates and places, by mentioning, that as regards such a
party the deed was signed or executed, on such a day and
at such a place, and that as regards such other party,
it was also signed or executed on such a day and at such
a place. And the deed shall not be closed and signed by
the notary, save on the day of the last signature thereto.

Exemption of
a witness or
a second
notary.

Notwithstanding the provisions of the second paragraph of article 1208 of the civil code, the presence and
signature of a second notary or of a witness, when the
parties to a deed are unable to sign, shall not be requisite
to complete and make authentic a deed passed before any
notary, save in the case of wills.

54. Commercial firms, which have filed their declarations, where the law requires, are sufficiently designated by the name of the firm, and may act in any notarial deed under such name of the firm, mentioning in the deed the place where they carry on business, and the names, additions and residence of such of the partners as represent them. Designation of commercial firms.

55. Notarial deeds must be written without abreviations, blanks or spaces; they may, however, be prepared on printed or written blanks, on filling up the blank spaces by a heavy stroke of the pen. Sums, dates and numbers, which are other than simple indications or references not absolutely essential, must be written in full. No spaces, abreviations, &c.
Blanks.
Dates, &c.

56. Procurations or other documents, of which there are minutes, and in virtue of which the principal deed is executed, if sufficiently described, need not be annexed. Procurations and other documents *en brevets* or *sous seing privé* must be when produced also sufficiently described, and then annexed to the minute. The latter only must be admitted as true, and be signed by the parties in the presence of the notaries and the subscribing witnesses. Procurations, etc.

57. Notes, additions and lengthened lines, with the exception hereinafter mentioned, must be written in the margin only; they are signed by the *paraphes* or initials of the subscribers to the deed, under pain of the nullity of such notes and lengthened lines; and if the length of the note or the narrowness of the margin, require it to be placed at or carried to the end of the deed, it must be also signed by the *paraphes* or initials of the subscribers in the same manner as marginal notes, under pain of the nullity of such part of the note so placed or carried over; the same rule applies to foot notes and other notes, which the margin cannot contain, and which are written at the end of the deed. Notes, additions, &c.

58. There must not be in the body of the deed, or in the marginal or foot notes, any words written over, interlineations or additions; and the words written over, interlined, or added, are null. Erasures are made in such manner, that the words erased or struck out may be counted. Words written over.
Interlineations, &c.
Erasures.

59. The reading of a will or codicil is performed by the acting notary; as respects ordinary deeds, it is indifferent whether they are read by the notary, or by any other person. Reading.

60. The locality where the deed is passed is sufficiently indicated by specifying the city, town, parish or other place. Locality indicated.

Number.   .**61.** The minutes of deeds are numbered consecutively.

Minutes kept.   **62.** Notaries are bound to keep the minutes of all acts which they receive, except those hereinafter mentioned, which they may execute and deliver *en brevets*, if the parties so require.

SECTION SECOND.

OF DEEDS *en brevet.*

Deeds which may be exe-cuted *en bre-vets.*   **63.** There may be executed and delivered, on demand of the parties, *en brevets*, singly, in duplicate, or in multiple, life certificates, partial releases, procurations, powers of attorney, acts of notoriety, discharges of rent or farm rent, of salaries, of arrears of rents or pension, obligations or agreements purely personal, unless their effect is to be perpetual and pass from the contracting parties to their heirs or representatives, declarations, notices of family councils, appointments and reports of experts, attestations, disavowals, releases, discharges in respect of papers and moveables, and other documents the effect whereof must not be perpetual, or which do not confirm or discharge the effect of a deed executed *en minute.*

SECTION THIRD.

OF COPIES AND EXTRACTS.

64. Copies are the faithful reproduction of the minute, or annex made according to the provisions prescribed by the civil code ; extracts are also made in accordance with the provisions of the same code.

Extracts.   The right of furnishing such copy or extract vests only in the notary or prothonotary who is the custodian of the original.

SECTION FOURTH.

REPERTORIES AND INDICES.

Repertory.   **65.** Every notary is obliged, under disciplinary penalties and fine, to have and to keep in good order and proper state of preservation, a repertory of all deeds passed by him *en minutes*, in which he enters consecutively, their dates and numbers, their nature or kind, and the names of the parties.

Index.   **66.** With the same care, and under the same penalties, he must make and preserve an index to the repertory.

Special repertory.   **67.** Every notary may keep a special repertory, with or without an index, as he chooses, for notes, protests of bills of exchange and bills and other papers of the same nature.

SECTION FIFTH.

68. Except in cases of lawful transfer of notarial *greffes*, as hereinafter provided, and the transfer under section ten, the minutes, repertories and index of every practising notary who leaves the province, or who becomes unable to act as such, on account of performing functions inconsistent with practice, which places him on the list of non-practising notaries, or of any notary interdicted or removed from office, or who dies, or voluntarily ceases practising, the whole under the restrictions set forth in this act, are deposited by him, or by the party to whose care he has left them, or by his curator, his widow, his children, his heirs or legatees, as the case may be, in the office of the prothonotary of the superior court for the district in which such notary last practised and resided. *Deposit of the minutes, index, &c., in the office of prothonotary.*

69. Upon the refusal or neglect of any person obliged thereto, to make such deposit, the prothonotary is bound, within thirty days from the notice which is given to him by the syndic of the board of notaries, to proceed, in a summary manner, to recover and obtain possession of such minutes, repertories and index, by an action in revendication, before a judge of the superior court of the said district, either in term or vacation ; and he is also bound to report the proceedings to the president of the board of notaries. In default of the prothonotary fulfilling this duty, he is personally liable to a penalty of fifty dollars for each month of delay, counting from the day of the service of notice of the syndic. *The prothonotary must recover them on refusal. Penalty.*

70. Saving the case of the legal transfer of notarial *greffes*, every person obliged to make the deposit, who refuses or neglects to make the same, is liable to a penalty of from fifty dollars to one hundred dollars for each month of delay, counting from the day on which he has been called upon to make such deposit ; the notary himself is further subject to the disciplinary penalties hereinafter mentioned ; the whole without prejudice to any action of damages on the part of the party injured. *Penalty. Damages.*

71. The widow of a notary, whether she be in community with her husband, or separated as to property, or has accepted or repudiated the community,—or the legal representatives of the deceased notary, during the ten years next after his decease, if his *Rights of the widow, &c., to half the fees received by the prothonotary.*

widow dies before the expiration of the said ten years, and whether such representatives accept or repudiate the succession of such notary, or the representatives, or assigns of any absent notary,—or the notary himself who does not wish to practise, or refuses to do so, or who is interdicted or suspended,—shall receive, every six months, counting from the day of the deposit of his minutes, repertories and index, from the prothonotary of the superior court in the district where such deposit has been made, half the fees and emoluments which the prothonotary shall have received for searches, copies or extracts of or from any deed out of the *greffe* of such notary, whereof he is the custodian.

Fees which the prothonotary is entitled to receive for copy of deeds deposited.

72. The prothonotary of the superior court of any district is entitled to receive for every copy or extract of any notarial or annexed deed, whereof he is custodian, and by him delivered, fifty cents for the first four hundred words or under, ten cents for every additional hundred words, and fifty cents for the certificate of authenticity ;

Searches.

and a further sum of twenty cents, for each year searched in the repertory and index collectively.

Minutes, &c., deposited, form part of the records of the office.

73. The minutes, repertories and indices of notaries transferred to the prothonotary of the superior court, form part of the records of his office.

Greffe deposited can be retaken.

74. Whenever any notary, interdicted or absent, is anew admitted to practice, he shall be entitled again to obtain possession of his minutes, repertory and index deposited, as shall also any notary who has voluntarily ceased to practise, and has transmitted his *greffe* as aforesaid, if he desire again to practise within the limits of the district wherein his *greffe* has been deposited.

Greffes and safes not liable to seizure.

75. Notarial *greffes* and the safes in which the deeds are placed are not liable to seizure, except in the cases provided for in this act.

SECTION SIXTH.

TRANSFER AND ASSIGNMENT OF NOTARIAL *greffes.*

Transfer of the greffes.

76. The minutes, repertory and index of any notary deceased since the twenty-fourth of February, eighteen hundred and sixty-eight, or who dies after the passing of this act, or of any notary who has resigned and abandoned practice, may, under the conditions and formalities hereinafter set forth, be assigned and transferred to another notary, who either resides or will fix his residence, in the district of the professional domicile of the notary deceased or giving up practice.

77. It shall be lawful for the lieutenant-governor in council, upon application which shall be to him made, to permit or refuse, as he shall deem expedient, and according to the conditions hereinafter set forth, that the minutes and repertories of any notary, deceased since the twenty-fourth day of February, eighteen hundred and sixty-eight, or who shall die after the passing of this act, or of any notary resigning or who is desirous of ceasing to exercise his functions, or who shall have left his judicial district, be, with the consent of such notary, or of his heirs or representatives, transmitted to any other notary who resides, or who shall fix his residence in the district of the professional domicile of the notary deceased or resigning.

Power of the lieutenant-governor in council.

78. Such other notary and every successor thereof, who shall have in the same manner obtained such minutes and repertories, may deliver signed and certified copies thereof, and such copies shall be authentic for all purposes whatsoever; provided that in certifying the same he shall have made mention of the date of the order in council, under which the minutes were placed in his possession.

Copies delivered by the notary assignee.

79. Before granting such permission, the provincial secretary shall publish a notice of such application, for one month in the *Quebec Official Gazette*, and the permission granted under section 77 shall not take force and effect, until after the publication thereof in the said *Quebec Official Gazette*.

Notice required.

80. Application for such permission shall be made in the form of a petition, and the lieutenant-governor in council shall not grant the same unless the notary assignee has complied with the following conditions:

Petition.

1. To produce a certificate of the board of notaries, signed by the president of the said board, establishing that he is not undergoing any censure or punishment on the part of the said board of notaries;

Certificates.

2. To accompany the said petition by a report signed by the notary assignee, specifying the number and condition of the said minutes, together with the minutes missing, and the provincial secretary shall inform the prothonotary of the district of such transmission;

Report.

3. To provide a vault or safe sufficient as a protection against fire or damp, therein to deposit the said minutes, repertory and index; and so often as he shall be required he must permit such inspection of the vault or safe, as the board of notaries may from time to time require by an order under the signature of the president or vice-president of the said board, countersigned by one of the secretaries. The first inspection is always made at the cost

Vault or safe.

Inspection

of the applicant who shall pay them immediately and before he is entitled to obtain possession of the notarial *greffe* ceded and transferred to him.

CHAPTER THIRD.

GOVERNMENT OF THE NOTARIAL PROFESSION.

SECTION FIRST.

BOARD OF NOTARIES.

Board of notaries.

Powers.

81. There exists in the province of Quebec a board of notaries, designated as "The board of notaries." It is a corporation, and as such, enjoys all the privileges confered by law upon such bodies ; it may acquire, possess and enjoy real and personal estate, provided the same do not exceed in value the sum of fifty thousand dollars.

Services.

82. Any service on the said board made at the office of one of the secretaries is a good and valid service.

Formation of the board.

83. The board of notaries is constituted or composed of forty-three members, elected in the manner hereinafter prescribed, and distributed as follows : nine for the district of Montreal, eight for that of Quebec, four for that of Three-Rivers, three for that of St. Hyacinthe, two for each of the districts of Richelieu, Iberville, Joliette and Kamouraska, one for each of those of Ottawa, Terrebonne, Montmagny, Beauce, Arthabaska, St. Francis, Bedford, Beauharnois, Rimouski and Gaspé, and one for the united districts of Chicoutimi and Saguenay.

Quorum.

84. Twelve form a *quorum* for the despatch of business, and eight for the examination of candidates for the study of, or admission to, the notarial profession.

Election of the members of the board.

Time, place, mode.

85. The members of the board are elected by the practising notaries residing in the above named districts respectively, at general meetings in each of the said districts, in the district of Chicoutimi as regards the united districts of Chicoutimi and Saguenay, and at New-Carlisle in the county of Bonaventure, as regards the district of Gaspé, at the times and places hereinafter prescribed ; the election is held at the court house, at one o'clock in the afternoon, on the first Wednesday of the month of June, by the majority of votes of the notaries present, and by ballot ; and the prothonotary of every district shall be bound, subject to a penalty of twenty dollars, to point out a fit and proper room for every such meeting.

86. Such general meetings are held every three years, to which period the functions of the members of the said board are limited ; nevertheless, the same members may be re-elected, with their own consent; the elected members remain in office until their successors are elected or appointed in their place. *Every three years.* *Re-eligibility.*

87. Each such meeting is presided over by a notary, chosen by the majority of the notaries present, entitled to vote at such meeting. The notary chosen to preside at the meeting, after drawing up and signing the minutes of the proceedings, files the same in the records of the superior court for the district, and at once or within fifteen days, delivers a certified copy thereof to the president of the board of notaries, addressed to one of the secretaries, after giving notice of their election to each of the members elected ; under a penalty of twenty dollars, against any one of the officers mentioned in this section for refusal or neglect, in respect of the duties imposed on him by this section. *Meetings.* *President.* *Minutes.* *Copies to members elected.* *Penalty.*

88. The next general meeting of notaries for the election of members of the board, shall take place on the first Wednesday of the month of June, eighteen hundred and seventy-six, and the subsequent triennial meetings for the election of members of the board, shall be held at the same places, at the same time, and in the same manner as the first; and if such day be a holiday, such meetings shall be held on the next following juridical day. *Years in which meetings are to be held.*

From this present time, till the first Wednesday in June, eighteen hundred and seventy-six, the notaries of this province who now form the provincial board of notaries, shall be members of the board of notaries established by this act, and shall exercise and perform all powers and duties thereunder, as if they had been elected under its provisions, and shall continue in office till they be replaced under this act. *Former members, continued.*

89. The existing officers of the provincial board of notaries also remain in office, as officers of the board of notaries hereby established, till their replacement by such latter board. *Existing officers.*

90. All the by-laws, and regulating resolutions of the provincial board of notaries shall be also those of the board of notaries now constituted, till their revocation or modification by the latter. *By-laws, &c., in force.*

91. The general meetings of the board of notaries are held, alternately, at Quebec, on the third Wednesday in May, at ten o'clock in the forenoon, and at Montreal, on the first Wednesday in October, at ten o'clock in the *Meetings are held in Quebec and Montreal, alternately.*

forenoon, in each year ; if such day be a holiday, the meeting is held on the next juridical day.

If in a district there has been no election of members. **92.** If at the time of the first meeting of the board,
immediately following a triennial election, or if at the
time of any subsequent meeting, it appears that in any
district or territory there has been no election of a member to represent such district or territory in the board,
the board may, on information thereof, appoint a member,
or the number of members required to represent such
district or territory ; every member so appointed has the
same powers, privileges and duties as those elected by
notaries at a general meeting.

Extraordinary meetings of notaries. **93.** Extraordinary general meetings of notaries may
take place whenever circumstances require, and the
board deems desirable.

Other extraordinary general meetings of notaries may
also be called by either of the secretaries of the board on
a written request addressed to such secretary and signed
by twenty-five notaries, qualified to vote at meetings
for the election of members of the board. All such meetings, asked for in either manner, are summoned by
Mode of summoning. advertisements inserted, in the French and English languages, in two newspapers published in each of the
districts of Quebec and Montreal, at least fifteen days
Places. before such meeting ; they are held alternately at Quebec
and Montreal.

Adjournment. **94.** Every meeting of the board of notaries, and every
general meeting of notaries, may be adjourned by consent
of those present, to such place, day and hour, as shall be
then decided upon.

Officers. **95.** The board elects :
President ; his powers, &c. 1. A president, who votes only when the votes are
equally divided, who calls special meetings of the board
when he deems it expedient, or on the justified requisition
in writing of two members, or of the syndic hereinafter
Vice-president. named, and who preserves order at all meetings ; also a
vice-president to represent him, in case of sickness,
absence or otherwise ; they may be replaced, in case of
the absence of both, by a temporary president, appointed by the members present ;
Two secretaries ; their duties, &c. 2. Two secretaries, one of whom must reside in the
city of Montreal, and the other in the city of Quebec ;
they draw up and preserve the records of the proceedings of the board, have the custody of all archives, and
deliver copies thereof ; they collect the facts relative to
any charges brought against a notary, and report the same
to the board. Each of them may appoint a deputy to
represent him in case of illness, absence or detention,

with the approbation of the board, or in vacation with that of the president, or of the vice-president if the president is absent or unable to act; such deputy is so appointed by a certificate signed by the secretary in his own name, and which is recorded in the minutes of the board; Assistant-secretary.

3. A treasurer, who has charge of the common fund hereinafter established, who receives and pays money upon the order of the board, and accounts for the same as the board directs; Treasurer.

4. A syndic, who acts as prosecutor in the case of notaries accused before the board, or before the commission of accusations hereinafter established. Syndic.

96. The out-going president shall also at the meeting held in the month of October following a g neral election of its members, submit a report of the principal facts and proceedings of the board, during his term of office, and a general statement of the affairs under the control of the board up to that date. Report of the out-going president.

97. The *procès-verbal* of every meeting of the board is signed on the minute book of the proceedings by the president of the meeting, and countersigned by the secretary. Nevertheless the omission, for any reason whatsoever, of the signature of the president of the meeting, does not invalidate the authenticity of the *procès-verbal* when signed solely by the secretary. Entry of the *procès-verbal* of the meetings.

98. When the board of notaries holds its meetings in either of the cities of Montreal or Quebec, the secretary residing in such locality, or his deputy, draws up minutes of the proceedings and keeps the register thereof; but each of the secretaries is bound, as soon as possible, to transmit to the other a certified copy of the proceedings, and it shall be the latter's duty to enter such copy in his register. Which secretary is bound to act.

99. In addition to the special powers assigned to the officers aforesaid, each of them, if he is a member of the board, may vote as such with the other members, at all meetings thereof; except that with regard to any matter relating to any charge against a notary, the syndic, who conducts the prosecution, if he is a member of the board, forms one of the *quorum*, and takes part in the proceedings, but has not the right to vote on any decision taken by the board, on the matter of the accusation and the procedure consequent thereon. Other powers of the officers.

100. In case of any of the officers aforesaid being absent, or prevented from acting, th ir places may be supplied by the appointment of others, *pro tempore*, by the majority of Case of absence, &c.

the members present, at any meeting at which there is a *quorum*.

Who may be officers. **101.** The president and vice-president, or *pro tempore* president, are always chosen from among the members of the board ; the other officers may be chosen either from among the members of the board or from among other notaries practising within its jurisdiction.

Removal of the officers. **102.** The board may remove any officer at pleasure, and appoint another in his stead ; but no officer is so removed except by the vote of the absolute majority of the members of the board.

Time of the election of the officers. **103** The election of the president and other officers is made by the members of the board every three years ; the same persons being capable of re-election, and the senior in age having the preference, in case of equality of votes.

Penalty for refusal. **104.** Any notary refusing to accept the office of member of the board, or to perform the duties of president. vice-president, *pro tempore* president, secretary-treasurer, or syndic, is liable to the disciplinary penalties and fines hereinafter mentioned, unless he has already filled one of such offices, or has attained the age of sixty years.

Penalty for absence, &c. **105.** Any notary elected or appointed a member or an officer of the board, who does not attend regularly at the meetings of the board, or who neglects to fulfil the duties of his office, after accepting the same, is liable to the disciplinary penalties and fines hereinafter provided, unless he has been prevented from attending through illness or other serious cause, and any member or officer of the board, who after having been elected, or re-elected with his own consent, refuses to act, is liable to the same penalties.

Vacancies. **106.** If any vacancy occurs in the board of notaries. by the death of one of the members thereof, or by absence from the meetings for any time not less than one year, or by resignation, or otherwise, the board may fill such vacancy by the majority of votes of the members present forming a quorum. The same rule applies in relation to any officer who is not a member of the board.

SECTION SECOND.

POWERS OF THE BOARD OF NOTARIES ; MODE OF PROCEDURE ON ACCUSATIONS.

Functions of the board. **107.** The functions of the board of notaries are :

1. To maintain internal discipline among notaries within Discipline. its jurisdiction, and finally to award censure, and enforce other disciplinary provisions;

2. To prevent and reconcile all differences between no- Differences, taries, and all complaints and claims by third persons complaints, against notaries, concerning their functions; to express an &c. opinion respecting the damages which may thence arise, and to repress by censure or other means of discipline, Repression. even including suspension and removal, whatever offence may be the subject thereof, without prejudice to any right of action before a court of justice, if any such there be ;

3. To grant or refuse, after examination, all certificates Certificates. of qualification and admission required by applicants for admission, either as students or notaries, and to take full cognizance thereof;

4. To summon before it when necessary, any notary Summons. within its jurisdiction;

5. To alter from time to time, if it thinks proper, its *quorum* for the dispatch of routine business, but such *quo-rum* shall not be less than five members present ; and whenever any decision is required to be taken on any matter brought before the board, the *quorum* shall consist Quorum. of twelve members present for the dispatch of business, and eight for the examination of candidates for admission to the study or practice of the profession ;

6. According to the gravity of the offence and according Punishments. to the provisions of this act, to punish by itself or through the action of the commission of accusations, any notary within its jurisdiction, by the imposition of all or any of the disciplinary penalties defined and enumerated in section 177 of this act, and of the several fines prescribed by this act in the various sections thereof;

7. To make such by-laws and orders as from time to By-laws. time are found requisite for the administration and regulation of all matters under its control, and for the due execution of this act.

108. In the case of accusations brought against notaries Accusations. and for the mode of procedure therein, there is appointed, at the ordinary meeting of the board of notaries, held in October of each year, a commission of five members chosen Commission from among the members of the board itself, of which three of 5 members. are a *quorum*, which commission has by the present act, power to investigate, hear and decide, in the manner and form hereinafter provided, any accusation against a notary for breach of his professional duties or for all acts derogatory to the honor of the profession. The secretary of Secretary. the board, or his deputy, as the case may be acts as its clerk *ex-officio*.

109. The powers of such commission expire at the an- Commission nual meeting which follows its nomination ; the m embers is for a year.

Proviso.

who compose it are however, eligible to re-election, if they are qualified and consent.

The commission which has heard an accusation on the merits, must render judgment, notwithstanding the expiration of its powers.

Place of its sitting.

The commission must sit at Montreal or Quebec, whenever so required by its chairman, by two members, or by one of the secretaries of the board.

Rules.

The board is authorized to make rules to define the proceedings for convening the commission, and the latter has power to make by-laws to regulate its proceedings, and the procedure to be adopted before it.

Complaints admitted by the board.

The board of notaries may, by resolution, cause to be brought before the commission of accusations, any complaints and accusations received and admitted by the provincial board of notaries up to the time of the coming into force of the present act. From such time, the commission, its officers, and the officers of the board, each in so far as concerned, take up the proceedings on such accusation, in the state in which it is, and continues them in the manner prescribed by this act, till final judgment; without prejudice, however, to the right of appeal hereinafter provided.

Decision.

110. In every case where a notary is accused before the commission of accusations of any offence or of any action derogatory to the dignity, and honor of the profession, or of any contravention of the provisions of the present act, the accusation is decided *vivâ voce*, "guilty" or " not

Absolute majority.

guilty," by the absolute majority of the commission appointed by the board.

Power of the syndic.

111. The syndic may, *ex-officio* and on the sole authority of the board, bring, in the name of the board, before the commission, an accusation against any notary who violates any one or more provisions of this act, which violation entails the infliction of disciplinary penalties, and he may conduct in his own name as complainant all the proceedings according to the procedure prescribed by this act.

Mode of proceeding.

112. The mode of proceeding on all accusations brought by the syndic is as follows:—whenever the syndic receives, on the oath of one or more credible persons, (the oath to be administered by any justice of the peace,) a complaint against a notary, reflecting on the honor, dignity or duties of the profession, he, without delay, lays such complaint before a meeting of the commission of accusations, called for that purpose, by its chairman, two of its members, or one of the secretaries of the board, on the demand of the syndic ; and if the commission deem that there is matter for investigation, it orders the trial of such notary.

113. When the syndic *ex-officio*, takes proceedings against a notary, on the sole authority of the board, the commission of accusations is relieved from deciding whether there be matter for investigation, and from ordering the trial of such notary. Idem.

114. The complaint must briefly mention the time, place and circumstances of the charge. Allegations of the complaint.

115. The syndic then draws up the act of accusation in the form of schedule No. 3, of the present act. Act of accusation.

Such act of accusation is transmitted to the secretary of the place where the commission must sit, which secretary makes a copy, which he certifies, and causes to be served on the accused, with an order in the name of the president of the board enjoining him to appear in person or by attorney before the clerk of the commission, on the day and hour mentioned in the said order, which is drawn up in the form of schedule No. 4 to this act. Order to the accused.

116. There must be a delay of ten days between the service of the order and the appearance of the accused, if the latter has his elected domicile within five leagues of the place of meeting of the commission ; and if the distance exceeds five leagues, the delay is increased by one day for each additional five leagues. Delay.

117. The service of the act of accusation and of the order to appear is made by a bailiff of the superior court, by delivering certified copies as aforesaid to the accused in person, or to a reasonable person of his domicile, and the said bailiff, under his oath of office, makes a return of such service on the original of the said order to appear, which original, with the papers annexed, he transmits to the secretary at least two days before the date fixed for the appearance of the accused. Service made by a bailiff of the S. C.

118. The complainant transmits to the secretary, on or before the day of return of the act of accusation, the exhibits in support of his complaint, and the list of witnesses to the charge, stating the domicile of his witnesses. Exhibits and list of the witnesses filed.

119. The complainant may appear personally or by attorney, on the day of the return of the act of accusation, if not, the syndic represents him. Appearance.

120. The reply to the accusation is made in writing and is signed by the accused or by his attorney ; it may contain a general denial of the accusation or a special answer to all or any part thereof ; in any case it is communicated, either personally or through attorney, to the secretary, within the eight days following the return of Reply. Delay.

Exhibits and list of the witnesses filed.   the act of accusation, together with the exhibits in support thereof, and also a list of the witnesses of the accused, with their respective domiciles.

Issue joined.   **121**. Issue is joined,

1. By the act of accusation, the answer of the accused, and the replication of the complainant, or of the syndic when he acts *ex-officio ;*

2. It is equally so by foreclosure from pleading or in the absence of a replication ;

3. Nevertheless on petition justified to that end, the delegate of the commission may accord leave to produce further pleadings.

Record ; communication thereof ; exception.   **122**. In any case brought before the commission of accusations :

1. The list of witnesses produced by either side, must not be communicated to the other party ;

2. The papers produced cannot be withdrawn except with the written consent of both parties, the written permission of the delegate of the commission, and upon receipts therefor ;

3. Each paper filed in a case (excepting the lists of witnesses,) is common to both parties in the case, and they may order copies to be forwarded to them, by the clerk so long as he is the custodian thereof ;

4. Until the last and final judgment is rendered, every paper filed forms part of the record, and after the cause is definitely concluded cannot be returned to the party who filed it, except by the written permission of the delegate of the commission, or of the president or vice-president of the board when an appeal has been instituted.

Presumed domicile of the parties.   **123**. The domicile of the complainant and of the accused, for the proceedings on the accusation, is deemed to be at the office of the secretary of the board, at the place where the commission is to sit.

Foreclosure.   **124**. If the accused does not answer the accusation within the delay established, he is foreclosed from doing so, and the complainant proceeds to proof in the manner hereinafter mentioned.

Inscription for proof.   **125**. Within six days from the filing of the replication or other pleading authorized by the delegate of the commission or from the foreclosure of the accused, the complainant or syndic, when acting *ex-officio*, or on their default the accused may inscribe the cause for proof, mentioning the place where the evidence on either side is to be taken, and the secretary transmits the record to the commission, in order to proceed to proof.

126 At the first or any other meeting of the com- Delegate of mission of accusations, for the reception of, or for taking the commission: his into consideration, any complaint or accusation against a powers.; notary, it may appoint one of its members as a delegate, and to him it may transfer all its powers, or a part thereof only, moment to the decision and regulating of any incident which may arise in the procedure and at *enquête*, from the period of his appointment as delegate, till the case be definitely ready for final hearing on the merits.

127. If, by his nomination, the powers of such dele- Idem. gate are not defined, they include all that the commission may itself exercise, from the date of his appointment, till the case be ready for final hearing on the merits.

128. The commission also appoints at its first meeting *Commissaire-* a *commissaire-enquêteur*, whose powers are indicated and *enquêteur.* duties prescribed by the sections of this act.

129. The order appointing such commissioner must Mention re- specify the place where the investigation shall be held, quired in the order. and the delay within which it shall be completed. Such delay may be extended, on sufficient cause, by the delegate of the commission.

130. The delegate superintends the proceedings and Duty of the the investigation, and any decision rendered by the delegate. *commissaire-enquêteur*, on any objection made during the investigation on any point of procedure, is subject to revision by the delegate, at the instance of either of the parties. The judgment of the delegate is in such case final and conclusive.

131. Paragraph 6 of section 3 of chapter 6 of the Para: 6, s. 3, first title of the first book of the second part of the code c. 6, T I. B. I. part 2 of the of civil procedure, and the amendments to such por- c. c. p. shall tion of the code apply to the duties of the *commissaire-enquê-* apply. *teur* under this act, and to the procedure at the investigation before him, in so far as other provisions are not laid down in respect thereof by this act.

132. The witnesses are summoned by writ of *subpœnâ* Witnesses. in the form of schedule No. 5 of this act, in the name of the president of the board, and signed by the secretary ; and their refusal to appear before the *commissaire-en-* *quêteur*, is equivalent to a refusal to appear before a court of justice, and the commissioner has, by this act, the same powers to compel witnesses to attend and give evidence, as courts of justice.

Such writ of *subpœnâ*, as are all other pieces of pro- *Subpœnâ.* cedure under this act, is served by a bailiff of the superior court.

Powers of the commissaire-enquêteur.   The *commissaire-enquêteur*, during the investigrtion, has the same power to fine witnesses for non-attendance, and to imprison for contempt of court, as a judge sitting in any court of justice, in the province of Quebec.

Commissaire-enquêteur administers the oath to witnesses.   **133.** The *commissaire-enquêteur* is empowered by this act to administer the oath to the witnesses ; and any person guilty of any false declaration, in any oath required, is guilty of perjury, and punished by the penalties by law inflicted, in cases of perjury.

Enquête taken at length.   The *enquête* before the *commissaire-enquêteur* must be taken down at length, in the same manner as that specified in the code of civil procedure, in relation to an *enquête* before the superior court.

Expenses of the witnesses.   The expenses of the witnesses are taxed by the *commissaire-enquêteur*, subject to revision by the delegate, if occasion require.

Enquête declared closed.   **134.** If five days elapse, and neither party proceeds with his *enquête*, the *commissaire-enquêteur* may *pleno jure* declare closed the *enquête* of the party in default, and may grant act thereof to the other party, upon his demand. He may also declare the *enquête* closed generally, if neither party proceed within such delay.

Report of the commissaire-enquêteur.

Inscription for hearing on the merits.   **135.** So soon as the *commissaire-enquêteur* has closed the *enquête* generally, he reports his proceedings, the secretary inscribes the cause on the roll for hearing on the merits, and gives notice to the parties, and to the members of the commission, at least ten days previously, of the day fixed for such hearing.

Counsel heard.   **136.** At the hearing of the cause, not more than two counsel are heard on either side, and one only in reply.

Judgment rendered, with grounds thereof.   **137.** The commission, after deliberation, must give its judgment in writing, together with the grounds thereof, and if the accused is declared guilty, the judgment at the same time pronounces the punishment which the commission intends to inflict.

Its effect.   The judgment of the commission pronouncing sentence of suspension or removal only takes effect on the day after the expiration of the delay to appeal therefrom.

Costs in the proceedings.   **138.** The costs incurred in the proceedings are taxed in the judgment against the party liable for the same, at the discretion of the commission.

Taxation.   2. Such costs are taxed according to the tariff established by the board, as well for costs incurred in the first instance, as for those of appeal.

Tariff.   3. Such tariff may be modified by the board when it deems it expedient.

4. The costs taxable according to such tariff, are the travelling expenses of the members of the commission of accusations, of their delegate, of the *commissaire-enquê-teur*, of the secretaries of the board acting as such or as clerks of the commission, of the syndic, of the counsel of the parties, of the writers at *enquêtes* if any are employed, of the bailiffs and of the witnesses. Taxable costs.

5. If a fee is not provided in the tariff for any necessary or useful service rendered in relation to the case, the commission, the delegate thereof or the board, according to circumstances and the position of the case, may allow a fee for such service, and tax the same against such of the parties to the cause as they may deem meet. Fees not provided for.

139. The prothonotary of the superior court of the district where the party condemned resides is authorized and enjoined, on production of a certified copy of the judgment, which then forms part of the archives of the court and remains of record, to issue a writ of execution for the recovery of the costs of judgment and subsequent costs, as in judgments of the superior court ; in the case of an opposition, the costs are as in a cause of the lowest class in the superior court. The same proceedings are had in relation to the costs of the judgment in appeal, before the assembled board. Execution issued by the prothonotary.

140. The commission is hereby authorized, and according to the gravity of an offence against discipline, or of any action derogatory to the honor of the profession, to impose : Powers of the commission.

1. Censure, deprivation of the right to vote at any meeting of notaries, ineligibility to the board of notaries for a period more or less extended, at the discretion of the commission, removal as a member of the board of notaries, if the party found guilty is then a member thereof, suspension for any time not exceeding five years, or absolute removal. Censure.

2. The judgment inflicting such penalties is given at the first ordinary meeting, following the date of the judgment, which imposes the same. It is pronounced in a loud voice by the chairman of the meeting, the offender having been previously summoned to appear for that purpose by the clerk Judgment.

3. At the expiration of fifteen days after the judgment pronouncing censure, suspension or removal, if the party condemned has not appealed therefrom, execution follows. In the case of a judgment pronouncing sentence of suspension or removal, a copy thereof, certified by one of the secretaries of the board, is served by a bailiff upon the prothonotary of the superior court of the district in which the notary condemned is resident. Execution. Service in certain cases.

Service to the prothonotary. **4.** Together with such copy of judgment, an order is served upon the prothonotary, enjoining him in the name of the board to take possession of the *greffe* of the notary condemned, and retain it for the future if the latter is removed, or for the whole period of his suspension, if he is merely suspended.

Return. **5.** The bailiff makes a return of the service of such copy of judgment and of such order upon the original of the said order.

Duties of the prothonotary. **6.** And to the end hereof, the prothonotary is bound to take proceedings, to obtain possession of the *greffe* of the condemned notary, as in the ordinary cases provided for by section 69 of this act.

Idem. **7.** The prothonotary is bound to report his proceedings to the president of the board of notaries.

Publication in the Official Gazette. **8.** The suspension or removal of a notary, is published for one month in the *Quebec Official Gazette*, immediately after the expiration of the delay to appeal, if no appeal is instituted, and immediately after the judgment of the board sitting as a court of appeal, if the judgment originally rendered is confirmed.

9. The notary who after suspension or removal, during such suspension, or after his removal, takes fees as a notary, for any deed executed after his suspension, is deemed to have taken them under false pretences, and is punishable in the same manner as persons obtaining money under false pretences.

Appeal to the board of notaries. **141.** Any notary accused, who considers himself aggrieved by the final judgment rendered by the commission on the charge brought against him, can only appeal therefrom to the board of notaries, in the manner hereinafter set forth, and no judgment of the commission rendered under this act can be set aside by other means than that of the appeal therein mentioned.

Deposit of $50.00. **2.** With the view of obtaining such appeal, the notary aggrieved must, within fifteen days after the pronouncing of the judgment, deposit fifty dollars with the treasurer of the board. Such sum is returned to the appellant, if the judgment of the commission is set aside or altered, together with the costs, but in the contrary case, goes in part payment of the costs of the appeal, and no record or copy of proceedings is transmitted to the board, unless the deposit hereinabove required is made, and the inscription for appeal duly served upon the respondent or his attorney, and no inscription is received previous to such deposit and service. In the event of no appeal having been instituted, within fifteen days after the rendering of the judgment, such judgment is final and executory without delay.

Service. Delay.

Duties of the secretary. **3.** The service of the inscription and the deposit have the effect of compelling the secretary to transmit to the board, the record of the charge instituted against the appellant, together with the inscription and the certificate of deposit, as also the proceedings and copies of all judgments and orders in the cause, and to enter the cause upon the appeal roll.

4. On the inscription of the cause on the roll of appeal, the secretary must lodge in Her Majesty's post office, post-paid, a notice of such appeal and of the day fixed by him for the hearing thereof, which hearing shall not take place before the expiration of fifteen days after the deposit of the notice in the post office ; such notice is addressed to the appellant, to the respondent, to the president, and to the members of the board, requiring their attendance at the day, place and hour specified. *Notice to the members of the board.*

5. The members of the commission cannot sit in the board constituted into a court of appeal. *Inability of cert. members.*

6. The *quorum* of the board sitting as a court of appeal consists of twelve members present. *Quorum.*

7. At the time of the hearing in appeal, the complainant and accused must file statements or factums to the number of fifty copies, which they transmit at least eight days before the hearing to the secretary of the board, at the place where it is about to sit as a court of appeal. The said secretary, (who acts as clerk of the court of appeal), distributes copies of the *factum* to the members of the board who are to constitute the court of appeal, and to the parties interested. *Factum.*

8. If such statement or *factum* is not produced within the said delay, on the part of the appellant, the appeal is held to be abandoned, and the secretary must strike the inscription, and notify the members of the board not to assemble, in relation to the said cause. *Default of factum.*

9. If such statement or *factum* is not produced within such delay, on the part of the respondent, the appellant is notified thereof by the secretary, and the appeal is heard *ex parte* without the intervention of the respondent.

142. The record of the proceedings in the first instance before the commission, and the factum of the parties shall be the only documents produced in appeal, or *Documents to be submitted.*

1. On the day fixed for hearing, if neither of the two parties appear before the assembled board, the case is struck from the roll, and cannot be again inscribed except on payment of a further deposit, if the first is not sufficient to cover the expenses incurred and to be incurred for another meeting of the board ; which costs the latter must tax in striking the case from the roll ; *Default to appear.*

2. If the appellant do not appear, the appeal on the respondent's application is dismissed with costs ;

3. If the respondent do not appear, the appellant, on demand, is heard *ex-parte* and judgment rendered.

Counsel heard.   **143.** In any appeal, not more than two counsel may be heard on the side of each party, and one only in reply.

Judgment.   **144.** Judgment must be rendered within the shortest delay possible ; it is publicly rendered, and is recorded in the minutes of the board, and transmitted, as the case may be, as aforesaid, to the prothonotary.   '

Judgment.   **145.** The board confirms, disaffirms, or modifies the final judgment rendered in the first instance, and pronounces the judgment which should have been rendered by the commission, and adjudges costs, as well in the first instance, as in appeal.

If the judgment decree suspension, it must fix the days on which such suspension commences and ends.

If the judgment decree removal, it takes immediate effect.

Tariff of fees.   **146.** The board is authorized to prepare and establish a tariff of fees, as well in respect of proceedings in the first instance, as in appeal.

Punishment in case of absence.   **147.** Any member, who without valid reason absents himself from the meetings of the board of notaries or of the commission of accusations, is liable to the disciplinary penalties hereinafter mentioned, in section 177 of the present act.

2. In regard to members of the commission of accusations, such absence is established by the *procès-verbal* of the meetings of the commission, in which must be entered the names and surnames of the members present at each sitting.

3. The absence of a member of the commission, established by the *procès-verbal* of the meetings and proceedings thereof, is the only proof required to authorize the commission of which such member formed part, to impose disciplinary penalties on such absent member, the latter

Appeal.   being previously heard or duly summoned according to rules which the board may make from time to time, in reference thereto; saving an appeal to the board by the commissioner condemned.

Proceedings.   4. In the event of appeal by the latter, the appeal will be proceeded with as hereinbefore prescribed in relation to any appeal from a judgment of the commission of accusations, in an ordinary case.

Substitute.   5. If suspension be decreed, the commission (of which three form then a quorum) appoint *ex-officio* a substitute duly qualified in this respect, to replace the absent member, so as not to retard the trial and decision, in an action then pending; if otherwise it is necessary to wait till the board appoint one to replace such member, at its first meeting after the vacancy has occurred.

148. The board of notaries may, as often as it deems Inspectors of fit, choose amongst its members, or amongst other notaries *greffes*, appointed by the board. under its jurisdiction, one or more practising notaries not exceeding three, to inspect the offices or *greffes*, minutes, repertories and indices of one, or more or all the notaries, with the view of establishing whether they conform to the laws of this province, and to the provisions of the present act, and to collect information on all matters and things, contained in the instructions they receive from the board of notaries, to which they report under their oath of office.

The inspectors thus appointed cannot be compelled to Case of exact as such, if they fall within the class exempted from emption. accepting office by this act.

149. Any notary who refuses either to receive the Penalty for visit of the notary or notaries thus appointed, or to grant refusal. communication of his official papers and registers, incurs for each refusal or neglect, the pains and penalties imposed by this act.

150. Any notary thus appointed to make such inspec- Exception. tion, cannot be compelled to make more than one visit during three years; and he is entitled to receive from the common fund of the board of notaries, any renume- Costs. ration deemed sufficient by the board.

SECTION THIRD.

TARIFF OF NOTARIAL FEES.

151. The board of notaries may make one or more Tariff of fees tariffs of fees, which may be exacted by notaries for pro- exacted by notaries. fessional services, and it may increase, diminish or otherwise modify them from time to time.

152. Such tariffs, so made or modified, enter into force Published in only after they are published in the *Quebec Official Gazette* the Official Gazette. for four consecutive weeks, and fifteen days after the last publication; any notary contravening them, by exceeding such tariff, is subject to the disciplinary penalties and fines hereinafter prescribed.

The board of notaries is bound to print copies for the Penalty for use of notaries inscribed as practising, and address to each contravention. a copy authenticated by one of the secretaries of the board, as also to each prothonotary of the superior court, who must exhibit it in a prominent place in his office.

SECTION FOURTH.

COMMON FUND OF THE BOARD OF NOTARIES.

153. The board of notaries may establish a common Common fund, which is formed by subscriptions from the several fund.

practising notaries of the province. In order to assist in forming this common fund, and to meet the annual

Annual contribution. and extraordinary expenses of the board, there shall be paid, in advance, each year, on the first of March, by each practising notary, at the office of the treasurer of the board, a fixed subscription of four dollars. This subscription may be augmented or decreased by by-law of the board, as it deems advisable.

Arrears due to the old boards. **154.** The arrears of subscriptions established by former laws, to be paid into the common fund of the notaries of the heretofore district boards of notaries or into the common fund of the provincial board of notaries, in this province, if they have not already been paid and discharged, are the property of the board of notaries created by this act, and are payable at the office of its treasurer in office for the time being.

Recovery of the contribution and arrears. **155.** The fixed subscription, increased or diminished as provided for in section 153 of this act, and the arrears of former subscriptions mentioned in the preceding section, are, in default of payment, recoverable by the syndic, by action in the name of the board of notaries before any competent court of the place where the treasurer of the board in office for the time being may reside.

Penalty for refusing to pay. **156.** Any notary who refuses or neglects to pay, at the times or places hereinabove mentioned, the subscription and arrears mentioned in the three preceding sections is subject to the disciplinary penalties hereinafter mentioned, in the section 177 of this act.

Annual statement of receipts and expenditure. **157.** A statement of receipts and expenditure is, each year, submitted to the board by the treasurer, at its first meeting, under the pains and penalties hereinafter provided.

Fiscal year. **158.** The fiscal year of the board of notaries dates from the first of March.

By a by-law of the board the commencement of the fiscal year may be altered from time to time.

If the board makes such change, the subscription of the year commencing at the newly-established date, is payable in advance.

SECTION FIFTH.

EXAMINATION AND ADMISSION OF CANDIDATES TO STUDY AND PRACTISE AS NOTARIES.—FEES.

Admission as a student. **159.** No person shall be admitted as a student with any notary unless he has previously undergone a public examination before the board of notaries, in relation to his qualifications and capacity, nor unless he establishes that he has received a liberal education, which must include a complete course of classical studies, that is to say : latin elements, syntax, method, versification, belles-lettres, rhetoric and philosophy inclusive, or any other complete course of classical studies taught in colleges, seminaries, or any incorporated university, nor unless he produces a certificate to such effect, nor unless he has given the notice required by section 164 hereinafter specified. Knowledge required.

Notice required.

160. Any candidate may undergo an examination to be admitted as a student of the profession, at any ordinary and regular meeting of the board of notaries, and, if it consent, at any extraordinary or special meeting. Meetings.

161. After the examination of the candidate, and the production of the requisite certificates, if the board deem him sufficiently qualified and capable, he is admitted to the study of the notarial profession. Examination.

A certificate thereof is delivered to such candidate in the form of schedule No. 1, of this act or in any other analogous form. Certificate.

Such certificate must be annexed to the minute of the deed or articles of clerkship, in which mention must be thereof made, as also of the date of such certificate, and of that of the board's admission of the candidate to the study of the profession.

162. To be entitled to the certificate of admission to practise as a notary, the candidate must prove before the board : Conditions required for a certificate to the admission as a student.

1. That he possesses the qualities required by the thirtieth section of this act ;

2. That he has been regularly admitted to study as a notary ;

3. That he has *bonâ fide* served a regular clerkship under a practising notary, during four consecutive years ; or during three years, if he has at the same time, and to the satisfaction of the board, followed an univers ty course ;

4. That he has thus served during such time of his clerkship, under a notarial deed or *brevet portant minute ;*

5. His good moral conduct during such clerkship ;

6. His knowledge of law and notarial practice, in an examination before the board ;

7. His practical knowledge of the drawing up of notarial deeds, by drawing up at once any part of a deed which the board may direct him.

If a candidate has terminated his time of clerkship since twelve months. **163.** Twelve months after the expiration of his clerk ship, the candidate cannot be admitted to prove befor< the board what is required of him by the preceding sec tion, unless upon:

1. Obtaining from it a by-law permitting him t< proceed to such proof ;

2. Paying to its treasurer and for the use of the board as special compensation, the sum of twenty-five dollars ;

8. Fulfilling the conditions and defraying the expense: which the board, according to the circumstances, ma) ordain by such by-law.

Notice required from the candidate to the practice. **164.** The candidate for admission to practise as a no tary must give to the secretary of the board, at the plac< where it is to hold its next meeting, a written notice, a least one month in advance, containing :

1. His name and surname, as entered in his certificat< of baptism or birth;

2. Mention of his intention of submitting to the exam ination required in a candidate for practice.

This notice must be signed by the candidate, and be ac companied by a sum of fifteen dollars to cover the expens< of the publication of the notice prescribed by the follow ing section.

Notice to be given by the Secretary. **165.** The secretary of the board, at the place where i is to hold its next meeting, must give notice for thre weeks, of the day and hour at which the examination wil take place, and of the name, surname and residence o each candidate.

This notice must be drawn in the French and Englis] languages, and be posted up as notices in the offices of the two secretaries of the board, and then published in one or more newspapers, in the manner prescribed by the rules of the board.

Meetings. **166.** Each candidate may obtain a certificate of admission to practise as a notary, at the ordinary meeting of the board nearest to the date of the expiration of his articles of clerkship, whether such meeting be held before or after such expiration ; nevertheless the certificate is not given before the expiration of such articles.

Power of the board to summon witnesses. **167.** The board of notaries may summon before it, by an order under the hand and seal of the president, or on his default, of the vice-president, and the countersignature of one of its secretaries, any person, whom the candidate or those opposing his admission, wish to call in support of or in opposition to the allegations concerning his mode of **Oath.** life and qualification. The oath is administered to the witness in this case by the person presiding at the board, when such oath is required.

168. If the candidate has complied with all the con- Certificate of ditions required by law, is found capable and qualified admission. by the board of notaries, and has paid to the treasurer of the board a sum of fifty dollars, he is entitled to obtain a Payment of commission to practise as a notary, in the form of schedule $50. No. 2 of this act, or in any form having the same effect. He is bound to enregister such commission, in the office of Registration. the registrar of the province.

169. The word "consecutive," in paragraph 3, of Interpreta- tion of the section 162 of this act, and applying to the length of word "conse- clerkship required, signifies that there has not been cutive." any interruption throughout longer than three months in the studies of the candidate, and an interruption of not more than three months in all, in the studies of a candidate to practise as a notary, does not prevent his admission to examination, and is not in any manner injurious to him, at whatever time the interrup- tion may have taken place.
If the interruption be more than three months, the Case of inter- board may use its discretion as to what it is best to do. ruption of more than
To do away with the necessity of the candidate apply- three months. ing to the legislature for relief, the board may make a by-law to do away with such default, the candidate who wishes to benefit by it, paying to the treasurer of the board a sum of twenty-five dollars to the profit of the common fund, without prejudice to the payment of the other sums which each candidate is obliged to pay before obtaining his commission.

170. The examinations of candidates for study or prac- Examina- tice as notaries, are held at a meeting of the board in tions. *quorum*, and are conducted as well in writing, as publicly and *vivâ voce.*

171. A candidate to practise as a notary who, after If candidate examination, has been thrice refused on account of incapa- is thrice re- city, is not again permitted to undergo an examination fused. or to be admitted as a notary.

172. In addition to the examinations hereinabove The board required the board of notaries may, by regulations made may order several exam- from time to time, subject the candidates for admission inations. to the practice of the notarial profession, to one or more examinations on the study and practice of law, during their time of clerkship.

173. The three or four years of clerkship required shall When clerk- be computed from the date of the articles, and not from ship begins. the date of the admission to the study of the profession by the board of notaries.

Registration
of articles and
transfers.
174. All articles and transfers of articles must be enregistered in the office of one of the secretaries of the board of notaries, within a delay of thirty days from their date, under pain of the nullity of such articles or transfers; nevertheless the board of notaries may allow the registration of any such deed after such delay, on the special application of the person in default, on condition of his paying a sum not exceeding ten dollars; but such enregistration must be made at least within six months before the expiration of such articles.

Secretaries'
fees.
175. The secretaries of the board of notaries, or their deputies, shall be entitled to demand and receive the following fees, which the board may, from time to time, modify :

1. For the certificate of capacity and admission to the profession, delivered to the candidate, five dollars, over and above the cost of publication of the advertisement ;

2. For the entry of any declaration in the cases provided for by the present act, fifty cents ;

3. For every summons, twenty-five cents ;

4. For enregistering any articles, or transfer of articles, and the certificate substantiating it, one dollar for the first four hundred words or under, and ten cents for every additional hundred words ;

5. For a certificate of any copy asked for and certified, fifty cents.

Tariff of fees
payable to
officers.
176. The board may also, from time to time, by by-law make and modify as it pleases, a tariff of fees to be paid to any of its officers, or officers of the commission of accusations, for any papers and other acts required of them, in the performance of their respective duties, and in respect of which this act does not otherwise provide.

Disciplinary
penalties.
177. The disciplinary penalties mentioned in the several sections of this act, are the following :

1. Deprivation of the right of voting at elections of members of the board, as also at the general meetings of notaries, during a certain period ;

2. Deprivation of eligibility to the office of member of the board ;

3. Calling to order a member of the board, which prevents him attending the meeting in which he is called to order, unless he apologizes to the board ;

4. Censure ;

5. Forfeiture of membership of the board of notaries ;

6. Suspension from the right of practising the profession of a notary, which *ipso facto* removes him from membership of the board ;

7. Removal from the office of notary.

178. All these disciplinary penalties are imposed at the discretion of the board, or the commission of accusations, according to their powers. And they are imposed separately or simultaneously. Penalties imposed.

179. Any notary who is guilty of any infraction of the provisions of the sections hereinafter specified of this act, incurs one, or more, or all of the disciplinary penalties mentioned in section 177 aforesaid, and is at the same time amenable to the following pecuniary penalties : Penalties.

SECTION SIXTH.

IMPOSITION AND RECOVERY OF PENALTIES ; MISCELLANEOUS PROVISIONS.

180. 1. For contravening section twenty, in reference to the list of interdicted persons, curators or judicial advisers, a penalty of from ten to twenty dollars ; Fines for contravening sections 20.

2. For contravening the provisions of sections 32, 33 and 34, respecting the taking of the oath of office, and the other things to be performed before commencing practice, a penalty of from twenty to one hundred dollars; 32, 33 and 34.

3. For contravening sections 53 and 55 referring to the drawing up of deeds, a penalty of from ten to twenty dollars ; 53 and 55.

4. For contravening sections 65 and 66 referring to the keeping of repertories and indices, a penalty of from twenty to fifty dollars; 65 and 66.

5. For contravening the provisions of sections 104 and 105, referring to the refusal of accepting the office of member of the board of notaries, or of officer thereof, or negligence after accepting in fulfilling the duties, without sufficient cause, a penalty of from ten to twenty dollars ; 104 and 105.

6. For contravening section 148 in relation to the inspection of notarial *greffes*, a penalty not exceeding twenty-five dollars; 148.

7. For contravening section 149 respecting the refusal to receive such visit and to communicate official papers and registers, a penalty not exceeding forty dollars; 149.

8. For contravening the provisions of section 152, relative to the tariff of fees of notaries a penalty of from twenty to thirty dollars ; 152.

9. For contravening section 157 respecting the annual account to be rendered by the treasurer, a penalty of from ten to twenty dollars, for each week during which he neglects to make the same. 157.

181. Any fine or penalty imposed by the present act is sued for and is recoverable by the syndic, in the name and with the previous authorization of the board, or of its Fines recovered by lawsuit.

president or vice-president, before any competent civil court; and when recovered, it is paid by the syndic into the hands of the treasurer of the board, to form part of the common fund.

Use.

Archives of old boards.

182. The registers, books and archives which belonged to the former boards of notaries if not heretofore transferred, shall be transferred to the board of notaries, within thirty days from the coming into force of this act, under a penalty of fifty dollars against the custodian for each month during which he neglects to fulfil such duty.

Indemnity to members of the board.

183. The members of the board of notaries are entitled to be indemnified for their costs and travelling expenses during the whole period of their attendance at its meetings, or at those of special committees sitting in vacation; which expenses in the first instance must not exceed two dollars, and in the second four dollars a day, computing from the day of departure from their residence to that of return, over and above travelling expenses, which are also to be repaid.

These costs and expenses are paid by the treasurer from the common fund, on a certificate taxing the said costs and expenses, given and signed by the president, in his absence by the vice-president, or in their absence by the *pro tempore* president of the meeting, and as regards a special committee sitting in vacation, by the chairman of the committee. The board may, by by-law, increase the indemnity.

Idem.

184. Saving the exception hereinafter made, all the members of the board of notaries, over and above necessary disbursements really paid for expenses and travelling, and which shall be refunded to them, are entitled to an indemnity of two dollars *per diem,* for all the time absolutely required to take them to the place of meetings of the board, give their attendance and return; the day of leaving their residence and the day of return count as two whole days.

Exception.

The following persons are exempted from benefiting by the preceding provision : 1. the members of the board who reside in the town where the meeting is held ; 2. those who reside in suburban municipalities and in the immediate vicinity of the town.

Special committees.

The members of the board of notaries who attend, when it is not in session, according to its instructions at meetings of special committees appointed by it, are also entitled to travelling expenses and an indemnity, to be fixed by the board, at the time of the appointment of the committees, or later at its discretion.

Accounts attested.

Such expenses and indemnity are paid by the treasurer, from the common fund of the board, on a detailed account, attested by the declaration prescribed by the statute of Canada, 37 Vict., chap. 37, of the member who produces it, before the treasurer, and on receipt to the satisfaction of the latter.

The treasurer is himself sworn as to his account, before one of the secretaries of the board, or his deputy.

185. Practising notaries have alone the right of voting Voters at at meetings of notaries, and at meetings for the election of meetings. members of the board, and further practising notaries are alone eligible as members of the board of notaries, Eligibility. provided always, that in either case, they have before the first of April preceding such meetings, paid their subscription to the common fund of the board, to the last day of the month of February preceding.

FINAL PROVISIONS ; LAWS REPEALED.

186. The acts of the legislature of this province, thirty- 33 v., c. 28 ; third Victoria, chapter twenty-eight, and thirty-fourth 34 v., c. 13 ; C. Victoria, chapter thirteen, as also chapter seventy-three of and 27–28 the consolidated statutes for Lower Canada, as amended v., c. 45, re- by the act twenty-seven and twenty-eight Victoria, pealed. chapter forty-five, are hereby repealed.

187. All other laws in force respecting the notarial Other laws re- profession, at the time of the coming into force of the pealed in cer- present act, are also repealed in cases :
1. Where it contains a provision which has expressly or impliedly such effect ;
2. Where they are contrary to or inconsistent with the provisions it contains ;
3. Where it contains an express provision on the special subject of such laws.

188. This act shall come into force on the day of its Act in force. sanction.

SCHEDULE No. 1.

Schedule 1.

CERTIFICATE OF ADMISSION TO THE STUDY OF THE NOTARIAL PROFESSION.

Province of Quebec. }   BOARD OF NOTARIES.

This is to certify to all whom it may concern, that of in the district of hath passed his public examination before the board of notaries, and hath been found duly qualified, according to the requirements of the law in this behalf, to study the profession of notary in the province of Quebec.

In witness whereof, we have signed these presents at
in the district of
in the province of Quebec, the
day of the month of   eighteen hundred
and sixty

President.

Secretary.

SCHEDULE No. 2.

CERTIFICATE OF ADMISSION TO PRACTISE AS A NOTARY.

FORM OF CERTIFICATE OR COMMISSION.

Province of Quebec, Board of Notaries.

This is to certify to all whom it may concern, that A. B.
of   in the district of
Esquire, hath duly ·passed his examination before the
board of notaries, and hath been found qualified to fulfil
the office and duties of a notary, he having complied with
all the requirements of the law in that behalf.

Wherefore the said A. B. is admitted by the board to
the profession of a notary, and is in virtue of the law
authorized to practise the profession of a notary in this
province, and to enjoy all the rights and privileges attached to such office.

In witness whereof, we have signed these presents, at
the   day of
in the year eighteen hundred   and
have thereto set the seal of the board.

(L. S.)

C. D.
President.

E. F.
Secretary.

SCHEDULE No. 3.

ACT OF ACCUSATION.

Province of Quebec, Board of Notaries.
To the president and members of the Board of Notaries.

A. B , Syndic of the board of notaries, informs, by these
presents, the said board, that G. H. Esquire, residing at
in the district of   is ac-
cused under oath of N. B.

as follows, to wit: that the said G. H. (*here set forth the offence.*)

Wherefore the said A. B. prays that there issue an order from the said board, enjoining the said G. H. to appear before it, in due course of law and justice.

Done at   this   day of
               eighteen hundred
                                              A. B.
                                                Syndic.

SCHEDULE No. 4

SUMMONS OF THE ACCUSED.

Province of Quebec, Board of Notaries.

By the president and members of the board of notaries, to G. H., Esquire, residing at   in the district of
                                              greeting :
You are by these presents required to appear in person before us at our board, in the city of
on the   day of   instant
(*or next*), at   o'clock of the   noon then and there to answer to the complaint, a copy of which is annexed, brought against you by A. B., Esquire, syndic.

And you are informed that, in default of appearing before us, at the day, hour and place mentioned, proceedings will be had by default on the said complaint.

Given at   under the seal of the said board, the signature of our president and the counter-signature of one of our secretaries, this   day of   eighteen hundred

(E. F.)   C. D.
    Secretary.   *President.*

SCHEDULE No. 5.

SUBPŒNA.

Province of Quebec, Board of notaries.
By the president, &c., (*or in the preceding form.*)
A. B. C., (*additi n, residence*) greeting :
We enjoin you by these presents, that you and each of you, do appear in person before us, at our board, in the city of ·   on the   day of
instant (*or next,*) at   o'clock   in the noon, to give your evidence and notify the truth of all you know of a complaint brought before us by
Esquire, syndic of the said board, against G. H., Esquire, and therein fail not under penalty of law.

8

Given at the city of   under the seal of the
said board, and the signature of one of our secretaries, this
·   day of   eighteen hundred
(L. S.)   F. E.,
Secretary.

CAP. XXXIV.

An act to amend chapter 77 of the consolidated statutes of Canada, respecting land surveyors and the
survey of lands.

[*Assented to 24th December*, 1875.]

HER MAJESTY, by and with the advice and consent
of the Legislature of Quebec, enacts as follows :

C. S. C., c. 77, **1.** Section 6 of chapter 77 of the consolidated statutes
s. 6, repealed. of Canada is repealed ; and in future, no person shall be
admitted as a surveyor's clerk unless he has previously
undergone, before the board of examiners of surveyors, an
Knowledge examination with respect to his knowledge of the French
required of or English language, according as the candidate is of
surveyors' French or English origin ; in the first instance the exa-
clerks. miners shall require of him a knowledge of the
Examination. elements and syntax of the French language, and his capacity of translating correctly from English into French ;
in the second case a knowledge of the elements
and syntax of the English language and his capacity
of translating correctly from French into English ; in either
case, candidates for the study of land surveying must be
able to write correctly from dictation, each in his mother
tongue ; and further no person shall be admitted as a surveyor's clerk, unless he possess a fair knowledge of the
geography of the globe in general and of Canada in particular, nor unless he is well versed in vulgar and deci-
mal fractions, the extraction of square and cube roots,
the rules of proportion and progression, the elements
of geometry and of plane trigonometry, the mensuration
of superficies and solids, and the use of logarithms.

Id. s. 9, **2.** In addition to the matters required by section 9· of
amended. chapter 77 of the consolidated statutes of Canada, in the
Other know- examination which every surveyor's clerk must undergo
ledge requir- before being admitted to practise as a land surveyor, the
ed of survey- candidate shall be examined and shall reply in a satisfac-
ors. tory manner, on the elements of mineralogy and botany,
(on the forest flora of Canada in particular,) on the mode to
be pursued in conducting a *bornage*, on all questions referred to in this act, and in chapter 77 of the consolidated
statutes of Canada, on the investigation of titles to pro-

perty, and generally on all fundamental questions of law connected with the admeasurement and bounding of land, before being entitled to the diploma specified in the ninth section aforesaid.

3. No member of the board of examiners of surveyors shall be permitted to prepare a student for undergoing the preliminary examination required for admission to the study of surveying. These members are only permitted to prepare their own clerks for undergoing the necessary examination to be admitted to practice; and the commissioner of crown lands, on satisfactory evidence, may dismiss from his functions any member of the board of examiners who may act in contravention of this enactment. *An examiner cannot prepare for admission to the study.*

4. The privileges granted by section 17 of chapter 77 of the consolidated statutes of Canada, to those who have followed a course of study in a university, and have there received their degree or diploma in the manner therein specified, are extended to those who have followed a regular and complete course in a college or school where surveying and civil engineering are taught, and who have received a certificate or diploma from the said college or school; provided that the said college or the said school has been previously approved for this purpose by the lieutenant-governor in council. *Privileges extended to other colleges, &c.*

5. The words "surveyors clerk" are substituted for the word "apprentice" wherever the latter occurs in chapter 77 of the consolidated statutes of Canada. *C.S.C., c. 77, amended. Name of the surveyor's clerk.*

6. Hereafter, and notwithstanding the usage that may have prevailed in certain parts of the province, all the side lines of lots of land of regular form, in the townships of this province, shall be established and traced on the bearing or course of the exterior lines of the township whereof such lots form part, when they are parallel to the lines of such sub-divisions as set forth on the plan and in the description contained in the proclamation erecting such township. *Mode of establishing side lines.*

7. When the exterior lines of a township are not parallel to the internal sub-division of the lots, the guiding line shall be the centre line drawn on the course or bearing of the side lines of the said lots, in each range which it affects, as set forth on the plan and in the description aforesaid. *Guiding lines in certain cases.*

8. The said division lines shall be drawn on the said course or bearing from the posts or division pickets planted or established on the front of each range or concession. *Division lines.*

Front of a range.

9. The front of each range shall be understood to be the lowest range line in the series of numbers designating the several ranges of a township. Thus the front of the first range of a township shall be the division line which separates it from the township, seigniory or river, upon which it rests; the front of the second range shall be the division line between the first and the second range; the front of the third range shall be the line between the second and the third ranges, and so on.

Front line, how referred in certain cases.

10. When the front of the first range happens to be a line on which no sub-division posts have been planted, (for the township which may be in question), or should it be formed by the shore of a lake or water-course, on which there is no post marking the said lots, the front line shall be referred to the range line next above the first, and the side lines of the lots shall be traced from the posts planted thereon, (or from those which have been lawfully substituted for them,) on either side in opposite directions, for the first and the second ranges, the front being common to both.

If the posts are destroyed.

11. If it happen, that at the same time, both on the front and rear lines of any range, the entire series of posts marking out the lots has been destroyed, either by lapse of time, or by fire, or from any other cause, the sub-division of such lots shall be made *de novo*, in conformity with section 47 of chapter 77 of the consolidated statutes of Canada, and with the official plan of the original survey, and the side lines of the lots in such range shall be established and drawn from the posts so planted, as above prescribed.

Limits of the lots.

12. These side lines thus established from the posts which mark out a lot on the front line of a range, and drawn parallel to the lateral lines or to the centre line of the township in which such lot is included, in conformity with the proclamation erecting such township, or with the plan annexed to the official description of the erection of the township, produced to meet the rear line of the said range, shall, together with the portion of such latter line, comprised between such side lines, and that part of the front line between the posts aforesaid, form the boundaries of the said lot.

Lines drawn according to a certain special system.

13. If before the passing of the present act the lateral lines of one or of several lots comprised in the range of a township should have been traced in accordance with the system adopted in certain parts of the province, from a post on one range line to the corresponding post on the range line immediately above or below, all the lots in the said range whose lateral lines remained to be drawn on

the ground shall be drawn in accordance with the same
system, and on the same principle ; as the division lines
between the said lots are not affected by the provisions
of the present act.

14. The commissioner of crown lands, when he shall
deem it necessary in the interests of his department, may
exact from any provincial land surveyor, any certified
copy of plans or minutes of any survey, which the latter
may have performed at the request of any person ; and
if such surveyor refuses to deliver certified copies thereof
as requested, he shall be liable to the penalties set forth
in section twenty-five of chapter 77 of the consolidated
statutes of Canada. · *Copies of plans or minutes of survey may be exacted by the Com. C.L.*

15. From and after the coming into force of this act,
any provincial land surveyor who may be called upon to
grant a certificate setting forth that the conditions of
settlement required by the act 32 Vict., chap. 11, and by
the regulations of the crown lands department, have been
complied with, on any lot purchased from the crown, the
purchaser whereof desires to take out letters patent therefor, shall grant such certificate in the form A, hereunto
annexed. *Certificate of the performance of the conditions required by 32 v., c. 11, &c.*

16 Any surveyor, wilfully inserting in the said
certificate any untrue statement, may under and in virtue of the act hereinbefore cited, be condemned by the
board of examiners to the loss of his diploma. *Untrue statement in the certificate.*

17. Any surveyor who, in any report of inspection
or valuation respecting crown lands, whether vacant
or held under location ticket, shall wilfully lead into error
the commissioner of crown lands, or his representatives,
by means of false information, shall be also liable to the
penalties set forth in section twenty-five of the act aforesaid. *False information given in any report of inspection or valuation.*

18. After the word " government " in the third line of
section twenty-six of chapter 77 of the consolidated statutes of Canada, are added the following words, " or a
member of the legislature." *C. S. C, c. 77, s. 26 amended.*

19. Paragraph 5 of section 108 of chapter 77 of the consolidated statutes of Canada is hereby amended, by substituting the figure 5 in place of the figure 4, which occurs
in the column of figures in the said paragraph. *Id. s. 108 § 5 amended.*

FORM A.

I, the undersigned provincial land surveyor, certify that on the   18   , I visited lot No.
of the   range of the township of   , in the county of   , where I ascertained that the purchaser M.   or his (or her) representatives M. (or MM.)

has (or have) been resident upon the said lot during the   years last past, and that M.   is at present in the locality, the recognized possessor of the said lot.

I further certify, upon inspection, that there are upon the said lot   acres under cultivation, and that a habitable house occupied by the said   or his (or her) representatives, the dimensions whereof are at least 16 feet by 20, has been erected on the same.

Signature, A. B.

Provincial Land Surveyor.

CAP. XXXV.

An Act to amend the act of this province 38 Vict., chap. 29.

[*Assented to 24th December*, 1875.]

Preamble. WHEREAS by section four of an act of the legislature of this province, 38 Vict., chap. 29, intituled : " An act to amend chapter 18 of the consolidated statutes for Lower Canada," it was enacted that meetings for the election of church-wardens, for the rendering of accounts and for all purposes requiring a general parish meeting, in the five parishes civilly recognized by such act, should be composed of the old and new church-wardens and of persons elected in compliance with the ordinance of the bishop, to form the board or body of the *fabrique* ;

And whereas it is advisable that such provisions should apply to all other parishes detached from, or which may hereafter be detached from, the old parish of *Notre-Dame de Montréal*, which are or may hereafter be formed, either in whole or in part, out of the territory of the said parish of *Notre-Dame de Montréal*, so that the mode of holding the said meetings be uniform throughout such parishes ; Therefore, Her Majesty, by and with the advice and consent of the Legislature of Quebec, enacts as follows :

38 v., c. 29, s. 4, shall apply to parishes to be erected.
1. The provisions of section four of the act of this province, 38 Vict., chap. 29, intituled : " An act to amend chapter 18 of the consolidated statutes for Lower Canada," and

which section reads as follows: " The meetings for the erection of church-wardens, for the rendering of accounts and for all purposes requiring a general parish meeting, in these parishes, shall consist of the old and of the new church-wardens, and of the persons elected in compliance with the ordinance of the bishop, to form the board or body of the *fabrique*" apply and shall apply to all parishes, detached or which may hereafter be detached, which are or may hereafter be formed, in whole or in part, out of the territory of the old parish *of Notre-Dame de Montréal,* and are recognized as being lawfully binding therein; provided that in any case the church-wardens so Payment of elected, or the *fabriques* so constituted, shall not oblige or debts. bind the parishioners to pay debts contracted by the said church-wardens or the said *fabriques*, without the previous consent of the said parishioners declared at a general parish meeting, duly called by a notice of at least eight days."

2. The said meetings shall be convened by notice from Meetings. the pulpit (*prône*) on the Sunday preceding that on which the meeting is held, and they shall take place at the hour and in the place mentioned in the notice.

And whereas doubts have arisen respecting the validity of the elections of church-wardens held before the passing of this act, in certain parishes detached from the old parish of *Notre-Dame*, and it is expedient to remove such doubts, it is further enacted as follows:

3. All elections of church-wardens held before the Elections of passing of this act, in all parishes detached, in whole or church-war- in part, from the territory of the old parish of *Notre-Dame,* dens already are hereby declared valid, and the church-wardens so elect- clared valid. ed duly possessed of all the powers and functions attached to the office of church-warden, whatever may have been the mode pursued in such elections.

4. Nothing in this act contained shall affect pending Pending cases. cases.

5. This act shall come into force the day of its sanction. Act in force.

CAP. XXXVI.

An Act for the civil erection of several parishes cut off from the territory of the old parish of Notre-Dame of Montreal.

[Assented to 24th December, 1875.]

WHEREAS the civil erection, under chapter 18 of the Preamble consolidated statutes for Lower Canada, of the

parishes hereinafter named, and comprised within the old
limits of the parish of Notre-Dame of Montreal, would be
very costly and very difficult, owing to the large population of these parishes, to act in conformity with the said
chapter 18 of the consolidated statutes for Lower Canada,
and whereas it is necessary to civilly acknowledge the
said parishes ; Therefore, Her Majesty, by and with the
advice and consent of the Legislature of Quebec, enacts
as follows :

Erection of catholic parishes. 1. The parishes hereinafter described, erected for religious purposes, only by the ecclesiastical authority, with
the limits and boundaries assigned to them by the canonical decrees respecting the same, are declared to be and are
recognized as catholic parishes, as fully and to the same
effect, as if they had been recognized, erected and ratified,
for all civil purposes under chapter 18 of the consolidated
statutes for Lower Canada.

St. Gabriel. " 1. The parish of St. Gabriel, erected by a decree of
Monseigneur Ignace Bourget, Roman Catholic bishop of
Montreal, dated December 10th, 1875, comprising the
south eastern part of the parish of *St. Henri des Tanneries,*
and bounded on the north by the Lachine canal, from the
bridge crossed by the Grand Trunk railway to the
actual limits of the city of Montreal, on the east by the
said limits to the river St. Lawrence, thence, on the south,
by the said river in following its upward course, up to the
property actually occupied by J. H. Mooney excluded,
on the west, by a boundary line starting from the said
river from the Mooney property, passing through the
centre of the highway called No. 1, following it upwards,
thence passing to the west of the waterworks buildings,
including the reservoir, and thence to the said bridge on
the canal included.

St. Paul. 2. The parish of St. Paul, erected by a decree of the
same bishop, dated December 10th, 1875, comprising the
south-western part of the parish of *St. Henri des Tanneries,*
part of the river St. Pierre, and part of the Côte St. Paul,
and bounded on the south, by the river St. Lawrence,
starting from the property actually occupied by J. H.
Mooney included, and running upwards to the property of John Crawford included ; on the west, by the
actual limits of the Lachine parish to the Lachine railway, on the north, from the property of Dame widow
McNaughton excluded, by following the said railroad
until its junction with the Côte St. Paul road, thence by
a straight line crossing the Lachine canal, following
then the south of the said canal, as far as the Grand
Trunk railway bridge crossing the said canal ; thence, on
the east, by a line running down to the river and which is
to pass to the west of the waterworks buildings ; thence
in the middle of a highway called No. 1, and thence, to
the St. Lawrence river.

3. The parish of Ste. Cunégonde erected by a decree Ste. Cuné-
of the same bishop, dated december 11th, 1875, com- gonde.
prising the eastern part of the parish of *St. Henri des
Tanneries*, and bounded on the south by the Lachine
canal from Atwater street to the actual limits of the city
of Montreal ; on the east by the actual limits of the city
of Montreal from the Lachine canal to Dorchester street ;
on the north by a line passing through the middle of Dorchester street, and extending from the limits of the city
of Montreal to Atwater street ; on the west by a line
passing through the middle of Atwater street, and extending from Dorchester street to the Lachine canal.

4. The parish of St. Jean Baptiste, erected by a decree St. Jean-
of the same bishop, dated december 11th, 1875, com- Baptiste.
prising the southern part of the parish of St. Enfant
Jésus, and bounded on the north by the Tanneries road,
now called Mount-Royal ; on the east by the centre of
the Papineau road ; on the south by the city of Montreal ;
on the west by the mountain or Mount Royal.

5. The parish of Sacré-Cœur de Jésus, erected by a Sacré-Cœur
decree of the same bishop, dated december 11th, 1875, de Jésus.
comprising the northern part of the parish of St. Bridget,
and bounded on the north by the present limits of the
city of Montreal ; on the east by the middle of Colborne
street, going downwards till its junction with Logan
street; on the south, by the middle of the said Logan
street to Visitation street; thence, by a straight line
supposed to be also the middle of Logan street, to
Amherst street ; on the west, by the middle of the said
Amherst street in an upward direction to the aforesaid
limits of the city.

2. Nothing in this act contained shall have the effect Municipal
of changing in any manner the limits of the city of limits, not
Montreal, and of the various other municipalities in changed.
which such parishes are situated. Such municipalities
shall continue to exist, with the same limits and boundaries, as if the present act had never been passed.

3. Each parish so recognized is so, subject to the pro- Decree of
visions set forth in the decree of erection which respects erection.
the same.

4. Every parish which the ecclesiastical authority may Recognizance
erect for religious purposes, within the limits of the of the parish-
parishes of the ancient territory of Notre-Dame of es erected in
Montreal, already dismembered and civilly recognized, the future.
or which are so by section one of this act, shall be a catholic parish, from and after the insertion in the *Quebec
Official Gazette*, of a notice of the issue of the canonical Notice re-
decree which erects the same, and that as fully and with quired.
the same effects as if it had been recognized and rati-

fied for all civil purposes, under chapter 18 of the consolidated statutes for Lower Canada, subject to the provisions of section two of this act, and to the provisions set forth in the decree of erection, which respects the same.

Meetings of the parishioners. 5. Meetings for the election of church-wardens, for the rendering of accounts, and for all matters which require the convening of a parochial meeting, in such parishes, shall be composed of the old and new church-wardens, and of persons elected in conformity with the ordinance of the bishop, to constitute the board or body of the **Payment of debts.** *fabrique* ; provided that in any case the church-wardens so elected or the *fabriqual* so constituted shall not have power to oblige or bind the parishioners to the payment of debts contracted by the said church-wardens, or the said *fabriques*, without the previous consent of the said parishioners declared at a general meeting of the parish duly convened after eight days notice.

Act in force. 6. This act shall come into force the day of its sanction.

CAP. XXXVII.

An Act to annex certain islands in the parish of Sorel, county of Richelieu, to the parish of *la Visitation de l'Ile du Pads*, in the county of Berthier, for parliamentary, municipal, school and registration purposes.

[*Assented to* 24*th December*, 1875.]

Preamble. WHEREAS certain inhabited islands situate at the south-west entrance of lake St. Peter, in the river St. Lawrence, are not included in the limits of the several surrounding parishes ; and it is important to define the limits of the parish of *la Visitation de l'Ile du Pads* and of the parish of *St. Pierre de Sorel*, situated respectively, the former in the county of Berthier, and the latter in the county of Richelieu, in such locality ; Therefore, Her Majesty, by and with the advice and consent of the Legislature of Quebec, enacts as follows :

Certain islands annexed to the parish of l'Ile du Pads. 1. The islands hereinafter named situated at the south-western entrance of lake St. Peter, in the river St. Lawrence, comprised within the limits of the parish of *la Visitation de l'Ile du Pads* recognized by the proclamation of the lieutenant-governor of this province, bearing date the fourth day of june, 1875, that is to say : *l'Ile des Plantes, l'Ile Ducharme, l'Ile Manon, l'Ile à l'Orme, l'Ile au Noyer,* *l'Ile Lamarche, l'Ile a la Cavalle*, situate between *l'Ile Madame, l'Ile à l'Ours* and *l'Ile du Pads*, and also the small islands and battures, comprised in the same territory, shall in future form part of the said parish of *la Visitation de l'Ile du Pads* for the same purposes as those mentioned in the following sections.

2. The islands hereinafter named situate in the same place, that is to say, *l'Ile du Nord, les Iles de la battures aux carpes, la Girodeau, l'Ile Milieu, la Grande Ile, l'Ile Latraverse, les Iles au Sable*, and all the small islands and battures, comprised in the territory included by the said islands hereinabove named and situated to the north thereof, and to the south of the islands *à l'Aigle* and *à la Grenouille*, shall in future form part of the said parish of *la Visitation de l'Ile du Pads*, in the county of Berthier, for all municipal, school, electoral and other purposes. *Certain islands annexed to the same parish.*

3. The islands hereinafter named situate in the same place, that is to say : *l'Ile de Grâce, l'Ile aux Corbeaux, l'Ile à la Pierre, l'Ile du Moine, l'Ile des Barques, l'Ile aux Raisins*, and all the small islands and battures comprised within the territory included by such islands, and situate to the south thereof, shall in future form part of the parish of *St. Pierre de Sorel*, in the county of Richelieu, for the same purposes as those mentioned in the preceding section. *Certain islands annexed to the parish of Sorel.*

4. The division line of the counties of Berthier and Richelieu, in such locality of the parishes of *la Visitation de l'Ile du Pads* and *St. Pierre de Sorel*, shall be as follows : from the limits of the parish of *Ste. Geneviève de Berthier*, the said line shall follow the ship channel in the river St. Lawrence, to the south of *l'Ile St. Ignace, l'Ile Madame, l'Ile Ronde, l'Ile à l'Ours* and *les Iles au Sable* extending to lake St. Peter, and to the north-western limits of the county of Maskinongé. *Division of the counties of Berthier and Richelieu*

CAP. XXXVIII.

An Act to detach from the county of Terrebonne, the part of the parish of Ste. Monique, situate in such county, and to annex the same to the county of Two Mountains, and to annex certain lands detached from the domain of the lake of Two Mountains, to the parish of St. Benoît, county of Two Mountains, for parliamentary, registration, municipal and school purposes.

[*Assented to 24th December, 1875.*]

HER MAJESTY, by and with the advice and consent of the Legislature of Quebec, enacts as follows:

Part of Ste. Monique annexed to the county of Two Mountains.

1. All that part of the parish of Ste. Monique, now in the county of Terrebonne, is detached from such county, and annexed to the county of Two Mountains, for municipal, school and registration purposes, and for parliamentary representation.

C.S.C., c. 2, s. 1, and C.S.L C., c. 75, s. 1, Ss. 13, 14, amended.

2. Section one of chapter two of the consolidated statutes of Canada, and sub-sections thirteen and fourteen, of section one of chapter seventy-five, of the consolidated statutes for Lower Canada, shall be read and interpreted in-so-far as they apply to this province, in conformity with the preceding section of this act.

Municipal purposes.

3. The part of the parish, hereby annexed to the county of two Mountains, shall form part of the municipality of the parish of Ste. Monique, in the same manner and with the same effect as if such annexation had been made under the municipal code.

Part annexed to the parish of St. Benoît

4. The lot of land occupied by Moise Brayer *dit* St. Pierre, containing twelve arpents in width by thirty-two arpents in depth, extending at one end to the *trait-quarré* of the lands of côte St. Jean, in the said parish of St. Benoit, on the other to a proposed base line, or to the line of demarcation between the parish of the Annunciation and the said parish of St. Benoît, on the north-east side to the seigniorial domain, and on the south-west side to the *Baie* road, as also a lot of land of twenty-four arpents in front, owned as follows: nine acres in front, to Jean Baptiste Waddel, twelve arpents in front to Damase Boileau, and three arpents in front to Felix Angrignon, by thirty-two arpents in depth, the whole front of the said lot being upon the high road, bounded in rear by the *trait-quarré* of the lands of Côte St. Ambroise, or by the line of demarcation of the said parish of the

Annunciation, on the north-east side by Gatien Husereau, and on the south-west side by the land of Basile and Magloire Bertand, shall be and they hereby are annexed to the said parish of St. Benoît, in the county of Two Mountains, for all parliamentary, judicial, municipal, school and registration purposes.

5. The lots of land hereby annexed to the parish of St. Benoît, shall form part of the municipality of the parish of St. Benoît, in the same manner and to the same effect as if such annexation had been made in virtue of the municipal code. Municipal purposes.

CAP. XXXIX.

An Act to detach from the county of Dorchester, a part of the parish of St. Anselme, situate in that county, and to annex it to the county of Bellechasse, for all parliamentary, municipal, school and registration purposes.

[Assented to 24th December, 1875.]

H ER MAJESTY, by and with the advice and consent of the Legislature of Quebec, enacts as follows :

1. The whole of that part of the parish of St. Anselme, called the "North-East of the Mountain" and divided into two ranges, whereof one is known as "range of St. Matthew" and the other as "range of St. Paul" the whole comprising an extent of territory of about thirty arpents frontage by about sixty arpents in depth, bounded as follows, to wit : towards the north-west by the boundary line which separates the said St. Paul concession from that styled "La Grillade" in the parish of St. Henri ; towards the north-east, by the boundary line separating the said parish of St Anselme from that of St. Gervais ; towards the south-east by the boundary line separating the said concession of St. Matthew from that called St. Mark ; towards the south-west partly by the line separating to the south-west the property of Ignace Morency from that of Jean-Baptiste Boutin, in the said concession of St. Matthew, and partly by the line which also to the south-west separates the property of Michel Morency from that of the said Jean-Baptiste Boutin, in the said concession of St. Paul ; the said territory, as at present annexed to the parish of St. Gervais, county of Bellechasse, for religious purposes, is detached from the said county of Dorchester, and is annexed to the said county of Bellechasse, for municipal, registration and school purposes, and for the purpose of parliamentary representation Part of St. Anselme annexed to the county of Bellechasse.

S. 1, of c. 2,
C S. C. and
Ss. 42, 44, of
s. 1, of ch. 75,
C. S. L. C.,
amended.

2. Section 1 of chap. 2 of the consolidated statutes of Canada, and sub-sections 42 and 44 of section 1 of chap. 75 of the consolidated statutes for Lower Canada, shall be read and interpreted, in so far as they apply to this province, in conformity with the preceding section of this act.

Municipal purposes.

3. The part of the parish of St. Anselme, in the said county of Dorchester, annexed by the present act to the county of Bellechasse, shall form part of the municipality of the parish of St. Gervais, in the same manner and to the same effect as if such annexation had been made in virtue of the municipal code.

Pending cases

4. Nothing contained in the present act shall in any way affect pending cases.

Act in force.

5. The present act shall come into force on the day of its sanction.

CAP. XL

An Act to annex certain parts of the territory of St. Maurice to the county of Champlain, for the purposes of representation in the legislative assembly, and for municipal and registration purposes.

[*Assented to 24th December,* 1875.]

HER MAJESTY, by and with the advice and consent of the Legislature of Quebec, enacts as follows :

Parts annexed to the county of Champlain.

1. All parts of the townships of Lejeune, Mekinac, Boucher and Polette, not comprised in the county of Champlain, and all the territory annexed to the district of Three-Rivers by the act of the legislature of this province, passed in the thirty-seventh year of the reign of Her Majesty Queen Victoria, chap. 18, are by the present act annexed to the county of Champlain, for the purposes of representation in the legislature of this province, and for municipal and registration purposes.

Act in force.

2. This act shall come into force on the day of its sanction.

CAP. XLI.

An Act to annex certain portions of the township of
Shawinigan, in the county of St. Maurice, to the
parish of Ste. Flore, in the county of Champlain,
for school, municipal and registration purposes, and
for the purposes of parliamentary representation.

[Assented to 24th December, 1875.]

WHEREAS by proclamation of His Excellency, the **Preamble.**
lieutenant-governor of the province of Quebec,
bearing date the twentieth day of April, 1875, the portions hereinafter mentioned of the township of Shawinigan, in the county of St. Maurice, have been detached
from the said township, and civilly annexed to the parish
of Ste. Flore, in the county of Champlain ; Therefore,
Her Majesty, by and with the advice and consent of the
Legislature of Quebec, enacts as follows :

1. All the lots of the first range of the township of **Parts annex-**
Shawinigan, to lot thirty-nine inclusive, all range A, and **ed to the**
the piece of land known as the land of the late Ed. **county of**
Greaves, situate between the rivers Shawinigan and St. **Champlain.**
Maurice, shall be, from and after the passing of this act,
detached from the county of St. Maurice and annexed to
the county of Champlain, for all school, municipal and **Municipal**
registration purposes, and for the purposes of parliamen- **purposes.**
tary representation, and shall form part of the municipality of the parish of Ste. Flore, to the end that the **Boundaries of**
said municipality of the parish of Ste. Flore shall be **the munici-**
bounded to the south-west by the parish of St. Mathieu de **pality of Ste.**
Caxton, which coincides with the south-west lateral line of **Flore.**
Cap de la Magdaleine, to lot thirty-nine of the first range
of the township of Shawinigan inclusively, from thence
by the line which separates the thirty-ninth lot from the
fortieth lot of the said first range, by the line which
separates the said first range from the second range of
the township of Shawinigan, to the river Shawinigan,
and thence by the rivers Shawinigan and St. Maurice.

2. This act shall come into force on the day of its **Act in force.**
sanction.

CAP. XLII.

An act to detach a certain portion of the county of
Lotbinière and to annex it to the county of Beauce,
for school, municipal and registration purposes, and
for those of parliamentary representation, and to
civilly erect the parish of St. Sévérin.

[Assented to 24th December, 1875.]

Preamble.

WHEREAS by a decree, dated the twentieth day of
September, 1872, the Right Reverend Elzear
Alexander Taschereau, Archbishop of Quebec, was
pleased to annex and erect, for religious purposes, the
parish of St. Sévérin, in the county and district of Beauce,
including therein a portion of the seigniory of Beaurivage,
in the county of Lotbinière ; Therefore Her Majesty, by
and with the advice and consent of the Legislature of
Quebec, enacts as follows :

St. Severin
recognized as
a civil parish.

1. From and after the coming into force of this act, the
parish of St. Sévérin, thus erected by religious authority,
shall be recognized as erected for all civil purposes whatever, and that in as full and complete a manner as if it
had been erected under chapter 18 of the consolidated
statutes for Lower Canada.

Limits.

2. The boundaries of the parish of St. Sévérin are the
following, that is to say : towards the south-east, partly
by the line separating the said seigniory of Linière from
that of Fleury, from St. Jacques range to the township
of Broughton, partly by the line separating the land of
sieur Joseph Lacroix from that of *sieur* Bénoni Paré,
in the first range of the said township, the land of George
Henry Pozer, esquire, from that of *sieur* Rager Vachon, in
the second range of the said township, the land of *Sieur*
John Cryan from that of *Sieur* Ferdinand Laplante, in the
third range also of the said township, the lot number five
from lot number six, in the fourth range of the said township ; towards the south-west, partly by the line which
separates the said fourth range of the township of
Broughton, from the fifth range of the said township, and
partly by the line which separates the Ste. Catherine
range from the St. Thomas and Ste. Marguerite ranges, in
the said seigniory of Beaurivage, from the said township
of Broughton, to the line separating the land of
sieur Patrick McShea from that of *sieur* Thomas
Stephenson, in the said Ste. Marguerite range ; towards
the north-west, partly by the line which separates the lands
of the said *sieurs* Patrick McShea and Thomas Stephenson,
partly by the line which separates the range known as

Fermanagh's Hope from the range known as Egypt or
Killarney, in the said seigniory of Beaurivage, partly by
the line which separates the land of *sieur* Augustin Couture from that of *sieur* Michel Marcoux in the St. André
range, in the said seigniory of Linière, partly by the line
which separates the land of *sieur* Louis Lefebvre from
that of *sieur* Auguste Couture, in the Ste. Anne range in
the said seigniory, partly by the line which separates the
land of *sieur* Jean-Baptiste Labbé from that of *sieur*
William Boyce, in the St. Olivier range, also in the said
seigniory ; towards the north-east by the line which
separates the said St. Olivier range from the said St.
Jacques range also in the said seigniory.

3. That portion of the parish of St. Séverin, situate in Portion an-
nexed to the
county of
Beauce.
the county of Lotbinière, shall be detached from the
county of Lotbinière, district of Quebec, and shall be annexed to the county of Beauce, and district of Beauce, for
electoral, municipal, judicial, registration and other purposes.

4. The parish of St. Séverin aforesaid shall form a Municipal
purposes.
separate and distinct parish municipality, in the same
manner and with the same effect as if it had been erected
into a parish municipality, under the operation of the
municipal code.

5. The present act shall in no manner affect pending Pending
cases.
cases or proceedings.

6. This act shall come into ιοιce on the day of its sanc- Act in force.
tion.

CAP. XLIII.

An Act to detach a certain part of the county of Bellechasse, and to annex the same to the county of
Montmagny, for parliamentary, registration, municipal and school purposes.

[*Assented to 24th December*, 1875.]

HER MAJESTY, by and with the advice and consent
of the Legislature of Quebec, enacts as follows :

1. All that north-east part of the township of Armagh, Portion an-
nexed to the
county of
Montmagny.
which extends from lot number one to lot number thirty,
inclusively, in the first range, to the north-west of the
river *du Sud*, and in the second and first ranges, to
the south-east of the said river *du Sud*, and all that part of
the township of Mailloux, which is to the north-east of

the north-east range of the Mailloux road, comprising lots from number forty to forty-six, inclusive, of the first, second and third ranges, and lots from number thirty-four to forty-six, inclusive, in the fourth, fifth, sixth and seventh ranges, in the said township of Mailloux, are detached from the county of Bellechasse, and annexed to the county of Montmagny, for all parliamentary, registration, municipal and school purposes.

Municipal purposes.

2 The part so annexed to the county of Montmagny, shall, from and after the coming into force of this act, form part of the municipality of the township of Montminy, in the same manner and with the same effect, as if such annexation had taken place under the municipal code.

Act in force.]

3. This act shall come into force on the day of the sanction thereof, except in so far as regards parliamentary purposes, and for the said purposes this act will only come into force at the end of one year after the sanction thereof.

CAP. XLIV.

An Act to divide the municipality of Newport, in the County of Gaspé, into two separate municipalities.

[*Assented to 24th December, 1875.*]

Preamble.

Considering that the council of the municipality of Newport, in the county and district of Gaspé, has prayed that an act be passed to divide such municipality into two separate municipalities, and that it is expedient to grant the prayer of the petition ; Her Majesty, by and with the advice and consent of the Legislature of Quebec, enacts as follows :

Division of the municipality of Newport into two.

1. The municipality of Newport, for the future, shall cease to form one municipality, and shall be divided into two separate municipalities, which shall be known and described as follows : " municipality of Newport, " and " municipality of Pabos."

Limits.

2. The municipality of Newport shall in future comprise the whole division of the township of Newport.

The municipality of Pabos shall comprise the seigniory of Pabos, as actually bounded.

Municipal code shall apply.

3. All the provisions of the municipal code shall apply to such municipalities, as also to the corporation and council of each of them, as if they had been separated in virtue of such code, save in so far as the same are incompatible with the present act.

4. A general election of municipal councillors shall be Municipal held in each of these municipalities, on the second Monday elections. of the month of February which follows the coming into force of this act, at which election seven councillors shall be elected in the manner prescribed by the municipal code.

The general elections, afterwards, in these municipalities, shall be held as in other local municipalities.

5. The by-laws, orders, rolls or municipal acts which Old munici-governed the municipality of Newport, before the coming pal acts into force of this act, shall continue to be in force in each of such two municipalities, until they are repealed or amended by the council of the municipality.

6. The present act shall come into force on the first Act in force day of January, eighteen hundred and seventy-six.

CAP. XLV.

An Act to erect the village of Bagotville into a separate municipality.

[Assented to 24th December, 1875.]

WHEREAS the inhabitants of the village of Bagot- Preamble. ville, in the county of Chicoutimi, have by their petition represented that the present population of the said village is four hundred souls, that such part of the township of Bagot has already, by order of the government, been laid out in park and village lots, with a view to subsequently becoming a separate and distinct municipality, and in view of the rapid extension of the said village, which further includes lots numbers 1, 2, 3, 4 of the fourth range north-east of the river *à Marse*, as also lots numbers 15, 16, 17 and 18 of the *Anse à Philippe* range, in the township of Bagot, to assimilate the said municipality to that already established for school purposes; and whereas it is requisite to establish certain by-laws to promote the interests of the said village and to favor its development, and whereas the inhabitants thereof have by their petition prayed that the said village be erected and constituted into a village municipality; and whereas it is expedient to grant the prayer of their said petition; Therefore, Her Majesty, by and with the advice and consent of the Legislature of Quebec, enacts as follows:

1. From and after the first day of February, 1876, the Municipality village of Bagotville, including therein lots numbers 1, of the village of Bagotville.

2, 3 and 4 of the fourth range north-east of the river *à Marse* and lots numbers 15, 16, 17 and 18 of the *Anse à Philippe* range, in the said township of Bagot, county of Chicoutimi, shall form a village municipality separate and distinct from the municipality of Bagotville, the north-west portion of the township of Bagot, in which the said village is situate, under the name of "municipality of the village of Bagotville," and the inhabitants and rate-payers are hereby constituted into a corporation, under the name of " The corporation of the village of Bagotville."

Names of the municipality and corporation.

2. The municipality of the village of Bagotville shall be composed of all that portion of the township of Bagot, divided into park and village lots and designated and known under the name of the " village of Bagotville," and further of the lots numbers 1, 2, 3 and 4 of the fourth range north-east of the river *à Ma·se*, and the lots numbers 15, 16, 17 and 18 of the *Anse à Philippe* range.

Extent thereof.

3. The first general meeting of the election of councillors for the said municipality, shall be held at ten of the clock in the forenoon of the first Monday in March, eighteen hundred and seventy-six, and shall have the same effect as if it were held at the period mentioned in article 298 of the municipal code ; but such election shall not have the effect of preventing the general election following taking place, as required by article 292 of the said code, and at the period therein specified.

Election of the councillors.

4. The municipal council of the said village may impose upon merchants and traders strangers to the said municipality and who trade there, such duties and taxes as the said council may deem expedient, and compel them to pay for their license the sum so imposed.

Power to impose duties.

5. All the provisions of the municipal code of the province of Quebec, and the acts which amend the same applicable to village municipalities, shall apply to the municipality of the village of Bagotville.

Municipal code shall apply.

6. The movable property, assets and liabilities of the municipality of Bagotville, north-west portion of the township of Bagot, shall be divided between the said municipality and that of the village of Bagotville, in conformity with the said municipal code and the acts which amend the same ; and the two municipalities shall equally benefit by the wharf within the limits of the said village.

Division of the debts.

Wharf.

7 The municipal council of the village of Bagotville shall have the right to abate, remove and prevent all encroachments made or which shall hereafter be made

Encroachments.

in and upon the lands that have been set apart for the
opening of front and cross roads in the said village ; and
any suit for such purpose shall be instituted, conducted
and decided in virtue of the said municipal code and the
acts which amend the same.

8. The bridge over the river *à Marse*, within the limits Bridge of the
of the said village shall continue to be one-half, at the river *à Marse*.
charge of the municipality of the said village of Bagotville, and of the municipality of Bagotville, and the other
half at the charge of the municipality of *Grande Baie*.

9. This act shall come into force on the day of the Act in force.
sanction thereof.

CAP. XLVI.

An Act to amend the incorporation act of the town
of Longueuil, 37 Victoria, chapter 49.

[*Assented to 24th December,* 1875.]

HER MAJESTY, by and with the advice and consent
of the Legislature of Quebec, enacts as follows :

1. The second section of the act of this province, 37 Vic- 37 V.,c. 49, s.
toria, chapter 49, is amended by striking out all the words 2 amended.
comprised between the word " by " in the second line of Limits.
the said section, and the word " and " in the ninth line
of the same section, exclusively, and substituting therefor
the following words : " the centre of the river St. Lawrence, to the north-east, partly by the land heretofore
belonging to Adolphe Trudeau, by the lands of John
Donnelley and Pierre E. Hurteau, Esq., and by part of
the land of Joseph Dubuc, to the south-east, partly by
the Gentilly road, and partly by the *trait-quarré* line of
the first concession of lands in the seigniory of Longueuil,
and to the south-west by the stream running along the
south-west side of the line of the old track of the Grand
Trunk Railway Company of Canada, heretofore forming
the north-east division line separating the land heretofore
belonging to Joseph Goguet, Esquire, from the former
village of Longueuil. "

2. The fourth section of the said act is amended by Id. s. 4
striking out the words " sign his name " in the second line amended.
of the first paragraph of the said section, and substituting
therefor the words " read and write," and in like manner
by striking out the words " write his name " at the end
of the second and beginning of the third line in the
second sub-section of the same section, and by substituting therefor the words " read and write."

Id. s. 9 amended.

3. The ninth section of the said act is amended by striking out, in the second sub-section of the said section, all the words from the word "votation" in the fourth line thereof, to the end of the said sub-section, and adding after the said word "votation" in the said fourth line of the second sub-section of the said section, the words "all his municipal taxes or assessments, or other municipal rates then due."

Id. s. 26 amended.

Oath of voters.

4. The twenty sixth section of the said act is amended by striking out the form of oath there given, and substituting the following therefor :

"You swear that you are a subject of Her Majesty, "that you are entitled to take part and vote at this elec- "tion, that you have, before the thirty days immediately "preceding this day, paid all your municipal taxes and "assessments or other municipal rates then due and "payable ; (if the oath is taken by a tenant) that you "have resided and paid rent in the town of Longueuil for "at least six months before this day, " (if there is a list of "the municipal voters) " that it is your name that is en- "tered in the list of the municipal voters of the ward "(east, centre *or* west *as the case may be*) of this town, "that you have not received anything, nor has anything "been promised to you either directly or indirectly, to "vote at this election, and that you have not already voted "at this election (for the mayor of the said town, *or* for a "councillor for any ward thereof *as the case may be*.) So "help you God."

Id. s. 30 amended.

5. The thirtieth section of the said act is amended by striking out all the words in the said section after the word "act" in the fourth line of such section, and by substituting therefor the following words : "draw up under his signature, a certificate showing the total number of votes enregistered in the poll-book kept by him or by his poll clerk, and given to each of the candidates for mayor of the said town, or for councillor or councillors of a ward thereof, for which he shall act ; which certificate shall be annexed to the said pol -book and form part thereof."

Id. s. 34 amended.

6. The thirty-fourth section of the said act is amended by striking out after the word "prepared" in the sixth line thereof the words " on his poll-book and."

Id. s. 49 amended.

7. The forty-ninth section of the said act is amended by striking out the word "a " after the word "to" in the second line thereof, and substituting therefor the word "any."

8. The fifty-third section of the said act is amended by Id. s. 53 adding after the word "open" in the fourth line of the amended. said section the words "or take into consideration."

9. The following section shall be, in the said act, in- 53a inserted. serted immediately after the fifty-third section thereof :

"53a. The said council may exercise the powers conferred upon it by the two immediately preceding sections of this act, by a resolution of the said council adopted during their sittings authorizing the mayor of the said town, or councillor presiding at the time of the adopting of such resolution, to exact within such delay as may be fixed by such resolution, from any person having incurred any of Payment of the penalties mentioned in the said sections, the payment the fine. of such fine, the amount wherof shall also be fixed by such resolution, and in default of payment of the said fine, within the delay above mentioned, authorizing the said above-mentioned persons to sign and issue against such person having incurred the said fine, a warrant of im- Imprison- prisonment for the period fixed in the said resolution, ment. which warrant shall be addressed to any policeman or constable, or to any peace officer of the said town and to the gaoler of the common gaol of the district of Montreal, or authorizing by the said resolution, the said mayor or presiding councillor to give effect, in the manner above prescribed, to both penalties at once, against the person having incurred the same. "

10. The following section shall be inserted immediate- S. 102a in- ly after the hundred and second section of the said act : serted.

" 102a. For annual, general, or partial elections for mayor and councillors of the said town, the secretary-treasurer shall, within the fifteen days immediately following the last day allowed to municipal voters, whose names are inscribed on the list of such voters for each ward of the said town, to qualify themselves as such, as regards payment of their municipal taxes or assessments or Revised copy other municipal rates, be obliged to make a copy of the of the list of said list for each ward of the said town, and he shall strike voters. out from the said copy the name of any voter, appearing on such list as proprietor of any land, whose municipal taxes or assessments, or other municipal rates due and payable on the said day, appear on the collection roll of the said town as not having been paid on or before the said day ; and such copies of the list thus corrected shall be sent to the various persons presiding Transmission over the election, in each ward of the said town entitled thereof. thereto, on the day of, and immediately before the voting ;

2. The secretary-treasurer shall certify under oath to Corrections be taken before the mayor, or any councillor of the said certified. town, or any justice of the peace for the district of Mont-

real, the accuracy of the corrections made by him as aforesaid on the copies of the said lists, and such copies shall alone be used for the municipal elections above mentioned ; provided, however, that if such copies of lists be not completed or prepared at the time of any municipal election aforesaid, no such election shall be thereby prevented, but in that case, the qualification of voters shall be established by the oath of the voter, and by the original list of municipal voters, for each ward of the said town, if such original list exists, or in default thereof, by the valuation roll of the said town then in force."

If revised copies do ᵣₒₜ ₐₓᵢₛₜ

12. The following section shall be inserted immediately after the hundred and fifty-sixth section of the said act :
" 156a. When the proprietor of any land or part of a land which the said town council wishes to acquire, either to open or enlarge any street within the limits of the said town, or for any other useful public purpose whatever, shall refuse to sell by agreement, or when such proprietor is absent from the province, or when such land or piece of land belongs to minors, issue unborn, idiots, insane or interdicted persons, women under authority of their husbands, or to any corporation, the said town council shall have the power to obtain such land or piece of land by means of expropriation ;

S. 156a inserted.

Expropriation.

2. The said town council, upon such refusal, in case of refusal, or in the other cases above specified, on a resolution passed at any regular meeting of the said council, deciding that such land or piece of land shall be expropriated, shall notify, through its secretary-treasurer or any of its officers authorized for that purpose, before taking and entering into possession of any such land or piece of land, such proprietor, or the tutor or curator of such minor, unborn, idiot, insane or interdicted person, or the husband of the wife proprietor, or in the case of a corporation the president, secretary or other officer of such corporation, by notice served to any such person and placed postpaid, in the post office of the said town, or if the proprietor of such land or piece of land is absent from the province, by an advertisement to be once inserted one month previously in the English language in a newspaper published in that language in the district of Montreal, and in the French language, in a newspaper published in that language in the said district, that the said council shall, on such day which shall be fixed in the said letter of notification or advertisement, demand, from any judge of the superior court for Lower Canada, sitting in chambers in the district of Montreal, or from the said superior court, the nomination of three arbitrators, to make such expropriation. The appointment of one of such arbitrators may be made by the town council, the nomination of the second by the other party interested, and the judge of the said

Proceedings.

Notices.

Arbitrators.

superior court, or the said court shall nominate, without any suggestion from any of the parties interested, the third of such arbitrators; and in the case in which the town council or the other party interested, does not suggest the name of any qualified person to be an arbitrator, at the time the demand for the appointment of arbitrators shall be made as aforesaid, then the judge or the court may of its own motion nominate two or all the arbitrators ;

3. The persons appointed to act as arbitrators in any Their qualification matter of expropriation, must be proprietors in possession of real estate in the town of Longueuil, (which real estate shall not be situate in the ward of the said town in which the improvement necessitating the expropriation is to be made,) entered in the last valuation roll in force in the said town, at a real value of at least one thousand dollars ;

4. The said arbitrators shall, within eight days after Oath. having received special notice of their appointment as such, present themselves before the prothonotary of the said court, and subscribe before him an oath to well and truly perform the duties imposed upon them, as such arbitrators ; and if the said arbitrators or any of them, shall make default to so present himself within the above-men- Refusal. tioned delay, before the prothonotary of the said court, or if having presented themselves, they refuse to take the oath above-mentioned, they shall then be liable to a penalty not exceeding one hundred dollars, recoverable Penalty. by suit in the usual manner ;

5. Within the fifteen days immediately after the day in Visit of the which the three arbitrators shall have been sworn, as lands. above-mentioned, the said arbitrators shall personally and together, visit the land or lands or portions of lands to be expropriated, and shall within the delay of twenty two days, from the day upon which they were sworn, make and transmit to the said judge or court, their report in writing, Report. or their reports in writing if they do not agree, upon the amount at which they estimate the value of the land or lands or pieces of land to be thus expropriated, which report or the report of the majority of such arbitrators, if it is not contested within fifteen days immediately after the day of the giving of the notice hereinafter mentioned, of the deposit of the said report in the hands of the said judge Homologa- or in the said court, shall be held and considered to be tion. and shall be virtually, homologated ;

6. Any proprietor, whose land or lands or pieces of land Opposition. shall be expropriated, who shall consider himself aggrieved by the report of the said arbitrators or of the majority thereof, may within the fifteen days above mentioned, file before the said court an opposition to the said report, which should afterwards be served upon the said council, who shall appear and answer thereto within the ten days immediately after such service ; and such oppo-

Proceedings. sition shall be subject to the same rules of procedure as ordinary actions for the same amount, and in such opposition the report of the arbitrators, or of the majority thereof, may be confirmed or amended by the said superior court;

Notice of the report of the rbitrators. 7. Public notice shall be given by two advertisements drawn up in the English language, and inserted in a newspaper published in that language, in the district of Montreal, and by two advertisements drawn up in the French language, and inserted in a newspaper published in that

Deposit of the sum adjudicated. language in the aforesaid district, of the deposit of the report of the said arbitrators, or of the majority thereof, as also of the deposit made by the council of the town of Longueuil, of the sum at which the said arbitrators, or the majority thereof, shall have valued the said land or lands or portions of land to be expropriated; and any creditors of any proprietor, whose land or portion of whose land shall have been thus expropriated, shall have a right to file within the said delay of fifteen days in the office of

Opposition afin de conserver. the prothonotary of the said court, an opposition for the payment of his claim, and may be contested or homologated in the same manner as ordinary oppositions *afin de conserver ;*

Taking possession. 8. Upon the deposit being made in the aforesaid place, by the town council, of the amount fixed by the report of the said arbitrators or of the majority thereof, as being the value of any land thus expropriated, the said town council shall have the right to enter upon and take possession of such land or portion thereof, as the proprietor thereof ;

Costs of expropriation. 9. In the case in which the arbitrators or the majority thereof shall by their report, declare, that the price at which a proprietor shall have offered to sell by agreement to the town council, the land or lands or portion thereof, forming the subject of expropriation for which they act, is not above the value of such land, the town of Longueuil shall then be obliged to pay the cost of such expropriation, including such fees as the court or judge shall allow the said arbitrators for their services ; in all other cases the court or judge shall decide as to who shall pay such costs, which may be recovered by an execution in the same manner as in ordinary actions ;

Indemnity, how paid. 10. The amount fixed to be paid for any land expropriated shall be paid out of the general funds of the town, if such expropriation is for public improvements in which the said town generally is interested ; but if such expropriation takes place for local improvements, by which only a portion of the said town benefits, the price of such expropriation shall be borne by the proprietors of the lands situate in the vicinity of the place in which such improvement takes place and within such radius as the council shall determine ; and such amount, in the first case, shall be included in the annual general or special tax levied by the said council, and in the latter case, it shall be divided among the parties interested, according to the actual value of their respective real estate;

11. No street shall be widened and no new street shall Demand be opened by means of expropriation, unless such improve- required. ment shall have been demanded by a majority of the proprietors interested."

. **13.** The hundred and fifty-eighth section of the said S. 158, act is amended by adding after the words " may be " in of 37 V, the second line thereof, the words " unless it is otherwise chap. 49, provided by some special provision of this act." amended.

14. The hundred and sixty-first section of the said act S. 161 is repealed and is replaced by the following: replaced.

"161. The said town council shall have full power and au- Winter road thority to cause to be opened and maintained during win- on the river. ter, a road on the river St. Lawrence, to communicate with the city of Montreal. The expenses of opening and maintaining such road shall be borne by the corporations of the city of Montreal, of the county of Chambly, and of the Costs of main. town of Longueuil, in the following proportions, half tenance, by of such expenses shall be paid by the city of Montreal, whom paid. three-eighths of the said expenses shall be paid by the county of Chambly, and one eighth of the said expenses shall be paid by the town of Longueuil."

15. The hundred and sixty-third section of the said S. 163 amend- act is amended, by striking out all the words in the said ed. section immediately after the words " above mentioned " in the eighth line thereof.

16. All the foregoing provisions of the present act Citation and form part of the act of the legislature of this province, application of 37 Victoria, chapter 49, incorporating the village of Lon- the acts of gueuil as a town, shall take in the body of the said act, chap. incorpora- 49, the places assigned them by this act, may be cited tion. under the numbers given them, and shall apply to the same subjects as the provisions for which they are substituted, or to which they are added, or which they amend, and shall in general have the same force or application as the said act, 37 Victoria, chapter 49.

17. The present act shall come into force on the day Act in force. of its sanction.

CAP. XLVII.

An act to amend the act twenty-seventh Victoria, chapter twenty-three. entitled : "An act to incorporate the town of Joliette."

[*Assented to 24th December, 1875.*]

Preamble.   WHEREAS the "mayor and corporation of the town of Joliette " have by their petition represented that the act twenty-seventh Victoria, chapter twenty-three, intituled : "An act to incorporate the town of Joliette," should be amended ; and whereas it is expedient to grant the prayer of the said petition ; Therefore Her Majesty, by and with the advice and consent of the Legislature of Quebec, enacts as follows :

27 V.,c. 23, s. 1, amended.   **1.** The first section of the said act is amended by striking out the words "mayor and" at the end of the fourth and beginning of the fifth line.

S. 3 amended.   **2.** The third section of the said act is amended by striking out in the first line the words " from time to time," and substituting therefor the words " in the month of January in each year," and by adding further to the said section, the following sub-sections :

Election of councillors.   " Of the seven councillors to be elected in the month of January next, two shall be replaced in the month of January, 1877, two shall be replaced in the month of January, 1878, the three others shall also be replaced in the month of January, 1879, and so on in January in every subsequent year, so that two councillors shall be elected two years in succession, and three councillors every third year.

Selection by lot.   " The councillors to be replaced in the months of January, in the years 1877 and 1878, shall be chosen by lot, in the council during the sitting thereof, in the month of December preceding the month fixed for the said election ; in default of so doing, the lots shall be drawn by the officer presiding at the election, in presence of the municipal electors at the opening of the election."

S. 4 amended.   **3.** The fourth section of the said act is amended by adding after the word " members, " in the third line, the words " of the parliament of Canada and members."

S. 5 replaced.   **4.** The fifth section of the said act is repealed and the following substituted therefor :

Right to vote.   " The persons who shall have the right of voting at any municipal election and at all meetings of electors of the said town of Joliette, shall be those whose names have been regularly inscribed upon the list of parliamentary electors in force at the time of the said election or meeting, and who List. have all the qualities required by the Quebec election act, to vote at an election of a member of the legislative assembly of this province ; and the said list of parliamentary electors made for the said town of Joliette, shall be at the same time the list of municipal electors of the said town, to all lawful intents, provided always that no person qualified to vote at a municipal election in the said town shall have the right to have his vote recorded if he has not paid his municipal and school taxes due before such election, and this under a penalty of twenty dollars, and it shall be lawful for any candidate at such election to demand the production of the receipts establishing the payment of such taxes due as aforesaid."

5. Section seven of the said act is amended by striking s. 7 amended. out in the second line, the words "in the month of January every second," and substituting therefor the following " in the manner hereinabove established, on the second Wednesday in January in each."

6. Section eight of the said act is amended,   S. 8 amended; **1.** By striking out in the ninth line the words "seven councillors," 'and substituting therefor the words "the number of councillors who are to be elected;" **2.** By striking out in the tenth line the word " seven ;" **3.** By striking out the fourth subsection thereof and substituting the following : " Every councillor shall remain in office until replaced."

7. Section ten of the said act is amended by adding s. 10 amend-the following thereto: " provided also that it shall be ed. lawful for the said council to accept the resignation of any councillor, when the reasons given in support thereof are found to be sufficient."

8. Section twenty-one of the said act is amended by s. 21 amend-striking out the last seven words and substituting therefor ed. the following : "every year."

9. The twenty-third section of the said act is amended S. 23 amend-by striking out in the third line the word : "six," and ed. substituting therefor, the word "four."

10. Section twenty-four of the said act is amended :   S. 24 amend-**1.** By striking out in the sixteenth line the words "exces- ed. sive valuation," and substituting therefor : "unjust valuation and one not proportionate to the valuation of other properties ;" **2.** By adding in the twenty-first line thereof after the words "presiding councillor," the following : "and also the assessors whenever the said council shall deem it necessary to call upon them ;"

3. By striking out in the twenty-first line the words "or alter" and substituting therefor the words "increase or diminish ;"

4. By striking out in the twenty-fourth line the words "two years," and substituting the following therefor : "one year, and the roll shall remain in force until such time as another has been made."

S. 28 replaced   **11.** Section twenty-eight is repealed and the following substituted therefor :

Mayor and councillors are justices of the peace.   "The mayor and councillors of the town shall, during their continuance in office, be justices of the peace for the said town, provided always that they shall not be bound to take any other than the official oath of office, to act as such, any law to the contrary notwithstanding."

S. 30 amended.   **12.** Section 30 of the said act is amended by striking out in the eleventh and twelfth lines, the words : " the Lower Canada consolidated municipal act and its amendments," and by substituting therefor the following : " the municipal code of the province of Quebec and its amendments."

Ss. 26 a, b, c, d, e, added to s. 33.   **13.** Section 38 of the said act is amended by adding thereto, immediately after sub-section twenty-six, the following provisions :

Water-works.   "26a. To make by-laws for the protection and management of all water-works, public wells or reservoirs which may have been established, built under the provisions of the preceding sub-section, to prevent the public water from being dirtied or wasted, or in contravention of such by-laws, to restrain the use thereof, according as circumstances may require, in the opinion of the said council ; to prohibit all persons from giving water to, or allowing the taking it by, whom the said corporation had taken away the same as hereinafter provided, and to impose a penalty upon any infraction of any of the said by-laws."

Special tax.   "26b It shall be lawful for the said council, with a view of meeting the interest upon moneys expended for the establishment or construction of such water-works, public wells or reservoir, and to create a sinking fund, to impose upon all proprietors or occupants of any immoveable property in the said town, whether such proprietor or occupant makes use of the said water or does not do so, an annual special tax not exceeding one-quarter of a cent on the dollar of the value, according to the valuation roll then in force, of such immoveable property, house, store or

Collection.   other similar building, and the land upon which it is built, which taxes shall be levied and collected under the same obligations and rules, and in the manner provided for the collection of the general taxes of the said town ,

but such annual special taxes shall not be payable until
the said council shall have given notice to such proprietor Notice.
or occupant of such immoveable property, or to the proprietors of such stocks of goods, that it is ready at its own
cost to bring the said water in or near such real property,
store, house or other building ; it shall be lawful for the
said council irrespective of, and in addition to, such annual
special tax to provide for the payment by all persons Compensa-
making use of such water, of a compensation based upon tion.
such tariff or scale as shall be fixed by the said council ;
provided always that the said town council shall have the
power to compel the payment of such compensation by
all proprietors, tenants or occupants, whether such water Right of the
is used by them or not and this so soon as the said council council.
shall have notified such proprietor, tenant or occupant
that it is ready to bring at its own cost the said water to
the house occupied by such proprietor, tenant or occupant
and the proprietor of any habitation, house or store, with
one or more tenants, sub-tenants or occupants, shall be
liable for the payment of such compensation, if he refuses
or neglects to give to each such tenant, sub-tenant or occupant a separate and distinct distributing pipe, and it shall
further be lawful for the said council to enter into special
arrangements with the parties interested, to furnish such
water to any person whomsoever outside the limits of the
said town, provided that they conform to the by-
laws of the said town concerning the management of
such water-works, public wells or reservoir, and also to
supply the said water for the use of steam-engines, brew-
eries, distilleries, tanneries, manufactories, mills, livery-
stables, hotels or any other special cases."

" 26c. It shall be lawful for the said council to stop the Power to stop
supply of water, to any person refusing or neglecting to the supply of
pay such annual special tax or the said compensation for water.
the use of the said water, and of all persons wasting such
water, or using the same contrary to the by-laws of the said
town, or refusing to admit, as hereinafter provided, into
his house or upon his property, the officers appointed by
the said council for the administration and supervision
of the said water-works, public wells or reservoir, and
such person shall nevertheless continue to be responsible
for the said arrears of taxes and obliged to pay the same,
and shall be also obliged to pay all such annual special
tax as aforesaid, which shall become due in the future, as
if such person made use of the water ; and the said council shall not be responsible for the quantity of water to Quantity of
be supplied under the present section, and no person shall, water.
on account of the insufficiency of the supply of the said
water, refuse to pay such annual special tax, or such compensation for the use of the water as aforesaid."

26d. The said council may appoint such officers as they Officers for
may deem necessary, for the management of such water- the management of the
water works

works, public wells or reservoir, and such officers shall
have the right to enter into any house or building whatever, or upon any property in the said town, and outside
of the said town, to ascertain that the public water is not
lost, and whether the by-laws of the said council concerning such water-works, public wells or reservoir, are
faithfully executed, from eight o'clock A. M., until six
o'clock P. M., and it shall be the duty of all proprie-
Admission, tors or occupants of any such house, building or proof the officers perty, to allow the said officers to visit such house, build-
in the houses. ing or property as aforesaid, under the penalty of being
deprived of the use of the water, during all such time that
they do not permit or prevent such visit of such officers,
and in addition under a penalty not exceeding twenty
dollars, or imprisonment not exceeding one calendar
month."

Power of the] "**26e.** And it shall be lawful for the said town council to
council to transfer by by-law to that effect, its rights and powers
transfer its hereinabove enumerated, with reference to the water sup-
rights. ply of the said town, to any person or company desirous
of undertaking the same, provided that such person or
company shall not increase the rates to be levied by
virtue of the provisions of this act, on persons obliged
to receive the water, which rates the said town council
shall establish by the said by-law."

S. 35 amend-   **14.** Section thirty-five of the said act is amended:
ed.   1. By adding in the fourth line of the second sub-
section after the words: "so in arrears' the following:
"residing in the said town of Joliette; "
   2. By adding after the said second sub-section and as
forming part thereof, the following:
Report of the   "As to persons residing outside the said town, the secre-
sec.-treas. as tary-treasurer shall report to the council in writing the
to certain ar- amount of taxes due by them, with the property affec-
rears. ted by such taxes, and the said council may order any
such persons to be sued in the ordinary manner before the
circuit court of the district of Joliette, for the recovery of
such taxes according to the procedure usually followed
in the circuit court, but at the end of the eight days which
follow the judgment, execution may issue ;"
Ss. 4, 5, and   3. By striking out at the end of the third subsection, all
6, inserted. the words after the word "manner," in the twelfth line
thereof ;
Power of the   4. And by adding as sub-sections 4, 5 and 6, the following:
bailiff.   "4. The bailiff entrusted with the execution of such
warrant shall be invested with all the powers conferred by
article 965 of the municipal code ;"
Opposition.   "5. Within the three days which follow the seizure made
under a warrant as above mentioned, any party interested
may oppose the sale to be made under the said seizure ;"
Deposit in   "6. All oppositions to annul to be received, shall be ac-
such case and companied by a deposit sufficient to cover the amount

claimed and the costs to be incurred by the council, in case proceedings. such opposition be not maintained; and no opposition to withdraw shall be received unless the opposant first pays, saving his lawful recourse, the amount due, together with the costs up to the date of the said opposition; the allegations of all such oppositions shall be attested on oath taken before a judge, or the clerk of the said circuit court; it shall be served upon the secretary-treasurer of the corporation and other parties interested, if there are any, and shall be returned without delay, before the said circuit court. Within the three days after the signification of any such opposition, the corporation and all other parties interested shall appear and declare, without it being necessary to compel them to do so, by a rule, whether or not they intend to contest the opposition produced; they shall file at the same time their contestation with reasons in support thereof, if any they have, after which one day's notice will suffice to inscribe the opposition so made for proof and hearing; and such oppositions, as well as the actions to be brought before the said court, in virtue of section thirty-five as amended by this act, shall be summarily heard and decided at any time and even between the tenth of july and the first of september, without it being necessary to wait for the regular term of the said court."

16. Section thirty-seven of the said act is repealed and s. 37 of said the following substituted therefor: act, amended.

"**37.** The secretary-treasurer shall, at the end of the three Report of the months next after the making of his collection roll, persons indebted. report in writing the persons still indebted to the corporation, with the amount due by each, the lands upon which such arrears are due, the date of any judgment rendered in the circuit court in suits or oppositions; and the reasons preventing the recovery of the said arrears.

"Upon such report the said council may order the sale of Sale of lands. all or any of the said lands, at a time to be fixed by the said council. The secretary-treasurer shall publish such sale in the official gazette of this province, and in another newspaper published in the said town of Joliette, or in the nearest place thereto, if no newspaper is published in the said town, by a notice specifying the day, hour and place of the sale, and in separate columns the name of each proprietor, the description of each land, and the amount due, and notifying all hypothecary or privileged creditors, to file their oppositions *afin de conserver*, in the event of its being necessary so to do, in his office, within the fifteen days next after such sale; such notice shall be published twice, the last publication shall be at least one month before the day of sale; and shall in addition be published in the said town of Joliette as prescribed by section seven of the said act of incorporation.

"On the day fixed, the sale of the said lands shall be By whom made by the secretary-treasurer to the highest and last made.

bidder for cash, and a title to the property in the said land, signed by the mayor and secretary-treasurer, shall by this latter be furnished to the purchaser (*adjudicataire*) within the fifteen days next after the said sale.

Adjournment of the sale.   " If at the end of the sale there remain some lands unsold through there being no bidders, or because the purchase price shall not have been paid in cash by the *adjudicataire*, the secretary-treasurer shall adjourn the said sale to another day, within eight days, and shall recommence the sale of such lands on the day so fixed by him, and this for the same purposes and with the same authority.

Council may bid upon.   " The town council may bid upon any land, through the mayor or any other councillor specially authorized to that purpose.

Proceeds of the sale.   " The secretary-treasurer shall, out of the proceeds of the sale, retain the amount due for taxes and costs by each proprietor, or other person bound for the payment of the said taxes and costs, on account of the lands thus sold, and such sum shall be entered by him in his books, in discharge of the said taxes and costs, and shall form part of the funds of the said corporation; And in all cases, in which there is a surplus, immediately after the sale the secretary-treasurer is bound to procure from the registrar, a certificate of the hypothecs and privileges affecting the immoveable sold, and which have been registered, up to the day of sale; and he shall make a return of such sale to the superior court, in the district of Joliette, as soon as possible after the expiration of fifteen days from such sale, and he shall transmit to the said court at the same time the said certificate and such oppositions as may have been filed with him, and proceedings shall be had upon such return in the same manner as on the return made by a sheriff of any sale by him made; and the surplus shall remain in the hands of the secretary-treasurer, until a copy of the judgment of distribution shall have been transmitted to him, and he shall then pay over such surplus as ordered by the said judgment.

Surplus.

Effect of the sale.   " The sale so made shall have all the effect of a forced sale and cannot be annulled except in the manner and for the reasons for which a sheriff's sale may be annulled."

Fees.   " A tariff of the fees payable to the secretary-treasurer shall be made by the council."

S. 45 amended.   **16.** Section forty-five of the said act is amended by adding thereto the following subsection:

Right to borrow.   " Notwithstanding the provisions of the preceding subsection, the said town council may, however, contract a loan to the amount of forty thousand dollars, with a view of constructing waterworks, public wells or a reservoir for supplying the said town with water; but such loan can be contracted only after having obtained the approval of the majority proportionately to the value of the real estate

Approval.

of the electors of the said town to be taxed for such purpose, by a by-law authorizing such loan, within the thirty days after the passing thereof by the said council, such approval shall be expressed in a general meeting, presided over by the mayor, or in his absence by the pro-mayor, the secretary-treasurer acting as secretary, and duly called by advertisement signed by the mayor or the secretary-treasurer, published and posted in the manner provided by section seven of the said act; provided always that any six qualified municipal electors present at the said meeting may demand the holding of a poll to estab- Polls. lish such majority, and on such demand the holding of such poll shall be granted by the mayor, or in his absence by the pro-mayor, and shall be held immediately after such demand, the secretary-treasurer acting as poll clerk, under the direction of the mayor or pro-mayor as the case may be; each elector shall present himself in his turn, and shall give his vote by "*yea*" or "*nay*" the word "*yea*" signifying that he approves of the said by-law, and the said word "*nay*" signifying that he disapproves of the said by-law, but the vote of no person shall be received unless he has all the qualities required for a municipal elector, provided always that such poll shall be held during two consecutive days, not being non-juridical days, from the hour of ten in the morning to the hour of four in the afternoon, and at the close of the poll, the mayor or pro-mayor, as the case may be, shall sum up the "*yeas*" and the "*nays*," and at the next following sitting of the said council he shall submit a statement showing the value of the immoveable property of each of the voters according to the roll then in force, and shall certify for the information of the said council, if the majority in value of the real property of the electors of the said town approve or disapprove of Certificate. the said by-law, and such certificate signed by the mayor or pro-mayor, as the case may be, and countersigned by the secretary-treasurer shall, by this latter, be kept with the poll-list and the said statement, among the archives of his office, and if the said by-law is approved as aforesaid, then the said town council may after having by resolution ratified the approval of the said by-law and having published it in the ordinary manner, effect the said loan.

17. This act shall form part of chapter 23 of 27th Vic- Interpre- toria, 1863, intituled : "An act to incorporate the town of tation. Joliette," and shall come into force immediately after it Act in force. shall have been sanctioned.

CAP. XLVIII.

An Act to amend the Act 22 Victoria, chap. 106,
incorporating the Town of St. John.

[*Assented to 24th December*, 1875.]

HER MAJESTY, by and with the advice and consent
of the Legislature of Quebec, enacts as follows:

S. 3 of 22 v.,
c.106, amended.

1. Section 3 of the act 22 Vict., chap 106, is amended
by substituting the word "twelve" for the word "eight"
in the fourth line.

S. 7 replaced.

Municipal
elections.

2. Section 7 of the said act, is wholly repealed and
replaced by the section following :
" The municipal elections of the said town shall take
place in the month of february of each year, and shall
be announced at least eight days before the nomination
of the candidates, by a notice published in a french journal
and an english journal of the said town, and posted up on
the church doors and on public squares in the said town.
The nomination of candidates shall take place eight days
before the voting.

If there are
only two candidates nominated.

If there are
more than
two.

" If at the time of the nomination of candidates for the
election of february, 1877, there are only two candidates nominated for any one ward, the person presiding
over the election shall at the meeting declare such two
candidates elected for such ward, and if at the time of
nomination at subsequent elections, only one candidate
is nominated for such ward, the person presiding shall,
at the meeting, declare such candidate elected for such
ward. When at the nomination, more than the number
of candidates hereinabove prescribed are nominated for
any ward, the person presiding over the election shall
grant a poll, and the voting shall take place eight days
after the nomination, in the manner prescribed by the
said act, 22 Vict., chap. 106."

§ 4 of s. 8,
replaced.

Time of the
office of the
mayor and
councillors.

3. Subsection 4 of section 8 is repealed, and the following substituted therefor :
" The mayor shall be elected for one year, until his
successor replace him, and the councillors elected at any
of the municipal elections shall remain in office for three
years, except those who shall have been elected at the
first election after the passing of this act, of whom four
shall retire from office at the expiration of the second
year ; and it shall be declared by lot in the manner established by the council, which of the councillors shall
retire from office at the end of the said second year."

4. Subsection 5 of section 9 of the same act is amended, § 5, s. 9, by substituting the word " seven " for the word " five." amended.

5. Sub-section 2 of section 10 is repealed, and replaced § 2 s. 10, by the following : replaced.

" In case of the death, absence from the town or absolute Vacancies. incapacity from acting as such, of the mayor or any councillor, a new election shall be held to replace such mayor or councillor unable to act as such, and in case of the resignation of the mayor, the council shall have the right to judge, accept or regulate such resignation, for which reasons must be given ; and such election to replace such mayor or councillor, who has become unable to fulfil his duties as such, shall take place within one month from the date of the inability of such mayor or councillor, except in the case of absence from the town, and in this latter case the election shall be held at the end of three months, instead of one month as aforesaid. And such election shall take place by the majority of the councillors, who shall appoint from among the inhabitants of the town, another person to replace such mayor or councillor, who is absent or has become unable to act as such, and such person may be chosen from among the members of the council, or from among the electors qualified and capable of being elected mayor or councillors, as the case may be."

5. The council shall, at its first general meeting and Pro-mayor. every three months during the year, choose among its members and elect a person to be pro-mayor for three months ; and such pro-mayor, in the absence of the mayor, shall have the same powers and shall exercise His powers. the same municipal functions.

6. The twenty-second section of the same act is amended §§ 3, 4, 5 and by repealing sub-sections 3, 4, 5 and 6, and substituting 6 of s. 22, re-for them the following sub-section : placed.

" The secretary-treasurer shall furnish security not ex- Security of ceeding one thousand dollars, for every five thousand the sec -treas. dollars of the city revenue ; such security may be represented by a guarantee policy of assurance."

7. The twenty-third section of the same act is amended §§ 3, 4, 5 and by adding the words " or more" in the second line, after 6, of s 23, the word " three" and by adding the following words replaced. at the end of the said twenty-third section : " and it shall be the duty of the secretary-treasurer to notify the said Duties of the assessors of their appointment within eight days after sec.-treas. their appointment."

8. The twenty-seventh section of the same act is s. 27, amend-amended by adding the following words: " It shall ed. be the duty of the secretary-treasurer to notify the said Duties of the sec.-treas. auditors of their appointment, within eight days next after their said appointment. And such auditors, within the thirty days next after their appointment, shall take the oath proscribed in the twenty-seventh section of the said

Auditors. act. And on the refusal by the persons named as auditors to act as such, they shall incur a penalty not exceeding twenty dollars for each refusal."

S. 34 amended. **9.** The thirty-fourth section of the same act is amended by wholly repealing the second sub-section and by striking out the following words from sub-section seven, in the eleventh line thereof : " carters and livery stable keepers" and substituting therefor the following words: " and on all horses or vehicles of any kind kept for pleasure, use, work or hire."

Rates on certificates of licenses. **10.** The council shall have the power to establish the rates payable on certificates of licenses for taverns or houses of public entertainment at any sum not exceeding one hundred dollars, and any existing law contrary to the present provision shall not have effect within the limits of the town of St. Johns. This provision shall extend to permits granted to houses known as temperance houses.

Time for petitions, limited. **11.** No petition to obtain a certificate to keep a tavern or house of public entertainment shall be granted by the council, after the general meeting in the month of April.

Publication of the lists of demands. **12** Within the eight days which shall precede the meeting above mentioned, the secretary-treasurer shall publish in the two english and french newspapers of the said town, a list of the persons applying for certificates to keep a tavern or house of public entertainment, at the same time notifying the public to present and support their objections to the granting of such certificates to the applicants. The preceding provisions shall not apply to transfers of licenses.

§ 29 of s. 35, replaced. **18.** The thirty-fifth section of the same act is amended by striking out the whole twenty-ninth sub-section and substituting the following therefor: "The council may tax the proprietors of real estate to the amount of the sum or sums that may at any time be necessary to defray

Drainage, &c. the expense of building or repairing any public drain, in any public street or highway in the town of St. John, immediately in front of such real estate respectively.

Taxes. The cost of the construction or repair of any public drain shall be borne, one-third by the corporation, and the other two-thirds by the rate-payers of the street in which such drain is constructed or repaired. In the case of the diameter of any public drain exceeding two feet, the cost of such excess shall be borne wholly by the corporation."

14. Any law to the contrary notwithstanding, the cor- Right to buy poration of the town of St. John shall be entitled to and borrow, take, buy or sell shares in regularly incorporated indus- limited. trial or railroad companies; to borrow or to contract a debt to the extent of one hundred thousand dollars, for the following purposes : for the construction or repair of public drains, street improvements, the purchase of water works or public bridges, or for any other purposes which the council may deem necessary.

15. No by-law passed in virtue of the preceding Approval. section shall have any force or effect until it shall have been approved by the majority in number and by the value of the assessed real property of the electors being proprietors in the said town, within the thirty days after the passing of such by-law. This approbation shall be expressed in a public meeting presided over by the mayor, or, in his absence, by the senior councillor of the said town, the secretary-treasurer acting as secretary, and duly called by notices signed by the mayor or by the secretary-treasurer, published and posted up in the manner prescribed for the publication and posting up of the public notice required by the provisions of this act, for the publication of by-laws ; provided always, that six qualified municipal electors present at the said meeting, may demand a poll to establish such majority ; and a poll shall Poll. be granted by the mayor, or, in his absence, by the presiding councillor, on being so demanded, and shall be held within four days next after such meeting, the secretary-treasurer acting as poll clerk under the direction of the mayor or of the presiding councillor, as the case may be. Each elector shall then present himself in turn and shall give his vote by " yea " or " nay " ; the word " nay " signifying that he disapproves of the by-law ; but no person's vote shall be received unless the name of such person be inscribed on the municipal voters' list then in force, if such list exists, and if there be no such list, no person shall be entitled to vote unless it appears, by the valuation roll then in force in the said town, that he is duly qualified to vote as municipal elector, and unless he has paid all his municipal taxes, at least three clear days before the day of such voting ; provided always, that such poll shall be held during one day, being a juridical day, from ten o'clock in the morning until four o'clock in the afternoon. At the close of the poll, the mayor, or the presiding councillor, as the case may be, shall count the " yeas " and the " nays, " and within four days thereafter, he shall lay before the town council, a statement showing the value of the real pro-

Certificate.

party of each of the voters, according to the valuation roll then in force, and shall certify, for the information of the town council, whether the majority in number and value of assessed real property of the electors of the town approve or disapprove of the said by-law. This certificate shall be countersigned by the secretary-treasurer of the town, and preserved by him with the poll-list and the aforesaid statement among the archives of his office, and if the said by-law is approved of as aforesaid, the said by-law shall have full force and effect.

Limits.

16. The east side of Longueuil street, from St. James street, and thence to its end towards the south, shall for the future be comprised within the limits of the east ward of the town of St. John.

Power to acquire bridges, &c.

17. The corporation of the town of St. John shall have the power to acquire the bridges built in whole or in part within the said city, or which cross the Richelieu river in front of the said town.

Drains already constructed.

Taxes.
Proviso.

18. The corporation shall be entitled to tax the owners of real estate, situate immediately opposite the drains already constructed in St. James, St. Charles and Champlain streets, in the said town, up to an amount not exceeding two-thirds of the cost of such drains, provided that the diameter thereof does not exceed two feet.

CAP. XLIX.

An Act to amend the Act of this Province, 38 Vict., cap. 79, entitled : " An act to incorporate the City of Hull."

[*Assented to 24th December, 1875.*]

Preamble.

WHEREAS " the mayor and the aldermen of the city of Hull" have by petition represented that the act of this province, 38 Vict., chap. 79, entitled : " An act to incorporate the City of Hull," should be amended, and whereas it is just to grant the demand contained in the said petition ; Therefore, Her Majesty, by and with the advice and consent of the Legislature of Quebec, enacts as follows :

Interpretation of the act 38 V., c. 79.

1. In order to remove all doubt on the interpretation to be given to the said act, it is declared that the said corporation of the city of Hull is separated from the county of Ottawa for municipal purposes, save for the business commenced before the incorporation of the said city of Hull, in which the mayor of the said city of Hull shall have the same position, and the same rights as the mayors of the other municipalities of the county of Ottawa, and as if the said act of incorporation had not been passed.

2. Section 10 of the said act is repealed, and the following is substituted therefor : S. 10 repealed and replaced.

" The persons who shall have the right to vote at the municipal elections of the said city, shall be the freeholders of the full age of twenty-one years, in usual possession of real estate in the said city of the value of two hundred dollars, or of the annual value of twenty dollars, and also tenants of twenty-one years of age whose names are on the valuation roll, at the time of the election, as paying a rent of not less than twenty dollars yearly for the premises occupied by them respectively, which qualification shall be established by the valuation roll, which it shall be the duty of the council to amend and complete every year ; provided always that any person having the right to vote at such municipal election in the said city, shall not vote, unless he shall have paid before the first day of voting, all the municipal and school assessments then due, and any candidate at any such election or the chairman of the same may require the production of the receipts for the payment of such assessments due as aforesaid ; and each and every elector shall vote in the ward in which his property or lease hold is situated, and at the poll held for such ward, and in favour of the candidates duly nominated for such ward. Electors must be of the male sex."

Right to vote

Payment required.

Production of receipts.

Place of votation.

3. Section 11 of the said act is amended by adding at the fifth line after the words, " in the french and english languages" the following words : " in the english language in an english paper, if such english paper exist within the limits of the said city, and in the french language in a french paper, if such paper exist within the limits of the said city." S. 11 amended.

4. Section 14 of the said act is amended by adding at the beginning of the said section the words : " The nomination of candidates for the office of alderman, shall take place in each ward at nine o'clock in the forenoon," and by substituting in the second line for the words, " from nine of the o'clock in the forenoon," the words : "from ten o'clock in the forenoon." S. 14 amended.

5. Section 15 of the said act is repealed, in so far as it relates to the hour of the " nomination of candidates for the office of alderman." S. 15 amended.

S. 16 amended.   **6.** Section 16 is amended by adding at the tenth line after the word, "shall," the following words : "immediately after having received the poll-books."

S. 19 amended.   **7.** Section 19 of said act is amended in striking off in the eighth and following lines to the end of the section, the words : " and the said alderman shall make a proclama-·tion of the person elected, in the same manner, at the same hour, and in the same place, as the registrar for the first election."

S. 65 amended.   **8.** Section 65 of the said act is amended by adding the following words at the end of the said section : "but the said council shall at least once a year proceed to the revision of the said roll in the manner, and after having given notice as provided by law for the making and homologation of the valuation roll in force previous to such revision, and

Revision of the roll.   such revision and homologation shall be made in such manner as to be completed on the first day of august, of each year."

Right of appeal to the circuit court.   **9.** An appeal shall lie to the circuit court from any decision of the council of the said city of Hull, with reference to any valuation roll, *procès-verbal*, expropriation of property, or any other matter or thing with regard to which any party shall deem himself aggrieved ; the decision of the court shall be binding upon all parties. Such appeal shall be prose vuted in the manner provided by sections 1064 to 1079 inclusive of the municipal code relative to appeals from decisions of county councils.

S. 68 amended.   **10.** Section 68 is amended by striking off at the tenth and eleventh lines the words "such meeting," and in substituting therefor the words : "the date of the notice."

§§ 82, 83, 84, and 85, replaced.   **11.** Sections 82, 83, 84 and 85 of the said act are repealed, and the following section substituted therefor :

School taxes.   " Every school tax or assessment, in the city of Hull, shall be payable by the occupant of the land assessed, whether he holds the same as tenant or otherwise, if there be such occupant, and in default of such occupant, by the proprietor.

Commissioners.   The common school commissioners and the trustees of dissentient schools are authorized to impose, levy and collect, on any occupant of land, or any proprietor in the absence of such occupant, any assessment or tax for the support of their respective schools, without taking into consideration the title to the property under which such occupant holds.

Levying of taxes.   Every school tax or assessment shall be imposed and levied on and collected from all occupants of land, in the same proportion and according to the same rules, as it now is from proprietors under the common school law, and the same shall be done by the board of commissioners or the board of trustees, according as such occupant falls within the jurisdiction of one or other of such boards.

No tax or assessment for school purposes shall be imposed, levied or collected, from any proprietor in respect of any real estate, already assessed, taxed or rated in the name of the occupant of such real estate.

In the case of the real estate taxed, assessed or rated belonging to a proprietor, who falls within the jurisdiction of a school board different from that which has jurisdiction over the occupant, such tax or assessment upon such real estate, shall not convey a hypothec upon the real estate so assessed, taxed or rated, but merely upon the rights and improvements of the occupant. And this provision shall take effect even for the current year."

12. This act shall come into force the day of its sanc- Act in force. tion.

CAP. L.

An Act to incorporate the City of Sherbrooke.

[*Assented to* 24*th December,* 1875.]

WHEREAS the provisions of the municipal code do not Preamble. meet the present requirements of the town of Sherbrooke ;

And whereas it has become necessary that more ample provisions should be made for the internal government of the said town ;

And whereas the inhabitants of the said town are desirous that the same should be constituted a city and have a special act of incorporation ; Therefore, Her Majesty, by and with the advice and consent of the Legislature of Quebec, enacts as follows :

1. The inhabitants of the said town of Sherbrooke, as here- Corporation inafter described, and their successors, shall continue to be, continued. and are hereby declared to be, a body politic and corporate, by the name of "The corporation of the city of Sherbrooke," and Name. by that name, they and their successors shall have perpetual succession, and shall have power to sue and be sued, to implead and be impleaded in all courts and in all actions, causes, and suits at law whatsoever ; and shall have a common seal, with power to alter and modify the same at their General pleasure ; and shall, in law, be capable of receiving by powers. donation, of acquiring, holding and parting with any property, real or moveable, for the use of the said city ; of becoming parties to any contracts or agreements in the management of the affairs of the said city, and of giving or accepting any notes, bonds, drafts, obligations, judgments, or other instruments or securities for the payment of, or securing the

Loan.

payment of, any sum of money borrowed or loaned, or for the execution of any other duty, right or thing whatsoever; and for borrowing any sum of money required for any purpose within the jurisdiction of the council of said city, either upon the debentures of the said city, to be issued and executed as hereinafter provided; or by hypothecating the immoveable property of the city for that purpose.

Engagements of the town, continued.

2. All by-laws, ordinances, agreements, dispositions and engagements whatever, passed and entered into by the municipal council of the said town of Sherbrooke, as heretofore existing, shall continue to have full force and effect; as though such by-laws, ordinances, agreements, dispositions and engagements had been passed and agreed to by the council of the said city of Sherbrooke, as hereby constituted, until such time as such by-laws, agreements or engagements shall be formally rescinded, abolished or amended by the council of

Obligations of the town, transferred to the city.

the said city, or fulfilled ; and the said corporation, as continued by this act, shall succeed and be substituted for all purposes whatsoever, in the engagements, rights, debts and obligations of the corporation of the said town of Sherbrooke, as now existing under the municipal code.

By-laws of the town, &c., continued.

3. The by-laws, orders, rolls and municipal acts, which governed the territory heretofore constituting the said town of Sherbrooke, before the passing of this act, shall continue in force until they are amended or repealed by the city council to be hereinafter chosen ; and the mayor and councillors of the said town of Sherbrooke, as now existing, shall remain in office until the elections, which are to take place under this act, have taken place ; and all the municipal officers of the said town of Sherbrooke, as now existing, shall continue in office until their successors are chosen or appointed, under the provisions of this act.

Limits of the city.

4. The boundaries and limits of the said city of Sherbrooke, shall be those of the present town of Sherbrooke as defined by proclamation on the 28th day of June, eighteen hundred and fifty-two, of His Excellency the Governor-General of the late province of Canada ; but the said city of Sherbrooke shall be divided into four wards ; known as the north ward, the south ward, the east ward and the centre ward,

North ward.

bounded as follows : North ward to comprise all that part of the said city lying north of the river Magog and west of the

South ward.

river St. Francis ; South ward to comprise all that part of the said city lying south of King street and west of the river St.

East ward.

Francis ; East ward to comprise all that part of the said city

Centre ward.

lying east of the river St. Francis ; and the Centre ward to comprise all that part of the said city lying north of King street and between King street and the river Magog and St. Francis.

Councillors.

5. There shall be elected, at such time as shall be fixed by this act, seven fit persons, who shall be and be called the

"Councillors of the city of Sherbrooke," and such councillors for the time being shall form the council of the said city and shall be designated as such, and shall represent, for all purposes whatsoever, the corporation of the said city of Sherbrooke ;

2. Of the said councillors, two shall be elected for the North ward, one for the South ward, one for the East ward, and three for the Centre ward, the said seven councillors shall as hereinafter provided, elect one of their number as mayor, and the said mayor shall be designated "The mayor of the city of Sherbrooke." *Number of councillors for each ward. Mayor.*

6. No person shall be capable of being elected mayor of the said city of Sherbrooke, unless he be possessed, as owner of real estate within the said city of the value of one thousand dollars after payment or deduction of his just debts. *Qualification of mayor.*

No person shall be capable of being elected a councillor of the said city, unless he shall have been a resident of the said city for one year immediately preceding such election, nor unless he be possessed as owner, either in his name or in his wife's name, of real estate within the said city, of the value of six hundred dollars, after deduction of his just debts. *Of the councillors.*

2. No person shall be capable of being elected councillor of the said city of Sherbrooke, unless he be a natural born or naturalized subject of Her Majesty, and of the full age of twenty-one years. *Persons who may not be councillors.*

3. No person being in holy orders nor the ministers of any religious belief whatever, nor the members of the executive council, nor judges, district magistrates, sheriffs, or clerks of any court of justice, nor officers on full pay in Her Majesty's army or navy, nor any person accountable for the revenues of the said city, nor any other person receiving any pecuniary allowance from the said city for services, nor any keeper of a tavern, hotel or house of public entertainment nor any person who has acted as such, within the twelve months preceding, nor any officer or person presiding at the election of the councillors, while so employed, nor any person who shall have been convicted of treason or felony in any court of law within any of Her Majesty's dominions, nor any person having directly or indirectly, in person or through his partner, any contract whatever, or interest in any contract with or for the said city, shall be capable of being a councillor for the said city. *Idem.*

4. Provided however that no person shall be held incapable of acting as mayor or councillor for the said city, from the fact of his being a shareholder in any incorporated company which may have a contract or agreement with the said city. *Proviso.*

5. The following persons shall not be obliged to accept the office of councillor of the said city nor any other office to be filled by the council of the said city :—members of the provincial legislature, or of the parliament of the dominion, practicing physicians, surgeons, and apothecaries, schoolmasters actually engaged in teaching, persons over sixty years of age, and the members of the council of the said *Exemption from office.*

city at the time of the coming into force of this act or who have been so the two years next preceding, or members of the said city council, and the person who shall have filled any of the offices under such council, or paid the penalty incurred for refusal to accept such office, shall be exempt from serving in the same office during the two years next after such service or payment.

Right to vote.   **7.** The persons entitled to vote at the municipal elections of the said city shall be of the male sex of the age of twenty-one years, and possessed at the time, either in their own name or that of their wife, of real property in the said city of the value of two hundred dollars ; and also the male tenants of the age of twenty-one years, who shall have resided in the said city and paid rent during the year immediately preceding an election, on a dwelling house or part of a dwelling house, or other real property therein, at the rate of not less than twenty dollars per annum, and the qualfication in all cases referred to in this act, shall be determined by the valuation roll then in force in said city.

Proviso.   **2.** Provided always, that no person qualified to vote at any municipal election in the said city shall have the right If taxes are of having his vote registered unless he shall have paid his not paid. municipal taxes due, before offering to vote at such election ; and it shall be lawful for any candidate at the said election, and for the person presiding over the said election, to require Production of the production of the receipts setting forth the payment of receipts. such taxes, as aforesaid, before registering such vote, and in case the same is not produced, such vote shall not be register-ed, unless such person make oath before the person presiding at such election that he has paid such taxes.

Time of elec-   **8.** The municipal elections for the said city, under this tions. act, shall be held on the second monday in the month of january of each year, at nine o'clock in the morning, and public notice thereof shall be given at least eight days previous to such election, in the french and english lan-Notice. guages, by notices posted up at the doors of the churches, and at other places which may be determined by the council of the said city, by resolution for that purpose, and the said notice shall be signed for the first election under this act, by the then mayor of the town of Sherbrooke, and shall specify the day, place and hour upon which the said election for the said city shall take place ; and for all the following elections the said notice shall be signed by the mayor or secretary-treasurer of the said city, and shall also specify the day, places and hour upon which the said elec-tions are to take place.

Presiding   **9.** Before the publication of the notices announcing such officer at the election, the present council of the town of Sherbrooke, for election. the first election to take place on the second monday of the month of january next, and afterwards the council of the said city, for the following elections, shall appoint a pre-siding officer for each of the wards within which an election

is to be held to preside at and to conduct such election, and
to specify in the said four wards of said city, the place
where the same shall be held in the several wards of the said
city ; such presiding officer shall appoint a poll clerk for his Poll clerk.
ward, where an election is to be held, under his own hand-
writing, and the poll shall be open for the reception and
registration of votes, when a poll is demanded, from ten of
the clock in the forenoon until five of the clock in the afternoon, of the day appointed for such election,/

1. Provided however that the election shall not have taken Voting.
place by acclamation ; and at such election each elector shall
be entitled to vote for the councillor or councillors to be
elected in the ward in which such elector is entitled to vote,
and each elector shall be entitled to vote in each ward where
he is a qualified elector ; and, at the closing of the poll in any
ward, the officer presiding at such poll shall declare the
person or persons who shall have received the largest number Persons elect-
of votes, to be duly elected members of the said council ; and ed.
in case two or more candidates have received an equal
number of votes, the said officer shall be entitled to vote—
but in this case only, and he shall then give his casting vote Case of equal-
in favor of the candidate or the candidates, whom he shall ity of votes.
think fit to choose, and he shall have the right to give such
casting vote and shall be bound to give the same, immediately
after the votes shall have been counted ;

2. If at any time after the votes have commenced to be Duty of the
polled, one hour elapses without any vote being polled, it person pre-
shall be the duty of the person presiding, after the expiration siding in cer-
of the said hour, to close the said election and declare duly tain cases.
elected as councillors as aforesaid, such candidates as shall be
entitled to be so declared elected ; provided that no person
shall have been, within the last hour, prevented from approach-
ing the poll by violence, of which notice shall have been given
to the person presiding ;

3. The mayor shall be elected by the council for one year Duration of
only, (but he shall be eligible) for re-election, and remain in the office of
office until his successor shall have entered in charge : the mayor.
councillors elected at any of the municipal elections shall remain
in office during three years, except those who shall be elected at the first election, of whom two shall retire at the expiration of the first year, and two at the expiration of the second
year, and three at the expiration of the third year, and it shall
be declared by lot, in the manner established by the council,
which of the councillors shall thus retire from office, at the
end of the first and second years ;

4. The subsequent annual elections of councillors for the Subsequent
said city shall take place in the same manner and within elections.
the same delays as the first ;

5. Before proceeding to the holding of any election under
this act, the presiding officer and his deputies and poll clerks
shall take the following oath, which any justice of the peace
is hereby empowered to administer ;—to wit :

" I do solemnly swear that I will, to the best of my judg- Oath of pre-
" ment and ability, faithfully and impartially perform the siding officers
" duties of presiding officer (or of deputy presiding officer or and poll clerks.

" poll clerk) at the election which I am about to hold (or which is about to be held) of a person or persons to serve " as councillors for the said city of Sherbrooke. So help me " God."

Powers of presiding officers.

6. The persons who shall preside at an election, in the several wards where elections are being held, shall, during such election, be guardians of the peace, and shall be invested with the same powers for the preservation of the peace and the apprehension, imprisonment, and holding to bail, of persons charged with violations of the law and breakers of the peace, as are vested in justices of the peace, and this, whether the said persons do or do not possess the property qualification of a justice of the peace, as required by law; and it shall be lawful for the presiding officer and his deputies at an election, to appoint special constables in sufficient numbers to preserve peace at such election, if he or they shall think it necessary, or be required to do it by five electors ;

Hotel keepers &c., bound to close.

7. Every hotel, tavern and saloon keepers shall close their bars during the days of voting under a penalty of fifty dollars, or imprisonment in the common jail for three months in default of payment ;

Penalty.

Notice to elected.

8. The presiding officer at any such election, shall, within three days from the closing of the election, give each' of the councillors so elected special notice of his said election, as well as of the place, the day and the hour appointed by him for the first session of the council to take place after the said election, which shall be not more than eight days from the

Entry and duration of office.

giving of the notice. The councillors so elected shall enter respectively into office as such, at the said first meeting, and shall remain in office until the appointment of their successors ;

Delivery of poll books to secy.-treas. &c.

9. The person so presiding at any such election, shall deliver up immediately to the secretary-treasurer of the city council, if there be such officer, and, if not, then, as soon as such officer shall be appointed, the poll-books kept at such election, together with all other papers and documents relating to the said election, certified by himself, to form part of the records of the said council; and copies of the same, certified by the secretary-treasurer, shall be authentic in any court of justice ;

First session of council after first election.

10. The first session of the council, after the first election, shall take place within eleven days immediately following such election, and at such meeting or prior thereto, the councillors elected shall take the following oath before a justice of the peace :

Oath of councillors.

"I (A. B.) do solemnly swear faithfully to fulfil the duties " of member of the city council of the city of Sherbrooke, " to the best of my judgment and ability. So help me God!"

Quorum. Election of mayor.

12. And the members then present, provided they form a majority of the council, which number shall constitute a quorum under this act, shall be authorized to act as the council, and shall immediately proceed to elect one of their number as mayor : and the members absent, without just cause, shall be held to have refused office and shall be liable to the fine

hereinafter provided for in like cases, unless they be persons exempt from serving;

13. The councillors elected at the elections subsequent to the first, shall enter into office upon receiving notice from the presiding officer as aforesaid, and upon taking the oath aforesaid, and a meeting of the council shall take place within eleven days after, in the same manner as after the first election, and the councillors elected shall take the same oath, and those absent without just cause, shall be held to have refused the office, and shall be liable to the penalty hereinafter provided in such case, unless they be persons who are exempted from serving; Session after subsequent elections.

14. The expense of every election shall be defrayed out of the funds of the corporation. Election expenses.

10. The general sessions of the council of the city of Sherbrooke shall be held on the first monday in each month at such hour as shall be fixed by resolution of the council, and in case the said first monday, shall be a holiday, then the session shall be held on the next following juridical day at the hour fixed for other general meetings. Time of general sessions.

11. It shall be lawful for the mayor of the said city, whenever he shall deem it necessary or useful, to call special meetings of the said council, and whenever two members shall be desirous of obtaining such special meetings, they shall apply to the mayor to call such meetings, and in the absence of the mayor, or on his refusal to act, they may call such meeting themselves, on stating in writing to the secretary-treasurer of the said council their object in calling such special meeting and the day on which they are desirous that it shall be held, and the said secretary-treasurer shall, upon receipt of such written notification, communicate the same to the other members of the council, and shall give public notice of the same, and no other business shall be transacted at such meeting, except the business mentioned in such notice. Special meetings. Business transacted.

12. In any case in which one of the persons so elected shall refuse to act as councillor, or in case his election shall be declared null, the electors of the ward for which such election is necessary, shall proceed to a new election and elect a person to replace the said councillor within one month after the said refusal shall have been made known. Case of refusal to act.

2. In case of the death of a councillor, or in case of his absence from the city, or incapacity, sickness, or any other cause, during two calendar months; the other councillors, at the first meeting of the council which shall take place after such decease, or at the expiration of the said period of two months, shall declare the seat of such councillor to be vacant and a new election shall immediately take place in the ward represented by such person for the purpose of filling such vacant seat in the usual way; provided that notwithstanding the decease, absence or inability to act, of the said councillor, the remaining councillors shall continue to exercise the same powers, and fulfil the same duties which they would have had Vacancies.

to exercise and fulfil, had not such decease, absence or inability to act, on the part of the said councillor, taken place.

Councillors elected in place of others.   3. Every councillor elected or appointed to replace another, shall remain in office for the remainder of the time for which his predecessor had been elected or appointed, and no longer.

Oath of person presiding at election.   13. Before any person shall proceed to hold an election in conformity with this act, he shall take the following oath, which any justice of the peace is hereby authorized to administer, that is to say :

" I do solemnly swear that I will faithfully and impartially, " to the best of my judgment and ability, discharge the duties ".of presiding officer at the election which I am about to hold " of a person (or persons) to serve as members of the city coun- " cil of the city of Sherbrooke. So help me God."

His powers and duties.   14. The officers presiding at any election under this act, shall have authority, and are hereby required, at the request of any persons qualified to vote at such election, to examine upon oath (or affirmation, when the party is allowed by law to affirm), any candidate for the office of member of the said council, respecting his qualification to be elected to the said office, and shall also have authority, and are hereby required upon such request as aforesaid, to examine upon oath (or affirmation) any person tendering his vote at any election, and the oath to be administered by the presiding officers in both cases, shall be in the form following :

Voter's oath.   " You shall true answer make to all questions put to you " by me, in my capacity of presiding officer respecting your " qualification to be elected a member of the city council " (or respecting your qualification to vote at this election—as " the case may be.) So help you God."

Questions.   2. And the presiding officer shall himself put the questions when he shall think necessary, but in no case shall the presiding officer at any ward have the power to refuse or reject the nomination of any person duly nominated, or to refuse to record the votes cast for such candidate, and the fact that the person was sworn shall be entered in the poll-book.

Contestation of elections.   15. If the election of all, or of one or more of the councillors be contested, such contestation shall be conducted and decided according to the provisions of the municipal code, except in so far as the same is provided for, in and by the following section.

Failure of annual election.   16. In case it shall at any time happen that an annual municipal election shall not be held for any reason whatever, on the day when, in pursuance of this act, it ought to have been held, the said city council shall not, for that cause, be deemed to be dissolved, and it shall be lawful for such members of the said council as shall not have retired from office, to meet again, for the purpose of fixing as early as possible a day for the holding of such annual municipal election ; and

in such case, the notices and publications required by this
act, shall be published and posted up, not less than eight clear
days before the election, and if, within fifteen days after the
day in which such election ought to have been held, the members of the said council shall have neglected to appoint a day
for such election, they shall be liable to a fine of twenty
dollars each. Penalty.

17. The mayor of the said city, if he be present, shall pre- Duties of the
side at the meetings of the council, shall maintain order thereat mayor.
and shall have a right to express his opinion, but not to vote
on all questions which shall be brought before the said council ; provided always, that when the said councillors, after
having voted on any question, shall be found to be equally
divided, then and in that case only, the mayor shall; decide
the question by his vote, giving his reasons for it if he thinks Casting vote.
proper; and neither the mayor nor the councillors shall
receive any salary or emoluments from the funds of the city
during the time they shall remain in office ; provided also, Absence of
that whenever the mayor shall not be present at any regular mayor.
or special meeting of the said city council, the councillors
present shall choose one of their number to fill the place of the
mayor during the sitting.

18. The council, at its first general session, or at a special Secretary-
session held within the fifteen days which shall follow the first treasurer.
day of such general session, shall appoint an officer who shall
be called the " secretary-treasurer ."

2. The secretary-treasurer shall be the custodian of all the His duties in
books, registers, valuation rolls, collection rolls, reports, pro- general.
cès-verbaux, plans, maps, records, documents and papers kept
or fyled in the office or archives of the council ; he shall attend all sessions, and shall enter, in a register kept for the purpose, all the proceedings of the council, and he shall allow
persons interested therein to inspect the same at all reasonable
hours, and every copy or extract of or from any such book or
register, valuation roll, collection roll, report, procès-verbal, Authenticity
plan, map, record, document or paper certified by such of his certifi-
cates.
secretary-treasurer shall be deemed authentic.

3. Every person appointed secretary-treasurer shall, before His security.
acting as such, give such security as shall be fixed and determined by the council ; provided such security shall be
hypothecary or by a guarantee company.

4. The secretary-treasurer of the council shall receive all Receives and
moneys due and payable to the corporation ; and he shall, pays over
after having been authorized to that effect by the council or by moneys.
the mayor, be bound to pay out of such moneys all drafts or
orders drawn upon him by any person thereto authorized by
this act, for the payment of any sum to be expended or due
by the corporation, whenever thereunto authorized by the
said council ; but no such draft or order shall be lawfully paid
by the said secretary-treasurer, unless the same shall show Proviso.
sufficiently, the use to be made of the sum mentioned in such
draft or order, or the nature of the debt to be paid thereby.

Their oath.

"I (A.B.) having been appointed to the office of auditor of
" the city of Sherbrooke, do hereby swear that I will
" faithfully perform the duties thereof, according to the
" best of my judgment and ability; and I do declare that I
" have not directly or indirectly, any share or interest what-
" ever in any contract or employment with, by or on behalf
" of the city council of the said city of Sherbrooke. So help
" me God."

Their duties.

24. It shall be the duty of the auditors to examine, approve
or disapprove of and report upon all accounts which may be
entered in the books of the said council or concerning the
latter, and which may relate to any matter or thing under the
control of, or under the jurisdiction of, the said city council,
before the annual municipal elections.

Persons who
cannot dis-
charge such
duties.

25. Neither the mayor, councillors nor secretary-treasurer of
the said city, nor any person receiving any salary from the said
council, either for any duty performed under their authority,
or on account of any contract whatsoever entered into with
them, shall be capable of discharging the duties of auditor for
the said city.

Mayor is a jus-
tice of the
peace.

26. The mayor of the said city shall, during the period of
his office, be a justice of the peace within the limits of the said
city; provided always that he shall not be bound to take
any other oath than the official one to act as such, any law to
the contrary notwithstanding.

Persons who
cannot serve
as councillors

27. Every person holding the office of councillor of the
said city, who shall be declared bankrupt or shall become
insolvent, or who shall apply for the benefit of any of the laws
made for the relief or protection of insolvent debtors, or who
shall enter into holy orders, or become a minister of religion
in any religious denomination, or who shall be appointed a
judge, district magistrate or clerk of any court of justice, or a
member of the executive council, or who shall become responsible for the revenues of the city, in whole or in part, or
who shall make any contract with the said corporation to
execute work or furnish supplies, or who shall absent himself
from the said city without the permission of the said council
for more than two consecutive months, or who shall not be
present at the meetings of the said council for a like period of
two consecutive months, shall, by virtue of any of these
causes, become disqualified, and his seat in the said council
shall become vacant, and such person shall be replaced in
accordance with the provisions of this act; provided always
that the word "judge" employed in any part of this act,
shall not apply to a justice of the peace.

Proviso.

General
power to
make by-
laws.

28. It shall be lawful for the said city council from time
to time to make such by-laws as may seem to them necessary
or expedient for the preservation of order at the sittings of the
council, for the internal government of the city, for the

improvement of the place, for the maintenance of peace and
good order, and for the good repair, cleansing and draining of
the streets, public squares and vacant or occupied lots, for the
prevention or suppression of all nuisances whatsoever, for
the maintenance and preservation of the public health, and
generally for all purposes connected with or affecting the
internal management or government of the said city.

29. It shall be lawful for the said city council to appoint, Power to
remove and replace, when they shall think proper, all such name officers,
officers, constables and policemen as they shall deem necessary &c.
for the due execution of the laws and by-laws now in force or
to be by them enacted hereafter; and to require from all persons employed by them, in any quality whatsoever, such
security as to them shall seem meet, to ensure the due execu- Their securi-
tion of their duties. ty.

30. In order to raise the necessary funds to meet the ex- To levy taxes;
penses of the said city council and to provide for the several
necessary public improvements in the said city, the said
city council shall be authorized to levy annually on persons,
and on moveable and immoveable property in the said city,
the taxes hereinafter designated, that is to say:

2. On all lands, city lots and parts of city lots, whether On lands, &c;
there be buildings erected thereon or not, with all buildings
and erections thereon, a sum not exceeding two cents on the
dollar on their whole value, as entered on the assessment roll
of the said city;

3. On all stocks in trade or goods kept by merchants or
traders and exposed for sale on shelves in shops or kept in Stocks;
vaults or storehouses, a tax of not more than one quarter *per
cent,* on the estimated average value of such stock in trade,
and in case any person or persons shall come temporarily into
the said city to dispose of any bankrupt or other stock of
goods, wares and merchandize, either at public auction or at
private sale, the said council may, by resolution passed as soon
as convenient, after the same shall come to their knowledge,
levy on such person or persons a license fee of not less than License;
twenty dollars, and not more than fifty dollars, for the sale of
said goods so brought into the said city and exposed for sale
therein, such duty to be payable by such person or persons
on demand being made therefor by the secretary-treasurer,
and if not paid when demanded, the same may be collected by Recovery of
distress warrant issued under the hand and seal of the mayor duties in cer-
or pro-mayor, immediately after such failure to pay, and said tain cases;
goods may be attached and shall be held for the payment of
the same;

4. On each tenant paying rent, an annual sum equivalent
to two *per cent* on the amount of his rent; On tenants.

5. On each male inhabitant of the age of twenty one years
who shall have resided in the said city for six months, not Capitation;
being a proprietor, tenant, an apprentice, nor a domestic
servant, an annual sum of one dollar;

Dogs;

6. On every dog kept by persons residing in the said city, an annual sum of not less than one, or more than three dollars, and if the proprietor or harborer of any dog shall fail to pay the said tax when legally notified so to do, by the municipal officer entrusted with the collection of the said dog-tax, then it shall be lawful for the said council to order the said dogs upon which the tax has not been paid, to be killed by poison or otherwise, and the council shall have the power to order

Destruction of dogs ;

dogs to be kept muzzled or tied up, and to cause to be destroyed such as are vicious or dangerous ;

On proprietors of houses of public entertainment ;

7. And it shall be lawful for the said city council to fix by a by-law or by-laws, and to impose and levy certain annual duties or taxes in the discretion of the said council, on the proprietors or occupants of houses of public entertainment, taverns, coffee-houses and eating-houses, and on all retailers of

Pedlers ;

spirituous liquors, and on all pedlers and itinerant traders selling in the said city, articles of commerce of any kind what-

Keepers of theatres, &c ;

soever, and on all proprietors, possessors, agents, managers and keepers of theatres, menageries, circuses, billiard rooms, ten-pin alleys, or other places for games or amusements of any

Auctioneers, grocers, &c ;

kind whatsoever, and on all auctioneers, grocers, bakers, butchers, hawkers, hucksters, carters and livery-stable keepers,

Yard keepers;

and on all traders and manufacturers and their agents, and on all proprietors or keepers of wood-yards or coal-yards and slaughter-houses in the said city, and on all money-changers or

Brokers ;

exchange-brokers, pawn-brokers and their agents, and on all bankers and agents of bankers and banks, and on all insurance companies or their agents, and generally on all commerce,

Manufacturers, &c ;

manufactures, callings, arts, trades and professions which have been or which may be introduced into, or exercised in the said city, whether the same be or be not mentioned therein.

Tax on liberal professions.

31. Every person in the said city practicing the profession of an advocate, physician, land surveyor, notary or any other liberal profession within the limits of the said corporation, shall be assessed at the sum of not less than three dollars annually, and the said city council may name a person or

Roll of moveable property:

persons, to make the roll of the persons and moveable property, mentioned in the different parts of the foregoing sections.

By-laws respecting ;

32. The said council shall also have power to make by-laws :

Opening of streets ;

2. For opening new streets in the said city, to such extent as may from time to time, be required ;

Markets ;

3. For establishing market-places and for extending them hereafter ;

Duties of clerks, &c ;

4. For determining and regulating the duties of the clerks of the market in the said city, and all other persons they may deem proper to employ to superintend the said markets, and

Stalls ;

for letting the stalls or places for selling upon and about the said market-places, and for fixing and determining the duties to be paid by any person selling on any of the said markets any provisions or produce whatever, and for regulating the

Conduct ;

conduct of all such persons in selling their goods and all produce whatever offered for sale on the said markets ;

5. For amending, modifying or repealing all by-laws made **Amendments**
by the municipal council who have had the management of **to by-laws ;**
the internal affairs of the said city ;

6. For regulating and placing all vehicles in which any **Vehicles on**
article shall be exposed for sale on the said markets ;   **markets ;**

7. For compelling proprietors to cause trees to be planted **Trees ;**
in front of their properties ;

8. For preventing persons bringing articles into the said **Sale of mer-**
city, from selling or exposing them for sale in any other place **chandize ;**
than the markets of the said city, or for making all other by-
laws, which they shall judge requisite to regulate the sale of
such articles, and for punishing by confiscation of their **Confiscation ;**
articles, goods or provisions, persons who in exposing them
for sale in the markets or streets of the said city, contravene
the by-laws passed by the said council as to the weight or
quality of such articles, goods or provisions ;

9. For the establishment of public weigh-houses ;   **Public weigh-**
10. For preventing obstructions of any nature whatsoever **houses ;**
in the streets ;   **Obstructions**
11. For preventing the sale on the public highway of any **on public**
wares or merchandize whatsoever ;   **streets ;**

12. For restraining, regulating or prohibiting the sale of **Sale of spiri-**
any spirituous, alcoholic or intoxicating liquors ;   **tuous liquors;**
13. For regulating and governing shopkeepers, tavern
keepers and other persons selling such liquors by retail, and in **Hotelkeepers;**
whatever places such liquors may be sold, in such manner as
they may deem expedient to prevent drunkenness ;

14. For taxing saloons and saloon keepers ;   **Saloons ;**
15. For preventing the sale of any intoxicating beverage
to any child, apprentice or servant ;   **Sale of spiri-**
16. For regulating, fixing and determining the weight and **tuous liquors**
quality of bread, sold or offered for sale, within the limits of **&c ;**
the said city ;   **Bread ;**

17. For regulating the conduct and duties of ap-
prentices, domestics, hired servants and journeymen in the **Masters and**
said city, and also duties and obligations of masters and **servants ;**
mistresses towards their servants, apprentices, journeymen
and domestics ;

18. To prevent the keeping of gaming houses, places for
gambling, or any description of house of ill fame in the said **Gaming**
city ;   **houses ;**

19. To establish as many public pounds, as the said council **Public**
shall deem expedient to open, for the impounding of animals **pounds ;**
of any species which may be running at large in the said
city ;

20. For regulating, arming, lodging, clothing and paying a
police force in the said city, and for determining their **Police ;**
duties ;

21. To compel the proprietors of all land and real property
within the said city, their agents or representatives, to enclose **Enclosure of**
the same, and to regulate the height, description and material **lands ;**
of every such enclosure ;

22. To compel the proprietors or occupants of lots of land
in the said city, upon which is stagnant or filthy water, to **Drains ;**

drain or raise such lands, so that the neighbours may not be
incommoded nor the public health endangered thereby, and
in the event of the proprietors of such lands being unknown
or having no representative or agent in the said city, it shall
be lawful for the said council to order the said lands to be
drained or raised, or to fence in and enclose them, at the cost
of the proprietor, if they are not already fenced in and enclosed; and the said council shall have a like power, if the
proprietors or occupants of such lands are too poor to drain,
raise or fence in the same, and in every case, the sum expended by the said council in improving such lands, shall
remain as a special hypothéc on such lands and have privilege
over all other debts whatsoever without its being necessary
to register the same.;

23. To oblige all proprietors or occupants of houses in the
said city to remove from the streets all encroachments or obstructions of any sort, either hanging over, or placed thereon,
such as steps, galleries, porches, posts, sign-boards or other
obstacles whatsoever;

24. To cause to be pulled down, demolished and removed,
when necessary, all old or dilapidated walls, chimneys, and
buildings of any description which may be in a state of ruin,
and to cause to be removed from the streets, all sheds, stables
and other buildings erected on the line of any street, and to
determine the time and manner in which the same shall be
pulled down, demolished or removed, and by whom the expense thereof shall be borne;

25. For regulating the width of the streets to be opened
hereafter in the said city, and for increasing the width of those
already opened, for regulating and altering the height or level
of any street or sidewalk in the said city; provided that if
any person shall suffer real damage by the widening, length-
ening or altering the level of any street in the said city, after
a grade has been established, such damage shall be paid to
such person after having been assessed by arbitrators, if any
of the parties shall require it;

26. For assessing the proprietors of property situate in any
street or portion of a street of the said city for the purpose of
making sewers or drains in said street or portion of street, such
assessment being in proportion to the assessed value of such property, and for regulating the mode in which such assessment
shall be collected and paid; provided always that the said
council shall not be authorized so to assess the proprietors
in any street or portion of a street, for making such common sewers, unless the majority of the proprietors in such
street or portion of a street, shall have prayed for such
undertaking, or called for such assessment;

27. For assessing, at the request of a majority of the citizens
residing in any street or portion of a street or public square of
the said city, all the citizens residing in such street or portion
of a street or public square in any sums necessary to meet the
expenses of sweeping, watering and keeping clean such street
or portion of a street or public square, and for removing the
snow from any such street or portion of a street, lane or public

Marginal notes:

Low lands, &c;

Fences;

Special Hypothec;

Encroach- ments;

Old walls;

Width and level of streets;

Drainage tax on proprie- tors;

Idem to water the streets;

Removal of snow;

place, such assessment being in proportion to the assessed value of the property therein ;

28. To prohibit the erection of steam-engines within the limits of the city for manufacturing or other purposes, except by leave of the council ; Steam-engines ;

29. To fix the place for the erection of any manufactories or machinery worked by steam in the said city ; Manufactories ;

30. For establishing a board of health and investing them with all the privileges, powers, and authority necessary for the fulfilment of the duties entrusted to them, or for acquiring all useful information on the progress or general effects of all contagious diseases, or for making such regulations as such board of health shall deem necessary for preserving the citizens of the city from any contagious diseases or for diminishing the effects or the danger thereof. Board of health ;

33. For the better protection of the lives and property of the inhabitants of the said city, and for more effectually preventing accidents by fire, the said council may make by-laws for the following purposes, to wit : By-laws against fire ;

2. For regulating the construction, dimension, height and elevation of chimneys above the roofs, or even, in certain cases, above the neighbouring houses and buildings, and within what delay they shall be raised or repaired ; Height of chimneys ;

3. For defraying out of the funds of the said city, any expenses that the council shall deem necessary to incur, for the purchase of fire-engines or apparatus of any kind, to be used at fires, or for taking such means as shall appear to them most effective for preventing accidents by fire, or arresting the progress of fires ; Fire-engines ;

4. For preventing thefts and depredations which may be committed at any fire in the said city, and for punishing any person who shall resist or illtreat any member or officer of the said council in the execution of any duty assigned to him, by the said council under the authority of this section ; Thefts at fires ;

5. For making or authorizing, or requiring to be made, after each fire in the said city an enquiry into the cause and origin of such fire, for which purpose the said council or any committee thereof, authorized to the effect aforesaid, may summon and compel the attendance of witnesses and examine them on oath, which oath they are empowered to administer ; Enquiry into cause of fire ;

6. For regulating the manner in which, and the periods of the year when chimneys shall be swept, and for granting licenses to such number of chimney-sweeps, as the said council shall think proper to employ, and for obliging all proprietors, tenants or occupants of houses in the said city, to allow their chimneys to be swept by such licensed chimney sweeps, and for determining what rates shall be paid either to the council or to such chimney sweeps, and for imposing a penalty of not less than one dollar, nor more than five dollars, on all persons who shall refuse to allow their chimneys to be swept as aforesaid, and all persons whose chimneys may have caught fire after any refusal to allow them to be swept, such penalty to be recovered before any justice of the peace ; and whenever any Sweeping chimneys ;

chimney which shall have caught fire as aforesaid, shall be common to several houses, or be used by several families in the same house, the said justice of the peace shall have power to impose the above penalty in full on the occupant of each house or family, or to divide the same among them in proportion to the degree of negligence, shown on proof before him ;

Keeping of ashes and quick-lime ;

7. For regulating the manner in which ashes and quick lime shall be kept in the said city, and for preventing the inhabitants of the said city from carrying fire in the street without necessary precaution, from making a fire in any street, or from going from their houses to their yards and outbuildings

Lights generally ;

and entering therein with lights not enclosed in lanterns, and generally for making such regulations as they may deem necessary for preventing accidents by fire ;

Conduct of persons present at fires ;

8. For regulating the conduct of all persons present at any fire in the said city, for obliging idle persons to assist in extinguishing the fire or in saving effects which may be in danger, and for obliging all the inhabitants of the said city, to keep at all times upon and in their houses, ladders and fire-

Ladders, &c ;

buckets, in order the more easily to check the progress of fire;

Aid to wounded, &c ;

9. For defraying out of the funds of the said city any expenses which the said council shall deem expedient to incur in aiding or assisting any person in their employ, who shall have received any wound or contracted any severe disease at any fire in the said city, or in any other service for the city, or in assisting or providing for the family of any person in their employ who shall perish at any fire, or in any other service for the city, or in bestowing rewards in money or otherwise upon persons who shall have been particularly useful or zealous at any fire in the said city ;

Demolition in case of fire ;

10. For vesting in such members of the said council, or in the fire inspectors or in the said members and inspectors who shall be designated in such by-laws, the power of ordering to be demolished during any fire, any houses, buildings, outhouses or fences which might serve as fuel to the fire and endanger the other property of the inhabitants of the said city, saving the obligation of paying to the proprietors of the buildings so demolished, the damages to which they may be entitled ;

Appointment of officers ;

11. For appointing all such officers as the council shall deem necessary, for carrying into execution the by-laws to be passed by them, in relation to accidents by fire, for prescribing their duties and powers, and providing for their remuneration, if they think fit, out of the funds of the said city ;

Inspection of houses, &c ;

12. For authorizing such officers as the council shall think fit to appoint for that purpose, to visit and examine at suitable times and hours, that is to say : between nine o'clock in the morning and four o'clock in the afternoon, either the inside or the outside of all houses and buildings of any description within the said city, for the purpose of ascertaining whether the rules and regulations passed by the said council, under the authority of this act, are regularly observed, and for obliging all proprietors or occupants of houses in the said city to admit all officers of the corporation for the purpose aforesaid ;

13. For imposing a penalty, of at least one dollar and not Penalty. more than twenty dollars, for any infraction of by-laws legally made.

34. The secretary-treasurer, when he shall have completed Collection of his collection-roll, shall proceed to collect the rates therein rates. mentioned, according to the manner provided by the municipal code.

35. Every tax or assessment imposed under this act upon Recoverable any property or house in the city may be recovered either from whom. from the proprietor, tenant or occupant of such property or building.

36. All the debts now due or hereafter to become due to Taxes privi-the said corporation, for all taxes or assessments imposed leged. upon moveable or immoveable property in the said city shall, under this act, be privileged debts according to the municipal code.

37. All the fines and penalties recovered under the provisions Penalties, to of this act shall be paid into the hands of the secretary-treasurer whom paid. of the said city council, and the proceeds of all licenses granted under this act shall form part of the public fund of the said Licenses. city, any law to the contrary notwithstanding ; also all fines and penalties sued for and recovered, in the magistrates' Other penal-court in the said city of Sherbrooke (save and except for the ties. infraction of the laws relating to the sale of liquors,) under and by virtue of this act and under the summary convictions act, shall belong to and form part of the general funds of the said city of Sherbrooke and shall be paid over to the secretary-treasurer of the said city council, by the justice rendering Employment judgment, and in all such cases the evidence may be taken thereof. *vivâ voce* and need not be reduced to writing, unless at the Proof *vivâ* time of the fyling of the plea, the defendant requests the same *voce.* to be taken in writing.

38. Before any by-law of the said council shall have force Publication or be binding, such by-law shall be published by publication of by-laws. for two consecutive weeks in two newspapers published within the limits of the said city, in one newspaper in the french language, and in the other in the english language.

39. The said council may contract loans for all objects Power to falling within the scope of their power, by complying with borrow. the provisions of the municipal code, and may make a by-law or by-laws granting such bonus or bonuses, as they may think desirable and proper in aid of any manufacturing company Aid to manu-or companies as may be established within the limits of the said facturing city of Sherbrooke ; but no such by-law shall be operative companies. until the same shall have been approved of by the municipal Approval. electors of the said city under and by virtue of the provisions of the municipal code ; provided however, that none but owners Proviso. of real property who by the valuation roll are entitled to vote at other municipal elections under this act shall be entitled to vote, either for or against any by-law for the purposes aforesaid.

Issue of debentures.

40. The said council may issue debentures for the purpose of raising money upon the credit of the city for all objects falling within the scope of their powers, such debentures to be issued subject to the provisions of the municipal code, and the amendments thereto; provided however,

Mode of issue. that none but owners of real property as aforesaid shall be entitled to vote for or against any by-law passed for the pur-

Proviso. poses aforesaid;

Issue of debentures for $25,000, without approval of rate-payers.

2. But inasmuch as the said town of Sherbrooke has promised by way of bonus to the Canadian meat and produce company, the sum of eight thousand dollars, and inasmuch as there is due by said town, certain other debts which are now due and exigible, amounting in all to a sum not exceeding twenty-five thousand dollars, the said council may and they are hereby authorized to issue debentures for the purpose of raising money to pay these debts upon the credit of the city and without submitting the same to the rate-payers of the said city to an amount not exceeding twenty-five thousand dollars, such debentures to be issued in the form and under the provisions set forth in the municipal code and its amendments; save and except however, that they may be issued by virtue of a resolution of the council of the said city of Sherbrooke, and such resolution shall not require the sanction or approval

Mode of issue. of the municipal electors of the said city nor of the lieutenant-governor of this province, but such debentures shall have the same validity as though sanctioned by the lieutenant-governor.

Properties exempt from taxation.

41. The following property shall be exempt from taxation in the city of Sherbrooke:

All lands and property belonging to Her Majesty, Her heirs and successors, held by any public body or office or person, in trust for the service of Her Majesty, Her heirs and successors;

2. All provincial property or buildings;

3. Every place of public worship, presbytery, parsonage or manse and appurtenances and every burying-ground;

4. Every public school house and the ground on which the same is constructed, provided that such ground does not exceed one acre;

5. Every educational establishment and the ground on which the same is constructed, provided that such ground does not exceed two acres;

6. All buildings, grounds and property occupied or possessed by hospitals or other charitable institutions, not exceeding three acres.

Encroachments upon the streets.

42. It shall be lawful for the said city council to order the inspector of the said city to notify any parties who shall have made or shall hereafter make encroachments upon the streets or public squares of the said city by means of houses, fences, buildings or obstructions of any kind, to cause the removal of **Power to** such encroachments or obstructions, by giving to such per- **cause the re-** sons a reasonable delay for the purpose, which delay shall be **moval of them** specified by the said city inspector in giving his notice, and **cases.** if such persons shall not have removed such encroachments or obstructions within the delay specified, the said corporation may itself remove the same and shall recover the sum expended for such purpose from the person in default.

43. From and after the passing of this act, every proprie- **False repre-** tor or agent who shall wilfully grant a certificate or receipt **sentation.** setting forth a less sum than the rent really paid or payable for the premises therein mentioned or referred to, and every tenant who shall present to the assessors of the said city such a receipt or certificate falsely representing the value of the rent paid by such tenant in order to procure a diminution or abatement of his assessment, or who shall directly or indirectly deceive the said assessors as to the amount of such rent, shall be liable, on conviction thereof before the mayor or a **Penalty.** justice of the peace, to a penalty of twenty dollars currency or less, with costs, or in default of payment to imprisonment during one calendar month or less, according to the judgment of such mayor or justice of the peace.

44. The said council shall have full and unlimited power to **Power to ac-** purchase and acquire out of the funds of the said city all **quire land** such lots, lands and real property whatsoever within the said **for the** town, as they shall deem necessary for the opening or enlarge- **streets, &c.** ment of any street, public square or market place, or for the erection thereon of a public building, or generally for any object of public utility of whatsoever nature.

45. When the proprietor of a lot which the said council **Expropria-** shall be desirous of purchasing, for any object of public uti- **tion for pub-** lity whatsoever, shall refuse to sell the same by private agree- **lic utility.** ment, and also refuses or neglects within ten days after notification, to appoint an arbitrator to act jointly with an arbitrator chosen by the corporation, and to enter into a bond with the corporation to accept the award of the said arbitrators as compensation for said land, or in case such proprietor shall be absent from the province or in case such lot of land shall belong to minors, issue unborn, lunatics, idiots, or *femes covert*, the said council may apply to any judge of the superior court for Lower Canada in and for the district of Saint Francis after having given notice of such application to the party interested, an absentee in such case being notified by a notice for such object published during two months in the newspapers, one published in the english language and the other in the french language in the district of Saint Francis, for the appointment of an arbitrator by the said judge, to make, conjointly with the arbitrator appointed by the said council, a valuation of such lot, with power to the said arbitrators however appointed, in case of a difference of opinion, to appoint a third, without being bound, in case of such latter appointment, to notify the parties ; and when the said arbitrators or two of them shall have made their report to the said council, at a regular meeting thereof, it shall be lawful for the said council to acquire such lot on depositing the price at which it shall have been valued by the said arbitrators, in the hands of the prothonotary of the superior court, for the district of St. Francis, for the use of the person entitled thereto ; provided always, that in all matters of expropriation it shall be the duty of the said arbitrators in making their valuation, to declare if the residue of the said land, part whereof has been detached, is benefitted by the expropriation, and if such be the case, such value so given to the residue of the land shall be by them taken into consideration, in making the estimate of indemnity, and shall be deducted therefrom, and the decision of the said arbitrators, or of a majority of them, shall be final, and within ten days after notification of the deposit of such money, with the said prothonotary, which notification in the case of an absentee shall be published in the newspapers as required by this section, the owner of such land shall be bound to execute a deed of sale of said land to and in favor of the corporation, and in case of his failing to do so, then the registration in the registry office of the proper registration division, of the said award, and a certificate from the prothonotary of the deposit of such money, shall constitute a good and sufficient title to said land in the said corporation.

Penalty for refusal of charge or neglect. **46.** Every person who, being elected or appointed to any of the offices mentioned in the following list, shall refuse or neglect to accept such office or to perform the duties of such office during any portion of the period for which he shall have been so elected or appointed, shall incur the penalty mentioned in such list, or designation of such office, that is to say :

Mayor ; 1. The office of mayor, fifty dollars ;

Councillors ; 2. The office of councillor, twenty-five dollars ;

Valuators ; 3. Whenever the valuators neglect to make the valuation which they are required to make under this act, or neglect to draw up, sign and deliver the valuation roll to the secretary-treasurer of the council within two months from the date of their appointment, every such valuator shall incur a penalty of fifty dollars ;

Members of the council ; 4. Every member of the council, every officer appointed by the council, who shall refuse or neglect to do any act or perform any duty required of or imposed upon him by this act shall incur a penalty not exceeding twenty dollars and not less than one dollar ;

Voters not qualified ; 5. Every person who shall vote at any election of councillors, without having at the time of giving his vote at such election, the qualification by law required to entitle him to vote at such election, shall thereby incur a penalty not exceeding twenty dollars ;

Road inspectors ; 6. Every inspector of roads or road-officer who shall refuse or neglect to perform any duty assigned to him by this act, or by the by-laws of the council shall, for each day on which such offence shall be committed or such neglect shall continue incur a penalty of two dollars, unless some other and heavier penalty be by law imposed on him for such offence

7. Every person who shall hinder or prevent, or attempt to Preventing hinder or prevent, any officer of the council in the exercise of an officer any of the powers or in performance of any of the duties his duty; conferred or imposed upon him by this act, or by any by-law or order of the said council, shall incur a penalty not exceeding twenty dollars for every such offence ;

8. Any person contravening any of the provisions of this Contravention act, the penalty for the infraction whereof is not already tion of this prescribed by any provision of this act, shall incur a penalty act. not exceeding twenty dollars.

47. All the penalties imposed by this act, or by any by- Recovery of law made by the council, shall be recovered in the manner penalties. provided by the municipal code ; provided however, that in all summary trials for such penalties had before the district magistrate or any two magistrates in the said city of Sherbrooke, the evidence may be taken orally, unless the party prosecuted do make a demand that the same shall be taken in writing, and in all such cases, conviction shall carry costs.

48. All the powers conferred by the municipal code of the Municipal province of Quebec and the amendments thereto, upon any code shall municipal council, and upon the councillors and officers of apply. such council and not inconsistent with this act of incorporation, shall apply to the corporation of the city of Sherbrooke, to the municipal council and to the councillors and officers of the said corporation ; and wherever this act is silent, all the provisions of the said code and its amendments shall apply, and be law, in relation to all municipal matters in the said city of Sherbrooke and to all matters and things provided for in the said code.

49. An appeal shall lie to the circuit court from any Appeal to the decision of the council of the said city of Sherbrooke with refer- circuit court. ence to any valuation-roll, *proces-verbal*, expropriation of property, or any other thing with regard to which any party shall deem himself aggrieved by the decision of the council, and the decision of the court shall be binding upon all parties ; such appeal shall be prosecuted in the manner provided by articles 1064 to 1079 inclusive of the municipal code relative to appeals from decisions of county councils.

50. This act shall come into force on the day of its Act in force. sanction.

CAP. LI.

An Act further to amend the provisions of the several
acts relating to the incorporation of the City of
Quebec.

[Assented to 24th December, 1875.]

H ER MAJESTY, by and with the advice and consent
of the Legislature of Quebec, enacts as follows :

38 V., c. 74, s. 9, replaced.

1. The ninth section of the act of the province of
Quebec, 88th Victoria, Chapter 74, is hereby repealed
and the following substituted therefor :

32 V., c. 16, s. 24 amended concerning Quebec.

" The twenty-fourth section of the act of the province
of Quebec, 82nd Victoria, Chapter 16, is hereby amended
so far as the city of Quebec is concerned, by adding the
following words at the end of the said section : "And the
said tax shall be imposed, levied and recovered as aforesaid by the said corporation of the said city of Quebec
without any other formality and without it being necessary for the said corporation to make a by-law to that

Tax.

effect. And the said tax shall be so imposed every year
according to the annual assessed value of the said real
estate in the said city of Quebec."

35 V., c. 12, s. 4, amended concerning Quebec.

2. The fourth section of the act of the province of
Quebec, 85th Victoria, Chapter 12, is hereby amended, so
far as the city of Quebec is concerned, by adding the
following words at the end of the said section :

Additional sum.

"And the said additional sum when demanded by either
the catholic or protestant board shall be levied annually in
the manner stated in the said fourth section above cited,

Tax.

by means of a tax to be imposed, levied and recovered by
the said corporation of the said city of Quebec on the
real estate within the said city of Quebec, at the same
time and in the same manner as the other taxes of the
said city, on real estate, without any other formality and
without it being necessary for the said corporation to
make a by-law to that effect. And the said tax shall
so be annually imposed according to the assessed
annual value of the said real estate within the said city
of Quebec ;

When imposed.

2. But this last mentioned tax may be imposed, levied
and recovered by the said corporation of the city of
Quebec, at the same time as the other taxes of the said
city of Quebec, as above stated, or at any other time after
the payment of any such additional sum made by the said
corporation to the said catholic or protestant board, or
to either of them ;

If demanded after the com-

3. And if the said additional sum be demanded at any
time after the completion of the assessment roll made every

year by the said corporation of Quebec, then and in such pletion of the case the said tax shall be imposed, levied and recovered, in rolls. the manner above stated, according to the assessment-rolls made for the year for which the application for the said additional sum shall be made, and may be then immediately levied and recovered by the said corporation ;

4. Provided that the demand for any additional sum be made prior to the thirtieth day of April of each year, and not afterwards ;

5. And in case the said corporation of the said city of Quebec shall have omitted to make the yearly statement required by the 27th section of the act 32 Vict., chap. 16, or in case the said statement should be incomplete, then and in such case it shall be lawful for the said corporation to make or complete the said statement, previously to the imposition of any tax to be imposed in virtue of the present act or in virtue of the acts hereby amended."

Statement required by 32 V., c. 16, s 27.

3. And whereas the said corporation of the city of Quebec, under the said fourth section of the said act 35 Vict., chap. 12, hath paid, in the course of the fiscal years, one thousand eight hundred and seventy-four, and one thousand eight hundred and seventy-five, to the protestant board of school commissioners of the city of Quebec, a sum of three thousand five hundred dollars, to which sum the said protestant board was entitled for the said two years according to law, and whereas the said payment was so made by the said corporation since the making of the said assessment-rolls made by it, for each of the said two years,—the said corporation do now levy the said sum of three thousand five hundred dollars by means of a tax to be imposed, levied and recovered by assessment on real estate in the said city of Quebec, in the same manner as above enacted, for the recovery of any additional sum, without any other formality, and without the necessity of passing a by-law to that effect. And the said tax shall be so imposed according to the assessed annual value of the said real estate, within the said city of Quebec, and the said corporation may impose the said tax, and exact its payment at any time after the passing of the present act.

Tax to be imposed to reimburse the corporation of the sum paid to the protestant board.

4. All taxes to be imposed, as well under the present act as under the acts hereby amended, shall be paid by the proprietor of the real estate whereupon they shall have been imposed, in the manner prescribed by the twenty-sixth section of the act 32 Vict., chap. 16, and shall form part of the city school tax.

By whom the taxes shall be paid.

5. And whenever it shall become necessary for the said corporation of the city of Quebec to impose and levy any of the said taxes, it shall be lawful for the said

Additional taxes for costs of imposi-

tions and of
collections.

corporation to impose and levy at the same time and in the same manner, an additional tax of one fourth of a cent in the dollar on the assessed annual value of the real estate in the said city of Quebec, to meet and defray the expenses to be incurred by the said corporation, for the imposition and recovery of any of the said taxes, and this last mentioned tax shall also form part of the city school tax.

Suits.

6. All actions for the recovery of taxes or assessments to be imposed by the present act or by the acts hereby amended, shall be brought in the name of the corporation of the city of Quebec before the recorder's court of the said city, in the same manner as all other actions for the recovery of other taxes and assessments of the said city, and proceedings shall be had thereupon according to the law regulating the said court.

38 V., c. 74, s.
26, amended.

7. The twenty-sixth section of the act 38 Victoria, chapter 74, is hereby repealed and the following substituted therefor :

Widening of
St. John and
Fabrique
streets.

" 26. The said corporation is hereby authorized to borrow $100,000 to be applied to the widening of St. John street, within, and Fabrique street, provided the widening of the said streets is decided by two-thirds of the council present.—The said sum shall form part of schedule B."

31 V , c. 33, s.
11, amended.

8. The eleventh section of the act 31 Victoria, chap. 33, is hereby amended by adding the following words at the end thereof: " without the need of other publication of the said by-law before its final adoption, unless the same be ordered by a resolution of the council."

FINANCES.

Stock of
$65,000 of the
water works.

9. The corporation of the city of Quebec is hereby authorized to issue stock or shares, to be known as " the Quebec Water Works Stock," to an amount of sixty five thousand dollars, to raise a like sum to be invested for the same purposes as mentioned in the 12th section of the act 38 Vict., chap. 74, according to the schedule A annexed to the present act.

Use of the
$216,000.

10. And the sum of two hundred and sixteen thousand dollars to be employed for the same purposes as mentioned in the thirteenth section of the same act, and according to the schedule B annexed to the present act ;

Shall bear
hypothec.

2. And the said sums so employed for the said purposes will bear the same hypothecs and carry the same privileges and guarantees as the debentures mentioned in the said twelfth and thirteenth sections of the above cited act.

11. And the said corporation of Quebec is further Debentures authorized to issue debentures at any time it may think of the water-fit, to be called "Quebec water works debentures," to the $1,100,000. amount of one million one hundred thousand dollars, to be employed to redeem the permanent stock class A, now issued and mentioned in the twelfth section of the said act.38 Vict., chap. 74, and also to pay the city stock to the amount authorized by the ninth section of the present act;

2. And the said debentures so issued for the said pur- Hypotheca. poses, shall bear the same hypothecs and carry the same privileges and guarantees as the debentures mentioned in the said twelfth section of the above cited act.

12. All the debentures issued under the present act Term of shall be redeemable within a period not exceeding thirty debentures. years from the date of the issuing thereof respectively, and shall bear interest at a rate not exceeding six per Interest. cent *per annum*, payable half yearly, and shall be signed Signed. by the mayor, city clerk and city treasurer, and under the seal of the corporation, and the payment of the said debentures and interest thereon shall be guaranteed by a sinking fund of one and a half per cent, on the amount of debentures issued, to be taken every year on or before the first of january by the city treasurer out of the annual revenues from the other funds of the corporation, and before the payment of any other appropriation whatsoever of the said revenues or funds, as more fully set forth in the twentieth section of the said act 38 Vict., chap. 74, which said section as well as the sections eighteen, twenty-one and twenty-two shall apply, *mutanda mutandis* to the debentures issued under the present act.

13. The said sum of two hundred and eighty one Such sums thousand dollars, amount of debentures to be issued form part of under the present act, shall form part of the consolidated dated fund. fund of the city of Quebec, created in virtue of the 11th section of the act 38 Vict., chap. 74.

14. The first section of the present act shall be con- Interpreta- sidered as forming part of the act 32 Vict., chap. 16, which tion. it amends.

15. And the sections 2, 3, 4, 5 and 6 of this act Idem. shall be considered as forming part of the act 35 Vict., chapter 12, which they amend.

16. And the sections 9, 10, 11, 12 and 13 of this act Idem. shall be considered as forming part of the act 38 Vict., chapter 74, which they amend.

Votes of two-thirds required. **17.** The item of seventy thousand dollars to establish a street parallel and to the north of St. Paul street, shall only be expended upon the vote of two-thirds of the council present; and the said street shall only be opened upon the same vote.

Interpretation. **18.** The present act shall be considered as forming but one and the same act with the acts hereby amended.

SCHEDULE A.

To amount authorized by Act 38 Vict., chap. 74..	$ 1,085,000 00
" expenses on sale of debentures, &c...	45,000 00
" amount required to introduce water in several streets................................	20,000 00
	$1,100,000 00

SCHEDULE B.

To amount authorized by act 38 Vict., chap. 74	$1,940,000 00
" enlargement of Jacques Cartier Market	20,000 00
" amount required to pave Cul-de-Sac street to Champlain street.............	11,000 00
" amount required to pave St. Paul street to St. Joseph street..........	20,000 00
" amount required to pave St Joseph street to Crown street.................	24,000 00
" complete Mountain Hill, Des Sœurs and Dalhousie streets.................	15,000 00
" amount to pave the street parallel and north of St. Paul street..............	70,000 00
" prolongation of Durham Terrace and the improvements suggested by Lord Dufferin..........................	40,000 00
" amount required to meet the expenses of widening Champlain street..	10,000 00
" amount required for macadamizing St. John street, from Sutherland street to toll gate	6,000 00
	$2,156,000 00

CAP. LII.

An Act to amend the acts concerning the Corporation
of the City of Montreal.

[Assented to 24th December, 1875.]

WHEREAS the corporation of the city of Montreal has Preamble,
by its petition represented that it is necessary, in the
interest of the citizens of the said city, to make certain amendments to its acts of incorporation, and to introduce certain
changes in the municipal administration of the said city;
Therefore, Her Majesty, by and with the advice and consent
of the Legislature of Quebec, enacts as follows :

TAXES AND CONTRIBUTIONS.

1. The seventy-eighth section of the act of the legislature s. 78, 37 v., c.
of this province, passed in the 37th year of Her Majesty's 5, replaced.
reign, chapter 51, is hereby repealed, and the following section substituted in its stead :

" 78. The said council may pass and promulgate a by-law Power to
or by-laws for the following purposes : make by-laws

1. To impose and levy an annual assessment on all real for:
property liable to taxation in the said city, or upon the owners Taxes on
or occupiers thereof, such assessment not to exceed one and a ties.
quarter per cent of the assessed value of such property ;

2. To impose and levy an annual tax (to be called " the Business tax.
business tax ") on hotel or tavern-keepers, brewers, distillers,
merchants, traders, manufacturers, banks, bankers, brokers
and money lenders, auctioneers, grocers, bakers, butchers,
hucksters, pawnbrokers, livery-stable keepers, tanners, inspectors of ashes, pork, beef, flour, butter or other produce,
or the agents thereof; on railway, telegraph, insurance,
steamboat, or steamship companies, or their agents, doing
business in the said city ; on proprietors or managers of
theatres, billiard rooms, ball alleys or other like games ;—and
generally on all trades, manufactories, occupations, business,
arts, professions or means of profits or livelihood, whether hereinbefore enumerated or not, which now are or may
hereafter be carried on, exercised, or in operation in the said
city ; provided that such business tax shall not exceed seven
and a half per cent on the annual value of the premises occupied by the said parties in the said city, in which they carry
on or exercise such trades, manufactures, occupations, business, arts, professions or means of profit or livelihood ;

3. To impose and levy an annual tax on pedlars and Business tax.
carters doing business in the said city ; on owners of horses,
vehicles and dogs in the said city ; on brokers, money-
lenders or commission merchants ; on pawnbrokers and auctioneers; on inn-keepers, brewers and distillers ; on theatres,
circuses, menageries and minstrels ; on billiard tables ; on
livery-stable keepers ; and on ferrymen or steamboat ferries,
plying for hire for the conveyance of travellers to the city,
from any place not more than nine miles distant from the

Proviso.

same ; provided such tax do not exceed those respectively imposed in the year one thousand eight hundred and seventy-four ;

Statute labor.

4. To fix the amount of the commutation money payable each year, by each person liable to statute labour on the highways in the said city, not to exceed one dollar ; and to compel every person, so liable, to pay the amount of such commutation money so fixed, without his being allowed to offer his personal labour on the said highways instead thereof ;

Tax on fire insurances.

5. To impose and levy an annual tax on fire insurance companies doing business in the city of Montreal, not to exceed four hundred dollars for each such company ;

Id. life and marine insurances, &c.

Proviso.

6. To impose and levy an annual tax not exceeding two hundred dollars on every life, marine, accident or guarantee insurance companies doing business and taking risks in the city of Montreal ; provided that when any insurance company combines two or more branches of any kind of insurance, but one tax only shall be levied upon such company, that is to say, the tax, the rate of which is the highest on the said branches of insurance respectively ;

Idem on banks.

7. To impose and levy an annual tax not exceeding four hundred dollars on every bank doing business in the said city, with a paid up capital of one million dollars or less; an annual tax not exceeding five hundred dollars on every such bank the paid up capital of which is more than one million, but does not exceed two million dollars, and a tax not exceeding six hundred dollars on every such bank the paid up capital of which is above two million dollars ;

Idem on gas companies.

8. To impose and levy upon all gas companies doing business in the city of Montreal, an annual tax not to exceed five thousand dollars, and no other tax or assessment can be imposed upon all such companies, save and except such as may be imposed on the immoveable property of all such companies ; but in no case shall the city of Montreal be held as having the right to impose a tax or assessment on the pipes laid in the streets."

Interpretation of s. 78 of 37 V., c. 51

2. The present act shall be read and interpreted as if section 78 of the 37th Vict., cap. 51 had not been repealed in so far as it relates to the Montreal city passenger railway company, and section one of the present act shall not apply to any such company.

S. 72 of 37 V., c. 51, replaced.

Mode of assessing.

3. Section 72 of the said act 37 Vict., cap. 51, is hereby repealed and the following substituted in its stead :

"72. The assessors in assessing real property in the said city shall take as the base of their assessment the actual value of such property at the time of making the assessment ; they shall moreover specify and include in the assessment roll the *bonâ fide* rent of such property ; and if the same be occupied by, or in the possession of the owner thereof, the assessors shall determine the rent of such property, according to the amount at which, in their judgment, the said property might be rented, or ought to produce, if it were rented."

4. If upon action taken in pursuance of sub-section 21 of section 176 of the 37th Vict., cap. 51, the compensation awarded by the commissioners be augmented, it shall be lawful for the corporation of the city, in cases where the whole or any part of the cost of the improvement is to be paid by the proprietors interested, to cause a supplementary assessment to be made to cover such increase of compensation, by following the formalities prescribed by law. *Supplementary tax in certain cases.*

5. The sub-section one of section 185 of the said act (37 Victoria, cap. 51) is hereby amended by striking out the word " shall," in the fifth line of the proviso in the said sub-section, and substituting the following words in its stead: " may, at their discretion, follow the former mode of assessment or." *Ss. 1 of s. 185 37 V., c. 51, amended.*

MISCELLANEOUS.

6. And whereas the commissioners appointed by one of the judges of the superior court for the district of Montreal, to appraise the value of the lands to be expropriated for the widening of St. Mary street, between Papineau square and the city limits, and for the extension of St. Catherine street, from Dufresne street to the eastern city limits of the said city, and to apportion and assess the cost or part of the cost of the said improvements upon the real property benefitted, have committed an error by taking as the basis of the assessment the actual value of such real property, exclusive of the buildings thereon erected, instead of taking as such basis the value of such real property as specified and established in and by the general roll of assessment of the said city last made and revised, as required by the above cited act ; and whereas the said error cannot but be highly detrimental to the interests of the said city if not rectified, and it is urgent, in the interest of the public, in consequence of the large sums which the corporation of the said city have advanced and deposited in the above cited cases, that new rolls of assessment be made with the least possible delay, in order that the said corporation may be in a position to re-imburse themselves the sums so advanced and deposited,—it is hereby declared and enacted, that the two rolls of assessment and apportionment aforesaid made and completed by the said commissioners, that is to say; that of St. Mary street, on the nineteenth of february last and that of St. Catherine street, on the tenth june last—are null and void, and that it shall be lawful for the corporation of the said city, to cause a new assessment and apportionment of two-thirds of the cost of each of the said improvements to be made by following the mode prescribed in and by section 187 of the said act 37 Vict., chap. 51, upon the real property which the new commissioners shall adjudge and declare to have been interested in and benefitted by the said improvements respectively, and according to the valuation of the said property as established in and by the general roll of *Certain assessment rolls rendered null.* *Right to proceed to a new assessment.*

Pending cases.

assessment of the said city, for the year one thousand eight hundred and seventy four; provided however, that it shall be lawful for the court before which actions are now pending based upon such error, to award costs at its discretion.

S. 192, 37 V., c. 51, amended.

Sidewalks.

7. The section 192 of the said act, 37 Vict., cap. 51, is hereby amended by striking out the words "flag-stone or asphalte sidewalks" in the second and third lines thereof, and substituting the following in their stead " sidewalks made of stone or asphalte, or both together, or of any other durable and permanent material to the exclusion of wood."

Loan.

8. It shall not be lawful for the corporation of the said city to effect any loan of money beyond the amount which it is authorized to borrow under sections 106, 114 and 120 of the said act 37 Vict., cap. 51, unless such loan shall have been previously submitted to and approved of by a majority of the owners of real property in the said city, in the manner and form specified in the said section 120 of the said act *mutatis mutandis.*

Approval required.

Construction of private drains.

9. The council of the said city is hereby authorized to regulate, by by-law, with the usual penalty, the time when private drains to be used for draining property in the said city shall be made, as also the manner and material with which the same shall be constructed, and to enact that such private drains shall be made by the corporation of the said city, from the line of the street to the common or public sewer, and to assess the cost of the same on the owners of such private property respectively.

Supp'y of water by gravitation.

10. The corporation of the said city is authorized to cause a survey to be made in any adjoining municipality with a view to ascertain the feasibility of obtaining for the said city, its supply of water by gravitation; and for that purpose to enter, by its officers or engineers, upon the lands of private individuals, free of charge and without the latter having the right to claim any indemnity except for actual damage caused.

Interpretation of the word "parsonages."

11. The word "parsonages" in the third section of the act of the legislature of this province, 88 Vict., cap. 73, shall apply to any house occupied as a residence by the officiating priest or minister of any church in the said city, either as proprietor or tenant; provided however, that but one parsonage for each church in the said city shall have the benefit of the exemption provided for, in the last cited section.

Lithographed receipts.

12. In all cases, proceedings or instances before the superior or circuit court wherein it is intended to prove the payment of municipal taxes or assessments in the said city, the production of lithographed or stamped receipts, as given in the office of the city treasurer, shall be held and taken as *primâ facie* evidence, of the payment of such taxes or assessments.

13. In cases of *saisie-arrêts* issued in the hands of the cor- Case of *saisie-* poration of the said city, it shall be lawful for the treasurer of *arrêts.* the said city to deposit in the *greffe* of the court from whence such *saisie-arrêts* shall have so issued, the sum of money which he may have in hand belonging or owing to the defendant, that the said sum may be paid to whom it may appertain, as the court shall order.

14. Sections one and three of the present act shall be Interpreta held as forming part of the said act 37 Vict., chap 51, tion. which they amend.

15. The present act shall be held as forming but one and Idem. the same act with the acts which it amends.

16. This act shall come into force immediately after its Act in force. sanction.

CAP. LIII.

An Act further to amend " The Quebec Railway Act, 1869," (32 Vict., chap. 51.)

[Assented to 24th December, 1875.]

HER MAJESTY, by and with the advice and consent of the Legislature of Quebec, enacts as follows:—

1. Paragraph twenty-eight of section nine of " The ¶28, s. 9, of Quebec Railway Act, 1869," is amended by the addition 32 Vict., c. 51, amended. of the words following : " But ten days previous notice of the time and place when and where application will be made for its granting, shall be served upon the owner of the land or upon the party empowered to convey the Notice land, or interested in the land to be taken or required by required in the company ; and the costs of the application to, and of case of expro priation. the hearing before the judge, shall be borne by the com- Costs of the pany, whenever the compensation awarded shall be more application. than they had declared their readiness to pay ; provided Proviso. however, that when such owner or party is absent from the district without having a known agent upon whom such service can be made, or when such owner or party is unknown, application for such warrant may be made at any time after the expiration of the month's notice mentioned in paragraph thirteen without any other or further notice."

CAP. LIV.

An act to change the name of " the Philipsburg, Farnham and Yamaska Railway Company" to that of "The Lake Champlain and St. Lawrence Junction Railway Company," and to allow the company to · change its line of road.

[*Assented to 24th December,* 1875.]

Preamble.

WHEREAS " the Philipsburg, Farnham and Yamaska Railway Company, a body politic and incorporated under an act of the legislature of the province of Quebec, to wit, chapter 31, of 35th Victoria, has, by its petition, prayed to be authorized to change its name, and to make certain changes in the line of its road to the north of the city of St. Hyacinthe, and whereas it is expedient to grant the prayer of the petition; Therefore, Her Majesty, by and with the advice and consent of the Legislature of Quebec, enacts as follows:

Former name, changed.

New name

Rights not affected.

Suits, &c.

1. The name of the said Philipsburg, Farnham and Yamaska Railway Company, is hereby changed to that of " The Lake Champlain and St. Lawrence Junction Railway Company," which name shall be and subsist instead of that up to this time belonging to the said company; but such change of name shall in no manner be interpreted as modifying or affecting any of the rights of the said company, or any of its obligations, or any suit, action, or proceeding pending or had at the time when the present act shall come into force, but all such rights and obligations shall subsist as if the present act had not been passed; and all such suits, actions or proceedings shall continue as if this act had not been passed; but any new proceedings which may hereafter be instituted either by or against the said company, shall be in the name assigned to it by the present act.

Certain line, not obligatory.

Power to make another.

Proviso :

2. The said company shall not be obliged to build the road to the north of the city of St. Hyacinthe, over the properties and at the places shown on the charts, plans or books of reference already made for that part of the road to the north of the said city, and now deposited in the office of the department of public works, but it may adopt such other line, as it may deem convenient, within the limits of the counties of St. Hyacinthe, Bagot, Drummond, Richelieu, Yamaska and Nicolet, provided that the northern and southern termini of the line be not changed, and provided also, that new plans, charts or books of reference, for that part of the road, be prepared and deposited as required by law, and the same shall be substituted to the first for all lawful purposes, and the properties that shall be designated on the new plans, charts and books of reference may be expropriated in the manner provided by the railway Act of 1869 and its amendments.

3. The present act shall come into force on the day of Act in force. the sanction thereof.

CAP. LV.

An Act further to amend the acts relating to the Stanstead, Shefford and Chambly 'Railroad Company.

[*Assented to 24th December*, 1875.]

WHEREAS the Stanstead, Shefford and Chambly Preamble. Railroad company have petitioned the legislature for certain amendments to their act of incorporation and the other acts relating thereto, and inasmuch as the said railroad has been completed and in good working order, as far as the village of Waterloo, in the township of Shefford, and the company are using their utmost efforts to reach the terminus originally proposed, either alone or with the corporation of the Waterloo and Magog railway company, which was incorporated, in the year 1871, it is expedient to grant the prayer of their petition ; Therefore, Her Majesty, by and with the advice and consent of the Legislature of Quebec, enacts as follows :

1. Notwithstanding anything in the act passed in the Provisions of 32nd year of Her Majesty's reign, chap. 61, or in any other acts, continued. act contained, and the non-completion of the said rail- road within the period limited by the said last mentioned act, the corporate existence and powers of the said Stanstead, Shefford and Chambly railroad company shall be held to have continued, and shall continue in full force and effect, and all proceedings taken and Proceedings things done by the said company, and the directors and declared good officers thereof, within the limits assigned to them by and valid. the said act of incorporation and other acts relating thereto, shall be held good and valid ; provided the said railroad be completed and put in operation within Delay extend- ten years after the passing of this act. ed.

2. Notwithstanding anything contained in the said act Time of the of incorporation, or in any other act, the next general general meeting of shareholders of the said company, for the elec- meetings of tion of directors, and for the transaction of the general holders.

business thereof, shall be held on the second wednesday
in november next, after the passing of this act, and
thence annually on the second wednesday in november
in each year thereafter; public notices of such annual
general meeting shall be given, and the election shall be
held in the manner provided by the said act of incorporation.

CAP. LVI.

An Act to amend the act incorporating the Montreal,
Portland and Boston Railway Company.

[*Assented to 24th December*, 1875.]

Preamble. WHEREAS the Montreal, Portland and Boston Railway Company have by their petition represented
that it is desirable to amend their act of incorporation,
and that it is expedient to grant their prayer; Therefore,
Her Majesty, by and with the advice and consent of the
Legislature of Quebec, enacts as follows :

Delay extended. 1. The time for completion of the works of the railway
is extended to two years from the passing of this act.

35 V., c. 29, s. 15, amended. 2. The following words in the fifteenth section of the
act incorporating the Montreal, Chambly and Sorel Rail-
way Company, 35 Vict., cap. 29, are struck out, to wit :
" the whole under pain of loss and deprivation of all the
rights conferred upon them by this act."

Issue of preferential debentures. 3. The directors of the said company shall have the
power to issue preferential bonds or debentures, signed by
the president or the vice-president of the said company,
and countersigned by the secretary and treasurer, or the
secretary-treasurer, as the case may be and under the seal
of the said company, for the purpose of completing and
equipping their railway, and such bonds or debentures
Privilege thereof. shall be and be considered to be first privileged claims
upon the property and rolling stock of the said company,
and shall bear a first mortgage or hypothec upon the said
railway, lands, bridges, buildings, and rolling stock, and
such preferential bonds or debentures shall form a first
charge on the tolls and income of the company, and
shall take precedence and priority over all or any of the
bonds or debentures already issued by the said company,
but no such bonds or debentures shall be issued without
Consent required. the consent in writing, first having been obtained from
the holders of all and every the first and second
mortgages, bonds or debentures which have heretofore
been issued by the said company, provided always that
the amount of such bonds or debentures hereby author-

ized to be issued, shall not exceed eight thousand dollars Proviso. per mile.

4. The board of directors shall hereafter be composed Number of of not less than seven and not more than nine members. the directors.

5. This act shall come into force immediately after its Act in force. sanction.

CAP. LVII.

An Act to further amend "the act incorporating the Levis and Kennebec Railway Company."

[Assented to 24th December, 1875.]

WHEREAS the Levis and Kennebec Railway Com- Preamble. pany have prayed, that the act to amend their act of incorporation be amended in the particulars hereinafter set forth, and it is expedient to grant their prayer ; and whereas it appears that a total length of forty-five miles of the company's line having been completed, a first and second issue each of one hundred thousand pounds of the company's debentures have been made, each of 'such issues consisting of one thousand debentures of one hundred pounds sterling each ; and whereas, since the passing of the said amended act, the subsidy granted by the provincial legislature has been increased to four thousand dollars per mile, and that further subsidies are about to be granted by various municipalities through which the line passes, thus providing a considerable portion of the amount required for the completion of the earthworks and bridges on the forty-five miles of lines remaining to be completed ; and whereas, to ensure the speedy completion of the said forty-five miles now incomplete, it is expedient that the rails and fastenings required should be provided without delay ; Her Majesty, by and with the advice and consent of the Legislature of Quebec, enacts as follows :

1. The following words in the twenty-second, twenty- 37 V., c. 23. third, twenty-fourth, twenty-fifth, twenty-sixth, twenty- amended. seventh, twenty-eighth, twenty-ninth and thirtieth lines in the first section of thirty-seven Victoria, chapter twenty-three, to wit : " And no more of such bonds shall be issued by the company until seventy-five miles of the said road (inclusive of the aforesaid forty-five miles) shall be complete and in running order as certified by the government inspecting engineer, and so soon as such seventy-five miles shall have been certified as completed and in running order as aforesaid, then the remaining one thousand bonds of one hundred pounds sterling each, to be termed the third issue, may be issued by the company." are struck out and the following are substituted therefor : " And so soon as the rails and fastenings required for the completion of the remaining forty-five miles or thereabouts of the company's line shall have been provided, then the remaining one thousand bonds of one hundred pounds sterling each, to be termed the third issue, may be issued by the company."

Time of the third issue.

CAP. LVIII.

An Act to grant to the " Union Navigation Company," incorporated by letters patent, a new charter of incorporation, with more extended powers.

[Assented to 24th December, 1875.

Preamble.

WHEREAS by letters patent issued under the great seal of the province, by order of His Excellency the lieutenant-governor in council, on the 6th august, 1874, a company having for its object the business of forwarding goods, the carrying of passengers, the building, owning, freighting and hiring of vessels, steamboats, wharves, roads and other things necessary for the purposes of the said company in this province, has been formed and incorporated in virtue of the provisions of the act concerning the incorporation of joint stock companies (31 Vict., chap. 25) ; whereas the said company having purchased vessels and other things necessary for its purposes, has been in operation and carried on business during two consecutive years, having established a new line of steamers between Quebec and Montreal ; whereas the president and the directors of the said company, after having caused to be subscribed by the shareholders of the said company the sum of $175,000 in the capital stock thereof, have represented that there remains a balance of $125,000 of the authorized capital stock of the said company, which has not yet been subscribed, that the said balance is indispensable for the operations of the said company, and that the present shareholders, consulted at a general meeting, were unanimously of opinion that it would be advisable, to the end that this balance of capital be more promptly subscribed, to authorize the said company to issue preferential shares to the amount of $125,000 currency ; and whereas the success of this new subscription would be better assured if the said company were incorporated by special and public charter recognizing their legal existence and granting in addition to the powers now possessed by them, the power to issue the said preferential shares ; and whereas it is expedient

to accede to the prayer of the said petition ; Therefore,
Her Majesty, by and with the advice and consent of the
Legislature of Quebec, enacts as follows :

1. The said " Union Navigation Company " and all the Corporation
present members and shareholders thereof, their succes- recognised
sors and assigns for ever, are by the present act recog- and consti-
nized to have been and are constituted into a corpora- Place of busi-
tion under his aforesaid name, having its principal place ness.
of business or office in the city of Montreal.

2. The said company has had and shall have the power Powers of the
of carrying on the business of forwarding goods and of company.
carrying passengers within the limits of this province,
and for this purpose the said company is authorized in
the prosecution of all matters within the scope of that
business, and to build, own, freight or hire all vessels,
steamers, wharves, roads or other things necessary for
the purposes of the said company.

3. The capital stock of the said company is and shall Capital stock.
be $300,000 divided into six thousand shares of $50 each.

4. The directors of the said company are hereby Preferential
authorized to issue for the balance of $125,000 of the said Stock.
hitherto unsubscribed capital stock, preferential shares,
conferring on the holders and proprietors thereof the privilege of receiving an annual dividend of eight per cent,
to be taken out of the net profits of the said company,
before the holders of the other shares of the said company can have and receive any dividend whatever ; pro- Proviso.
vided also that the said preferential shares shall not issue
or be made, until a by-law to that effect shall have been
adopted by two-thirds in value of the share-holders present Consent re-
or represented at a general meeting specially convened quired.
for the purpose of considering the same.

5. As soon as such dividend of eight per cent, granted Payment of
to the preferential shares, shall have been taken out of dividends.
the net profits realised by the company, the surplus of
the said profits shall be employed by the directors in Use of the
the payment of a dividend (at a rate to be by them fixed), surplus of the
upon the other shares of the company, but such dividend profits.
shall in no case exceed that of the preferential shares, and
if the profits realized by the company permit the directors
to pay a larger dividend than eight per cent, as well
upon the preferential as the ordinary shares, such dividend shall then be equal upon these different shares ;
but nothing shall prevent the directors, after the payment
of the dividend of eight per cent, upon the preferential
shares, from reserving each year out of the profits, a

13

Reserve in case of unforseen expenses.
reasonable sum to meet losses, accidents, unforseen expenses, &c.

Use of the sum subscribed.
6. The total amount of the sums subscribed for the said preferential shares, to wit, up to the said sum of $125,000, shall be exclusively employed by the directors of the said company either in repairing the steamers now owned by them or in building new ones.

Suit and transfer.
7. The said company may require and recover payment of the said preferential shares in the same manner, and with the same formalities as in respect of the payment of the ordinary shares, and the sale and transfer of the said shares shall be effected in the same manner as that of ordinary shares.

Investment of property.
8. All the moveable and immoveable property, assets and liabilities, rights and obligations generally of the said " Union Navigation Company," shall remain vested in the said company recognized and incorporated as aforesaid, under the same name, and shall continue to be held and prosecuted for, by, or against the said company, and thereto to belong for all lawful purposes, as if the present act had not been passed ; and all proceedings commenced by the said company may be continued without any change whatever.

Actual directors, officers and by-laws, continued.
9. The present president, directors and officers of the said " Union Navigation Company," shall remain in office for the said company, until they are replaced in conformity with the by-laws of the said company.

In a similar manner the present by-laws of the said company shall continue in force until they are modified, changed or repealed by the said company.

Interpretation.
10. All the provisions of the act 31 Victoria, chap. 25, which are not inconsistent with this act, shall be deemed to be incorporated therewith and shall form part thereof.

Act in force.
11. The present act shall come into force on the day of its sanction.

CAP. LIX.

An Act to amend the Act incorporating the Richelieu river hydraulic and manufacturing company.

[Assented to 24th December, 1875.]

HER MAJESTY, by and with the advice and consent of the Legislature of Quebec, enacts as follows:

1. The following words in the second section of the act 36 V., c. 74, s. of this province, 36 Vict., cap. 74, " provided that the 2, amended. lands so to be taken for the canals and for the ditches on either side thereof, and for such road or roads, shall not exceed six hundred feet, english measure, in width," shall be and the same are hereby struck out and omitted.

2. Section ten is hereby amended so as to read, instead S. 10. amend-of the words " after the whole capital stock of the com- ed. pany shall have been allotted or paid in," as follows : " after the whole capital stock of the company shall have been subscribed and one-fourth thereof paid in."

3. Section thirteen is hereby amended by adding after S. 13, amend-the words : " under the hand of the president," the words ed. " or vice-president."

4. Section fourteen is hereby amended by adding after S. 14, amend-the words : " support of the government," the words, ed. " and in default of payment of such forfeiture or penalty and the costs within fifteen days, from the rendering of the judgment, the person condemned may be imprisoned Imprison-for any time, not less than fifteen days and not exceeding ment. two months, which imprisonment, however, shall end on payment of the said sum."

5. Section fifteen of the said act is hereby repealed, and S. 15 replaced the following enacted in lieu thereof: " The powers granted to the company shall wholly cease, if their works Delay fixed. are not commenced within five years from the passing of this amending act."

6. The joint stock companies general clauses act shall General apply to and form a part of this act, except in so far as it clauses act is in contradiction to or inconsistent with any of the pro- shall apply. visions of this act, or of the act hereby amended, with the exception of clauses 32 and 39 thereof, the same not being applicable to this act, and the act hereby amended.

CAP. LX.

An Act to incorporate " the Patriotic Insurance Company of Canada."

[*Assented to 24th December,* 1875.]

WHEREAS Thomas Simpson, Angus R. Bethume, Preamble James P. Clark, Michael P. Ryan, Édouard J. Barbeau and Antoine A. Trottier, of Montreal, have petitioned for an act to incorporate them and others under

the name of "The Patriotic Insurance Company of
Canada," to enable them to carry on the business of Life
Insurance and Fire and Marine Insurance, and whereas
it has been considered advisable to grant the prayer of
the said petition ; Therefore, Her Majesty, by and with
the advice and consent of the Legislature of Quebec,
enacts as follows :

Incorporation.

1. The said parties and all other person and persons,
firm and firms and bodies politic, as shall from time to
time be possessed of any share or shares of the stock of the
said company, are hereby constituted and shall be a body

Name.

politic and corporate by the name of " the Patriotic Insurance Company of Canada," and by that name shall

General
powers.

have perpetuity and a common seal, with power to make
and alter such seal, and by that name may sue and be
sued, plead and be impleaded in all courts whatever.

Capital stock.

2. The capital stock of the said company shall be one
million of dollars, divided into ten thousand shares of one

Subscriptions

hundred dollars each, and books of subscription shall be
opened in the city of Montreal and elsewhere, at the discretion of the directors, and shall remain open so long as
and in the manner that they shall deem proper, after
giving public notice thereof for such period as the said
directors shall deem advisable, and such shares are hereby vested in the several persons, firms or corporations
who shall subscribe for the same, and their legal representatives and assigns, subject to the provisions of this
act ;

Increase of
the capital
stock.

Provided always that it shall be lawful for the said
company to increase its capital stock from time to time,
to a sum not exceeding the further sum of two millions
of dollars, or such portion thereof as the majority of the
stock-holders, at a meeting to be specially convened for
that purpose shall agree to.

Subscription.

3. It shall be lawful for any person or persons, firm or
body politic to subscribe for such and so many shares as
he shall or they may see fit ; five per cent shall be paid
at the time of subscription, five per cent in three months
thereafter, and the remainder shall be payable in such

Instalments.
Proviso.

instalments as the majority of the directors may determine upon ; provided always that no instalment shall be
called for nor be payable, in less than fifteen days after
public notice, given in two newspapers, english and
french, as the directors may direct.

Neglect to
pay instalments.

4. If any stockholder or stockholders, as aforesaid, shall
refuse or neglect to pay the instalment due upon any
share or shares held by him, her or them at the time required so to do, he, she or they shall *ipso facto* be and

become further liable to the payment to the company of interest on the amount of the unpaid call, from the date fixed for the payment of the same, at the rate of seven per cent per annum.

And the directors may declare such share or shares as aforesaid to be forfeited, together with the amount previously paid thereon, and such forfeited share or shares may be sold at a public sale by the said directors, after such notice as they may direct ; and the moneys arising therefrom shall be applied for the purposes of this act ; provided always that in case the money produced by any sale of shares, be more than sufficient to pay all arrears and interest, together with the expenses of such sale, the surplus money shall be paid on demand to the owner. *Forfeiture of shares. Use of the products of the sale. Proviso.*

5. Provided always that the company may, if the directors think proper, enforce payment of all calls and interest thereon, with costs of suit by action in any competent court ; and in such action it shall not be necessary to set forth the special matter, but it shall be sufficient for the company to declare that the defendant is a holder of one share or more, stating the number of shares, and is indebted in the sum of money to which the calls in arrear amount, in respect of one call or more on one share or more, stating the number of calls and the amount of each, whereby an action has accrued to the company to recover the same with interest for non-payment, and a certificate under the seal of the company, and purporting to be signed by one of its officers, to the effect that the defendant is a share-holder, that such call or calls has or have been made, and that so much is due by him, shall be received in all courts of law as *primâ facie* evidence to that effect. *Suits for recovery of the instalments. Certificates of the company received as evidence.*

6. A copy of any by-law, rule, regulation or minute, or of any entry in any book of the company certified to be a true copy or extract under the hand of the president or the vice-president, or the manager or secretary of the company, and sealed with the corporate seal, shall be received in all courts and proceedings as *primâ facie* evidence of such by-law, rule, regulation, minute or entry, without further proof and without proof of the official character or signature of the officer signing the same, or of the corporate seal. *Authenticity of the by-laws, books, &c.*

7. The company shall have power to make and effect contracts of life insurance with any person or persons, and to carry on the business of life insurance in all branches and modes of conducting the same, and on any plan or principle as the board of directors may determine and direct, and generally to enter into any transaction depend- *Life insurances.*

ent upon the contingency of life, and all other transactions usually entered into by life insurance companies;
Fire.   and shall also have the power and authority to effect contracts of insurance against loss by fire, or the perils of the sea and inland navigation, subject, however, to the provisions hereinafter mentioned, and the said company shall also have power to cause themselves to be insured against
Risks.   any loss or risk they may have incurred in the course of their business, and generally to do and perform all other necessary matters and things connected with and necessary to promote their objects.

Agencies and   **8.** For any or all of the purposes aforesaid, it shall be
local board of   lawful for the directors to establish agencies and local
directors.   board of directors for the carrying on of the business of the company, at any place it may be deemed advisable by the board of directors, and to appoint from time to time and to remove such agencies and local boards, as they in their discretion may deem advantageous, and to remunerate such agents and local boards, and to invest them with such powers as may be deemed necessary.

Commence-   **9.** It shall be lawful for the said company, so soon as
ment of the   one hundred thousand dollars shall have been subscribed,
business.   and twenty thousand dollars of that amount paid in, to carry on the business of life insurance ; and that as soon as a further sum of two hundred and fifty thousand dollars shall have been subscribed, and of the latter amount fifty thousand dollars paid in, the said company shall also be authorized to carry on the business of fire and
Separation of   marine insurance ; provided always, that before such bu-
the business.   siness of fire and marine insurance shall be commenced, separate books of accounts shall be opened and kept for all transactions connected with the said business of fire and marine insurance ; and further that the fund pertaining to the branch of life insurance shall be vested in trustees, not less than three in number, to be chosen by the directors, to be held by the said trustees for the benefit of life
Funds deri-   policy holders, and that all funds derivable from the life
vable from   branch shall be under the control of the said trustees, and
the life   be kept distinct and separate from the funds derivable
branch.   from the other branches of fire and marine insurance, and shall not in any way be held with or attached in any manner, for any liabilities incurred in either the fire and
Commence-   marine branches ; provided also, that ten directors may in
ment of the   the first instance carry on the business of fire and marine
business.   insurance so soon as the sum of two hundred and fifty thousand dollars has been subscribed, and fifty thousand thereof paid in ; and may afterwards carry on the business of life insurance if a further sum of one hundred thousand dollars has been subscribed, of which twenty thousand dollars is paid in, subject however to the provi-

sions above mentioned as to the appointment of trustees, the keeping of separate books for such life insurance business, and the vesting of the funds in such trustees for the exclusive benefit of life policy holders.

10. The said company shall have power to acquire and hold for the purposes of its business such real estate in the province of Quebec, to sell the same and buy others, as the directors may deem expedient; and the said company, in addition to the above mentioned real estate, may purchase and hold such other real estate on which it may hold mortgages or hypothecs, which may be brought to a forced sale; or it may take any real estate, with the approval of the majority of the directors, in payment of any debt due to it in the course of its legitimate business; but the said company shall sell such real estate, either so purchased or so taken in payment, and not acquired for offices or for the purposes of its business, as above provided, within five years after the same shall have been acquired. *Right to acquire properties, &c.* *Proviso.*

11. It shall be lawful for the said company to invest its funds in the debentures, bonds, stocks or other securities of the Dominion of Canada, or in the securities of any of the provinces comprising the Dominion, or in the securities of any municipal corporation in the Dominion, or in stocks of banks or building societies incorporated in Canada, or in stocks or debentures of companies incorporated in Canada, or to loan its funds on the security of such stocks, bonds or debentures, or on hypothecs or mortgages on real estate in the Dominion of Canada, or on its life policies to the extent of their surrender value, and it shall have power from time to time to dispose of such stocks, bonds or debentures and hypothecs, and replace them by others at the discretion of the directors. *Investment of the funds of the company in public stocks.*

12. The property, affairs and concerns of the said company shall be managed and conducted by a board of directors to consist of not less than five and not more than nine incorporators, as may be determined by the provisional board of directors hereinafter named, one of whom shall be chosen president and one vice-president by them, and they shall fix the quorum and procedure of their meetings; which boards in the first instance and until replaced by others, shall consist of Thomas Simpson, Angus R. Bethune, James P. Clark, Michael P. Ryan, Edouard J. Barbeau and Antoine A. Trottier, all of the city and district of Montreal. *Board of directors.* *President and vice-president.* *Provisional directors.*

13. The principal offices of the company shall be in the city of Montreal. *Place of business.*

General meetings.

Notice.

First election of the directors.

14. The said provisional directors may call a general meeting of the share-holders at some place, to be named, in the city of Montreal, a previous notice of ten days being given to such share-holders by mail, viz., such notice prepaid in the post office at Montreal to the address of such share-holders, at which general meeting the share-holders present in person or by proxy, shall elect not less than five, nor more than nine directors in the manner and qualified as hereinafter provided, who shall constitute a board of directors, and shall hold office until the annual general meeting in the year following the election.

General annual meetings.

Statement of the affairs.

Election.

Qualification.

15. The annual general meeting of the shareholders shall be held at such time as may be determined by the board of directors, at which meeting shall be submitted a statement of the affairs of the company. The annual election of directors shall take place at this meeting by ballot, which shall be kept open from two to three o'clock of the said afternoon, at the expiration of which time it shall be closed, and when so closed no person shall have a right to vote on any pretence whatever, and the persons who shall have the greatest number of votes at any such election shall be directors, except as hereinafter directed; and if any two or more persons have an equal number of votes, in such a manner that a greater number of persons than the requisite number shall appear to be chosen as directors, then the directors who shall have the greater number of votes or a majority of them, shall determine which of the said persons so having an equal number of votes shall be the director or directors so as to complete the whole number required; and no person shall be eligible to be, or shall continue as director, unless he shall hold in his name and for his own use, stock in the said company to the amount of twenty five shares, and shall have paid all calls made and due upon his stock.

Special meetings.

16. Special general meetings of the share-holders may be called for any day not a holiday, by order of the president, or in his absence of the vice-president, or on the requisition of share-holders representing one-fifth of the subscribed capital stock of the company; and on such requisition the directors shall be bound to call the meetings within the time specified therein,

Place of the general meetings.

Notices.

17. All general meetings of shareholders, whether for the annual election or special or other purpose, shall be held in such place in the city of Montreal, as the directors may select and indicate.

And notices of all such meetings shall be given by advertisement, during the ten days preceding the day fixed for the meeting in a daily english newspaper and a

daily french newspaper published in the city of Montreal.
The quorum at all such meetings shall consist of twelve Quorum.
shareholders duly qualified to vote. At all such general
meetings, whether for the annual election or for any other
purpose, each share-holder shall be entitled to give one
vote for every share held by him absolutely and in his Right to vote.
own name for not less than thirty days prior to the said
meeting, upon which all calls then due have been paid
up; such votes may be given in person or by proxy,
the holder of such proxy being himself a shareholder
qualified to vote; and all questions proposed for consideration shall be determined by the majority of votes, Decision.
the chairman presiding at such meeting having the casting
vote in case of an equality of votes.

18. In case it should at any time happen that an elec- Default of
tion of directors of said company should not be made on election.
the day appointed, it shall be lawfully held on any other
subsequent day appointed by the directors for the time
being; and they shall so continue in office until a new
election is made.

19. And if any vacancy should at any time happen Vacancy
amongst the said directors, such vacancy shall be filled amongst the
for the remainder of the year by the remaining directors directors.
or the majority of them electing in such place or places,
a shareholder or shareholders eligible for such ffioce.

20. Each share-holder shall be individually liable to Liability of
the creditors of the company, to an amount equal to the the share-
amount unpaid on the stock held by him for the debts holders.
and liabilities thereof, but no further; but shall not be
liable to an action therefor by any creditor before the
state of insolvency of the company be proved; and the Nature of the
shares shall be deemed personal estate. shares.

21. No transfer of any shares of the stock of the said Transfer of
company shall be valid until entered in the books of the shares.
said company, according to such form as may, from time
to time, be fixed by the directors; and until the whole of
the capital stock of the said company is paid up it shall be
necessary to obtain the consent of the directors to such
transfer being made,—provided that no transfer of stock
shall at any time be made until all calls due thereon have
been paid in.

22. The company shall not be bound to see to the ex- Execution of
ecution of any trust, whether express, implied or con- trusts.
structive in respect of any share, and the receipt of the
shareholder in whose name the same may stand in the
books of the company, shall be a valid and binding discharge to the company, for any dividend or money pay-

able in respect of such share, and his signature will suffice
for any transfer of such share or other thing concerning
such share, whether or not such notice of such trust shall
have been given the company ; •and the company shall
not be bound to see to the application of the money paid
upon such receipt or transfer.

Share of the holders in the profits.   **23.** It shall be lawful for the directors to return to the
holders of the policies or other instrument such part or
parts of the profits of the company in such parts, shares
and proportions, and at such times and in such manner,
as the said directors may deem advisable, and to enter
into obligations so to do, either by endorsement on the
policies or otherwise ;

Provided always that such holders of policies or other
instruments, shall not be held to be in any wise answerable for the debts or losses of the company, beyond the
amount of the premium or premiums which may have
been actually paid up by him, her or them.

Management of business.   **24.** The directors of the company shall have full power
in all things to administer the affairs of the company, and
may from time to time, if they deem advisable make by-
By-laws.   laws not contrary to law nor to this act, for the conduct
in all particulars of the affairs of the company and the remuneration of the directors, and may, from time to time,
repeal, amend or re-enact the same, but every such by-law
and every repeal, amendment or re-enactment thereof,
Approval.   unless in the meantime confirmed at a general meeting
of the company duly called for that purpose, shall only
have force until the next annual meeting of the company,
and in default of confirmation thereat shall at and from
that time only, cease to have force.

Transmission of shares, settled.   **25.** The transmission of the interest in any share of
the capital stock, in consequence of the marriage, death,
bankruptcy or insolvency of a shareholder, or by any
other lawful means than an ordinary transfer, shall be
authenticated and made in such form, by such proof, with
such formalities, and generally in such manner, as
the directors shall from time to time require, or by any by-
law may direct ; and in case the transmission of any
share of the capital stock of the company shall be by
Shares of married women.   virtue of the marriage of a female share-holder, it shall be
competent to include therein a declaration to the effect
that the share transmitted is the sole property, and under
the sole control of the wife, and that she may receive
and grant receipts for the dividends and profits accruing
in respect thereof, and dispose of and transfer the share
itself without requiring the consent or authority of her
husband and parties making the same, until the said
parties shall see fit to resolve it by a written notice to

that effect to the company, and the omission of a statement in any such declaration that the wife making the same is duly authorized by her husband to make the same, shall not cause the declaration to be deemed either illegal or informal, any law or usage to the contrary notwithstanding.

26. If the directors of the company shall entertain doubts as to the legality of any claim to and upon such share of stock, it shall be lawful for the company to make and file in the superior court of Montreal, a declaration and petition in writing, addressed to the said court, or to one judge thereof, setting forth the facts, and praying for an order or judgment adjudicating or awarding the said share to the party or parties legally entitled to the same ; and by which order or judgment the company shall be guided and held fully harmless and indemnified and released from all and every other claim for the said share or arising therefrom ; provided always, that notice of such petition shall be given to the party claiming such share, who shall upon the fyling of such petition, establish his right to the several shares referred to in such petition.; and the delays to plead and all other proceedings in such cases shall be the same as those observed in interventions in cases pending before the said superior court ; provided also, that unless the said court or judge otherwise order, the costs and expenses of procuring such order and adjudication shall be paid by the party or parties to whom the said shares shall be declared lawfully to belong ; and such shares shall not be transferred until such costs and expenses be paid, saving the recourse of such party against any party contesting his right.

If the Co.'y. has doubts as to certain claims. Proceedings. Notice. Costs. Recourse.

27. Any person who, as secretary, clerk or other officer of the company, shall be guilty of any designed fraud or falsehood, in any matter or thing pertaining to his office or duty, shall be guilty of a misdemeanor ; and any person offering to vote in person at any election of directors in the said company, who shall falsely personate another or who shall falsely sign or affix the name of any other person, a member of the company, to any appointment of a proxy, shall be guilty of a misdemeanor.

Persons in default.

28. In all actions, suits and prosecutions in which the said company may be at any time engaged any officer or stockholder in the said company shall be a competent witness, notwithstanding any interest he may have therein.

Competent witnesses.

29. During the hours of business every stock-holder of the said corporation shall have power to ask and receive from the president, secretary or other officer, the names

Information required.

of all the stock-holders of the said corporation, and the number of shares held by each of them.

Suits.

30. Any description of action may be prosecuted and maintained between the company and any shareholder thereof; and no shareholder not being himself a party to **Witnesses.** such suit shall be incompetent as a witness therein.

CAP LXI.

An Act to amend chapter 69 of the consolidated statutes for Lower Canada, respecting building societies, in providing for the means of their union or fusion.

[*Assented to 24th December, 1875.*]

Preamble.   WHEREAS it is expedient to provide for the union or fusion of building societies established in this province, under the provisions of chapter 69 of the consolidated statutes for Lower Canada, and with such view to amend such act; Therefore, Her Majesty, by and with the advice and consent of the Legislature of Quebec, enacts as follows:

Right of amalgamation.   **1.** It shall be lawful for two or more building societies established under the provisions of chapter 69 of the consolidated statutes for Lower Canada, to unite and join together to form one corporation, under the name of either of such societies, and to unite their capital, property, business, privileges, hypothecs, warranties, rights, powers and duties, by observing, however, the formalities hereinafter set forth:

Mode.   *a.* The directors of each of the societies desirous of uniting, shall fix and establish the terms of union, at one **Meetings.** of their respective meetings, held in the ordinary manner, at their respective offices or places of business. When the directors of each of such societies have settled the terms of union, the secretary of each shall convene a general meeting of the share-holders of the society, at the **Notice,** usual place of business of such society, by notice published in the french and english languages, twice in each language, during one month; in two newspapers, if there are two in the city, town, village or municipality, in which is situated the society's place of business, or in the same **How published and forwarded.** newspaper, if there is only one published in such locality, and in default of such newspaper there, in any other newspaper published in the neighborhood; and a copy of this notice shall be forwarded by mail to the address of each share-holder;

b. At such general meeting of the share-holders of each Approval. of such societies, (which shall be presided over by the society's president, or in default of him or in his absence, by a person to be selected by the meeting,) the draft of union settled and determined by the directors of such societies respectively, must be approved (if approved it Effect of the is), by at least two-thirds of the members and share-hold- approval. ers present, and each share-holder can be represented by a proxy, provided said proxy is a share-holder ; and at the same time, and at same meeting, the resolution, motion or by-law approving the draft of union submitted, either absolutely or with such modifications, as the meeting shall determine, shall contain, or shall be, an authorization to the president of such society, to sign any deed, document, resolution or by-law necessary to complete definitely the fusion of the societies.

2. When the draft of union shall have been so approved Deed of by the meeting of share-holders, the presidents of the union. societies about to unite, (each of which is thereunto authorized by this act), shall execute, either in notarial form or *sous seing privé*, (and in the latter case the deed shall be executed in triplicate), a deed of union, in conformity with the draft adopted by the meeting of the share-holders of each of the societies.

3. A copy of the notarial deed, or one of the triplicates, Deposit of shall be filed in the office of the prothonotary of the dis- the deed. trict wherein is the head office or principal place of affairs of the building society, the name of which is preserved. Another copy or one of the triplicates shall be filed in the registry office of the registration division, wherein is the head office or principal place of business of the society, the name of which is kept ; and such latter society shall retain the other triplicate, or a copy of the notarial deed, as the case may be, to form part of its archives.

4. After the execution or passing of the deed, the Name of the society, the name whereof shall have been retained for the gamated. purposes of the union, shall alone remain in existence, and the other societies united thereto shall be dissolved. The subsisting society shall thenceforward become and Effect of the be possessed, of all the assets and rights of the societies tion. so dissolved ; and the share-holders and members of the dissolved societies shall become and be members and share-holders in the subsisting society, on the terms stipu- lated in the deed of union. The rights of creditors of the dissolved societies shall Rights of the not be in any manner affected by such union, and they solved. may be enforced against the subsisting society, as the representative of the dissolved societies.

Pending
cases.
5. No proceedings pending, or judgment rendered against any of the societies united or dissolved, shall be affected by such union or fusion.

Such proceedings may be continued against the subsisting society, by suit or rule *en reprise d'instance* or by any other procedure permitted by law, and any judgment so rendered may be executed against the subsisting society.

Interpreta-
tion.
6. The provisions of this act shall form part of chapter 69 of the consolidated statutes for Lower Canada.

Act in force.
7. This act shall enter into force on the day of the sanction thereof.

CAP. LXII.

An Act to change the name of " The Provincial Permanent Building Society" to that of " The Provincial Loan Company," and to extend the powers thereof.

[*Assented to 24th December*, 1875.]

Preamble.
WHEREAS the Provincial Permanent Building Society, a body politic and corporate, have, by their petition, represented that they were incorporated under the authority of the legislature of the late province of Canada, consolidated statutes for Lower Canada, chapter 69, and that from the increase of their capital, the great extension of their business, and the nature and extent of their financial operations, it is desirable to change the name of the said corporation to that of " The Provincial Loan Company, " and to grant it additional and more extensive powers, and it is expedient to grant the prayer of their said petition; Therefore, Her Majesty, by and with the advice and consent of the Legislature of Quebec, enacts as follows :

Corporation
constituted.
1. The said " The Provincial Permanent Building Society," and all its members, their successors and assigns forever, are hereby constituted a body politic and corpo-

Name.
rate, under the name of " The Provincial Loan Company," having its principal place of business in the city of Montreal ; and under that name shall be capable of suing

Place of busi-
ness.
and being sued, pleading and being impleaded in all courts and places whatsoever.

Powers and
privileges,
continued.
2. The said " The Provincial Loan Company," shall not be deemed to be a new corporation, but it shall have, hold and continue to exercise all the rights,

powers and privileges that have heretofore been held and exercised and enjoyed by the said " The Montreal Permanent Building Society " in as full and ample a manner as if the said society had continued to exist under its original name; and all statutory provisions applicable to the said society shall continue applicable to the said " The Provincial Loan Company," so far as the same are not contrary to or inconsistent with the provisions of this act.

3. All the real and moveable property, shares or stock, Properties, obligations, debts, rights, claims and privileges of the said obligations, " The Provincial Permanent Building Society," shall be &c., transferand are hereby transferred to and vested in the said " The corporation. Provincial Loan Company :" and all the share-holders in the said society shall be share-holders for like amounts and with like rights, in the said "The Provincial Loan Company," but Suits already all legal proceedings heretofore begun by or against " The commenced. Provincial Permanent Building Society," may be continued and terminated under the name or style of cause in which they have been instituted, for the benefit of or against " The Provincial Loan Company."

4. The present President, Vice-President, Directors Actual offiand Officers of " the Provincial Permanent Building cers remain Society" shall continue in office as such in " The Provincial in office. Loan Company " with the names of President, VicePresident, Directors and Officers of " The Provincial Loan Company " until replaced in conformity with the bylaws of the said company and the provisions of the law.

5. All the present by-laws and rules of the said " The Actual byProvincial Permanent Building Society" shall continue laws, conin full force and effect, and shall be binding in law as tinued. regards " The Provincial Loan Company," its directors, officers, share-holders and borrowers, until modified, amended or repealed in conformity to law, and the provisions of this act.

6. The directors of the said " The Provincial Loan Com- Power to pany" may, from time to time, alter, amend, repeal or create change them, any regulation, rule, or by-law for the working of the said make others. company not contrary to law ; provided that such action of the directors shall be confirmed at the next general or annual meeting of the share-holders of the company, notice being given of the proposed changes in the notices calling Approval, resuch meeting, and shall if not so confirmed cease after quired. such meeting to have force ; and at all meetings of shareholders of the company, the share-holders shall have one vote for each share held by them respectively.

7. No share-holder of the company shall be liable for Liability of or charged with the payment of any debt or demand due the shareholders, limited.

from the company, beyond the extent of his shares in the capital of the company not then paid up.

Power to lend money.

Mode.

Proviso.

8. The said Provincial Loan Company may lend money upon hypothec or other security on real estate, or otherwise in conformity with the laws authorizing the establishment of building societies in Canada, and with the by-laws of the said company, to any person or persons, or body corporate, at such times and rates of interest as may be agreed upon, without requiring any of such borrowers to become subscribers to the stock or members of the said company; provided always, that all borrowers from the company shall be subject to all the rules of the company in force at the time of their becoming borrowers, but not to any other rules.

Power to purchase debentures, &c.

Advances.

9. The said Provincial Loan Company may purchase mortgages upon real estate, debentures of municipal or other corporations, dominion or provincial stock or securities, and stocks of incorporated bodies or companies, and they may re-sell all such securities, as to them shall seem advisable; and for that purpose, they may execute such assignments or other instruments as may be necessary for carrying the same into effect; they may also make advances to any person, or persons, or body corporate upon the same securities at such rates of discount or interest as may be agreed upon.

Power to act, &c., as agency, &c.

Guarantee.

10. The company may act as an agency and trust company, and may hold, invest and deal in its own name or otherwise, with such real estate, moneys, mortgages, hypothecs, securities or evidences of debt, debentures of municipal or other corporations, dominion or provincial stocks or securities, and stocks of incorporated bodies or companies, as shall, from time to time, be transferred or delivered to the company upon trust or as agents, and may exercise all the rights which the parties so transferring or delivering the same might or could exercise; and the company may give such guarantee as may be agreed upon for repayment of principal or interest or both of any such moneys, mortgages, hypothecs, securities, evidences of debts, debentures or stocks.

To receive on deposit.

Issue of debentures.

Interest.

Limits,

11. It shall be lawful for the said Provincial Loan Company to receive money on deposit and also for the board of directors of the company to issue debentures of the company for such sums, not being less than fifty dollars and in such currency as they may deem advisable, and payable in the Dominion of Canada, or elsewhere, not less than one year from the issue thereof, and allowing and bearing such rate of interest as may be deemed advisable; provided always that the aggregate

amount of money deposits in the hands of the company,
for which debentures may be issued and remain at any
time unpaid, shall not exceed double the amount of capi- Form.
talized, fixed and permanent stock of the company. 'The
debentures of the company may be in the form of schedule A to this act, or to the like effect.

12. The said Provincial Loan Company shall not be Execution of
bound to see to the execution of any trust, whether ex- trusts, &c.
pressed, implied or constructive, to which any share or
shares of its stock, or to which any deposit or any other
moneys payable by or in the hands of the said company
may be subject; and the receipt of the party in whose
name any such share or shares or moneys stand in the
books of the said company, or if the same stands in the
name of more parties than one, the receipt of one of the
parties, shall from time to time be sufficient discharge to
the company for any payment of any kind made in respect of such share or shares or moneys, notwithstanding
any trust to which the same may then be subject, and
whether or not the company has had notice of such
trust; and the company shall not be bound to see to
the application of the money paid upon such receipt.

13. The said Provincial Loan Company shall have Power to
power to acquire and hold by purchase, lease or other acquire.
legal title, houses, buildings and premises; and also
real estate for the purpose of constructing and building
houses and other buildings thereon, and to lease, let,
sell, convey and dispose of the said property, houses and
buildings, so acquired or erected by the said company;
provided always that the said company shall sell the Proviso.
property so acquired, within five years from the date of
the purchase thereof, and that any lease made according
to the provisions of section 14 of this act, shall be held to
be a sale within the meaning of this section.

14. Upon an agreement being made by the said com- Sale by lease.
pany for the sale of any house or other real estate held
thereby, it shall be lawful for the said company to
execute, in favor of the intending purchaser thereof,
a lease thereof, for the time stipulated in such agreement of sale, as the limit of delay thereby fixed for the
payment of the last instalment of the price therein
agreed upon, at a rental corresponding in the amount
and in the terms of payment thereof, with such price
and with the terms of payment of such price, and if
such lease appear by its terms to have been made
under the provisions of this act, it shall not be held to
convey, to such intending purchaser, any right in or to
the property intended to be sold, or any real right therein
whatever, nor shall the possession thereof by the intend-

14

ing purchaser be held to be a possession as proprietor, nor shall any legal right or hypothec be created or attached thereon (notwithstanding that such lease shall contain a direct promise of sale of such property so soon as the conditions thereof shall have been performed), until the sum of money in such lease stipulated for, and every part and portion thereof shall have been fully paid with all interest due thereon, nor until the charges, conditions and obligations created by or due under such lease shall have been fully paid, performed and fulfilled, and the agreement or promise of sale shall be conditional in the fulfilment of all the covenants of such lease.

Effect of the performance of the conditions of the lease, &c. **15.** If the intending purchaser or lessee, having accepted a lease under this act, of the property intended to be acquired by him from the company, shall make all the payments and perform all the conditions stipulated for by such lease, and shall fulfil all the obligations thereby imposed upon him, the said lease shall thereupon and thereafter be held to be, and shall be equivalent to a promise of sale of such property with possession, and shall vest the same in such intending purchaser in the same manner and to the same extent as if it were an ordinary promise of sale (*promesse de vente*), and shall give the right to the holder thereof, to demand and have, from the said company, a valid deed of sale of the property mentioned therein, containing warranty of title, and against all charges thereon, other than those disclosed and agreed to be permitted to remain thereon; and all hypothecs and privileges, whether conventional or legal, which were created for the intending purchaser, during the pending of the said lease, shall immmediately thereupon attach to such property, according to their rank and privileges and the date of their registration, in the same manner as if the same had been the property of such intending purchaser from the date of such lease.

Right to re-take possession of the property in certain cases. Notice. **16.** If at any time three months' arrears of the instalments stipulated for in any such lease shall become due and remain unpaid, the said company shall have the right to re-take possession of the property intended to be sold, upon giving to the intending purchaser or lessee ten days' notice to vacate and deliver back the same, and tendering to him the amount by him actually paid on account of the instalments agreed upon 'in the said lease, after the deduction therefrom of interest at the rate of ten *per centum* per annum on the price agreed upon remaining unpaid each year for the time during which the premises agreed to be sold remained in the occupation of the intending purchaser by way of rent for the use and occupation of such premises, and of ten *per centum* of the amount actually

paid in to be retained as a forfeiture and penalty for
non-performance of the agreement of purchase, of the
cost of such tender, of the expense of repairs, and
restoring all injuries and deteriorations suffered by the
premises so intended to be sold, reasonable wear and
tear excepted, and of all taxes, charges and assessments
which attached thereto by the occupation thereof by
the intending purchaser or lessee, and which shall then
remain unpaid, all which charges and deductions shall
be a first and privileged charge upon the amounts so
actually paid in by him. But if the instalments payable
annually under such lease shall amount to less than ten
per centum upon such price, then, and in that case,
the amount to be deducted for rental shall be the
amount of instalments stipulated for in such lease.

17. If at the end of ten days after service of such
notice and tender, the intending purchaser or lessees
shall not vacate and deliver back to the said company
the premises intended to be bought by him, the said
company shall have the right to cause him to be ejected
therefrom by proceedings to be taken under the provisions of the first chapter of the second title of the
second book of the code of civil procedure of Lower
Canada, commencing with article 887, in all respects
in the same manner and with the same delays as if
such lease were an ordinary lease. And the costs accrued
to the said company in any such action shall also be
a charge upon and be deducted from the amount of
money actually paid in by the intending purchaser.

18. Any tender made by the said company shall be
held to be sufficiently made if the company shall have
bonâ fide used diligence to ascertain the amounts which
they shall be entitled to retain out of the purchase money
paid in by the intending purchasers, notwithstanding
that the amount tendered may not be precisely that
which should have been so-tendered according to the
provisions hereof; and in such case the company, and
the intending purchaser shall have the right to recover
each from the other the amount which may have been
over or under tendered.

19. In the event of the surrender of any property so
leased as aforesaid, and of the sum of money actually
paid in by the intending purchaser being insufficient
to meet all the charges thereon and deductions therefrom herein provided for, the said company shall have
the same lien, privilege and remedies as an ordinary
lessor upon the effects of the intending purchaser or
lessee for the balance remaining due ; provided always,
that such balance does not exceed in amount the sum

Powers continued.

2. The said " the Montreal Loan and Mortgage Company," shall not be deemed to be a new corporation, but it shall have, hold and continue to exercise all the rights, powers and privileges that have heretofore been held and exercised and enjoyed by the said " the Montreal Permanent Building Society " in as full and ample a manner as if the said society had continued to exist under its original name ; and all statutory provisions applicable to the said society shall continue applicable to the said " the Montreal Loan and Mortgage Company, " so far as the same are not contrary to or inconsistent with the provisions of this act.

Properties, obligations, &c., transferred.

3. All the real and moveable property, shares or stock, obligations, debts, rights, claims and privileges of the said " the Montreal Permanent Building Society," shall be and are hereby transferred to and vested in the said " the Montreal Loan and Mortgage Company : " and all the shareholders in the said society shall be shareholders for like amounts and with like rights, in the said " the Montreal Loan and Mortgage Company, " but all legal proceedings heretofore begun by or against " the Montreal Permanent Building Society," may be continued and terminated under the name or style of cause in which they have been instituted, for the benefit of or against " the Montreal Loan and Mortgage Company. "

Proceedings commenced.

Actual officers, continued.

4. The present president, vice-president, directors and officers of " the Montreal Permanent Building Society " shall continue in office as such in " the Montreal Loan and Mortgage Company," with the names of president, vice-president, directors and officers of " the Montreal Loan and Mortgage Company," until replaced in conformity with the by-laws of the said company and the provisions of the law.

Actual by-laws, continued.

5. All the present by-laws and rules of the said " the Montreal Permanent Building Society " shall continue in full force and effect; and shall be binding in law as regards " the Montreal Loan and Mortgage Company," its directors, officers, shareholders and borrowers, until modified, amended or repealed in conformity to law; and the provisions of this act.

Power to make others, &c.

Approval.

6. The directors of the said " the Montreal Loan and Mortgage Company," may, from time to time, alter, amend, repeal or create any regulation, rule, or by-law, for the working of the said company not contrary to law ; provided that such action of the directors shall be confirmed at the next general or annual meeting of the shareholders of the company, notice being given of the proposed changes in the notices calling such meeting, and shall if not so confirmed cease after such meeting to have force ; and at all meetings of share-holders of the company, the shareholders shall have one vote for each share held by them respectively.

7. No shareholder of the company shall be liable for or charged with the payment of any debt or demand due from the company, beyond the extent of his shares in the capital of the company not then paid up. Liability of the share-holders, limited.

8. The said " the Montreal Loan and Mortgage Company " may lend money upon hypothec or other security on real estate, or otherwise in conformity with the laws authorising the establishment of building societies in Canada, and with the by-laws of the said company, to any person or persons, or body corporate, at such times and rates of interest, as may be agreed upon, without requiring any of such borrowers to become subscribers to the stock or members of the said company ; provided always, that all borrowers from the company shall be subject to all the rules of the company in force at the time of their becoming borrowers, but not to any other rules. Power to lend money. Mode. Proviso.

9. The said " the Montreal Loan and Mortgage Company " may purchase mortgages upon real estates, debentures of municipal or other corporations, dominion or provincial stock or securities, and stocks of incorporated bodies or companies, and they may re-sell all such securities as to them shall seem advisable ; and for that purpose, they may execute such assignments or other instruments as may be necessary for carrying the same into effect ; they may also make advances to any person, or persons, or body corporate upon the same securities at such rates of discount or interest as may be agreed upon. Purchase of mortgages, &c. Advances,

10. The company may act as an agency and trust company, and may hold, invest and deal in its own name or otherwise, with such real estate, moneys, mortgages, hypothecs, securities or evidences of debt, debentures of municipal or other corporations, dominion or provincial stocks or securities, and stocks of incorporated bodies or companies, as shall, from time to time, be transferred or delivered to the company upon trust or as agents, and may exercise all the rights which the parties so transferring or delivering the same might or could exercise ; and the company may give such guarantee as may be agreed upon for repayment of principal or interest, or both, of any such moneys, mortgages, hypothecs, securities, evidences of debts, debentures or stocks. The company may act, &c., as an agency. Guarantee.

11. It shall be lawful for the Montreal Loan and Mortgage company to receive money on deposit and also for the board of directors of the company to issue debentures of the company for such sums, not being less than fifty dollars and in such currency as they may deem advisable, and payable in the Dominion of Canada, or elsewhere, not less than one year from the issue thereof, and bearing such rate of interest as may be deemed advisable; provided always that the aggregate amount of money deposits in the hands of the company, for which debentures may be issued and remain at any time unpaid shall not exceed double the amount of capitalized fixed and permanent stock of the company. The debentures of the company may be in the form of schedule A to this act, or to the like effect.

12. The said Montreal Loan and mortgage Company shall not be bound to see to the execution of any trust, whether expressed, implied or constructive to which any share or shares of its stock, or to which any deposit or any other moneys payable by or in the hands of the said company may be subject; and the receipt of the party in whose name any such share or shares or moneys stand in the books of the said company, or if the same stands in the name of more than one, the receipt of one of the parties shall from time to time be sufficient discharge to the company, for any payment of any kind made in respect of such share or shares or moneys, notwithstanding any trust to which the same may then be subject, and whether or not the company has had notice of such trust; and the company shall not be bound to see to the application of the money paid upon such receipt.

13. The said Montreal Loan and mortgage company shall have power to acquire and hold by purchase, lease or other legal title, houses, buildings and premises; and also real estate for the purpose of constructing and buildings houses and other buildings thereon, and to lease, let, sell, convey and dispose of the said property, houses and buildings so acquired or erected by the said company; provided always that the said company shall sell the property so acquired within five years from the date of the purchase thereof, and that any lease made according to the provisions of section 14 of this Act, shall be held to be a sale within the meaning of this section.

14. Upon an agreement being made by the said company for the sale of any house or other real estate held thereby, it shall be lawful for the said company to execute, in favor of the intending purchaser thereof, a lease thereof, for the time stipulated in such agreement of sale, as the limit of delay thereby fixed for the payment of the last instalment of the price therein agreed upon, at a rental corresponding in the amount and in the terms of payment thereof, with such price and with the terms of payment of such price. And if such lease appear by its terms to have been made under the provisions of this act, it shall not be held to convey, to such intending purchaser, any right in or to the property intended to be sold, or any real right therein whatever, nor shall the possession thereof by the intending purchaser be held to be a possession as proprietor, nor shall any lien or hypothec be created or attached thereon (notwithstanding that such lease shall contain a direct promise of sale on such property so soon as the conditions thereof shall have been performed) until the sum of money in such lease stipulated for, and every part and portion thereof shall have been fully paid with all interest due thereon, nor until the charges, conditions and obligations created by or due under such lease shall have been fully paid, performed and fulfilled, and the agreement or promise of sale shall be conditional in the fulfilment of all the covenants of such lease.

15. If the intending purchaser or lessee, having accepted a lease under this act, of the property intended to be acquired by him from the company, shall make all the payments and perform all the conditions stipulated for by such lease, and shall fulfil all the obligations thereby imposed upon him, the said lease shall thereupon and thereafter be held to be and shall be equivalent to a promise of sale of such property with possession, and shall vest the same in such intending purchasers in the same manner and to the same extent as if it were an ordinary promise of sale (*promesse de vente*), and shall give the right to the holder thereof, to demand and have, from the said company, a valid deed of sale of the property mentioned therein, containing warranty of title and against all charges thereon, other than those disclosed and agreed to be permitted to remain thereon ; and all hypothecs and privileges, whether conventional or legal, which were created for the intending purchaser, during the pending of the said lease shall immediately thereupon attach to such property, according to their rank and privilege and the date of their registration, in the same manner as if the same had been the property of such intending purchaser from the date of such lease. *Effect of the execution of the conditions.*

16. If at any time three months' arrears of the instalments stipulated for in any such lease shall become due and shall remain unpaid, the said company shall have the right to re-take possession of the property intended to be sold, upon giving to the intending purchaser or lessee ten *Power to re-take possession in certain cases.*

days notice to vacate and deliver back the same, and tendering to him the amount by him actually paid on account of the instalments agreed upon in the said lease after the deduction therefrom of interest at the rate of ten *per cent* per annum on the price agreed upon remaining unpaid each year, for the time during which the premises agreed to be sold remained in the occupation of the intending purchaser, by way of rent for the use and occupation of such premises, and of ten *per centum* of

Forfeiture.
the amount actually paid in to be retained as a forfeiture and penalty for non-performance of the agreement of purchase, of the cost of such tender, of the expense of repairs, and restoring all injuries and deterioration suffered by the premises so intended to be sold, reasonable wear and tear excepted, and of all taxes, charges and assessments which attach thereto by the occupation thereof by the intending purchaser or lessee, and which shall then remain unpaid, all which charges and deductions shall be a first and privileged charge upon the amounts so actually paid in by him. But if the instalments payable annually under such lease shall amount to less than ten *per centum* upon such price, then, and in that case, the amount to be deducted for rental shall be the amount of instalments stipulated for in such lease.

Ejectment.
17. If, at the end of ten days after service of such notice and tender, the intending purchaser or lessee shall not vacate and deliver back to the said company the premises intended to be bought by him, the said company shall have the right to cause him to be ejected therefrom by proceedings to be taken under the provisions of the first chapter of the second title of the second book of the code of civil procedure of Lower Canada, commencing with Article 887, in all respects in the same manner and with the same delays as if such lease were an ordinary lease. And the costs awarded to the said company in any such action shall also be a charge upon and be deducted from the amount of money actually paid in by the intending purchaser.

Tender made by the company.
18. Any tender made by the said company shall be held to be sufficiently made if the company shall have *bonâ fide* used diligence to ascertain the amounts which they shall be entitled to retain out of the purchase money paid in by the intending purchasers, notwithstanding that the amount tendered may not be precisely that which should have been so tendered according to the provisions hereof; and in such case the company, and the intending purchaser shall have the right to recover each from the other the amount which may have been over or under tendered.

19. In the event of the surrender of any property so leased as aforesaid, and of the sum of money actually paid in by the intending purchaser being insufficient to meet all the charges thereon and deductions therefrom herein provided for, the said company shall have the same lien, privilege and remedies as an ordinary lessor upon the effects of the intending purchaser or lessee for the balance remaining due; provided always that such balance does not exceed in amount the sum chargeable against such intending purchaser, by way of rental for the use and occupation of the premises intended to be sold for expense of repairs and for the taxes, charges and assessments. Privilege of the company.

Proviso.

20. A copy of any by-law of the company purporting to be signed by any officer of the company, shall be received as *primâ facie* evidence of such by-law, in all courts of law or equity in this province. By-laws received as evidence.

21. If the directors of the company shall entertain doubts as to the legality of any claim to and upon any share or shares of the capital stock, it shall be lawful for the company to make and file in the superior court for Lower Canada sitting in the district of Montreal, a declaration and petition in writing, addressed to the Justices of the said court, setting forth the facts and praying for an order or judgment, adjudicating or awarding the said shares, to the party or parties legally entitled to the same, and by which order or judgment the company shall be guided and held fully harmless and indemnified and released from all and every other claim for the said shares, or arising therefrom; provided always, that notice of such petition, shall be given to the party claiming such shares, who shall upon filing such petition establish his right to the several shares referred to in such petition; and the delays to plead, and all other proceedings in such cases, shall be the same as those observed in interventions in cases pending before the superior court; provided also, that unless the said superior court otherwise order, the costs and expenses of procuring such order and adjudication shall be paid by the party or parties to whom the said shares shall be declared lawfully to belong; and such shares shall not be transferred, until such costs and expenses are paid, saving the recourse of such party contesting his right. Doubts as to certain claims.

Proceedings.

Notice.

Costs.

Recourse.

SCHEDULE A.

THE MONTREAL LOAN AND MORTGAGE COMPANY.

Debenture No.   Transferable
          Under the authority of an Act of the Legislature

of the Province of Quebec Dominion of Canada.
    The Montreal Loan and mortgage Company, promises
to pay to   or bearer the sum of   . on the
day of   , one thousand eight hundred and   , at
with interest at the rate of   *per cent per annum,* to
be paid . half-yearly on presentation of the proper coupon
for the same as hereunto annexed,
    Dated at   , the   day of   , 18 ·
    For the Montreal Loan and Mortgage Company.
    C. D.   A. B.
    Secretary.   President.

COUPON.

No. 1.
Half-yearly dividend due   of   18 ,   on
Debenture No.   issued by this Company on the
day of   , 18 , for   at   *per cent*
per annum, payable at
    For the Montreal Loan and Mortgage Co.
    C. D.   A. B.
    Secretary.   President.

CAP. LXIV.

An Act respecting a Company Incorporated under the
    name of " Le Crédit Foncier du Bas Canada,"

[Assented to 24th December, 1875.]

Preamble.   WHEREAS " Le Crédit Foncier du Bas Canada," a
    body politic and corporate, duly incorporated under
the statutes of Canada, 36 Victoria, chap. 102, have, by petition, represented that it is in the interest of such corporation, as well as in that of the public, that their act of
incorporation should be recognized by the legislature of
Quebec and the powers granted to them should be confirmed and legalized within the province of Quebec, in so
far as this legislature can grant powers to the said corporation, and that great advantages would result to the public
from the continuance of business within the province of
Quebec, of such landed credit company, with sufficient
capital for the making of loans for long periods, repayable
by means of sinking funds, or for short periods with or
without sinking funds, and that such an institution,
formed on the model of the best landed credit institutions
of Europe, is a boon to the province of Quebec, and have
prayed for the passing of an act recognizing that incorporation and confirming within the limits of this province
the powers conferred upon them in so far as this legislature can grant such powers, and whereas it is expedient

to grant the prayer of the said petition; Therefore, Her
Majesty, by and with the advice and consent of the Legislature of Quebec, enacts as follows:

1. The said company incorporated by chapter one hun- Corporation,
dred and two of the statutes of Canada, passed in the recognized.
thirty-sixth year of Her Majesty's reign, and known by
the name of "Le Crédit Foncier du Bas-Canada," is re- Name.
cognized as a body politic and corporate with all the rights,
powers and privileges incidental to corporations by the
laws of this province, and the said company shall, within General
this province, be governed by the provisions and possess powers.
and exercise the powers hereinafter mentioned, which are
those conferred by their act of incorporation and the act
amending it.

2. The business and affairs of the said company are Management
and shall be conducted and managed by a board of nine of the busi-
directors to be appointed by the shareholders as here- ness.
inafter provided.

3. The capital stock of the said company is and shall be Capital stock
one million of dollars, divided into ten thousand shares of
one hundred dollars each; but the directors of the said company may, in conformity to any decision come to by the
share-holders at a general annual meeting, increase the capi- Power to in-
tal stock by the issue of a new series of shares, provided that same.
each new series shall not exceed one million of dollars;
and provided also that no new series of shares shall be Proviso.
issued after the first, unless the full amount of the previous new series shall have been subscribed and paid up;
the subscribers to the first capital stock, their heirs and
successors, being entitled to take, by privilege, in the new Privileges of
issue of shares, an amount proportionate to their shares the first
in the first capital stock, and on the same terms and subscribers.
conditions.

4. No share-holder of the company shall be liable for Liability,
or charged with the payment of any debt or demand due limited.
from the company beyond the extent of his shares in the
capital of the company not then paid up.

5. Five directors shall form a quorum for the transac- Quorum, con-
tion of business. The directors shall name their presi- tinued.
dent and vice-president, and the said directors shall re- &c., duration
main in office until they shall have been replaced by their of the office.
successors in the manner hereinafter mentioned, unless
they cease to be so by one of the following causes,
namely : death, resignation, possession of less than ten
shares, insolvency, bankruptcy, or arrest for crime or misdemeanor.

Effect of the absence.

2. When a director has absented himself from the meetings of the board of directors during three consecutive months, the majority of a quorum of the other directors may, by resolution, declare his office vacant.

Resignation.

3. Every director shall have the right to give in writing his resignation of his office, and he shall be immediately replaced in the manner hereinafter provided.

Vacancy.

4. Every vacancy in the board of direction, happening in the course of the year, from whatever cause, shall be filled by the unanimous choice of the remaining directors, and the substituted director shall remain in office until replaced at the election of directors by the annual general meeting, but shall remain in office for the time for which the director he replaces had been elected.

Qualification of the directors.

Shares untransferable.

6. No person shall be elected a director who shall not be a proprietor of at least ten shares, on which all calls shall have been paid in full, a British subject, and a resident in the Dominion of Canada, and such number of shares shall remain untransferable during the time of his office.

Duration of charge.

Actual directors retiring.

7. The directors shall be elected for three years, but one third in number shall go out of office annually to be replaced by election at the annual general meeting of the present board of directors. Peter S. Murphy, François Benoit and the person who may be chosen to replace Charles J. Coursol shall remain in office for two years after the current year, and Michael O. Mullarky, William H. Hingston, Eugène H. Trudel, Edouard P. Lachapelle, Jeremiah Fogarty and the person who may be chosen to replace William Simpson, shall draw lots to decide which three shall retire at the end of the current year and which other three shall retire at the end of the next year.

Elections.

8. The election of directors shall be made at the annual general meeting and shall be by ballot, and decided by the majority of shareholders then present; voting either in person or by proxy.

Instalments.

Notice.

Restrictions

9. The board of directors may, from time to time, make such calls of money upon the respective shareholders in respect of the amount of capital respectively subscribed or owing by them, as they shall deem necessary; provided that thirty days' notice at least be given of each call, and that no call exceed the amount of ten dollars per share, and that successive calls be not made at less than the interval of three months, and that the aggregate amounts of calls made in one year, do not exceed the amount of forty dollars per share; and every shareholder shall be liable to pay the amount of calls so made in respect of the shares held by him, to the persons and

at the times and places from time to time appointed by the company.

10. If any person subscribing for shares in the capital stock of the company is desirous of paying up in advance, either at the time of subscribing, or at any other time, the full amount of his shares, the directors may at any time admit and receive such subscriptions, and the full payment or payments of any number of instalments, upon such conditions as they may deem expedient. `Payment in advance.`

11. If any share-holder or share-holders shall refuse or neglect to pay any instalment upon his, her or their shares of the said capital stock at the time or times required by the directors as aforesaid, such share-holder or share-holders shall be bound to pay thereon eight per cent interest per annum until effectual payment ; and moreover, it shall be lawful for the directors of the company without any previous formality other than thirty days public notice of the intention, to sell at public auction the said shares, or so many of the said shares as shall, after deducting the reasonable expenses of the sale, yield a sum of money sufficient to pay the unpaid instalments due on the remainder of the said shares and the amount of interest due on the whole of them ; provided that the said sale shall have been specially authorized by a resolution of the board of directors ; and the president, or the vice-president, or the cashier of the company, shall execute the transfer to the purchaser of the shares of stock so sold, and such transfer, being accepted, shall be valid and effectual in law as if the same had been executed by the original holder or holders of the shares of stock thereby transferred. The executors, administrators, curators, paying instalments upon the shares of deceased shareholders shall be indemnified for paying the same. `Default to pay instalments.` `Interests.` `Sale of the shares.` `Authorization to that office.` `Effect of the transfer.` `Indemnity in certain cases.`

12. Notwithstanding anything contained in the preceding section, the company may sue such shareholder, failing to pay, for the amount of the instalments due upon his shares, in any court having competent jurisdiction, and may recover the same with interest at the rate of eight per cent per annum from the day on which such call may have been made payable. `Recovery of the instalments.`

13. In any action to recover any money due upon any call, it shall not be necessary to set forth the special matter, but it shall be sufficient to declare that the defendant is the holder of one share or more, stating the number of shares, and is indebted in the sum of money to which the calls in arrear shall amount, in respect of one call or more upon one share or more, stating the number and amount of each of such calls, whereby an action hath accrued to the said company by virtue of this act. `Allegations in the suit.`

Proof required.

14. On the trial of such action it shall be sufficient to prove that the defendant, at the time of making such call, was the holder of one share or more in the company, and that such call was in fact made and such notice thereof given, as is directed by this act, and it shall not be necessary to prove the appointment of the directors who made such call nor any other matter whatsoever, and thereupon the company shall be entitled to recover what shall be due upon such call with interest thereon, unless it shall appear either that any such calls exceed the amount of ten dollars per share or that due notice of such call was not given, or that the interval of three months between the successive calls had not elapsed, or that calls amounting to more than the sum of forty dollars in one year had been made.

Register shall be evidence.

15. The production of the register book of shareholders of the company or a certified extract therefrom, signed by the cashier of the company, shall be *primâ faeie* evidence of such defendant being a shareholder, and of the number and amount of his shares and of the sums paid in respect thereof.

Registers of the shareholders.

16. The company shall keep a book, to be called " the register of share-holders," and in such book shall be fairly and distinctly entered, from time to time, the names and additions of the several persons being share-holders of the company, the number of shares to which such share-holders shall be respectively entitled, and the amount of subscriptions paid on such shares ; and such book shall Authentication thereof. be authenticated by the common seal of the company being affixed thereto.

Certificate of shares.

17. On demand of the holder of any share, the company shall cause a certificate of the proprietorship of such share to be delivered to such share-holder; and such certificate shall have the common seal of the company affixed thereto, and such certificate shall specify the number of shares in the undertaking to which such share-holder is entitled ; and such certificate shall be admitted in all courts as evidence of the title of such share-holder to the Authenticity thereof. share therein specified, nevertheless, the want of such certificate shall not prevent the holder of any shares from disposing thereof.

Nature of the shares.

18. The shares of the capital stock of the company shall be held and adjudged to be personal property, and shall be transmissible accordingly, and shall be transferable at the chief place of business of the company, or at any of its branches which the directors shall appoint for that purpose, and according to such form as the diTransfer. rectors shall, from time to time, prescribe; but no transfer shall be valid and effectual unless it be made and registered in a book or books to be kept by the directors for that purpose, nor until the person or persons making the same shall previously discharge, to the satisfaction of the directors, all debts actually due or contracted and not then payable by him, her, or them, to the institution which may exceed in amount the remaining stock (if any) belonging to such person or persons ; and no fractional part or parts of a share or other than a whole share shall be transferable ; and when any share or shares of the said capital stock shall have been sold Sale by execution. under a writ of execution, the officer by whom the writ shall have been executed shall, within thirty days after the sale, leave with the cashier of the company an attested copy of the writ, with a certificate of such officer endorsed thereon, certifying to whom the sale has been made, and thereupon (but not until after all debts due, or contracted but not then payable, by the original holder or holders of the said shares to the company shall have been discharged as aforesaid), the president, or vice-president, or cashier, shall execute the transfer of the share or shares Validity of so sold to the purchaser, and such transfer being duly exe- the transfer. cuted, shall be to all intents and purposes as valid and effectual in law as if it had been executed by the original holder or holders of the said share or shares ; any law or usage to the contrary notwithstanding.

19. Shares in the capital stock of the company may be Shares transmade transferable, and the dividend accruing thereon may ferable. be payable in the United Kingdom, or elsewhere, in like manner as such shares and dividends are respectively transferable and payable at the chief office of the company, and to that end the directors may, from time to time, make such rules and regulations and prescribe such forms, and By-laws to appoint such agent or agents as they may deem necessary. that effect.

20. If the interest in any share in the company become Transmission transmitted in consequence of the death, or bankruptcy, of interests in or insolvency of any shareholder, or in consequence of the the shares in certain cases. marriage of a female shareholder, or by any other lawful means than by a transfer according to the provisions of this act, such transmission shall be authenticated by a declaration in writing, as hereinafter mentioned, or in such other manner as the directors shall require ; and every such declaration shall be, by the party making and sign- Declaration. ing the same, acknowledged before a judge of a court of Acknowrecord, or before the mayor, provost, or chief magistrate ledgement of of any city, town, borough or other place, or before a tion. public notary where the same shall be made and signed ; and every such declaration so signed and acknowledged shall be left with the cashier, or other officer or agent of the company, duly authorized to that effect, who shall

15

Inscription. thereupon enter the name of the party entitled under such.
transmission in the register of shareholders; and until
such transmission shall have been so authenticated, no
party or persons claiming by virtue of any transmission
shall be entitled to receive any share of the profits, nor to
vote in respect of any such share as the holder thereof;
Proviso.   provided always, that every such declaration and instrument as by this and the following section of this act is
required to perfect the transmission of a share, which shall
be made in any other country than this, or some other of-
the British colonies in North America, or in the United
Kingdom of Great Britain and Ireland, shall be further
authenticated by the British Consul or Vice-Consul, or
other accredited representative of the British Government where the declaration shall be made, or shall be
made before such British Consul, or Vice-Consul, or other
Proviso.   accredited representative; and provided also, that nothing in this act contained shall be held to debar the
directors, cashier or other officer or agent of the company,
from requiring corroborative evidence of any such fact or
facts alleged in any such declaration.

Transmis-   **21.** If the transmission of any share of the company be
sion of shares by virtue of the marriage of a female shareholder, the de-
by virtue of
marriage or   claration shall contain a copy of the register of such mar-
by testament, riage or other particulars of the celebration thereof, and
&c.   shall establish the identity of the wife with the holder of
such share; and if the transmission has taken place by
virtue of any testamentary instrument, or by intestacy, the
probate of the will, or the letters of administration or the
act of curatorship, or any official extract therefrom, shall,
together with such declaration, be produced and left with
the cashier or other authorized officer or agent of the
company, who shall, thereupon, enter the name of the
party entitled under such transmission in the register of
shareholders.

Transmis-   **22.** If the transmission of any share or shares of the
sion of shares capital stock of the said company, be by the decease of
in virtue of
decease.   any shareholder, the production to the directors and
deposit with them of any probate of the will of the
deceased shareholder, or of letters of administration of his
estate granted by any court in the dominion of Canada,
having power to grant such probate or letters of administration, or by any prerogative, diocesan, or peculiar court of
authority in England, Wales, Ireland, India or any other
British Colony, or of any testament, testamentary, or
testament, dative expede in Scotland, or if the deceased
Decease out   shareholder shall have died out of Her Majesty's domi-
of Her Ma-   nions, the production to and deposit with the directors of
jesty's domi-
nions.   any probate of his will or letters of administration of his
property, or other document of like import granted by

any court of authority having the requisite power in such matters, shall be sufficient justification and authority to the directors for paying any dividend or transferring or authorizing the transfer of any share in pursuance of and in conformity to such probate, letters of administration, or other such document as aforesaid.

23. The company shall not be bound to see to the execution of any trust, whether expressed, implied or constructive, to which any of the shares of its stock shall be subject ; and the receipt of the party in whose name any such share shall stand in the books of the company, or if it stands in the name of more parties than one, the receipt of one of the parties shall from time to time, be a sufficient discharge to the company for any dividend or other sum of money payable in respect of such share, notwithstanding any trust to which such share may then be subject, and whether or not the company have notice of such trust, and the company shall not be bound to see to the application of the money paid upon such receipt, any law or usage to the contrary notwithstanding. *Execution of trust.*

24. The chief place of business of the said company shall be at the city of Montreal ; but the said company shall from time to time, and at all times hereafter, have power and authority, and they are hereby authorized to establish such and so many agencies in any part or portion of the dominion of Canada, or in England, and under such regulations for the management thereof, and to remove the same as the directors of the said company may deem expedient. *Principal place of business.* *Agencies.*

25. The company is authorized to loan and advance by way of loan or otherwise, on the security of immoveable property for a long term, sums of money to be repaid by way of annuities, or for a short term, with or without a sinking fund. *Loans and advances.*

It shall be lawful for the company to deduct previously from the amounts of its loans a bonus, which shall not at any time exceed two per cent, which bonus may be retained at the outset, or distributed over the whole period for which the loan is made, and in the last mentioned case shall form part of the annuity, the whole as may be settled in the deed between the company and the debtor. *Bonus.*

26. The annuity shall include : *Annuity.*

1. The interest on the capital, which shall not exceed eight per cent per annum ;

2. The costs of management, which shall not be more than one per cent ;

3. The amount for the sinking fund.

The annuity shall be stipulated in the instrument of loan, or the deed executed by the debtor in favor of the company.

Rate of payment.   **27.** The rate of payment of the sinking fund shall be calculated so as not to last more than fifty years, with power nevertheless, to the borrower to acquit himself of the whole, or any part thereof, at any time, giving three months' notice of his intention ; the rate of interest (if any) to be allowed by the company to its borrowers on payments made by them on account of sinking fund, shall be such as may be settled by the deeds between the company and its borrowers respectively.

Moneys required in advance.   **28.** The company is authorized to require and receive semi-annually and in advance, all interests, costs of management and annuities arising from its loans and disbursements.

Anticipatory payment.   **29.** In case of anticipatory payment, the company shall not be bound to accept and receive any sum under ten per cent of the amount of any loan made, and may require an indemnity which shall be calculated on the difference between the rate of interest stipulated in the deed or in the obligation, and that of the mortgage bond or debenture in circulation at the date of the anticipatory payment, and on the length of time the obligation has still to run, but such indemnity shall not exceed one per cent per annum on the amount of the anticipatory payment, for such time as the obligation or deed might have to run, and shall nŏt in any case exceed the losses which the company might incur in consequence of the said anticipatory payment ; Nevertheless the sum proceeding from such anticipatory payments may be invested in furthering new loans.

Amount of hypothecs, full privilege.   **30.** The company shall only lend and advance money on first hypothec of real estate, the value of which shall be at least double the amount of the loan and advance money, and any loan made on hypothec posterior only to the hypothec of the *rentes constituées* under the seigniorial act, or to any privilege or hypothec specially exempted from registration, shall be considered as made on first hypothec ; And the loans and advances to be employed in paying off obligations or debts already registered, shall also be considered as made on first hypothec, when by the effect of such payment, or of the subrogation arising therefrom in favor of the company, the claim of this latter shall rank first and not concurrently with that of any other creditor ; In this last case the company shall **Deed of sale as security.** keep in hand the necessary amount to effect such payment, but the company may, if it thinks fit, take a deed of sale of any immoveable property which it is desirous of having pledged to it as security in any transaction made, or to be made, and that subject to such clauses and conditions of lease and of reconveyance as may be settled in the deed between the company and its debtor, the clauses of such deed being indispensable and not comminatory. The company may possess any immoveable property so acquired during the whole of the time stipulated in the deed between it and its debtor ; but if the company finally becomes the actual owner of any such immoveable property unconditionally, it shall dispose thereof within five years.

31. The company shall require that property liable to be destroyed by fire be insured at the expense of the borrower, unless the said company holds as security for its claim apart from such property other real estate worth double the value of the sum loaned, and which is not liable to be destroyed by fire ; the deed of loan shall contain a transfer of the amount of the insurance in the event of loss, the property so pledged shall be kept insured during the whole term of the loan ; the company shall have a right to have the insurance made in their own name and the annual premiums paid through their hands ; in the case of a loan redeemable by annuity, such annuity may be increased by so much. *Obligation to insure.*

32. In the event of loss, the insurance money shall be paid directly to the company. During one year from the date of the settlement of loss, the debtor shall have the privilege of rebuilding. During that period the company may retain the insurance money, as security to the amount of their claims calculated up to the end of the year. *Indemnity recognised in case of fire.*

After the rebuilding, the company shall pay over the insurance money to the debtor, deducting, however, whatever may be due to it, and if, at the expiration of the year, the debtor has not availed himself of his right to rebuild, or if before that time, he has notified the company that he did not intend to avail himself thereof, thereupon the insurance money shall finally inure to the benefit of the company and shall be imputed on their claim as a payment by way of anticipation.

33. The anticipated payment which shall arise from loss by fire shall not give rise to the indemnity authorized by section 29 of this act in favor of the company ; Nevertheless, whenever the company shall deem that by the effect of the loss, their security shall have been jeopardized, they shall have the right at any time to exact the payment of the balance due. *Anticipated payment.*

Effect of the mutation of properties affected.

34. Every mutation, either by sale, promise of sale, exchange, donation or other way, of any immoveable charged for the guarantee of any claim of the company shall confer upon the latter the right to exact at any time, the total payment of such claim without any notice or signification; unless the debtor shall, at his own expense, within a month's delay, deposit with the company a registered copy of the deed causing any such mutation, and the new proprietor of such immoveable shall pass in favor of the company, within the same delay and also at his own expense, a new deed or act acknowledging such claim, and have it duly registered; And in the event of such payment for want of compliance with any of the formalities hereinbefore enumerated, the company shall have a right to claim the indemnity authorized in their behalf by section 29 of this act.

Loan to corporations.

35. The company shall also have the power to loan and advance to municipalities, corporations and *fabriques* whatever sums they may be authorized to borrow according to the laws and by-laws by which they are governed.

Issue of debentures, &c.

36. The company for the purpose of procuring capital, is authorized to issue and negotiate mortgage bonds or debentures, (*lettres de gage,*) either in or out of this province.

How payable and made.

37. The mortgage bonds or debentures shall be payable either to order or to bearer, and shall bear interest; and the bearers of such mortgage bonds shall have for the payment of the amount thereof, a priority of claim on the capital of the company over all other creditors.

Lettres de gage payable to order shall be transferable by indorsement, without any other warranty on the part of the indorser than that he is the holder thereof in good faith.

Circulation of the debentures.

38. The company shall not issue mortgage bonds to a larger amount than that of its hypothecary mortgage claims, of which they shall be deemed to represent the value; and the amount paid in on the subscribed stock of the company shall be kept at all times at one-tenth at least of the amount of such bonds in circulation.

Form, &c.

39. The mortgage bonds shall be in sterling money or currency, and may be delivered in sub-divisions at the option of the directors, and as they may think best for their negotiation.

Interest coupons.

40. The directors may attach interest coupons to the mortgage bonds, and such interest shall not exceed eight per cent per annum.

41. A portion of these mortgage bonds, proportioned to Recovery of the amount of the sinking fund paid in, shall be annually debentures. withdrawn from circulation, the number of those to be redeemed being ascertained by lot (*tirage ou sort*), so that all the bonds which have been issued may be withdrawn from circulation at the expiration of the time fixed for their becoming due.

42. The mortgage bonds so designated by lot, as well Idem. as those becoming due, shall be redeemed at par with interest in specie to the bearers, at the day and place appointed by the company in notices to that effect published in two newspapers, and they shall cease to bear interest from such day.

43. The mortgage bonds bearing different rates of interest, or payable at different periods, may be classified thereof. separately, and shall be redeemed proportionately to the amount received on the sinking fund, and applicable to each class.

44. The company shall keep a book, to be called "the Debenture mortgage and debenture book," and in such book shall be book. successively entered the date of loans, and names, occupation and residence of borrowers; the amount of mortgage money advanced; the amount of mortgage bonds or debentures issued; the value, situation and extent of the real estate hypothecated as security, and all other brief particulars deemed necessary.

45. The company may receive deposits bearing or not Power to bearing interest, and shall have the right of retaining from receive deposits the amount which shall be due by the depositor. deposits. Money received in deposit by the company may be invested in or loaned upon the debentures or other securities of this province, or in any municipal debentures.

46. On the fifteenth day of january annually, or such Annual day being a legal holiday, then on the next following day report. not being a legal holiday, there shall be a general meeting of the shareholders of the company for receiving a report of the state of affairs from the board of directors, electing the directors and transacting any other matter of general interest relating to the management of the company.

47. All meetings of the company, or of the directors Meetings. shall be presided over by the president, and in his absence, by the vice-president, and if both are absent, by a president *pro tempore*, chosen by the majority of the members present, and the cashier shall be *ex-officio* secretary of all such meetings, and in the absence of this latter, the assistant-cashier shall take his place, and the minutes of

these meetings shall be made and inscribed in a book call-
Record of the ed " The record of the deliberations of the shareholders
deliberations. and of the directors," and shall be certified, attested and
signed in such record by the president of the meeting,
and by the secretary of that same meeting.

Right to vote.   **48.** At all meetings of the company every shareholder
shall be entitled to one vote for every share held by him;
and no shareholder shall be entitled to vote at any meeting unless he shall have paid all the calls then payable
upon all the shares held by him.

Debenture-   **49.** No person shall, in right of any debenture, be
holders not   deemed a shareholder, or be capable of acting or voting
voters.   as such at any meeting of the company.

Mode of   **50.** The votes may be given either personally or by
voting.   proxy, every such proxy being a shareholder, authorized
by writing under the hand of the shareholder nominat-
Decision.   ing such proxy; and every proposition at any such meeting shall be determined by show of hands, or upon de-
mand of any shareholder after such show of hands, by the
majority of the votes of the parties present, including
proxies, the chairman of the meeting being entitled not
only to vote, but to have a casting vote if there be an
equality of votes.

Proxy.   **51.** No person shall be entitled to vote as a proxy unless the instrument appointing such proxy have been
transmitted to the clerk or cashier of the company two
clear days before the holding of the meeting at which
such instrument is to be used, and no person shall at any
one meeting represent as proxy more than ten share-
holders.

Votes of   **52.** If several persons be jointly entitled to a share,
copartners.   the person whose name stands first on the register of
shareholders as one of the holders of such 'share shall,
for the purpose of voting at any meeting, be deemed the
sole proprietor thereof, and on all occasions the vote of
such first named shareholder alone, either in person or by
proxy, shall be allowed as the vote in respect of such
share, and no proof of the concurrence of the other holders
thereof shall be required.

Power of the   **53.** The directors may, from time to time, make rules and
directors.   by-laws for the transaction of the affairs of the company,
which rules and by-laws shall be adopted at a general
meeting of shareholders, and they shall have and may exercise the powers, privileges and authorities set forth and
vested in them by this act, and they shall be subject to and
be governed by such rules, regulations and provisions as

herein contained with respect thereto, and by the by-laws made and to be made for the management of the said company, and the directors shall and may lawfully exercise all the powers of the company except as to such matters as are directed by this act to be transacted by a general meeting of the company ; they may call any general, special or other meetings of the company, or Meetings. of the directors which they may deem necessary ; and they shall, upon requisition made in writing by any number of shareholders holding in the aggregate one-fifth part of the shares of the company, convene an extraordinary general meeting ; and such requisition so made by the shareholders shall express the object of the meeting proposed to be called, and shall be left at the company's office, and if the directors do not convene such general meeting within twenty-one days from the date of the requisition, the requisitionists, or any other shareholders having the required number of shares, may themselves convene a meeting. Notice of Notice. all extraordinary general meetings shall be published in two newspapers published in the city of Montreal, the one in french and the other in english. The directors may use and affix or cause to be used and affixed the seal of the company to any document or paper which in Seal. their judgment may require the same ; they may make Instalments. and enforce the calls upon the shares of the respective shareholders ; they may declare the forfeiture of all shares Forfeiture. on which such calls are not paid ; they may make any payments and advances of money as they may deem expedient, which are or shall at any time be authorized to be made by or on the behalf of the company, and enter into all contracts for the execution of the purposes of the company, and for all other matters necessary for the transaction of its affairs ; they may generally deal with, treat, sell and dispose of the lands, property and effects of the company for the time being, in such manner as they shall General deem expedient and conducive to the benefit of the com- management. pany, as if the same lands, property and effects were held and owned according to the tenure, and subject to the liabilities, if any, from time to time affecting the same, not by a body corporate, but by any of Her Majesty's subjects being of full age ; they may do and authorize, assent to or adopt, all acts required for the due exercise of any further powers and authority which may hereafter at any time be granted to the company by the legislature of this province, or for the performance and fulfilment of any conditions or provisions from time to time prescribed by the said legislature in giving such further powers and authority, or in altering or repealing the same respectively, or any of them ; but all the powers shall be exercised in accordance with and subject to the provisions of this act in that behalf ; provided always that all real Proviso.

estate acquired and held by the said company in virtue of this act, except such as is necessary for the use and occupation of the said company, and the purposes thereof, shall be sold and realized at public auction or private sale by the company at any period not later than five years from the acquisition of such real estate.

Appointment of officers.
Salaries.
Security.

54. The directors shall name the cashier, assistant cashier and all other subordinate officers of the company, and shall fix their respective salaries and remuneration, and shall take from the cashier security for not less than five thousand dollars, and security for not less than two thousand dollars from any other officer having control of the cash or any monies of the company.

Entries in a book, required.

55. The directors shall cause notices, minutes or copies, as the case may require, of all appointments made or contracts entered into by the directors, to be duly entered in books to be from time to time provided for the purpose, which shall be kept under the superintendence of the directors ; and every such entry shall be signed by the chairman of the meeting at which the matter in respect of which such entry is made was moved or discussed at or previously to the next meeting of the company or directors, as the case may be ; and a copy of such entry so signed,

Authenticity.

shall be received as evidence in all courts, and before all judges, justices and others, without proof of such respective meeting having been duly convened or of the persons making or entering such orders or proceedings being shareholders or directors respectively, or of the signature of the chairman, and which last mentioned matters shall be presumed; and all such books shall at

Books open for inspection.

any reasonable time be open to the inspection of any of the shareholders.

Dividends, limited.

56. The company shall not declare any dividend whereby their capital stock may be reduced, and shall not pay any dividend exceeding eight per cent per annum, as long as their reserve fund shall not have reached twenty-five per cent of the paid up capital stock.

Contingencies and improvements.

57. Before apportioning the profits aforesaid, the directors may, if they think fit, set aside thereout such sums as they may think proper to defray preliminary expenses and to meet contingencies, or for enlarging or improving the estate of the company or any part thereof, or promoting the objects and purposes for which they are incorporated, and may divide the balance only among the proprietors, subject nevertheless to the provisions of the next preceding section relating to the reserved fund.

58. No dividend shall be paid in respect of any share Dividend. until all calls then due in respect of that or any other share held by the person to whom such dividend may be payable, shall have been paid.

59. To the payment of the expenses of the company Sums affected shall be applied in the following order :   to the pay-
1. The amount received for preliminary expenses ;.   ment of
2. The amount received for costs of management.   expenses.

60. To the payment of the debts and losses there shall Debts and be applied in the following order: losses.
1. The revenues and profits ;
2. The reserve fund ;
3. The shares.

61. It shall be lawful for the directors from time to Appointment time to appoint such and so many officers, solicitors and of officers. agents, either in this province or elsewhere, and so many servants as they deem expedient for the management of the affairs of the company, and to allow to them such sa- Salaries. laries and allowances as may be agreed upon between them and the company, and to make such by-laws as By-laws. they may think fit for the purpose of regulating the con- duct of the officers, solicitors, agents and servants of the company, and for providing for the due management of the affairs of the company in all respects whatsoever, and from time to time to alter and repeal any such by-laws and make others, provided such by-laws be not repug- nant to the laws of this province or to the provisions of this act ; and such by-laws shall be reduced into writing, and shall have affixed thereto the common seal of the company, and a copy of such by-laws shall be given to every officer and servant of the company, and any copy or extract there- from certified under the signature of the cashier shall be By-laws make evidence in all courts of justice in this province, of such proof. by-laws or extracts from them, and that the same were duly made, and are in force; and in any action or ju- dicial proceedings it shall not be necessary to give any evidence to prove the seal of the company, and Seal. all documents purporting to be sealed with the seal of the company, shall be held to have been duly sealed with the seal of the same.

62. With respect to any notice required to be served Service of by the company upon the shareholders, it shall be suffi- notice by cient to transmit the same by post directed according to mail. the registered address or other known address of the shareholder, within such period as to admit of its being delivered in due course of post within the period [if any] prescribed for the giving of such notice, and in order to prove the giving of such notice, it shall be sufficient to prove that such notice was properly directed, and that it was so put into the post-office.

Signature of the notices.

63. All notices required by this act to be given by advertisement in newspapers, shall be signed by the chairman of the meeting at which such notices shall be directed to be given, or by the cashier or other officer of the company, and shall be advertised in such newspapers as the directors shall order.

Authentication of the documents.

64. Every summons, demand, or notice, or other such document requiring authentication by the company, may be signed by one director, or by the cashier of the company, and the same may be in writing or in print, or partly in writing and partly in print.

Signature of the deeds.

65. The president, or in his absence, the vice-president, and the cashier, or, in his absence, the assistant cashier, shall sign all deeds and documents to which the company shall be a party ; and in the event of both the president and the vice-president, or both the cashier and the assistant-cashier, or all of them, being prevented from signing any such deed or document, either by absence, personal interest, or any other cause whatsoever, such deed or document shall then be signed by such person or persons as the board of directors shall authorize to that effect.

Interpretation.

66. In this act the following words and expressions shall have the several meanings hereby assigned to them, unless there be something in the subject or context repugnant to such construction, that is to say : words importing the singular number shall include the plural number ; and words importing the plural number shall include the singular number ; the word "month" shall mean calendar month ; the word "cashier" shall include the word "clerk" ; the term "real estate" shall extend to lands, tenements, and hereditaments of any tenure ; the word "company" shall signify "*Le crédit foncier du Bas-Canada*" ; the word "dominion" shall mean "the Dominion of Canada" ; the word "province" shall mean the "province of Quebec," the words "mortgage bonds or debentures" shall also apply to sub-divisions (*coupures*) of said mortgage bonds.

Elections and deeds legalized.

67. The elections heretofore made of directors of the company are hereby legalized and confirmed, as are also the nominations and appointments by them of the president, vice-president, notary and other officers of the company, and all deeds, documents and agreements entered into and executed by such directors or officers, on behalf of the said company, are also hereby confirmed and shall be deemed good and valid, without prejudice to pending causes (if any.)

ᵃ **68**. The said company shall be known as and under the name of "*Le crédit foncier de Montréal,*" should the parliament of Canada pass an act to change their name to that name; and this change of name shall be operated at such time as may be provided by such act.

Name of the company.

CAP. LXV.

An Act respecting the Canada Tanning Extract Company, (limited).

[Assented to 24th December, 1875.]

WHEREAS the Canada Tanning Extract Company, limited, have shown by their petition, that they have obtained under the statute of Great Britain, known as the companies act of 1862, an incorporation under the name of the Canada Tanning Extract Company, limited, to acquire and carry on the trade and business of manufacturing an extract of bark, for tanning, in the province of Ontario and elsewhere;

That the capital of the said company is £100,000 sterling, divided into ten thousand shares of £10 each;

That the said company have acquired lands and buildings and constructed large works and machinery, and acquired patents and patent rights, in the province of Quebec, where they carry on an extensive business and where most of their operations are carried on;

That it is expedient for the said company to carry on their operations, in the province of Quebec, that they should obtain an act confirming their existence and recognizing their incorporation;

That moreover, according to their charter and to the laws of Great Britain, under which they exist, the directors are authorized to borrow such sums of money as they may think proper, so that no more than £10,000 be owing at one time over and above such sums of money as may have been borrowed with the sanction of a general meeting; but that the company may in a general meeting authorize the borrowing of such sums of money, as it shall think fit;

That the money borrowed for the purposes of the company may be raised by a mortgage of the whole or any part of the company's property, or upon such terms or security, as the directors may think fit, and that there may be a stipulation, if approved by a general meeting, that the security may be converted into preference or other shares of the stock of the company;

That by their charter and by-laws they are authorized
to mortgage their property, and to issue debentures,
securing to the holders the benefit of such mortgages,
or hypothecations, the company being bound to keep
and register all such hypothecations in their office, in
England ;

That by the law under which the said company has been
incorporated, such mortgage can be effected by indenture of mortgage by the company made to trustees selected ·
by the company, or in the interest of the parties, who intend to advance such sums of money, as the company may
borrow, and the mortgage so given in favor of the said
trustees, subsists for the benefit of the debenture holders,
participating in such loan, and whereas it is expedient to
legalize the hypothecation of the said company's real estate in this province ; therefore, Her Majesty, by and with
the advice and consent of the Legislature of Quebec, enacts
as follows :

Incorpora-
tion.

1. The said company under its name, to wit : " The
Canada tanning extract company, limited," is recognized
as a body politic and corporate, with power to sue and be
sued, to plead and be impleaded in all the courts of this
province, in the same manner as a corporation created by
the legislature of this province.

2. The said company shall have power and authority
within the limits of the province of Quebec :

Power of
manufactur-
ing extract of
bark for
tanning.

1. To acquire the trade and business of manufacturing
an extract of bark for tanning, and the lands, buildings,
patents, patent rights, licenses, trade secrets and privileges,
machinery, plant materials, stock in trade, in respect of
or in connection with the said manufacture, trade or business, or used for the purpose of carrying on the same ;

Or any other
extract.

2. To carry on the trade or business of manufacturers
and dealers in such extract of bark for tanning, or any
other extract or production for like purposes, or any
extract or production of bark ;

Goodwill.

3. To acquire the goodwill of, or any interest in, any
trade or business similar· or analogous to any trade or
business which the company is authorized to carry on ;

Working of
patents.

4. To acquire and work any patents, patent rights,
licences or other privileges for the manufacture of such
extract of bark for tanning or any other extract or production for a like purpose, or any extract or production
of bark ;

Material for
working, &c.

5. For the purposes aforesaid, to acquire and work all
necessary machinery, materials and things, and to take on
lease, purchase or otherwise acquire any land or buildings,
or to erect any buildings for any of the purposes of the
company ; provided that the value of the land (irrespec-

tive of buildings) held by the said company do not exceed one hundred thousand dollars ;

6. To develope, improve, manage, cultivate, maintain Management: let, mortgage, sell or otherwise deal with and dispose of all, or any parts of, or of the produce of the lands, and real and personal estate, properties and effects of the company, in such manner and on such terms and for such purposes, as the company may think proper ;

7. To amalgamate, unite or co-operate with any com- Amalgama-panies or associations already or hereafter to be established tion. for, or engaged in objects similar or analogous to those of the company or to acquire for the benefit of the company, and in the name of the company or otherwise, any shares, stock or other interest in any such other company or association ;

8. To do all such other things as are incidental or conducive to the attachment of the above objects.

8. The said company shall be regulated as to its capital Government. shares, calls on shares, the transfer and transmission of shares, and forfeiture of shares, the conversion of shares, meetings, funds, directors, the duties of directors and their powers, and disqualifications, proceedings, the seal of the company, dividends, accounts and notes, by the articles of association which constitute its charter, and the said company shall have the right and power to carry out the dispositions of their charter and to hypothecate its property in the province of Quebec, and to that end, the said directors may, from time to time, borrow for the purposes of the company, such sums of money as they may think proper, so that no more than £10,000 stg. be owing at any one time, over and above such sums of money as may have been borrowed, with the sanction of a general meeting, but the company may in general meeting authorize the borrowing of such sums of money as it shall think fit.

All money borrowed, for the purposes of the com- Loans. pany, may be raised upon hypothecation of the whole or any part of the company's property within the province of Quebec, or upon such terms or security as the directors may think fit, and there may be a stipulation, if approved by a general meeting, that the security may be Security. converted into preference or other shares or stock of the company. In the event of any money being borrowed for the purposes of the company, on the terms of the securities for such money being convertible into shares, the directors may create and issue such new shares either pre- Issue of new ferential, ordinary or deferred, as may be necessary for shares in cer-carrying such conversion into effect. tain cases.

4. The said company, in order to carry out the autho- Power to rity to them appertaining to raise such money by hypoth- hypothecate

for certain purposes. ecation of the whole or any part of the company's property, upon such terms as the directors may think fit, may from time to time do so, by giving a hypothec to trustees selected by the company, or by the parties advancing such money, by indenture made and executed in England, according to the forms there acknowledged, embodying a description of the property hypothecated, as required by **Issue of debentures.** article 2042 of the civil code, and mentioning the issue and the amount of the debentures to be secured thereby; and thereupon the said company may issue debentures for such amount, which hypothec will exist for the benefit of such debenture holders; provided the same be registered as hereinafter provided.

Transfer of hypothecs. 5. Such indenture of hypothec shall be attested by two subscribing witnesses and shall be executed in Parts and proved as required by articles 2141, 2142 or 2143 of the civil code, and shall be registered in the registration division in the province of Quebec in which such property so hypothecated is situate, together with a schedule in the form hereunto annexed, showing the number of debentures issued and the amounts thereof, secured by the said hypothec, the date at which the same falls due, and the yearly rate of interest payable thereon and the dates of payment thereof. One of the parts shall remain among the records of the registry-office and form part thereof; and a certificate of the registration shall be written upon the other duplicate.

Registration thereof. 6. The registration of such indenture shall secure to the holders of such debentures, the rank and privilege of a hypothec according to the laws of the province of Quebec, on the property so hypothecated; but all debentures secured by any hypothec shall rank concurrently.

Book kept for that purpose. 7. The registrar of such registration division as aforesaid, shall enter in a book kept for that purpose, at the request of the original holder or holders, or of any subsequent transferee or transferees of such debentures, the name of such original holder or holders, or of such subsequent transferee or transferees, and such holder or last registered transferee, in such book of registration, shall be deemed *prima facie* the legal owners and possessors thereof.

Fees of registrars. 8. The following fees shall be paid to registrars:—for the registration of each indenture $10;—for registration of the name of the holder or transferee of any number of debentures not exceeding five, $1; over five and not exceeding fifteen, $2; over fifteen and not exceeding thirty, $3; upwards of thirty, $4;—for making search and examining entries connected therewith, $2.

SCHEDULE.

Number of Debentures,
issued and amounts
number, and   amount
of each debenture.   Date at which they fall due.
Rate of interest and date of payments.

CAP. LXVI.

An Act to authorize the " V. Hudon Cotton Mills
Company, Hochelaga, " to issue debentures on
the security of the property of the said company
and for other purposes."

[Assented to 24th December, 1875.]

WHEREAS by letters-patent issued under the great seal Preamble:
of the province, on the 10th of february, 1878, a company having for its object the manufacture and sale of
cotton, was incorporated under the provisions of the act
respecting the incorporation of joint stock companies,
31 Vict., chap. 25, under the name of the "V. Hudon
Cotton Mills Company, Hochelaga," with a capital of
$200,000 ; and whereas by supplementary letters-patent,
issued on the 10th february, 1874, the said company
was authorized to increase its capital stock to the sum of
six hundred thousand dollars ; and whereas the said company has been since its said incorporation, and now
is in full operation ; and whereas the directors of the
said company have by their petition shown, that it
would be advantageous to the said company to allow
them in an easy and inexpensive manner to borrow, on the
security of the property of the said company, the sums
that may be required by them in the prosecution of their
works, by permitting them to issue debentures constituting a mortgage on the property of the said company ; and
whereas the directors of the said company have also
prayed for other powers ; and, whereas it is expedient
to grant the prayer of their petition ; Therefore, Her Majesty, by and with the advice and consent of the Legislature of Quebec, enacts as follows :

1. The said " V. Hudon Cotton Mills Company, Ho- The company
chelaga," is authorized to issue bonds or debentures, may issue de-
conveying a hypothec on their property, to the sum of bentures to
the amount
$250,000, in one or several distinct issues, as the directors of $250,000.
may deem expedient.

2. Every such issue of bonds or debentures shall, on The issue of
pain of nullity, be decided upon and authorized by a such deben-

16

tures shall be by-law of the directors of the said company ; and such
authorized by by-law shall contain:
by-law.   1. Mention of the amount up to which such debentures
shall issue ;
       2. An indication of the number in order of such issue
so authorized, whether it is the 1st, 2nd or 3rd, &c. ;
       3. The description, in accordance with the provisions of
the civil code of Lower Canada, of the property hypothecated for the payment of such debentures ;
       4. The time and place of payment of such debentures
and the *coupons* thereof, and the rate interest not exceeding **eight** *per cent* that they bear.
       Such by-law shall afterwards be approved by the
shareholders of the said company, at an annual general or
special meeting thereof, after fifteen days notice of such
meeting having been given to the shareholders.

Such by-law   **3.** As soon as such by-law shall have been passed, and
shall be en-   before any of the debentures the issue whereof has been
registered.   so authorized shall have been issued, negociated or placed
in circulation, a copy of such by-law duly certified by the
president and secretary of the said company, shall be enregistered in the office of the registration division in
which are situated the immoveable property or properties
to be affected for the payment of such debentures ; and
all debentures thereafter issued in virtue of such by-law
Debentures   shall convey a hypothec, from the date of such enregis-
shall convey   tration against the said immoveable property or proper-
a hypothec   ties in favor of any bearer thereof for the time being,
from the date without it being necessary to enregister the said, or any
of such enre- of the said debentures or to execute any other formality.
gistration.

Debenture   **4.** Every debenture issued as aforesaid shall, under the
states the   certificate of the president and secretary of the company,
date of the   state the date of the enregistration of the by-law authoriz-
enregistra-   ing the issue thereof.
tion of the
by-law.

Order of the   **5.** If the debentures issued are issued at one time, for
privilege of   the total sum authorized by this act, they and each of
the deben-   them shall have an equal privilege upon the immoveable
tures pro-   or immoveables affected for their payment ; but if they
ceeding from   are of different issues, for less sums, those of the first
different   issue shall each concurrently have the first hypothec
issues.   upon the said immoveable or immoveables, those of the
second issue the second hypothec and so on for the other
issues.

The hypothec   **6.** The word "immoveable" hereinabove employed shall
shall affect   mean not only the immoveable properties of the said com-
engines,   pany, but also all engines, mills, looms and other ma-
looms, &c.   chines used by the said company, in and upon the said
immoveable properties described in the by-law authorizing

the issue of the debentures, as being affected for the payment thereof.

7. Every debenture issued by the said company and made payable to bearer, or to a person therein named, or to the bearer, may be transferred by delivery ; and such transfer shall convey the property therein to the holder, and shall give him the right to bring and maintain a suit at law upon such debenture in his own name ; and every such debenture made payable to a person, or to a person, or his order, shall be transferable by the endorsement of such person; and such transfer shall transfer the property therein to the holder and shall give him the right to maintain an action upon the said debenture in his own name.

Debentures payable to the bearer transferable by delivery.

Payable to order transferable by endorsement.

8. In any suit or action upon such debenture, it shall not be necessary for the plaintiff to allege or prove the manner in which he became the holder of such debenture ; nor to allege nor prove the fulfilment of any of the formalities required for the issue of such debenture, but it shall be sufficient, if the plaintiff is described as the holder of such debenture, to allege briefly its legal effect and to make proof in consequence.

What shall be sufficient to allege in any suit upon debenture.

9. Every such debenture issued as aforesaid shall be valid and recoverable in its entirety, although it may have been negociated at a rate under par, or at a rate of interest more than six *per cent per annum.*

Debentures valid in their entirety.

10. Whenever any debenture issued as aforesaid shall have been redeemed or paid by the said company, it shall be cancelled and annulled by the president and the secretary of the said company, by their writing across the same the date of such payment, and the name of the person to whom it was made payable, and by making such other marks upon it as the directors shall deem necessary ; and the said company may afterwards on presentation of such debenture or debentures to the registrar of the registration division in which the by-law authorising the issue thereof shall have been enregistered, together with a declaration sworn to by the president and the secretary of the company, certifying that such debentures have been paid and redeemed as aforesaid; shall obtain the striking out and discharge of the hypothec created by the enregistration of such by-law, up to the amount of such debentures so redeemed and cancelled.

Recovery and annullment of the debentures.

Withdrawal of the hypothec in consequence.

11. Notwithstanding the declaration in the letters-patent incorporating the said company, that its affairs shall be managed by a board of five directors only, it shall be

Number of the directors.

may be fixed de nine. lawful for the said company, by a mere resolution of its board of directors to increase such number, provided always that it shall not at any time be fixed at more than nine.

Qualification of the direc· tors. **12.** The qualification of the directors of the said company established at $5,000 by the letters-patent incorporating the same, shall be reduced to the sum of two thousand dollars.

Shares reduced to $100 each. **13.** The shares in the said company, which are at present $500, shall for the future be only $100 each; the capital of the said company shall consequently be $600,000 divided into six thousand shares of one hundred dollars each; and any shareholders, owners of shares to the amount of five hundred dollars each, shall for the future be considered to be proprietors of the number of shares of $100 sufficient to make the total sum of his capital, in the capital stock of the said company.

Act in force. **14.** This act shall come into force the day of its sanction.

CAP. LXVII.

An Act to authorize the Paton Manufacturing Company of Sherbrooke to issue Preferential Stock of the said Company.

[Assented to 24th December, 1875.]

Preamble. WHEREAS the Paton manufacturing company of Sherbrooke, have by their petition represented that it is necessary in order to carry-out their undertaking, that the capital stock of the said company should be increased by the issue of preferential shares, and have thereby prayed for the passing of an act for that purpose, and it is expedient to grant the prayer of the said petition; Therefore, Her Majesty, by and with the advice and consent of the Legislature of Quebec, enacts as follows:

Increase of capital **1.** The capital stock of the said company may be increased to six hundred and fifty thousand dollars, of which stock, five hundred shares, amounting to two hundred and fifty thousand dollars shall be preferential stock, and the holders thereof shall be entitled in each and every year to a dividend at the rate of ten *per cent,* per *annum,* before any dividend is declared or paid upon the balance of the stock of the company, which shall be known as ordinary stock.

Use of the balance of the profits. After such rate is paid or set apart for dividends upon such preferential stock, the balance of profit applicable to

dividends shall be devoted to the payment of a dividend
not exceeding the said rate of ten *per cent per annum* upon
the ordinary stock, and after the payment of such rate of dividend on the ordinary stock, the whole capital stock shall
rank equally in respect of dividends, provided that if in Proviso.
any year the holders of the preferential stock do not receive a dividend or dividends amounting to ten *per cent
per annum*, the deficiency shall be made up in the future
before any dividends are declared upon the ordinary stock,
but without any interest upon any amounts so deficient;
Provided also, that the increase of capital stock authorised Proviso.
by this section, shall not be made until a by-law to that
effect shall have been adopted by two-thirds in value of
the shareholders present or represented at a general meeting specially convened for the purpose of considering the
same.

2. This act shall come into force immediately after its Act in force.
sanction.

CAP. LXVIII.

An Act to incorporate " The St. Henri Gas Company."

[*Assented to* 24*th December,* 1875.]

WHEREAS Anthony Force, Aubery Fitch, and Preamble.
Alexander W. Ogilvie, all of the city of Montreal,
in the province of Quebec, and Charles H. Nash, of
Chicago, in the State of Illinois, and Kerr Murray, of
Fort Wayne, in the State of Indiana, have by their petition prayed, that they and such others as hereafter may
be associated with them in their enterprise, may be
incorporated under the title hereinafter named, for the
purpose of furnishing gas and other illuminating material to the said town of St. Henri and adjoining
municipalities, exclusive of the city of Montreal, and it is
expedient to grant the prayer of said petitioners ; Therefore, Her Majesty, by and with the advice and consent
of the Legislature of Quebec, enacts as follows :

1. The said Anthony Force, Aubery Fitch, Alexander Incorpora-
W. Ogilvie, Charles H. Nash and Kerr Murray, together tion.
with all such persons as now are or hereafter may
become shareholders in the company hereby established,
shall be a body politic and corporate to the ends and for
the purposes in the preamble to this act stated, by the
name of " the St. Henri Gas Company, " and by that Name.
name shall have perpetual succession and a common Seal.
seal, with power to break and alter the same,—and by General
that name shall and may sue and be sued, implead and powers.

be impleaded in all courts of law and equity, with power
to purchase, take and hold, real and personal property of
every kind and description for the use of the said company, and the same to alienate and mortgage ; provided
always that the total annual value (over and above the
works thereon erected) of the lands or real estate to be so
acquired and held by the said company, shall not exceed
the sum of ten thousand dollars.

Proviso.

2. The head office and chief place of business of the
said company shall be in the town of St. Henri, but the
company's works and business may be carried on or
transacted in the said town of St. Henri, or in any of the
neighboring municipalities exclusive of the city of Montreal with the consent of such town, and such other
municipalities.

Chief place of business.

3. The capital stock of the said company shall be the
sum of one hundred thousand dollars divided into two
thousand shares of fifty dollars each ; the said capital
stock may be from time to time increased as the wants of
the company require, as hereinafter provided.

Capital stock.

4. The said Anthony Force, Aubery Fitch, Alexander
W. Ogilvie, Charles H. Nash and Kerr Murray shall be
the first directors of the said company, with power to
open stock books, allot stock, convene general meetings
of the company at such time and place as they shall determine, and generally to do and perform all matters and
things which any other board of directors is empowered
to do, and any other act necessary and proper to be done
to organize the company and conduct its affairs ; and they
shall continue in office until the first general meeting of
stockholders hereinafter mentioned.

Provisional directors.

5. The company may commence operations and
exercise the powers hereby granted, so soon as fifty
thousand dollars of the capital stock shall be subscribed
and ten *per centum* thereon paid up ; and over and above
the said ten *per centum* paid up capital, any stock paid
in part or in full, which may have been taken by parties
conveying rights, privileges, rights to patents, or any real
or personal property to the company, in part payment or
in full payment for such rights, privileges, rights to
patents or real or personal property, shall be held to have
been so paid in cash, for the purposes of this section.

*Commence-
ment of
operations.*

6. The first general meeting of stockholders shall take
place at the said town of St. Henri on a day to be named
by the said directors, but such meeting must be held
within six months from the passing of this act, and the
ensuing annual meetings shall be held on the same day

*Annual
meetings.*

in each year thereafter, at such a place and hour as may be appointed by the by-laws of the company, or by the directors in their default, but a failure to elect directors on the day and in the manner prescribed shall not dissolve the company, but such election may take place at any general meeting duly called for that purpose : and the retiring directors shall continue in office until their successors are elected.

7. At such first and subsequent meetings, five directors shall be elected to hold office, until their successors are appointed as above provided. Number of the directors.

8. Any three of the said directors, whether those appointed by this act or subsequently elected, shall form a *quorum*, and may exercise all the powers devolving upon and vested in the said directors. Quorum.

9. The shareholders of the said company shall be bound to pay the amount of their subscriptions as they may from time to time be called upon by the directors ; but the said directors shall only be bound to make calls at the times and in the manner they deem to be expedient for the purposes of the company, any law to the contrary notwithstanding. Calls.

10. It shall be lawful for the said company to break up, dig and trench so much and so many of the streets, squares, highways, lanes and public places within the limits of such municipalities, as may be necessary for laying down the mains and pipes to conduct the gas or illuminating material from the works, of the company to the consumers thereof, doing no unnecessary damage in the premises, and taking care as far as may be, to preserve a free and uninterrupted passage through the said streets, squares, highways, lanes and public places while the works are in progress. Execution of the works.

11. Where there are buildings within the said limits, the different parts whereof belong to different proprietors, or are in possession of different tenants or lessees, the company may carry pipes to any part of any building so situated, passing over the property of one or more proprietors, or in the possession of one or more tenants, to convey the gas or illuminating material to the property of another or in the possession of another. Idem.

12. The company may also break up and uplift all passages common to neighbouring proprietors or tenants, and dig or cut trenches therein for the purpose of laying down pipes or taking up or repairing the same, doing as little damage as may be in the execution of the powers granted Idem.

by this act, and making satisfaction thereafter to the
owners or proprietors of buildings or other property, or
to any other party, for all damages to be by them sustained, in or by the execution of the powers granted by
Proviƨo. this act; subject to which provisions this act shall be
sufficient to indemnify the company, their servants, and
those by them employed, for what they or any of them
shall do in pursuance of the powers granted by this act.

Works, &c.   **13.** The said company shall so construct and locate
their works, and all apparatus and appurtenances thereunto belonging or appertaining, so as not to endanger
the public health or safety, and the said works shall be
subject to and bound by the existing by-laws of the corpo-
Control of the ration, and of the corporations of the municipalities here-
municipa- inbefore mentioned, in so far as the said works may be
lities. situated within their respective limits; and the said gas
works, apparatus and appurtenances shall, at all reason-
Inspection. able times, be subject to the visit and inspection of the
municipal authorities of the corporation or corporations,
within the limits whereof they are situated, reasonable
notice thereof being previously given to the company;
and the company, their servants and workmen, shall at
Offences. all times obey all just and reasonable orders and directions
they shall receive from the said municipal authorities, in
Penalties. that respect, under a penalty of not more than one hundred
dollars nor less than five dollars, for each offence, in
neglecting or refusing to obey the same—to be recovered
at the suit and for the use of said municipality, in any
court of competent civil jurisdiction.

Watchmen,   **14.** In case the said company shall open or break up
lamps, &c. any street, square or public place, and shall neglect to
keep the passage of the said street, square or public
place, as far as may be, free and uninterrupted, to place
guards or fences, with lamps, or to place watchmen, or to
take every necessary precaution for the prevention of
accidents to passengers and others, or to close and replace
the said streets, squares or public places, without unnecessary delay, or when notified so to do, by the town
surveyor as hereinbefore provided, or to repair any
Damages. damages that may have been caused to such street, square
or public place, by reason of any work done therein by
the said company, such company shall be responsible for
all damages caused by such neglect, and the municipal
authorities of the corporation interested, after notice in
writing to the company, shall cause the duty so neglected
to be forthwith performed, and may recover the costs
thereof from the said company; and in default of payment
Costs. of the said costs by the latter within one month after
demand, they may be recovered by civil action in any
court of competent jurisdiction.

15. If any person lays or causes to be laid any pipe or _{Laying} main belonging to the said company, or in any way _{pipes.} obtains or uses its gas, or other illuminating material, without the consent of the company, he shall forfeit and pay to the company the sum of one hundred and twenty _{Penalty.} dollars, and also a further sum of four dollars for each day during which such communication remains, which sums, together with costs of suit in that behalf incurred, _{Costs.} may be recovered by civil action, in any court of competent jurisdiction.

16. If any person wilfully or maliciously breaks up, _{Breaking up,} pulls down or damages, injures, puts out of order or des- _{&c.} troys any main pipe, engine, pipe, plug or other works or apparatus, appurtenances or dependencies thereof, or any matter or thing made and provided for the purpose aforesaid, or any of the materials used and provided for the same, or ordered to be erected, laid down, or belonging to the said company; or in any wise wilfully do any other injury or damage for the purpose of obstructing, hindering or embarrassing the construction, completion, maintaining or repairing of the said works, or causes or procures the same to be done, or increases the supply of gas or other illuminating material agreed for with the company by increasing the number or size of the holes in the gas burners, or using the gas without burners, or otherwise wrongfully, negligently, or wastefully burning the same, or by wrongfully or improperly wasting the same, such person shall, on conviction thereof, before a justice of the peace, or any other person authorized to act in that capacity in the locality wherein the offence has been committed, be compelled to pay for the use of the company, a penalty not exceeding forty _{Penalty.} dollars, together with costs of prosecution, or be confined in the common gaol of the district for a space of time not exceeding three months, as to such justice shall seem meet.

17. Nothing in this act contained shall prevent any _{Rights pre-} person from constructing any work for the supply of gas _{served.} to his own premises.

18. Neither the service nor connecting pipes of the said _{Properties of} company, nor any meters, lustres, lamps, pipes, gas-fittings _{the company} nor any other property of any kind whatsoever of the com- _{not subject to} _{seizure for} pany, shall be subject to or liable for rent, notwith- _{rent.} standing article 1622 of the civil code, nor liable to be seized or attached in any way by the possessor or owner of the premises wherein the same may be, nor be in any way whatsoever liable to any person for the debt of any person, to and for whose use, or the use of whose house or building the same may be supplied by said company, notwithstanding the actual or apparent possession thereof by such person.

Damaging pipes, lamps, &c.

19. If any person, wilfully or maliciously, damages or causes, or knowingly suffers, to be damaged any meter, lamp, lustre, service pipe or fitting belonging to the said company, or wilfully impairs or knowingly suffers the same to be altered or impaired, so that the meters or meters indicate less gas than actually passes through the same, such person shall incur a penalty to the use of the company for every such offence, of not less than four dollars, nor exceeding twenty dollars, and shall also pay all charges necessary for the repairing or replacing the said meter, pipes or fittings, and double the value of the surplus gas so consumed; such damages, penalties and charges to be recovered with costs as hereinafter provided.

Penalty.

Costs.

Damaging pipes, post-plugs, &c.

20. If any person wilfully extinguishes any of the public lamps or lights, or wilfully removes, destroys, damages, fraudulently alters or in any way injures any pipe, pedestal post-plug, lamp or other apparatus or thing belonging to the company, he shall forfeit and pay to the use of the company a penalty not less than four dollars, nor more than twenty dollars, and shall also be liable to make good all damages and charges, to be recovered with costs, as hereinafter provided.

Penalty.

Neglecting to pay the rate.

21. If any person supplied by the company with gas neglects to pay the rent, rate or charge due to the company at any of the times fixed for the payment thereof, the company or any person acting under their authority, on giving forty-eight hours previous notice, may stop the supply of gas from entering the premises of the person in arrear as aforesaid, by cutting off the service pipe or pipes, or by any such other means as the company or its officers see fit, and may recover the rent or charge due up to such time, together with the expenses of cutting off the gas, in any competent court, notwithstanding any contract to furnish for a longer time.

Supply of gas, stopped.

Power to enter into the houses, &c.

22. In all cases where the company may lawfully cut off and take away the supply of gas from any house, building or premises, the company, their agents and workmen, upon giving forty-eight hours previous notice to the person in charge or the occupier, may enter into the house, building or premises, between the hour of nine o'clock in the forenoon, and four o'clock in the afternoon, making as little disturbance and inconvenience as possible, and may remove and take away any pipe, meter, cock, branch, lamp, fitting or other apparatus, the property of, and belonging to the company, and any servant of the company duly authorized may, between the hours aforesaid, enter any house in which gas has been taken, for the purpose of repairing and making good in any such house, building or premises, or for the purpose of examining any meter, pipe or apparatus belonging to the company or used for their gas ; and if any person refuses to permit, Refusing to permit. or does not permit the servants and officers of the company to enter and to perform the acts aforesaid, the person so refusing or obstructing, shall incur a penalty to the Penalty. company for every such offence, of forty dollars and a further penalty of four dollars for every day during which such refusal or obstructing shall continue, to be recovered with costs as hereinafter provided.

23. All fines, penalties and forfeitures imposed by this Recovery of the penalties. act may be sued for and recovered with costs by the company either in the manner hereinbefore directed, or before a justice or justices of the peace in the district where the offence has been committed, on oath of any one credible witness.

24. All actions for damages or penalties, or both, given Mode of recovery. by this act, shall be brought in courts having jurisdiction to the amount involved in such suit, unless otherwise provided by this act.

25. In any action brought by or on behalf of the com- Share-holders may be witness. pany, in any court, or in any proceedings before a justice of the peace, on behalf of such company, the president and any share-holder shall be competent witnesses, notwithstanding their interest in such suit or otherwise.

26. The directors of the said company, if they see fit, Increase of the capital stock. at any time after the whole capital stock of one hundred thousand dollars above mentioned, shall have been subscribed and paid in, but not sooner, may make a by-law for increasing the capital stock of the company to any amount not exceeding two hundred and fifty thousand dollars which they may consider requisite, in order to the due carrying out of the objects of the company. Such by-law shall declare the number and value of the shares of the new stock, and may prescribe the manner in which the same shall be allotted. But no such by-law shall have force and effect until after it shall have been sanctioned by a vote of not less than two-thirds in amount of the shareholders, at a general meeting of the company, duly called for considering the same.

27. " The joint stock companies general clauses act " Joint stock comp. gen. c. act shall apply. shall apply and be part of this act, except in so far as it is in contradiction to, or inconsistent with any of the provisions of this act.

Conditions
required.

28. The privileges and advantages granted to the company by this act shall cease and be of no effect if works are not established and in operation in virtue hereof, within three years from the passing of this act—capable of producing ten thousand cubic feet of gas *per diem.*

CAP. LXIX.

An Act to incorporate the Women's Christian Association of Quebec.

[*Assented to* 24*th December,* 1875.]

Preamble.

WHEREAS the persons hereinafter mentioned have, by petition, represented that they and others for some time past have maintained, by voluntary contributions, a certain institution in the city of Quebec, known as "The Women's Christian Association of Quebec," for the purpose of receiving young women, who come as strangers to the city, obtaining for them board and employment, attending generally to their temporal and moral welfare, providing a reading room and library for young women, and premises where meetings of ladies connected with different benevolent institutions may be held, and for other benevolent purposes of a like nature, and have prayed that for the better attainment of its objects the institution may be vested with corporate powers ; Therefore, Her Majesty, by and with the advice and consent of the Legislature of Quebec, enacts as follows :

Incorpora-
tion.

1. Mesdames Robert Cassels, Henry D. Powis, Joseph Whitehead, Richard M. Harrison, James Gibb, William F. Collins and Misses Emily Gillespie and Lucy E. Lamb, and such persons as are now or may hereafter be associated with them, in conformity with this act, and their successors, are hereby constituted a body corporate and politic with all the rights incident to corporations by the name

Name.

of "The Women's Christian Association of Quebec."

General
powers.

2. The said corporation shall have perpetual succession, and| may have a common seal, with power to change the same if they think proper, and may under the said name contract, sue and be sued, and may acquire by any legal title, hold, possess, and enjoy, to and for the use of such corporation, any moveable or immoveable property which may be sold, exchanged, given or bequeathed to the said corporation, or to

Proviso.

sell, hypothecate, convey, let or lease the same ; provided always that such real estate shall not exceed the annual value of five thousand dollars, beyond that actually re-

quired for the use of the said corporation ; provided also, Proviso.
that if the said corporation become possessed of real
estate, exceeding the annual value of five thousand dollars, apart from that actually used by the said corporation,
it shall be bound to sell such surplus property within
three years from the acquisition of the same, and invest
the proceeds thereof, in public securities of the Dominion,
in stocks of chartered banks, mortgages, or other approved securities, for the use of the said corporation.

3. The officers of the said corporation, shall consist of a Officers.
president, four vice-presidents, a treasurer, a secretary and
an assistant-secretary. The officers, with such other members as may be chosen for that purpose, shall form the
committee of management of the association.

4. The said corporation shall have power to make a Power to
code of by-laws, not inconsistent with the laws of this make by-
province or of the Dominion, for fixing the terms of ad- laws.
mission, for its committee of management, and determining
or changing the number thereof, and for the general regulation and management of its affairs, which, when adopted at a regular general meeting, shall, until modified or
rescinded, be equally binding as this act, upon the institution, its officers and members.

5. The by-laws of the said institution, not being con- Actual by-
trary to law, shall be the by-laws of the said corporation, laws contin-
until they shall be repealed or altered as aforesaid.   ued.

6. The said corporation shall be bound to make an Report to the
annual report to the legislature, containing a general legislature.
statement of the affairs of the corporation, within the first
twenty days of every session of the legislature.

CAP. LXX.

An Act to incorporate " The Church Home," of
Montreal.

[Assented to 24th December, 1875.]

WHEREAS the Most Reverend Ashton Oxenden, Lord Preamble.
Bishop of Montreal, and Metropolitan of Canada and
others, hereinafter mentioned, have by petition, represented that about twenty years ago, " the Church Home"
was founded by the late Mrs. Fulford, during the lifetime of her husband the Most Reverend Francis Fulford,
late Lord Bishop of Montreal, and Metropolitan of Canada,
the object of this institution being, to afford an asylum
to the aged and infirm members of the church of England,

and also⁷ a temporary home for convalescents from the general hospital, and that this institution has continued ever since to exist, and now exists under their control and management, and that of a general committee and sub-committee composed of ladies, members of the church of England ; and have prayed that the said institution be incorporated, with power to hold property and to receive donations, gifts and legacies in aid of the said institution, and for other purposes ; and whereas it is expedient to grant the prayer of the said petition ; therefore, Her Majesty, by and with the advice and consent of the Legislature of Quebec, enacts as follows :

Incorpora-
tion.

1. The Most Reverend Ashton Oxenden, lord bishop of Montreal and metropolitan of Canada, Mesdames Sarah Oxenden, Ann Anderson, Louisa Aspinwall Howe and Margaret Blackwood, and such other persons as now are, or may hereafter be associated with them, and their successors are hereby constituted and created a body corporate and politic with all the rights incident to corporations,

Name.

by the name of "The Church Home."

General
powers.

2 The said corporation shall have perpetual succession, and may have a common seal, with power to change, alter, break and renew the same when and as often as they shall think proper, and may, under the same name, contract and be contracted with, sue and be sued, implead and be impleaded, in all courts and places whatsoever in this province, and by the same name they and their successors from time to time and at all times hereafter, shall be able and capable to have, take, receive, purchase and acquire, hold, possess, enjoy and maintain to and for the use of the said corporation all lands or property, moveable or immoveable, which may hereafter be sold, ceded, exchanged, given, bequeathed or granted, to the said corporation, or to sell, hypothecate, alienate, convey, let or lease the same, if need be, provided always that such real estate shall not exceed the annual value of five thousand dollars, beyond that actually required for the use of the said corporation;

Proviso.

provided also that if the said corporation become possessed of real estate exceeding the annual value of five thousand dollars apart from that actually used by the said corporation, it shall be bound to sell such surplus property within five years from the acquisition of the same, and invest the proceeds thereof in public securities of the dominion, stocks of chartered banks, mortgages and other approved securities for the use of the said corporation.

Officers.

3. The officers of the said corporation shall consist of a president, first directress, second directress, secretary and treasurer and a committee of management of not less than ten members, and such other officers as shall, from time to time, seem necessary to the corporation. The foregoing officers shall be chosen from among the members of the said institution, and the president, first directress, second directress, secretary and treasurer, shall be *ex-officio* members of the said committee.

4. The said corporation shall have power to make by laws not inconsistent with the laws of this province, or of the Dominion, for fixing the terms of admission of its members, for the government of the same, for the election, and changing of the officers above named, and for the general regulation and management of its affairs, which by-laws, when formed and adopted at a regular meeting, shall, until modified or rescinded, be equally binding as this act, upon the institution, its officers and members. *Power to make by-laws.*

5. The by-laws of the said institution, not being contrary to law, shall be the by-laws of the corporation hereby constituted, until they shall be repealed or altered as aforesaid. *Actual by-laws continued.*

6. Until others shall be elected according to the by-laws of the corporation, the present officers of the institution shall be those of the corporation. *Actual officers continued.*

7. The said corporation shall be bound to make annual report to the legislature containing a general statement of the affairs of the corporation, which said reports shall be presented within the first twenty days of every session of the legislature. *Report to the legislature.*

CAP. LXXI.

An Act to incorporate the "Dunham Ladies' College."

[Assented to 24th December, 1875.]

WHEREAS the Most Reverend Ashton Oxenden, D.D., Lord Bishop of Montreal and Metropolitan, the Reverend David Lindsay, M. A., the Reverend Wm. Henderson, M. A., the Honorable Thos. Wood, M. L. C., J. B. Gibson, M. D., W. W. Lynch, Esq., M.P.P., and G. B. Baker, Esquire, M.P.P. and others, have, by petition, prayed that an act of incorporation be passed for the purpose of establishing and conducting a seminary of learning, of a collegiate character, for the education of the daughters of the clergy and laity of the Church of England, in Canada, under the name of the " Dunham Ladies' College," and whereas it is expedient to grant such prayer; Therefore, *Preamble.*

Her Majesty, by and with the advice and consent of the Legislature of Quebec, enacts as follows :

Incorpora-
tion.

Name.

1. A body politic and corporate shall be and is by the present act constituted and established in the village of Dunham, in the district of Bedford, under the name of " The Dunham Ladies' College," which shall consist of the Most Reverend the Lord Bishop of Montreal, for the time being, and his successors in office, the clergy of the several parishes and missions, in connection with the Church of England, within the limits of the deanery of Bedford, *ex-officio*, and one layman for each parish or mission in said deanery, who shall be elected annually by the several vestries of the said parishes and missions, at their annual meetings on Easter Monday.

Power to
make by-
laws.

2. The majority of the corporation for the time being, shall have power and authority to make and pass such statutes, rules, orders and by-laws, not contrary to the present act, or to the laws in force in this province, as they may deem useful or necessary in the interests of the said corporation and for the government thereof, and they may from time to time modify, repeal and change such statutes, rules, orders and by-laws, or any of them, as they may deem useful, for the management of the said institution.

General
powers.
Seal.

Revenues
limited.

Legacies, &c.

3. The said corporation shall have perpetual succession, and may have a common seal, with power to change, alter, break and renew the same at their will and pleasure, and the said corporation may, under the same name, con- tract and treat, sue and be sued, implead and be im- pleaded, summon and be summoned in all courts of law and places whatsoever in this province, and shall have power without any other authority to acquire by pur- chase, donation or otherwise, to receive by will, hold, possess, take and accept for the purpose of the said corpora- tion, all lands, tenements or hereditaments, and moveable and immoveable property, as also to sell, lease, change, alienate and dispose of the same, and to acquire others in their place, for the above mentioned purpose ; provided always, that the annual net revenue, fruits and profits from all immoveable property of the said corporation, other than the lands on which are erected the buildings and dependencies of the said college, and those which may be acquired in the vicinity of the said buildings, and which shall be adjacent to the lands already possessed by the said college, shall not at any time exceed the annual sum of ten thousand dollars current money of this pro- vince. In the event of the said corporation, receiving by donation or legacy any immoveable property, over and above that which it is allowed to possess, such donation or legacy shall not on this account be null, but the said corporation shall within the seven years next after taking possession thereof, be obliged to sell or alienate the said immoveable property, or its other immoveable property, so as not to exceed the amount hereinbefore specified.

The said corporation shall also have power to appoint an attorney or attorneys to manage its affairs, and generally it shall enjoy all the rights and privileges of other bodies corporate and politic recognized by the legislature. *Management of affairs.*

4. And all property which shall at any time be possessed by the said corporation as well as the revenues arising therefrom shall be always appropriated and applied solely to the advancement of education in the said college and for no other purpose, institution or establishment whatever, not attached or dependent thereto. *Use of the revenues.*

5. The real estate in the said village of Dunham, with the college and its dependencies being thereon constructed, as well as the moveable property of the said college, the whole as now possessed by the Lord Bishop of Montreal, are by the present act with the consent of the said Lord Bishop of Montreal, vested in the corporation established by this act. *Investment of the college &c.*

6. All subscriptions heretofore made for the erection and endowment of the said " Dunham Ladies' College," shall be, and are hereby declared to be to all intents and purposes as lawful, and binding upon the subscribers, as if this act had been previously passed. *Interpretation.*

CAP. LXXII.

An Act to incorporate the "Compton Ladies' College."

[Assented to 24th December, 1875.]

WHEREAS the Right Reverend James William Williams, D. D., Lord Bishop of Quebec, has represented that a college for the education of young ladies has been established in the village of Compton, in which instruction has been given for some time, and of which the said Lord Bishop of Quebec is trustee, and that wishing to give it a permanent governing body, he hath prayed that corporate powers may be conferred on the said college ; and that in consideration of the advantages already derived, and to be derived from the said establishment, it is expedient to grant the prayer of the said petition ; Therefore, Her Majesty, by and with the advice and consent of the Legislature of Quebec, enacts as follows : *Preamble.*

17 *

Incorpora-
tion.

Name.

Persons form-
ing part
thereof.

1. A body politic and corporate shall be and is by the present act constituted and established in the village of Compton, in the township and county of Compton, under the name of "The Compton Ladies' College," which shall be composed of the Lord Bishop of Quebec, *ex officio*, who shall always be president of the said corporation, and of four others to be from time to time appointed as hereinafter provided; who together with the Lord Bishop of Quebec, shall be trustees of the said Compton Ladies' College, and the first members of the corporation of the said Compton Ladies' College shall be together with the Lord Bishop of Quebec, *ex officio*, the Reverend Henry Roe, professor of divinity in Bishop's College, Lennoxville, the Honorable Matthew Henry Cochrane, senator, of Compton aforesaid, Robert Herbert Smith, of the city of Quebec, Esquire, merchant, and the Reverend John Foster, missionary at Coaticook.

Purposes of
said corpora-
tion.

2. The purposes of the said corporation shall be to maintain and perpetuate the college which has been established in the village of Compton for the education of young ladies, of which the Lord Bishop of Quebec is the trustee.

Election of
trustees.

3. The successors of such last-named four trustees shall be elected from time to time, as hereinafter provided, by the synod of the Anglican diocese of Quebec.

Number of
such trustees.

4. Such synod of the diocese of Quebec is hereby empowered, if it shall see fit, by a canon duly enacted for that purpose, to increase the number of such elected trustees to any number not exceeding twelve in all.

Term of
office of the
actual trus-
tees.

Of their suc-
cessors.

5. Two of the above four last-named trustees shall hold office only till their successors are elected by the synod of the diocese of Quebec, at its now next ensuing regular session; the remaining two of the four last-named trustees shall hold office till their successors are elected by such synod of Quebec, at the session next following; and the two trustees who shall so retire from office first shall be the Reverend Henry Roe and the Reverend John Foster; but the successors of such trustees, and all subsequent trustees, shall hold office for four years, and until their successors are duly elected by such synod of the diocese of Quebec. All retiring trustees may be again chosen by the synod of the diocese of Quebec as aforesaid.

Power to
make by-
laws.

6. The majority of the corporation for the time being, shall have power and authority to make and pass such statutes, rules, orders and by-laws, not contrary to the present act, or to the laws in force in this province, as they may deem useful or necessary in the interests of the said corporation and for the government thereof, and they may from time to time modify, repeal and change such statutes, rules, orders and by-laws, or any of them, as they may deem useful, for the management of the said institution.

7. The said corporation shall have perpetual succession, and may have a common seal, with power to change, alter, break and renew the same at their will and pleasure, and the said corporation may, under the same name, contract and treat, sue and be sued, implead and be impleaded, summon and be summoned in all courts of law and places whatsoever in this province, and shall have power to acquire by purchase, donation or otherwise, to receive by will, hold, possess, take and accept for the purpose of the said corporation, all lands, tenements or hereditaments, and moveable and immoveable property, as also to sell, lease, change, alienate and dispose of the same, and to acquire others in their place, for the above mentioned purpose; provided always, that the annual net revenue, fruits and profits from all immoveable property of the said corporation, (other than the lands on which are erected the buildings and dependencies of the said college, which lands have a superficial area of six and a quarter acres, more or less, and those which may be acquired for the use and purposes of such college in the vicinity of the said buildings, and which shall be adjacent to the lands already possessed by the said college,) shall not at any time exceed the annual sum of ten thousand dollars current money of this province; And in the event of the said corporation, receiving by donation or legacy any immoveable property, over and above that which it is allowed to possess, such donation or legacy shall not on this account be null, but the said corporation shall within the five years next after taking possession thereof be obliged to sell or alienate the said immoveable property, or its other immoveable property, so as not to exceed the amount hereinbefore specified.

To have a seal, &c.
To acquire.
Proviso.
Revenues, limited.
Legacies, &c.

8. All property which shall at any time be possessed by the said corporation as well as the revenues arising therefrom shall be always appropriated and applied solely to the advancement of education in the said college and for no other purpose, institution or establishment whatever, not attached or dependent thereto.

Use of the revenues.

9. The real estate of about six and a quarter acres in superficies above mentioned, with the college and its dependencies thereon constructed, as well as the moveable property of the said college, the whole as now pos-

Investment of the college, &c.

sessed by the Lord Bishop of Quebec, are with the consent of the said Lord Bishop of Quebec vested in the corporation established by this act.

Report to the Synod.   **10.** The said corporation shall lay before the synod of the diocese of Quebec annually a report exhibiting the financial and educational condition of the institution.

Detailed statement furnished to lieut.-gov. when required.   **11.** It shall be the duty of the said corporation to submit to the lieutenant-governor when thereunto required by him the said lieutenant-governor, a detailed statement of the number of members of the said corporation, of the number of professors employed in the various branches of instruction, of the number of pupils receiving instruction, of the course of study followed and of the immoveable property possessed by it, and of the revenues arising therefrom.

CAP. LXXIII.

An Act to declare and define the powers of the Trustees of the Free Church, côté street, of Montreal, in respect of its property.

[*Assented to 24th December,* 1875.]

Preamble.   WHEREAS the elders and deacons constituting the "Deacons Court" of the Free Church, Côté street, in the city of Montreal, in connection with the "Presbyterian Church in Canada," have by their petition represented that the said church is not conveniently situated; and that the question of changing its locality and selling the property on which it stands, is under consideration in the congregation thereof, and whereas doubts exist whether section seven of the act respecting the union of certain Presbyterian Churches therein named, 24 Vict., chapter 124, apply to the said case, and whereas the said petitioners have prayed that the powers of the said congregation in respect of the said property may be more clearly defined, and it is expedient to grant the prayer of the said petition and quiet the said doubts ; Therefore, Her Majesty, by and with the advice and consent of the Legislature of Quebec, enacts as follows :

24 Vict., c. 124, s. 7, shall apply to Free Church.   **1.** Notwithstanding anything in the deed of acquisition of the property in Côté street, in the city of Montreal, now known and described upon the *cadastre* of Saint Lawrence ward of the said city under the number six hundred and fifty-seven, to wit, in that certain deed of sale and conveyance executed on the thirteenth day of june, one thousand eight hundred and forty-eight, at Montreal aforesaid, by John Redpath, of the said city of

Montreal, esquire, of the one part, and Adam Stevenson,
and seven others, as trustees, of the other part, before
Maitre W. Ross and his colleague, notaries, the seventh
section of that certain act above mentioned of the parliament of the late province of Canada, duly made and
passed in the twenty-fourth year of Her Majesty's reign,.
intituled : " An act respecting the union of certain
Presbyterian Churches therein named, " shall apply to
the said Free Church, Côté street, and to the property
thereof ; and therefore upon obtaining the consent of the   Power of the
congregation thereof, or of a majority present of those   trustees.
entitled to vote at a meeting convened to consider the
matter, the existing trustees of the said church may exercise
any or all of the powers mentioned or referred to in the
said seventh section of the said act ; provided always that   Proviso.
the exercise of such powers be first sanctioned by the
presbytery of Montreal of the Presbyterian Church in
Canada.

CAP. LXXIV.

An Act to enable the Rector and Churchwardens of
Saint Stephen's Church, of the Parish of Saint Stephen, in the Diocese of Montreal, to sell the said
church and the property on which it is built, and to
erect a new church elsewhere.

[Assented to 24th December, 1875.]

WHEREAS the Rector and Churchwardens of Saint   Preamble.
Stephen's Church, in the parish of Saint Stephen, in
the diocese of Montreal, have by their petition set forth :
That by deed of donation made and executed on the
twentieth day of april, eighteen hundred and forty-three,
before J. J. Gibb and his colleague, notaries public, John
Crooks, of the said city of Montreal, miller, gratuitously
and irrevocably gave, granted, conferred, transferred, conveyed, assigned and made over unto the Reverend John
Bethune, doctor of divinity, rector of the parsonage or
rectory and parish church of Montreal, and his successors
in office, the rectors of the said parsonage or rectory, and
parish church of Montreal, from thenceforth for ever,
those certain lots or emplacements situate in the fief Na-
zareth, and known and distinguished on the ground plan
of the said fief, by the numbers one hundred and fifty-
three and one hundred and fifty-four, being contiguous,
and bounded in front by Dalhousie street, in the city of
Montreal, in this province, in rear by lots numbers one
hundred and thirteen and one hundred and fourteen, and
on one side by the property of one Robinson, and on the
other side by lot number one hundred and fifty-five, and

containing said two lots ninety feet in front by ninety feet in depth, and containing a superficies *in toto* of eight thousand one hundred feet, in trust to and for the uses and purposes of the United Church of England and Ireland, and especially for the erection thereon of a church for the performance of divine worship and the administration of the sacraments, and of other rites and ceremonies of the said united church.

That a church was accordingly erected and still subsists on the said lot, called and known as Saint Stephen's Church, and which has been at all times devoted to the performance of divine worship according to the rites and ceremonies of the said church;

That the said lots of land so given and granted as aforesaid, are presently known and designated as lot number sixteen hundred and thirty-six on the official plan, and in the book of reference of Saint Ann's ward, of the said city of Montreal, within which ward they are situate;

That under the powers conferred on "The Synod of the Diocese of Montreal," by the act of the legislature of this province, 35 Victoria, chapter 19, the said Synod divided the said parish of Montreal into several parishes, one whereof was designated by the said Synod to be the parish of Saint Stephen;

That the aforesaid property and church are situate within the said parish of Saint Stephen, and, by virtue of the said subdivision of the said parish of Montreal, became and were, and are now vested in the said petitioners and their successors in office;

That in the judgment of the said petitioners and of the members of Saint Stephen's Church, it is expedient to sell the said lot of land and the church thereon erected, and apply the proceeds of such sale towards the erection of a church, to be also called Saint Stephen's Church, on the lot of land called and known as lot number eighteen hundred and seventeen, on the official plan and in the book of reference of the said Saint Ann's ward, presently vested in the said Reverend Thomas Trife Lewis Evans, as such rector of said Saint Stephen's Church, under and by virtue of a deed of donation to him, made and executed by John Harris, esquire, of the said city of Montreal, on the twenty-first day of june, eighteen hundred and seventy-five before James Smith, notary public; And whereas it is expedient to grant the prayer of the said petition; Therefore, Her Majesty, by and with the advice and consent of the Legislature of Quebec, enacts as follows:

Power to sell a certain lot in Montreal.

1. The said rector and churchwardens of the said Saint-Stephen's Church and their successors in office, are hereby authorized, by and with the consent of the Lord Bishop of Montreal, to sell the said lot of land numbered

sixteen hundred and thirty-six on the official plan and
in the book of reference of Saint Ann's ward, of the said
city of Montreal, and the church presently erected thereon, and called and known as " Saint Stephen's Church,"
and other appurtenances thereto belonging, either at
public auction, or by private sale, for cash or on credit, or
part cash and part credit, secured in such manner as to
them the said rector and churchwardens and their successors shall seem meet, and as they may deem most advisable, and to execute and convey an absolute title
thereto, to the purchaser or purchasers thereof, and to
receive payment of the purchase money and grant all
necessary acquittances and discharges therefor.

2. The purchase money to be derived from the said Use of the
sale shall be applied by the said rector and church-price deriving
wardens, and their successors in office, towards the erec-from the sale.
tion of a church to be also called " Saint Stephen's
Church," on the said lot of land numbered eighteen hundred and seventeen, on the official plan and in the book of
reference of the said Saint Ann's ward, but no person or
persons, body or bodies politic, who shall purchase the said
lot six hundred and thirty-six and the said church thereon,
and other appurtenances, shall be in any way bound to see
to the application, or be answerable for the non-application
of the said purchase money, or any part thereof.

3. The said property so acquired for the purposes of Purpose of
erecting a new church as also the church and other build-such acquisi-
ings to be thereon erected, shall be vested in the said rec-tion.
tor and churchwardens of Saint Stephen's Church and
their successors in office in trust for the uses and purposes
ecclesiastical of the said parish of Saint Stephen.

CAP. LXXV..

An Act to incorporate " The Canadian Club " of Mont-
treal.

[*Assented to 24th December*, 1875.]

WHEREAS the persons hereinafter named, with a Preamble.
large number of others in the city of Montreal,
have associated themselves for the establishment of a club
for social purposes, and have prayed to be incorporated
by the name of " the Canadian Club," and it is expedient to grant the prayer of their petition ; Therefore, Her
Majesty, by and with the advice and consent of the Legislature of Quebec, enacts as follows :

1. The following persons, namely, G. Maurice Lafram- Incorpora-
boise, Esq., Patrick O'Meara, Esq., Alfred Brunet, Esq., tion.

Joseph N. Pauzé, Esq., and Hector Lamontagne, Esq., and such other persons as are now members or shall hereafter become members of the said association, under the rules and regulations of the said association, shall be and are hereby declared to be a body politic and corporate

Name. in deed and in name by the name of " the Canadian Club," for the above purposes, and shall, by the same name, from time to time, and at all times hereafter, be

Power to acquire, &c. able and capable to purchase, acquire, hold, possess and enjoy, and to have, exchange, take and receive, to them and their successors, all lands, tenements and hereditaments, and all real or immoveable estates being and situate in the city of Montreal or its vicinity, necessary for the actual use and occupation of the said corporation for the purpose for which they are created, and the said property to hypothecate, sell, alienate and dispose of, and to acquire other instead thereof, whensoever the said corporation

Annual value, limited. may deem it proper so to do, but such real estate shall not exceed the annual value of ten thousand dollars currency ; and the constitution, rules and regulations now in force touching the admission and expulsion of members and the management and conduct generally of the affairs and concerns of the said association, in so far as they are not inconsistent with the laws of this province, shall be the constitution, rules and regulations of the said corporation ; provided always, that the said corporation may, from time to time, alter, repeal and change, in whole or in part, such constitution, rules and regulations in the manner provided by the constitution, rules and regulations of the said corporation.

Use of the properties held in trust. **2.** All property and effects now owned by, or held in trust for the said association, are hereby vested in the said corporation and shall be applied solely to purposes of the said corporation, and all debts, claims for subscriptions or contributions of members and other rights accruing to the said association under its constitution, rules and regulations, shall be vested in the corporation constituted by this act ; and the said corporation shall be charged with the liabilities and obligations of the said association.

Liabilities, limited. **3.** No member of the corporation shall be liable for any of the debts thereof, beyond a sum which shall be equal to the amount of the original entrance fee and the respective share of every member in the amount of the subsequent contributions or divisions which might hereafter be levied or allotted between all the members of the club for

Power of the members of the corporation to retire therefrom. the time being, in equal shares, and which might remain unpaid by such member ; and any member of the corporation, not being in arrears, may retire therefrom, and shall cease to be such member, on giving notice to that

Notice. effect in such form as may be required by the constitution, rules and regulations thereof, and thereafter shall be wholly free from liability for any debt or engagement of the club ; and every member expelled or retiring from the club, or whose name shall have been struck out of the list of members, for any of the reasons mentioned in the constitution, rules and regulations of the club, shall, *ipso facto,* forfeit all rights of membership. *Effect of the retirement or expulsion.*

4. The said corporation shall have power to appoint such officers, administrators and servants as may be required for the due management of its affairs, and to allow them respectively a reasonable and suitable remuneration ; and all the officers so appointed may exercise such other powers and authorities, for the due management and administration of the affairs of the said corporation, as may be required of them by the constitution, rules and regulations of the said corporation. *Officers.*

5. The rents, revenues and profits arising out of every description of moveable and immoveable property belonging to the said corporation shall be appropriated and employed to the exclusive use of the said corporation, to the construction and repairs of the buildings required for the purposes of the said corporation, and to the payment of expenses legitimately incurred in carrying out any of the objects relating to the aforesaid purposes. *Use of the revenues.*

6. This act shall come into force the day of its sanction. *Act in force.*

CAP. LXXVI.

An Act to incorporate the Musical Band of the Village of Lauzon.

[*Assented to 24th December, 1875.*]

WHEREAS there exists in the village of Lauzon, an association whose aim is to found a musical band, and whereas the persons forming the said association have prayed for an act of incorporation, and it is just to grant the prayer of their petition ; Therefore, Her Majesty, by and with the advice and consent of the Legislature of Quebec, enacts as follows : *Preamble.*

1. The Reverend E. Fafard, priest, F. X. Couillard, L. P. Patry, Jean Julien, Dr. Wm. Lamontagne, T. N. Couillard, Dr. A. A. Marsan, Thomas Bégin, Edouard Bergeron, and all other persons who are now, or who may hereafter become members of the said association, are hereby constituted a body politic and corporate, under the name of the " Musical Band of the Village of Lauzon," *Incorpora-tion.* *Name.*

Power to acquire, limited.

and under such name, may at all times acquire and possess for them and their successors, real and immoveable property for the requirements of the said corporation, not exceeding in annual value, the sum of one thousand dollars, and may hypothecate or alienate the same ; and the said corporation may, from time to time,

Power to make by-laws, &c.

enact and establish such rules and by-laws, which shall not be contrary to this act, or the laws of this province, as it shall deem useful or necessary for the interests of the said corporation and the management of its affairs, and may change, modify or repeal the same.

Actual by-laws continued.

2. The rules and by-laws which are already established for the government of the said society shall be and continue to be the rules and by-laws of the said corpora-

Proviso.

tion, until they are changed, modified or repealed under the authority of the present act, provided they be not contrary to the laws of this province.

Irregular conduct.

3. The said association shall have the right to ordain that any musician whose conduct shall be irregular shall leave the band and return within a delay of eight days into the hands of the band-master, the instrument which he has received from the society, under the penalty of a fine of not more than two or less than one dollar, for each day during which he shall so refuse and neglect to return the said instrument after the expiry of the said delay, or of imprisonment for thirty days, or of both at once, in the discretion of the judge, the said fine recoverable to the benefit of the said musical band in the ordinary manner.

Power to annul sub-scription.

4. The said association shall also have the right to annul, without repayment, the share of any musician which he shall have subscribed and paid, on proof before the committee of the band, of the irregular conduct of such musician, or if such musician shall have abandoned the band without giving notice thereof to the committee.

CAP. LXXVII

An Act to incorporate the " Young Irishmen's Literary and Benevolent Association" of Montreal.

[Assented to 24th December, 1875.]

Preamble.

WHEREAS, the persons hereinafter mentioned have, by petition, represented that they and others for some time past have maintained by voluntary contributions a certain institution in the city of Montreal, known as the " Young Irishmen's Literary and Benevolent

Association," for the purpose of the diffusion of knowledge by means of debates, essays, recitations, music, and the cultivation of a social and fraternal spirit, and the mutual benefit of its members in the time of sickness or death, and for the due celebration of the festival known as St. Patrick's day, and have prayed that for the better attainment of its objects the association may be vested with corporate powers ; Therefore, Her Majesty, by and with the advice and consent of the Legislature of Quebec, enacts as follows :

1. J. Hogan, priest, director, Thomas Burke, William P. McNally, Edward Tobin, P. J. Brennan, John F. Campbell, James Downs, James Murphy, Thomas Mulcair, John Mulcair, James McGuire, James McCarreys, Daniel O. Shaughnessy, William Doheny, Joseph Boyle, C. McDonnell, P. H. Shea, P. Enright, and such persons as are now, or may hereinafter be associated with them in conformity with this act, and their successors are hereby constituted a body politic and corporate with all the rights incident to corporations by the name of the "Young Irishmen's Literary and Benevolent Association." Incorporation. Name.

2. The said corporation shall have perpetual succession and may have a common seal, with power to change the same if they think proper, and may, under the same name contract, sue and be sued, and may acquire by any legal title, hold, possess and enjoy to and for the use of such corporation, any moveable or immoveable property which may be sold, exchanged, given or bequeathed to the said corporation, or to sell, hypothecate, convey, let or lease the same ; provided always that such real estate shall not exceed the annual value of five thousand dollars beyond that actually required for the use of the said corporation, provided also, that if the said corporation shall become possessed of real estate exceeding the annual value of five thousand dollars, apart from that actually used by the said corporation, it shall be bound to sell such surplus property within three years from the acquisition of the same, and invest the proceeds thereof in public securities of the Dominion, in stocks of chartered banks, mortgage or other approved securities for the use of the said corporation. Seal. Power to acquire, &c. Annual value, limited. Proviso.

3. The officers of the said association shall be : a reverend director, a president, first and second vice-presidents, treasurer, recording-secretary, corresponding-secretary, collecting-treasurer, assistant-collecting-treasurer, librarian, assistant-librarian, marshall, and a hall committee of nine. Officers.

Power to
make by-
laws.

4. The said corporation shall have power to form a code of by-laws not inconsistent with the laws of this province for fixing the terms of admission of its members, for the election and guidance of its officers and committee of management; and determining or changing the number thereof, and for the general regulation and management of its officers which, when adopted at a regular general meeting, shall, until modified or rescinded, be equally binding as this act upon the association, its officers and members.

Actual by-
laws, conti-
nued.

5. The by-laws of the said association not being contrary to law, shall be the by-laws of the said corporation until they shall be repealed or altered as aforesaid.

Report to the
legislature.

6 The said corporation shall be bound to make an annual report to the legislature, containing a general statement of the affairs of the corporation, within the first twenty days of the session of the legislature.

CAP. LXXVIII.

An Act to incorporate "The St. Patrick's Literary Institute of Quebec."

[*Assented to 24th December*, 1875.]

Preamble.

WHEREAS an institute called the "St. Patrick's Catholic and Literary Institute" has been in existence in the City of Quebec, for over twenty-two years; And whereas it is expedient to accede to , the prayer of the members thereof, asking that it be incorporated under the name of "The St. Patrick's Literary Institute"; Therefore, Her Majesty, by and with the advice and consent of the Legislature of Quebec, enacts as follows:

Incorpora-
tion.

1. Jeremiah Gallagher, John Lane, William H. Laroche, Thomas Coolican, Thaddeus J. Walsh, Jeremiah Horan, John O'Dowd, John Dunn, Robert H. McGreevy, John Deegan, Owen Murphy, John Hearn, Robert Behan, Maurice O'Leary, Edward Burke, Edward Crean, William Quinn, Honorable Thomas McGreevy, M. P., Thomas Duhig, Robert Gamble, William Kirwin, Michael McNamara, Patrick W. McKnight, Francis McLaughlin, Patrick C. Murphy, Patrick M. Partridge, James A. Quinn, James Rafferty, John Roche, Mathew F. Walsh, John O'Leary, Patrick Shee, Mark McLaughlin, William Maguire, M. D., and such other persons as now are, or may be hereafter associated with them in conformity with this act, and their successors, are hereby constituted and created a body corporate and politic, with all the rights incident to corporations, by the name of " The St. Patrick's Literary Institute" for Name. the purposes of education and for the advancement of the sciences and literature.

2. Within six months of the coming into force of this Inventory of act, the said corporation shall be bound to make an in- the proper-ventory by notary of all the property now belonging to ties. it, valuing moveables and immoveables, and any of the present members wishing to withdraw from the said corporation shall have the right to do so and claim their share of the net property of the said corporation ; this intention to withdraw and claim their share shall be made in writing within six months after the completion of the aforesaid inventory.

2. The said corporation shall have perpetual succes- General sion, and may have a common seal, with power to change, powers. alter, break and renew the same, when and as often as they shall think proper, and may, under the said name, contract, and be contracted with, sue and be sued, implead and be impleaded, prosecute and be prosecuted in all courts and places whatsoever in this province ; and by the same name, they and their successors, from time to time, and at all times hereafter, shall be able and capable to have, take, receive, purchase and acquire, hold, Power to possess, enjoy and maintain, to and for the use of the said acquire, &c. corporation, all lands and property, moveable and immoveable, which are now held in trust for it, or which may hereafter be sold, ceded, exchanged, given, bequeathed or granted to the said corporation, provided that the annual Annual revenue of the said corporation do not exceed ten revenues, thousand dollars ; or to sell, alienate, convey, let or lease limited. the same if need be.

3. The officers of the said corporation shall consist of a Officers. president, vice-president, one secretary, a treasurer, a committee of management not to exceed five in number, and such other officers as shall, from time to time, seem necessary to the corporation. The said nine to be chosen by the association at an annual meeting called for that Annual purpose between the first of february and first of march meetings. of each year, and the said nine shall choose their officers as above from among themselves at a subsequent meeting. The persons hereinafter named to wit : Jeremiah Gallagher, Thomas Coolican, Jeremiah Horan, Thaddeus Provincial J. Walsh, John Dunn, William H. Laroche, John O'Dowd, committee. John Deegan, Robert H. McGreevy and John Lane, shall be a provisional committee for the purpose of carrying out the provisions of this act, namely : the preparing the necessary by-laws, and calling a meeting of the members of the said corporation for the purpose of electing officers.

4. The said corporation shall have power to pass by-laws not inconsistent with the laws of the province for fixing the terms of admission of its members, for the government of the same, for the election of, changing and altering the officers above named, and for the general regulation and management of its affairs, and for carrying out the object of the said act of incorporation, which by-laws, when passed and adopted at a regular meeting, shall, until modified or rescinded, be equally binding as this act upon the corporation, its officers and members.

CAP. LXXIX.

An Act to incorporate " *Les Frères du Sacré Cœur."*

[*Assented to 24th December*, 1875.]

WHEREAS the Reverend *frère* Jean François Bererd, in religion *Frère Arnauld*, Joseph Courtines, in religion *Frère Sauveur*, Jean Firmin Fournier, in religion *Frère Théophile*, Auguste Tressol, in religion *Frère Théodule*, and James Tyler, in religion *Frère Francis*, and others, *Frères et Religieux du Sacré Cœur*, residing at Arthabaskaville, form a body whose object is to propagate the Christian Religion, and to teach in and direct academies or commercial colleges ; and whereas in order to consolidate their establishment and favor its prosperity and progress, they have prayed to be constituted a corporation enjoying civil and political rights ; Therefore, Her Majesty, by and with the advice and consent of. the Legislature of Quebec, enacts as follows :

1. The above named petitioners and all other persons who may in future be legally associated with them in virtue of the present act, are hereby constituted a body politic, and shall form a corporation under the name of

" *Les Frères du Sacré Cœur."*

2. The said corporation shall, under the same name, have perpetual succession, and shall have all the rights, powers and privileges of other corporations, and particularly of those having a religious, spiritual or moral object. It may at all times admit other members and establish them in one or more places. It may also, at all times and places by purchase, gift, devise, assignment, or loan, or in virtue of this act, or by any other lawful means and legal

title, acquire, possess, inherit, take, have, accept and receive any moveable and immoveable property whatever, for the usages and purposes of the said corporation, and the same may hypothecate, sell, lease, farm out, exchange, alienate, and finally lawfully dispose of, in whole or in part, for the same purposes ; provided that such immoveable property shall not exceed in annual value, the sum of ten thousand dollars, over and above the value of the immoveables used for the purposes of the said corporation ; and provided also that if the said corporation shall become possessed of real estate, exceeding the annual value of ten thousand dollars, as aforesaid, it shall be bound to sell such surplus property within five years from the acquisition of the same, and to invest the proceeds thereof in mortgages or other valid securities. *Annual revenues, limited. Power to acquire.*

3. The said corporation shall have full power and authority to make, establish and sanction rules, regulations and by-laws, not contrary to this act, or to the laws in force in this province, but which it may deem necessary or advantageous for its proper administration either for the admission, resignation or the changing of the residence of its members, or for the acquisition, possession, administration and alienation of its moveable and immoveable properties ; or, lastly, for the appointment, removal from office and changing of its superiors, administrators, *procureurs,* directors or other officers, to whom it may confer or restrict its authority and powers to govern in its name, and to manage its affairs under its responsibility. It shall also have full power and authority to amend, correct and repeal, in whole or in part, the same rules, regulations, statutes and by-laws, and to substitute others in lieu thereof. *Power to make by-laws.*

4. All moveable and immoveable property whatever belonging to the said community shall be and are by this act devolved upon the said corporation, and the said corporation shall be charged with all the debts and obligations of the said community ; but the members of the said corporation shall not be held personally responsible of its obligations. *Properties vested in the said corporation.*

5. The said corporation shall be obliged to report upon the state of its affairs to the lieutenant-governor in council, annually, twenty days before the meeting of parliament. *Report to the legislature.*

CAP. LXXX.

An Act to incorporate the *" Frères des Écoles chrétiennes."*

[*Assented to 24th December,* 1875.]

WHEREAS the Reverend *Frères* Victor Nicolas Vigueulles, in religion *Frère* Armin Victor, visitor for *Preamble.*

Canada, Jean Routhier, in religion *Frère* Flamian, director of the principal house in Montreal, Pierre Louis Lesage, in religion *Frère* Adelbertus, director of the community *des anciens*, at Montreal, Joseph Panneton, in religion *Frère* Christian of Mary, director of the noviciate, at Montreal, and Jean François Narcisse Dubois, in religion *Frère* Aphraates, director of the principal house, at Quebec, have, by their petition, represented that the institute of the *Frères des Ecoles Chrétiennes*, has for its object the christian education of the young and various works of christian charity, and that it now has under its control educational establishments in the principal towns of this province ; whereas the said institute desires to extend the range of its teaching, improve the material conditions of its educational establishments, and to found new ones in which to impart superior education in commerce, industry and agriculture; and whereas it has prayed to have the powers of a corporation enjoying civil and political rights conferred upon it; Therefore, Her Majesty, by and with the advice and consent of the Legislature of Quebec, enacts as follows :

Incorporation.

Name.

1. The petitioners and the *Frères des Ecoles Chrétiennes*, and those who shall hereafter be lawfully joined to them, are constituted a body politic and corporate and shall form a corporation under the name of "*Les Frères des Ecoles Chrétiennes*" with all the usual civil and political rights, privileges, immunities and powers belonging to corporations.

General powers.

Right to acquire, &c.

2. The said corporation, under the same name, shall have perpetual succession and shall enjoy all the rights, powers and privileges of other corporations, and particularly of those whose object is spiritual, religious or moral. They may, at all times increase their number with other members, and establish them in one or more places.. They may also at all times and places, by purchase, donation bequest, cession, loan, or in virtue of the present act, or by any other lawful title, acquire, possess, inherit, take, hold, accept and receive any property moveable and immoveable whatever, for the uses and purposes of the said corporation, as also to hypothecate, sell, lease, farm out, exchange, alienate and finally dispose legally of the same, in whole or in part, for the same purposes ; provided that such immoveables shall not exceed in annual value the sum of twenty thousand dollars, over and above the value of the immoveables occupied for the purposes of the said corporation ; and provided also that if the said corporation

Annual value, limited.

become proprietor of immoveable property, exceeding in annual value the sum of twenty thousand dollars as aforesaid, it shall be obliged to sell such surplus property within five years from the date of so acquiring the same, and to invest the proceeds, in mortgages or other lawful securities.

3. The said corporation shall have a common seal and Power to shall have full power and authority to enact, establish have a seal and to make and sanction rules and regulations, orders and statutes by-laws. not contrary to the present act, but which it shall deem necessary or useful for its good government either for the admission, discharge, change and domicile of its members, or for the acquisition, possession, management and alienation of its moveable and immoveable properties. It shall also have full power and authority to amend, correct and repeal, in whole or in part, the said rules, regulations, orders and statutes and in their place to substitute others.

4. The *Frère Visiteur* for Canada, the *Frère Directeur* Council of of the principal establishment at Montreal, the *Frère* management. *Directeur* of the noviciate of Montreal, and the *Frère Directeur* of the principal establishment at Quebec, shall always be the council of management and shall be the sole administrators of the said corporation, of which they shall be the sole attorneys and agents, under and in conformity with the rules and statutes of their order actually in force and in operation, in the said institute, and which shall hereafter come into force, in accordance with changes made, in conformity with the constitution of the said institute then in force, and no other member of the said corporation shall be named or form the said council of management, nor be a member thereof, and the said council shall be called and known as "the council of management of the *Frères des Écoles Chrétiennes*," and as such shall make all deeds and agreements which it may deem Its name and in the interest of the said corporation, and which shall be powers. obligatory upon the said corporation, without any of the members of the said corporation, having the power to contravene the same in any manner whatever; and the said council of management may delegate its powers to one of its members, and the acts of the person thus authorized shall also be as binding, as if made and passed by the council of management itself.

5. No member of the said corporation shall under any Rights of circumstances whatever exercise for himself rights of pro- property, by whom exer- perty in the property of the corporation, nor the possession cised. thereof, such power being bestowed and attributed solely to the council of management, and the said corporation under the direction of the council of management, shall be charged with all the debts and obligations of the communities of the *Frères des Écoles Chrét ennes* contracted in the name of the said corporation solely, in conformity Members not with section 4 of the present act ; but the members of the personally liable. said corporation shall not be held personally liable for its obligations.   18

Report to the
legislature.
6. The said corporation shall be obliged to report upon the state of its affairs to the lieutenant-governor in council annually, twenty days before the meeting of Parliament.

CAP. LXXXI.

An Act to incorporate the College of *Notre-Dame, Côte des Neiges.*

[*Assented to 24th December, 1875.*]

Preamble.
WHEREAS the Reverend Fathers Camille Lefebvre, Julien Gastineau, Amédé Guy, and Messrs. Louis Derve, *dit Frère* Stanislas, and Donald McDonnell, *dit Frère* Gabriel, all religious of the congregation of Ste. *Croix,* have, by their petition, to the legislature of the province of Quebec, represented that for several years they have fixed, at *Côte des Neiges,* near Montreal, their chief establishment, the object whereof is the instruction of youth in all the branches of classical, commercial, industrial and agricultural education, the direction of the orphanages, of missions and of the instruction by the noviciate of persons who have in view the object aforesaid; and whereas they have prayed that the powers of a corporation be conferred upon the said institution, and whereas in view of the advantages which may result therefrom, it is expedient to grant such prayer; therefore, Her Majesty, by and with the advice and consent of the Legislature of Quebec, enacts as follows :

Incorporation.

Name.
1. The said establishment, composed of the said petitioners, and of those who hereafter shall legitimately be aggregated to it, is constituted into a body corporate and politic, under the name of the " College of *Notre-Dame, Côte des Neiges,*" and the number of the members thereof shall be at no time less than five.

Seal.
2. The said corporation may have a common seal with power to alter, change and renew the same, when and so often as it shall deem expedient.

Suits.
3. The said corporation may sue and be sued in all courts of justice, in this province, in the same manner as any other body politic and corporate.

Power to
acquire.
4. The said corporation may, at any time, purchase, acquire, hold, possess, occupy, have, take and receive, for itself and its successors, for the use and objects of the said corporation, all lands, tenements, hereditaments, moveables and immoveables whatsoever, and it may sell, alienate, transfer and assign the same, and purchase

others in lieu thereof; provided always that the net Revenues, limited. rents or revenues arising from the real estate of the said corporation, may not, at any time, exceed the annual sum of ten thousand dollars.

5. The majority of the members of the said corporation Power to shall have power and authority to make and pass such make by-statutes, rules and regulations, not contrary to the laws in laws. force in this province, as it shall deem to be useful or necessary for the interests of the said corporation, or for the government thereof, or for the admission or resignation of its members, and it may, at any time, modify, repeal and alter the said statutes, rules, orders and regulations, or any of them.

6. The majority of the members of the said corpora- Management tion may appoint one or more administrators for the of the affairs. management of the affairs of the said corporation.

7. From and after the coming into force of this act, all Certain pro-the real and personal estate, dues, rights and assets of the perties transferred. said establishment of *Côte des Neiges,* up to that time possessed and administered by and in the name of " the civil society of the provincial house, of the college of *Notre-Dame, Côte des Neiges,*" shall become the property of the said corporation of the " college of *Notre-Dame, Côte des Neiges,*" and the said corporation shall, at the same time, become liable for all the debts, charges and obligations of the said civil society, which shall thereafter cease to exist.

8. It shall be the duty of the corporation, whenever Report to the thereunto required, to submit to the lieutenant-governor legislature. a detailed statement of the real estate possessed thereby under this act, and of the revenue arising therefrom.

9. This act shall come into force on the day of the Act in force. sanction thereof.

CAP. LXXXII.

An Act to incorporate the College of St. Césaire.

[*Assented to 24th December,* 1875.]

WHEREAS there exists in the village of St. Césaire, Preamble. county of Rouville, province of Quebec, an educational establishment known under the name of the Commercial College of St. Césaire, in which for upwards of six years have been taught all the branches of a complete commercial education, both french and english, whereas several of the principal citizens of that locality have, by their petition prayed that the said establishment be incorporated under the name of the Commercial College of St. Césaire, so as to establish it on a firm basis, and whereas such an institution would be very advantageous to the parish of St. Césaire and the public in general, and it is expedient to accede to the prayer of the said petition ; Therefore, Her Majesty, by and with the advice and consent of the Legislature of Quebec, enacts as follows :

Incorpora-
tion.

1. The Reverend Joseph André Provençal, *curé* of St. Césaire, the provincial of the community of the *Religieux de Ste. Croix* in Canada, with power to appoint delegates to represent them at meetings of the said corporation, and three members to be chosen by the provincial, from the *religieux* staff of the college of St. Césaire are hereby constituted a body politic and corporate in fact and in name, under the name of the "Corporation of the commercial col-

Name.

Power to
acquire, &c.

Annual value,
limited.

lege of St. Césaire" and, under such name, may, from time to time, and at all times hereafter, purchase, acquire, hold, possess, exchange, sell, accept and receive for them and their successors, to and for the uses and purposes of the said corporation, or for the education of the young, all lands, tenements and hereditaments situate in this province and necessary for the use and actual occupation of the corporation, or all constituted or other rents, in the said province, and they may sell and alienate the same and acquire others by any lawful title whatever, for the same purposes, but the annual value thereof shall at no time exceed five thousand dollars, and they shall have full power and authority to make and establish such orders, rules, regulations and by-laws, as they may deem necessary for the good management and government of the said commercial college and the administration of the property thereof ; provided however, that such rules or by-laws shall not be contrary to the rules, canons and constitutions of the roman catholic church and the rules, constitutions and ordinances of the *majeurs* superiors of the community of Ste. Croix.

Model farm.

2. The said corporation may acquire and possess, and receive by bequest or otherwise, real property of sufficient size to establish a model farm, the purposes thereof being also to teach practical agriculture.

Report to the
legislature.

3. The said corporation shall, at all times, when thereunto required by the lieutenant-governor or either branch of the legislature, make a complete report of the moveable and immoveable property thereof, as also of the annual receipts and expenditure.

CAP. LXXXIII.

An Act to constitute the community of the nuns of the *Precieux Sang de Notre-Dame de Grâce,* diocese of Montreal.

[*Assented to 24th December,* 1875.]

WHEREAS there has existed for more than one year, Preamble. in the parish of *Notre-Dame de Grâce,* in the county of Hochelaga, in the diocese of Montreal, a branch of the community of nuns, known as *Sœurs du Précieux Sang de St. Hyacinthe,* whose members aim at devoting themselves in common to works of piety and charity consistent with the contemplative life led by them ; and whereas the said branch or community of the *Précieux Sang de Notre-Dame de Grâce,* have through their superior and other officers hereinafter named, represented to the legislature, that the incorporation of the said community would assure and increase the advantages derived therefrom, and have prayed to be incorporated according to the rules and regulations hereinafter mentioned ; Therefore, Her Majesty, by and with the advice and consent of the Legislature of Quebec, enacts as follows :

1. Mesdames Herminie Bourdon, known as *Sœur Marie* Incorpora-*du St. Esprit,* Superioress ; Amélie Davignon, known as tion. *Sœur Marie de l'Eucharistie,* assistant; Marie Pormélie Duguay, known as *Sœur St. Alphonse,* mistress of the novices :

Mary McManamy, known as *Sœur Marie du Crucifix,* depositary ;

Olympe Bourdon, known as *Sœur Marie Réparatrice ;* Joséphine Morin, known as *Sœur St. Hyacinthe ;*

Mélanie Gatien, known as *Sœur St. Louis de Gonzague ;*

Marie Louise Hudon, known as *Sœur St. Jean l'Evangéliste :* all now members of the community of the *Precieux Sang de Notre-Dame de Grâce,* and all other persons who may hereafter become members of the said community shall be, and they are hereby constituted a body politic and corporate, under the name of the "Nuns of the *Précieux Sang de* N Notre-Dame de Grâce,* Montreal," and under such name shall have perpetual succession and a common seal, and Seal. may for the ends and purposes of the said community acquire, hold, possess, accept and receive for themselves and the persons who shall succeed them, all moveable and immoveable property which may hereafter be sold, ceded, given and bequeathed to the said corporation for its use and the purposes of the said community, and the same to sell, lease and acquire others in place thereof for Power to the same purposes, provided that the annual value of acquire, &c.

the said property shall not exceed the sum of five thousand dollars, exclusive of the buildings necessary for the said community, and the land upon which the same are or may be built.

Use of the revenues.
2. Provided always that the rents, revenues and profits arising from every description of moveable and immoveable property belonging to the said community, shall be appropriated and used solely for the purposes of the said community.

Power to make by-laws.
3. The said community shall have full power and authority from time to time, to make by-laws and rules (not contrary to this act or the laws of this province) for the government of the said community, and for the management and administration of all the moveable and immoveable property belonging or which may hereafter belong to the said corporation.

Quorum.
4. Three members of the said corporation, the superior, the assistant, and the depositary, shall constitute a quorum for the establishment of rules and by-laws, and for the transaction of all business of the corporation.

Agent or attorney.
5. The said quorum may appoint an agent or attorney, and remove him at pleasure, and appoint another in his place to represent the said corporation, and take charge of and defend the interests thereof before any court of justice, and this by a simple delegation signed by the persons forming the said quorum ; and it is understood that the
Their powers.
powers of such agent or attorney shall extend only to the matters, and for the purposes mentioned in such delegation and to no other or further purposes.

Report to the legislature.
6. It shall be the duty of the said corporation, when thereunto required by the lieutenant-governor, to submit to His Excellency, and to each branch of the legislature of this province, a detailed statement of the funded and real property held and owned by them under the present act.

CAP. LXXXIV.

An Act to incorporate the congregation of the nuns
" *Carmélites déchaussées de Rimouski.*"

[*Assented to* 24*th December*, 1875.]

Preamble.
WHEREAS there is now at Saint Germain de Rimouski a congregation of *Religieuses Carmélites déchaussées*, with a noviciate formed, under authority of *Monseigneur* the Bishop of St. Germain de Rimouski ;

And whereas the said *religieuses* have represented that it is necessary that they be incorporated civilly, as well to receive the gift and grant of the convent and lands which they now occupy in the town of St. Germain de Rimouski, which the said bishop has promised to give them by a formal deed of donation, as to secure to their convent the necessary revenue which it requires, and whereas great advantages would arise from establishing this community on a sure basis, it is expedient, to grant the prayer of their petition; Therefore, Her Majesty, by and with the advice and consent of the Legislature of Quebec, enacts as follows :

1. Mesdames Anna Teresa Mudd, known as *Sœur Joseph* Incorpora-*du Cœur de Jésus*, prioress of the said convent, Anna Maria tion. Fitzpatrick, known as *Sœur Michel de Jésus-Marie-Joseph*, sub-prioress, Marie Antoinette Langevin, known as *Sœur Térèse de Jésus*, Elizabeth Repig, known as *Sœur Marie de l'Incarnation* and Joséphine Parent, known as *Sœur Jean du Sacré-Cœur, novice de cœur*, and all other persons who may hereafter become members of the said convent, in conformity with its rules and under the authority of the said bishop, shall be and are, by this present act, constituted a body politic and corporate under the name of " *Carmélites déchaussées de Rimouski.*" and under such Name. name shall have perpetual succession and a common Seal. seal, and for the end and purpose of the said convent may acquire, have, possess, accept and receive, for themselves Power to and their successors, any moveable and immoveable pro- acquire, &c., perty which may hereafter be sold, ceded, given and bequeathed to and for the uses and purposes of the said convent, and the same to sell and lease, and to acquire others in their place for the same purposes.

2. Provided always that the rents, revenues and pro- Use of the fits, arising from any moveable or immoveable property revenues. of any kind, belonging to the said convent, shall be exclusively appropriated and employed for the purposes thereof and for the payment of the expenses which may be incurred for legitimate objects relating to the above mentioned purposes; provided always that the annual revenue of Revenues such properties does not exceed the sum of ten thousand limited. dollars.

3. The said convent, as a corporation, shall have full Power to power and authority to make, from time to time, rules make by-and by-laws (not contrary to the present act or to the laws laws. of this province), for the government of the said corporation and for the admission of persons into the said convent, and for their rejection, in conformity with their rules and by-laws, and the same to amend.

Report to the   **4.** The said corporation shall be obliged to report upon
legislature.   the state of its affairs to the lieutenant-governor in council annually, twenty days before the meeting of the legislature.

CAP. LXXXV.

An act to authorize the roman catholic bishop, or the
roman catholic episcopal corporation of Montreal,
to sell an immoveable destined by the will of the
Reverend Louis Marie Lefebvre, for the establishment of an hospital in the parish of Ste. Geneviève.

[Assented to 24th December, 1875.]

Preamble.   WHEREAS by his will, in authentic form, received at
Montreal before Mtres. E. Moreau and A. Lyonnais,
notaries, on the 27th of august, 1861, the Reverend messire
Louis Marie Lefebvre, then *curé* of Ste. Geneviève, in the
district of Montreal, and now deceased, bequeathed to His
Grace the roman catholic bishop of Montreal, and to his
successors in the said episcopal see, a lot of one hundred
arpents in superficies, with a house and other dependencies, situated in the said parish of Ste. Geneviève, on
condition that the said legatee should convert the said
house into an hospital or house of refuge, for aged and
infirm persons; the said house to be, if possible, placed
under the management of the *Religieuses de la Providence*
or of the *Dames Grises* of Montreal ;

Whereas by an olograph codicil of the said testator made
at Ste. Genevieve on the 1st of july, 1869, duly admitted
to probate and verified before the prothonotary of the
superior court for Lower Canada, for the district of
Montreal, on the 11th of april, 1872, the said Reverend
Louis Marie Lefebvre substituted for the said *Dames Grises* and *de la Providence*, the *Dames Religieuses de Ste. Anne*
of Lachine, seeing that they already had a convent in the
said parish of Ste. Geneviève ;

And whereas the said *Dames religieuses de Ste. Anne* of
Lachine cannot accept the management of the said hospital or house of refuge, and the burden of maintaining
the same, unless it be united to the house already possessed by them in the said parish ; and whereas for this purpose, and to assure the maintenance and prosperity of the
said hospital or house of refuge, and thus to fulfil more
efficaciously the intentions of the testator, it is expedient
to sell the said immoveable and to apply the price thereof to
the support of the said institution ; Therefore, Her Majesty, by and with the advice and consent of the Legislature of Quebec, enacts as follows :

1. His Grace the roman catholic bishop of Montreal, Roman Cahis successors in the said Episcopal see, or the roman ca tholic bishop,
tholic episcopal corporation of Montreal, as far as needs authorized
be, are by the present act, authorized to sell on the terms to sell certain.
and conditions and for the price that they may deem most property for
advantageous, the immoveable bequeathed by the will of certain purposes.
the late Reverend messire Louis Marie Lefebvre, to found
an hospital in the parish of Ste. Geneviève, in the said district of Montreal, and described as follows in the said
will :

" A certain piece of land situate and being in the said Description.
parish of Ste. Geneviève, containing about one hundred
arpents in superficies and bounded in front by the river
des Prairies, in depth by the *Côte St. Charles*, on one side
by widow Bernard Paiement and on the other side, partly
by Jean-Baptiste Damon, Theodore Pressault and by Guillaume Gamelin Gaucher, with a stone house of one story
and attics, of seventy-two feet in front by about forty feet
in depth, and barns and other dependencies thereon erected," to receive the price of the said sale and give a discharge therefor, to stipulate that all or a portion of the
said purchase price be paid in cash, or by instalments,
with interest at the rate they may deem advisable to stipulate.

2. Any deed of sale of the real estate, drawn up Effect of the
and signed before a notary by the said roman catholic signature of
bishop, or by the said roman catholic episcopal corpora the bishop to
tion of Montreal, shall have the effect of transferring the the deed
absolute property in the said immoveable, to any purchaser
in whose favor such deed may have been passed, and to
constitute for such purchaser, a perfect title to the said
property.

3. The acknowledgment in the said deed, by the said Effect of the
bishop or the said corporation, that the purchase price acknowhas been paid in whole or in part, or any notarial dis ledgment by
charge subsequently granted by the said bishop or by the said bishop.
said corporation, for the whole or part of the said purchase
price, and for the interest accrued thereon, shall have the
effect of totally or partially discharging the purchaser of his
purchase price ; and the enregistration of such deed of discharge shall free the said immoveable of all hypothecs resulting from the said sale, for securing the payment of the
said purchase price.

4. The roman catholic bishop, or the roman catholic Use of the
episcopal corporation of Montreal, as the case may be, price of sale,
shall make such use of the said purchase price as they may &c.
deem best in the interest of the said hospital or house of refuge ; provided always that the purchaser of the said immoveable shall in no manner be obliged to oversee the said

employment of the said money, nor shall the said immoveable remain in anymanner affected to insure the judicious use of the said purchase price; provided also that any portion of the said purchase price may always be left on the said immoveable by the said vendors, if they deem it advisable, and that the repayment thereof with interest may be guaranteed by hypothec and by the privilege of *bailleur de fonds*, constituted by the purchaser on the said immoveable.

Interpretation.

5. Nothing in this act contained shall in any way modify the duties and obligations imposed by the said will, either upon any of the said legatees, or upon the testamentary executors therein named, and all the provisions of the said will and of the codicils thereto, with the exception of the change by this act authorized, shall have their full effect, as if the present act had not been passed.

CAP. LXXXVI.

An Act to authorize the sale of certain property substituted by the last will and testament of Dame Maria Orkney.

[Assented to 24th December, 1875.]

Preamble.

WHEREAS Mrs. Maria Orkney, widow of her first marriage of the late Frost Ralph Gray, in his lifetime of the city of Quebec, Esquire, merchant, and of her second marriage of the late Joseph Morrin, in his lifetime of the city of Quebec, Esquire, physician, by her last will and testament duly executed in notarial form on the 26th day of may 1868, before Ed. Glackemeyer and another, notaries public at Quebec and enregistered in the registry office for the city and district of Quebec, did devise and bequeath among other things as follows : "I do hereby give and bequeath unto Frost Wood Gray and Maria Gray my two children issue of my marriage with the said late Frost Ralph Gray, the usufruct and enjoyment during their lives, of all the property I may die possessed of, without any reserves or exceptions, to be possessed and enjoyed by them in common, *par indivis* ; on the death of either of them the said usufruct shall continue between the survivor of the two, and the children of any of the first deceased; if there be no children issue of the first deceased, then the survivor shall have the said usufruct and enjoyment of all the said property I may die possessed of, until his or her death ; and as to the proprietary right in all the property I may die possessed of, I do hereby give and bequeath the same unto the children issue of my said two children, by equal

halves to each family, to wit: the children of my said
son taking one half, and the children of my daughter
taking the other half, their possession of my said property, so far as the proprietary right is concerned, only
taking place after the decease of both my said son and
daughter; and whereas it is represented by the petition
of Frost Wood Gray and Maria Gray, now the wife of
Arthur Gascoyne Chapman, that it is to the interest of
the said petitioners, and of the children, that a certain property in the city of Quebec, situated in d'Auteuil street,
in the said city, and being the house and premises designated on the Cadastre of St. Louis Ward, as the Cadastral
number 2679 be sold, and the proceeds invested for the
purposes of the said will, and praying to be authorized
to make such sale; and whereas it is expedient to grant
the prayer of the said petition; Therefore, Her Majesty,
by and with the advice and consent of the legislature of
Quebec, enacts as follows :

1. The executors of the will of the said Maria Orkney, Persons au-
after being authorized thereto, by a judge of the superior thorized to
court, on the advice of the relations and friends, and with properties.
the assistance of the curator to be appointed to the substitution created by the said will, are hereby fully authorized
to sell and convey the said lot of ground and premises,
with the house and other buildings thereon erected situated in d'Auteuil street in the city of Quebec, and being
the cadastral number 2679 in St. Louis ward, and to give
as good and effectual title for the same, as might have been
given by the said Maria Orkney, in her lifetime.

2. The price of the said sale shall be invested by the Use of the
said executors in such way as they and the said curator revenues.
shall deem right, and shall be by them applied in the same
way and to the same purposes as the said will directs,
respecting the property belonging to the estate of the
said Maria Orkney.

3. This act shall take effect on the day of its sanction. Act in force.

CAP. LXXXVII.

An Act to authorize the Bar of the Province of Quebec, Section of the District of Montreal, to admit, after examination, Louis Philippe Guillet as one of its members.

[*Assented to 24th December*, 1875.]

Preamble.

WHEREAS Louis Philippe Guillet, of the city of Montreal, was duly admitted to the study of the profession of advocate, and has studied law under William McDougall, esquire, advocate, of the city of Three Rivers, and under the Honorable F. X. A. Trudel, advocate, of the city of Montreal; and whereas doubts have arisen whether the said L. P. Guillet, having been obliged to interrupt for some time his regular attendance in the office of his patrons, has complied with the requirements of the law, although he has studied law and assiduously attended the office of his patrons during two periods, which together more than exceed four years, as evidenced by the certificates of J. N. Bureau, *Bâtonnier* of the bar of the province of Quebec, section of the district of Three Rivers, and of the Honorable F. X. A. Trudel; Her Majesty, by and with the advice and consent of the Legislature of Quebec, enacts as follows:

Admission of P. Guillet as an advocate, after examition.

1. It shall be lawful for the bar of the province of Quebec, section of the district of Montreal, and the examiners thereof, at their next meeting, or at any time, after the usual examination, to admit the said Louis Philippe Guillet to the practice of the profession of advocate and attorney, notwithstanding any interruption that may have taken place in his law studies.

CAP. LXXXVIII.

An Act to authorize the provincial board of Notaries to admit Charles Euchariste Octave Thomas Tranchemontagne, to the practice of the Notarial Profession.

[*Assented to 24th December*, 1875.]

Preamble.

WHEREAS Charles Euchariste Octave Thomas Tranchemontagne, of the city of Montreal, has been duly admitted to the study of the notarial profession; and whereas, from an interruption in his clerkship, the provincial board of notaries of Quebec. declares itself to be unable to admit him to the profession of a notary, without contravening the law respecting such profession ; whereas such interruption was caused by illness ; whereas the provincial board of notaries of Quebec has declared, at the sitting thereof of the eighth october 1874, that it would view with pleasure the passage by the legislature of Quebec of a special bill to admit to the practice of the notarial profession the said ,Charles Euchariste Octave Thomas Tranchemontagne, after a satisfactory examination ; Her Majesty, by and with the advice and consent of the Legislature of Quebec, enacts as follows :

1. The provincial board of notaries of Quebec, and the examiners thereof may, at their next meeting, or at any time, admit the said Charles Euchariste Octave Thomas Tranchemontagne, to the practice of the notarial profession, after the usual examination, notwithstanding any interruption or irregularity in his clerkship. _{Admission of C. E. O. T. Tranchemontagne as a notary, after examination.}

2. This act will come into force on the day of its sanction. _{Act in force.}

TABLE OF CONTENTS.

INDEX

TO THE

STATUTES OF QUEBEC.

FIRST SESSION, THIRD PARLIAMENT, 39 VICTORIA.

A

B

C

D

I

T